KILL JOY

People call her a goody-goody, but Maggie just wants to do the right thing. Perhaps she shouldn't have left the comfortable employ at the Camford house, but Miss Dolly was so insistent that she needed Maggie to accompany her as her new secretary. But why did they need to leave in the middle of the night? When they arrive at their secretive destination, it's nothing but a rather decrepit cottage by a lake—and occupied by two men, the artist Neely and his inebriated companion, Johnny Cassidy. This wouldn't do!

The next morning Miss Dolly's lawyer, Mr. Angel, comes calling. Later that day Maggie finds him dead in one of the row boats, and Neely immediately tries to hide the body. But what should she tell the policeman, Captain Hofer? She wants to do right, but everyone works against her. Maggie doesn't want to get Miss Dolly in trouble. But something is very wrong here. Mr. Angel may be dead, but everyone treats *her* like the kill joy.

THE VIRGIN HUNTRESS

Women can't resist Monty. Gwen considers him her boyfriend. Flora was once his wife. And then there's Nellie, who's carrying his baby. Nellie wanted to marry him, to settle down. Monty loved the company of women but there was no way he was going to marry someone like Nellie. She was too possessive, too conniving, too. . . common. He'd finally made his escape and was now well clear of her. Or was he?

On V-Day Monty meets Dona Luisa, an older woman who is fascinated by him because he reminds her of a long-lost love. Monty also meets her niece, Rose, who takes an immediate dislike to him. As Luisa begins to fawn on him, Rose starts to ask questions. Questions about his character, about his past. With Rose the huntress now on his trail, he has to work fast. Because Monty has a little secret—and it all leads back to Nellie.

Kill Joy

The Virgin Huntress

by Elisabeth Sanxay Holding
Introduction by Jake Hinkson

Stark House Press • Eureka California

KILL JOY / THE VIRGIN HUNTRESS

Published by Stark House Press
1315 H Street
Eureka, CA 95501, USA
griffinskye3@sbcglobal.net
www.starkhousepress.com

ISBN: 1-933586-97-4
13-ISBN: 978-1-933586-97-7

Book design by Mark Shepard, SHEPGRAPHICS.COM

First Stark House Press Edition: June 2016

FIRST EDITION

Elisabeth Sanxay Holding
The Godmother of Noir

When you trace back the roots of literary noir far enough, eventually you run into the unlikely figure of Elisabeth Sanxay Holding. Although she has been overlooked for far too long, in the forties and fifties Holding was pivotal in the development of noir as a distinct literary genre. She began writing mysteries in the thirties, but she hit her stride during the war years, writing book after book about isolated and desperate characters. She was, in many ways, the godmother of noir.

In her time, Holding sold well and was highly regarded by her peers. Raymond Chandler famously called her "the top suspense writer of them all." The critic Christopher Morley wrote of one of her books, "This is the kind of thing I recommend to a few like myself who find the purest refreshment in hallucinations and horrors, in damnation, dipsomania, and dismay." And looking back on her career, the great Anthony Boucher (namesake of the Bouchercon World Mystery Convention) noted, "Before anybody had ever heard of 'psychological novels of suspense' Elisabeth Sanxay Holding was writing them, and brilliantly."

So why has she been mostly forgotten today? It's impossible to say, of course, though I wonder if it has something to do with the way "noir" has come to be associated, incorrectly with "hardboiled." (In my view, *hardboiled* stories are about toughness. *Noir* stories, on the other hand, are about weakness.) Perhaps for many critics, she struck a decidedly upper crust, matriarchal figure. Born in Brooklyn in 1889, she received a private boarding school education and then married a British government officer, gave birth to a couple of kids and then spent the next few decades traveling the world with her husband. She actually began her career in the twenties as the writer of romances, so maybe, on first glance, something about Holding's life and early work smacks of the cozy English mystery tradition. By the time "noir" became a term critics were tossing around, she was already a plump grandmother in her sixties.

None of that bullshit matters, though. I'd wager everything I own in the world that if you could have sidled up to Holding at some stuffy dinner party and asked her what she was really thinking the answer would have been darkly funny and perceptive.

Today, all that really matters are the books. Her best, undoubtedly, is the masterpiece *The Blank Wall* (1947) about a beleaguered housewife attempting to protect her teenage daughter from blackmailers (and the police) after the girl's shady older boyfriend disappears. The book is one of the finest of all American crime novels, and it represents the crown jewel of what Julia Crouch has dubbed "domestic noir," that subgenre of noir that brings murder and mayhem home to Main Street and has largely explored the hidden lives of women. Holding's work in this area is essential and belongs on the same shelf with other great classic domestic noirs like Margaret Millar's *Do Evil In Return* and Charlotte Armstrong's *Mischief*.

Yet much of Holding's work lurches outside the realm of domestic noir and reads as though it could have given birth to Jim Thompson's unhinged psychos. Like Dorothy B. Hughes's *In A Lonely Place* or Patricia Highsmith's *The Talented Mr. Ripley*, Holding's darkest novels follow a l'homme fatale as he descends into amoral madness. Take Holding's wonderfully acidic *The Innocent Mrs. Duff*, which assumes the perspective of a hateful alcoholic with a gut full of whiskey and head full of bad ideas. Jacob Duff is a drunken son of bitch who is getting tired of his much younger trophy wife. He concocts a plan to run her off by framing her for adultery, but when it doesn't work he starts hatching plans to get rid of her permanently. "If I could be free," Duff thinks at one point, "if I could get out of this situation and start over again I'd do very differently. None of this damn suburban life. None of this slavery."

Human beings railing against the damn suburban life, the slavery—that was Holding's perennial theme. Sometimes those people were women, sometimes they were men. Sometimes they were good people struggling with their own weaknesses. And sometimes they were real bastards.

*

The book you hold in your hands contains two excellent, if lesser known, Holding novels, *Kill Joy* and *The Virgin Huntress*. For newcomers to Holding's work, this book is nice introduction to the two spheres (domestic noir and psycho noir) that she helped to shape in the forties and fifties. For readers who are already fans of her better known works like *The Blank Wall* or *The Innocent Mrs. Duff*, it will be a welcome reminder of what makes her one of the greatest of all mystery writers.

Kill Joy

> "…one word, one gesture would bring the horrible
> hidden knowledge into the light."

The first, *Kill Joy*, was published in 1942 and was later republished as *Murder Is A Kill-Joy*. It fits in nicely alongside Holding's other domestic noirs. The story focuses on young Maggie MacGowan, a domestic servant enlisted to accompany the rich and beautiful Dolly Camford to the country. The reasons for Dolly's trip are a bit mysterious, and things take a sinister turn as soon as they leave New York. ("There was a glass partition behind the front seat; Maggie, alone in the back, was shut off in silence and moldy darkness.") Is Dolly running from something? Why does she want Maggie along? These questions become more urgent once dead bodies start popping up.

With its whodunit structure and its dark-and-stormy setting, *Kill Joy* is the kind of Holding book that has one foot in an Agatha Christie puzzler and the other foot in a gothic Edgar Allan Poe story. In truth though, it's really best described as an Elisabeth Sanxay Holding novel. Like all of her best work, it is about social isolation. Maggie is in over her head, desperate to impress her beautiful employer even as she feels herself growing in resentment at the rich woman's callous flights of fancy. From the beginning, in fact, Maggie is trapped by her unquestioning adherence to the social order that puts her at the mercy of the whims of "Miss Dolly" and her rambling cohort of the drunken, idle rich. Maggie's not just fighting against the swirl of events around her, she's fighting her own inborn tendency to accept whatever comes with docile acceptance. "She had been brought up with grave suspicion about happiness," Holding tells us at one point. "It was a dangerous and frequently a discreditable thing."

Reading *Kill Joy* it's easy to see why someone like Chandler, who loathed the work of Agatha Christie, so loved the work of Elisabeth Sanxay Holding. I think the key is found in the ending. I won't spoil the novel's surprises, of course, except to say that like all of her best work, the ending here is not the neat and tidy denouement that one finds in so many mystery novels. There's no sense at the end of a Holding novel that once the crime is solved the world returns to a nice orderly shape. There's nothing cozy about *Kill Joy*.

At one point in the midst of all the turmoil, Maggie walks down the street of a small town and sees a pleasant scene of mothers and children playing. "This was everyday life," the novel remarks for her, "and she was shut away from it, imprisoned in a world where nothing was ordinary and peaceful and seemly." Yes, by the end of the novel we'll find out *whodunit*, but in a deeper sense the book has no solution. It is about Maggie's loss of connection to the peaceful, seemly world she saw on the street—and it is her loss of innocence, her permanent plunge into that darker world, that puts the *noir* in this domestic noir.

The Virgin Huntress

"I've had a man's life…
And it's been hell, all of it."

The Virgin Huntress was first published in 1951, and it makes an excellent addition to Holding's impressive collection of books about no-good sons of bitches. The book follows the exploits of a shady ladies' man named Montford Duchesne. With a five dollar handle like Montford Duchesne, you'd expect him to be a classy guy but when we meet Monty he's working at the shipyards and riding his bicycle home to a boarding house where he's been halfheartedly seducing the landlord's daughter. The novel opens on V-J Day when everyone is celebrating the surrender of the Japanese—everyone, that is, except for Monty whose very first thought at the announcement of the end of World War II is, "There goes my job."

With the whistles and bells ringing in "the sound of a new world," Monty takes off and gets himself involved in a scrap with a drunken sailor trying to accost a couple of women in a chauffeured car. He gets coldcocked for his efforts, but one of the women takes an immediate liking to him. Her name is Luisa Brown, and Monty takes an immediate liking to her peaceful air of refined wealth. The other woman in the car is Luisa's niece, Rose. Rose takes one look at Monty and correctly sizes him up as a world class heel.

I shouldn't say too much more about the plot here since its twists and turns are a large part of the fun, though I will say that this firecracker of a novel grows progressively darker as Monty's past starts to resurface and the book races to a climax that may well be the bleakest ending that Holding ever wrote.

As a study in slow boiling misogyny, *The Virgin Huntress* deserves to be mentioned alongside something like Thompson's *A Hell of a Woman* or Hughes's *In A Lonely Place*. Monty doesn't really know how much he resents women. "It was his nature to help women," the limited POV tells us, "any women; he felt that way about them." That's what he tells himself, sure, but soon enough he's regarding the suspicious Rose and wishing "with all his heart, that he could smash his fist down on her upturned face." Like so many of Holding's protagonists, Monty is running not just from the past, but from himself.

In some ways, *The Virgin Huntress* is a perfect example of the way Holding's work presages much psycho noir. Although it moves with lighting acuity, it stays close to its protagonist, isolating him from everyone around him. Holding's antiheroes always live in tortured isolation—from their families, from their coworkers, from society itself. Monty, recoiling from a woman's attempt to get him to marry down and live the "happy" domestic life in a small town, thinks:

> "Happy? On that street, of cheap little houses, getting to know all the neighbors, going to the movies once in a while. Mowing the lawn on Sunday, drying the dishes after dinner…"

No, Monty will not be settling down to a simple life in the newly emerging suburbs of the late forties. He is condemned to live out the consequences of his actions, a prisoner of his own personality.

*

Together, *Kill Joy* and *The Virgin Huntress* constitute one of the best Holding collections currently available. If you want to deepen your understanding of noir's roots—and if you want to read some crackerjack storytelling along the way—dive into Elisabeth Sanxay Holding. The godmother of noir awaits you.

Jake Hinkson
Chicago, 2016

Kill Joy

By Elisabeth Sanxay Holding

Chapter One

It was nearly half-past two when Mrs. Crabtree and Maggie had finished their lunch and the last of the dishes was dried and put away.

"Are you coming upstairs now, Mrs. Crabtree?" Maggie asked.

"No," said Mrs. Crabtree. "No, Maggie, I think I'll stop here a bit and read my paper."

That was bad news for Maggie. Mr. Camford was home this afternoon, and she dreaded the prospect of meeting him alone in the hall. She hated his way of looking at her, an annoyed and embarrassed way, as if she were an intruder from another world. As if she were a servant, a mere servant. And she was not. She might be employed here as a maid; but that was of no significance, it was only temporary. She was a high school graduate, and a very proud girl.

"No," Mrs. Crabtree said again, "I want to read about this murder."

"Oh, Mrs. Amber?" said Maggie. "That's a terrible thing, isn't it?"

"Well," said Mrs. Crabtree, "she brought it on herself."

"Oh, d'you think so?" asked Maggie.

"They all do," said Mrs. Crabtree, settling herself in her rocking-chair with a comfortable creaking.

She was an Englishwoman of great dignity and composure, stout, high-waisted, with grey hair crimped and parted in the middle; when she put on her spectacles, she had the benign authority of a fairy godmother.

"Well, but how?" asked Maggie.

"These women that get themselves murdered ..." said Mrs. Crabtree. "When you study the cases like I do, you'll see how they've all been flouncing around in these pajamas and these shorts—and shorts they are. They all get themselves mixed up with men, one way or another."

"But *anybody* could get murdered," said Maggie.

"They could," said Mrs. Crabtree. "But they don't. They bring it on themselves."

"Well, I've read about girls, respectable girls—" said Maggie, resisting this new theory.

"Yes," said Mrs. Crabtree, "but study the cases, and you'll see they've done something very foolish like going down in a cellar with one of these foreigners, or taking a ride with a gunman. You'd better go up and change now, Maggie. It's getting on, and Mrs. Mayfield likes you to be ready in your black uniform by three o'clock."

It was hard to leave the neat tranquil kitchen and the company of the admirable Mrs. Crabtree. But it was Maggie's duty to go, and she always did her duty. Always. She went up the dark flight of stairs from the basement, and that was all right, these stairs belonged to Mrs. Crabtree and herself. But there were no back stairs in this house, and when she reached the top of this flight, she was in Mr. Camford's domain.

He might be right there in the sitting-room, she thought, and she wanted to run, she felt limp and bedraggled in her blue cotton dress. But she would not run, she walked straight as an arrow, a pretty little thing with vivid blue eyes and crisp coppery hair and a creamy skin dusted with tiny freckles.

I don't care, she told herself. I'm doing the job I'm paid to do, that's all. This is a democratic country. I don't have to stay—like this. Some day, who knows? I might meet Mr. Camford at a party some day, when I'm a private secretary, or married to somebody much better than *he* is.

She got safely past the sitting-room and mounted the second flight, and there in the hall she nearly ran into Mr. Camford coming out of the bathroom. He was in his dressing-gown, too, which made it worse. He stepped aside, and so did she, so that they still faced each other; he raised his eyebrows, a tall, lean, bald man, ineffably distinguished. Maggie stepped to one side again, and so did he, and there they still were.

He made a faint tut-tut sound and turned away, back toward the bathroom, as if he could not endure the sight of her, and she went on toward the last flight, her cheeks burning, a hot resentment in her heart. He's *mean*, she said to herself. He could speak, couldn't he? Or even smile. You'd think I was—I don't know what. Dirt beneath his feet. All right! One of these days, I'll show him, the mean old thing.

She went into her own small room and closed the door, she went to the chest of drawers, and leaning her elbows on it, looked at the picture of her mother which stood there in a leather frame, a sandy-haired little woman with a thin, fine face. Her mother's idea, this had been. You could get a nice place with a private family, she had said. You mean, be a servant? her daughter had demanded. Yes, Mrs. MacGowan had said. You'd learn more about life in that way than ever you could in an office, and when you come to figure it out, you get more money.

Maggie had utterly repudiated that suggestion. She had decided to get a nice job in an office, and why not? She had taken a commercial course in high school, and she had done well in it, as in all her studies; she had a good opinion of her abilities. The reception she got at employment agencies surprised and displeased her. It was undeniable that she had had no experience, but she sat and talked to other girls just out of business school who were sent out to get jobs. She had some interviews, but nothing came of them.

"I don't see why it is that I don't get a job," she said to another girl waiting in an agency.

"Well," said this other girl with impersonal candor, "I think it's because you're kind of old-fashioned."

"Old-fashioned?" Maggie repeated.

"Yes, kind of," this other girl said.

"There's nothing old-fashioned about *me*," Maggie said briefly.

But on the way home, she looked critically at herself in shop windows, and doubts assailed her, to see that straight small figure in a long grey coat and a round felt hat ... There was only one week left. Mrs. MacGowan was going off to Maine to keep house for a very exacting brother while his wife went to the hospital. You'll have to get yourself settled, Maggie, one way or another, she had said, or else come with me.

Maggie went to a domestic employment agency the next day, and the moment she set foot in it she was a valuable and interesting client. She was sent out to see Mrs. Mayfield, and Mrs. Mayfield had engaged her there and then. In a way, she thought, it's not such a bad job. I've saved twenty-one dollars out of my first month's pay, and I've learned quite a lot, listening to them talk and all that, and Miss Dolly has been sweet to me. But it's not what I want, and I won't stay.

She put on her black poplin dress and the little ruffled apron and the cap that was a frill with a black velvet band. It was becoming to her; she looked pretty. But she did not *want* to wear a cap and apron. I'm not going to be just a maid, she said to herself. I can do better than this for myself. A *lot* better.

She took out her Manual of Shorthand, and her notebook, and started down the stairs. It was not nearly so bad to meet Mr. Camford in the hall when she was wearing her black uniform and her best shoes; she felt almost professional. Let him come, the mean old thing....

"Maggie!" said a low and lovely voice, and she turned to see Miss Dolly in the doorway of her room. "Come in, will you, Maggie?" she said. "And close the door. I want to speak to you."

A woman of mystery, Miss Dolly was, and Maggie was deeply interested in her. Still young, handsome and elegant, she lived a curious and solitary life here with her aunt and uncle. She never went anywhere except sometimes to do a little shopping; no one came here to visit her.

But it had not always been like this. Maggie came in every morning to do the room, and she had found in it souvenirs of a very different kind of life, little things, bottles, boxes, ash-trays from Paris and London, and in the closet were lovely evening dresses and wraps and slippers, gold and silver. Sometimes Miss Dolly would come in while Maggie was busy there, she would sit down and light a cigarette and talk with a vague and melancholy kindness; she would ask Maggie questions about herself, sometimes she gave her a little present, a cake of perfumed soap, some writing paper, an embroidered handkerchief.

"I think she's had some great misfortune," Maggie said to Mrs. Crabtree.

"I don't know about that," Mrs. Crabtree had said. "What I do know is, that she wasn't living here when I first came a year ago. She had a place of her own somewhere, and I never saw her here, and never so much as heard there was such a person till the day she came, bag and baggage, to stay."

"It seems a strange way for anyone like her to live," Maggie had said. "She's very good-looking, don't you think, Mrs. Crabtree?"

"Yes," Mrs. Crabtree had admitted. "Though I must say I don't care for such a dark complexion. It always looks foreign to me. And she talks French; I've heard her on the telephone."

This made her still more interesting.

"Why ever do you suppose she came here to live in such a lonely kind of way?" Maggie had asked.

"I couldn't say," Mrs. Crabtree had answered.

"Mrs. Mayfield and Mr. Camford seem so sort of distant to her," Maggie had continued. "I don't think they're nice to her."

"That's something I shouldn't care to give any opinion on, Maggie," Mrs. Crabtree had said with a trace of severity. "Not knowing the circumstances."

But Maggie went right on having opinions. She looked over at Miss Dolly stretched out on her chaise-longue, supple and languid in her black chiffon negligee, smoking a cigarette, her dark eyes gazing steadily and sadly out of the window. It's some love affair, thought Maggie, waiting there with her Manual under her arm.

She turned her head toward Maggie.

"Maggie," she said, "I can trust you, can't I?"

"Yes, ma'am," said Maggie.

"Ever since you came here, I've been studying you, Maggie," said Miss Dolly, "and I think you're a very remarkable girl."

The color rose in Maggie's cheeks, her heart beat faster, with pleasure and a sort of relief. For this was what she had been waiting for, this praise, this recognition that she was not really just a maid.

"Thank you, Miss Dolly," she said.

"I'm going to translate a French book into English. It's a wonderful book and I think it'll make a sensation. I'm going away to the country to work on it, and I want you to come with me as my secretary."

This was almost too good to be true.

"Miss Dolly ... *Thank* you," said Maggie, a little unsteadily. "I haven't had much—I haven't had any real experience, but I can type pretty well.

I'm a good speller—"

"I know you're just the right person for me," said Miss Dolly. "You're young—how old are you, Maggie?"

"Nineteen, Miss Dolly."

"That *is* young, isn't it?" said Miss Dolly with a faint smile. "But I think you're very understanding, Maggie. I think we'll have a wonderful summer."

"Yes, Miss Dolly," said Maggie. "When did you think of going, miss?"

"I've got to go to-night."

"To-*night!*" said Maggie.

"Yes. There's a car coming for me."

"But Miss Dolly, I've got to give Mrs. Mayfield notice."

"She can easily find somebody else, Maggie."

"Yes, I know, Miss Dolly, but—well, I'm sure she wouldn't discharge me without notice, and I don't feel I ought to do that to her."

"We can arrange that."

"Shall I speak to her now, Miss Dolly, and see what she thinks?"

"No," said Miss Dolly, and fell silent for a time. "Maggie," she said, "I don't want my aunt or my uncle or *anyone* to know we're going."

"But, Miss Dolly!" cried Maggie. "You mean for me just to go, just to walk out, and not even tell Mrs. Crabtree?"

"Maggie, I've *got* to go to-night," said Miss Dolly, "and I've got to go—without anyone knowing. You can take my word for it, can't you, that I've got a good reason?"

"Yes, Miss Dolly, but—"

"But what?"

Maggie was almost too miserable to answer. This thing *was* too good to be true. Lots of things were. I ought to've known there'd be a catch to it, somewhere, she thought.

"Maggie," said Miss Dolly, "I'm going to trust you utterly. Hand me my bag, will you? Read this, Maggie." She took a typewritten letter out of an envelope and handed it to Maggie.

"Dolly, you Devil:

I'm not going to wait any longer. To-morrow I'm coming to the house—with a bottle of vitriol. Then you won't sneer at me any more, devil that you are.

Othello."

"But, Miss Dolly!" said Maggie, astounded. "It's some kind of joke, isn't it?"

"No," said Miss Dolly.

"But, Miss Dolly, if anybody means that—"

"He does mean it," said Miss Dolly.

"But then, Miss Dolly, you ought to tell somebody. Mr. Camford—"

"He's the last person I'd ever tell. He and my aunt would turn me out of the house if they knew anything about this, and they'd take all my money."

"They couldn't do that, Miss Dolly. Nobody's allowed—"

"Yes, they could. I've signed all sorts of papers ... Maggie, you *must* have noticed how it is here for me, how unwelcome I am. In this house—the house I was born in. It was my father's house, Maggie, and he meant me to have it. But I was very young—and very foolish.... I was so happy here with my mother and father when I was a child—and maybe that's not a very good preparation for the world.... My parents were so gay and generous and loving ... I didn't realize how different other people were. I trusted people—too much."

There were tears in her dark eyes, and Maggie felt very sorry for her—in a way. But she was more shocked than touched.

"Do you mean they—other people—have got your house and your money away from you, Miss Dolly?" she asked.

"Oh, I wouldn't *care* about that if they were only kind and understanding," said Miss Dolly.

"You have to care about things like that," said Maggie briefly. "You have to look out for yourself—"

"I'm not like that," said Miss Dolly. "I just want to get away, Maggie. I just want a little peace and quiet."

"But, Miss Dolly, that man, the one that wrote the letter, he'll find out where you are, and he'll come after you."

"He won't, if nobody here knows where I've gone. Oh Maggie, please don't argue any more! Please just be kind and friendly and come with me. Things are worse, much worse than you imagine. I'll tell you later, when we're out of this horrible house. Maggie, you're so sensible and well-behaved. I need you so. Won't you come with me, Maggie?"

What a strange thing, that anyone like Miss Dolly, beautiful and rich and aristocratic, should be begging and praying Maggie MacGowan to come away with her! It's like a story, Maggie thought. I know I'm sensible. I know if there's one thing I am, it's practical. I do know how to look out for myself and I dare say I could help Miss Dolly in more ways than one. I suppose she sort of felt that, by instinct.

Miss Dolly had laid the back of her hand against her forehead, her eyes were closed, one hand dropped over the arm of the chair; she looked exhausted and curiously helpless. Look what she's got herself into, thought Maggie. There's this man threatening to throw vitriol at her—and she's signed these papers and lost her house and her money. My goodness!

"Will you come, Maggie?" asked Miss Dolly.

"Yes, miss," said Maggie.

"Oh Maggie, I'm so glad! I'll talk everything over with you once we're away from here. Maggie, the car's coming at half-past eleven. Just pack what you'll need for a day or two, and meet me at the back door. I'm so glad, Maggie ..."

Chapter Two

I'm doing the right thing, to go with Miss Dolly, Maggie said to herself. She's in a great deal of trouble, and she needs me.

But just the same, she felt mean.

Mrs. Crabtree had gone up to her room for her afternoon rest, leaving the kitchen as neat as a pin, the dessert was all made and in the ice-box, the lettuce was washed and in a sieve, the leg of lamb stood on the table ready for the oven. Always leave your meat out of the ice-box two or three hours before you cook it, she had told Maggie.

It was quiet as the grave down here, not a sound but the loud ticking of the clock. Through the barred window you could see feet going by along the street, cracked old shoes, and gleaming new ones, gay high-heeled pumps and a child's little stubby brown shoes. Sometimes a truck passed with a hollow roar, shaking the walls, the windows rattled in a gust of wind. Mrs. Crabtree's newspaper lay neatly folded in the rocking-chair, and Maggie sat down to read it for a while.

There was a picture of that Mrs. Amber; pretty she was, and young. It's funny there's never a word about Mr. Amber, thought Maggie. Well, maybe she wasn't really married at all. Brought it on herself ... ? They all do, Mrs. Crabtree said, getting mixed up with men.... Miss Dolly must have got mixed up some way with the man who wrote that letter. Othello. Well, that was Desdemona's husband, and he smothered her with a pillow. Vitriol ... That's a terrible thing. It blinds you and eats away your flesh.... I don't think she realizes how serious it is. I don't think she realizes anything much. She's so helpless. She needs someone to look after her.

She sighed, and put down the paper and opened the Shorthand Manual. It's going to be wonderful experience, working on Miss Dolly's book, she thought. Maybe later on I can get to be a secretary for a famous author. I'll get to tea parties where there are famous people. Who know? I might even marry a great author.

At half-past five Mrs. Crabtree descended in a clean print dress; she moved about, amiable, superbly adequate.

"Just the three of them for dinner," she observed. "I never like to work for three. Two is all right, and four is all right, and more than four. But three is awkward."

Maggie set the table as Mrs. Mayfield wanted it; real old-fashioned, she would not have any of the nice things you saw in the magazines. A fine damask cloth, the ornate old silver, the French china with a band of deep blue and gold, and right in the middle a white bowl of red carnations. A few moments before seven, Mrs. Mayfield herself came into the dining-room in a black dinner dress, a tall woman with an ungainly stoop forward from the waist, and dark hair grizzled at the temples. She looked at the table in her peering, absent-minded way.

"You're learning to do very nicely, Maggie," she said. "You can light the candles now."

Maggie lit the four candles in the chased silver holders, and the family entered. Mr. Camford, in a dark purple smoking-jacket, sat at the foot and his sister opposite him and poor Miss Dolly at the side. She had a queer look to-night, Maggie thought; maybe because she had her raven-black hair brushed back from her forehead, making her face look thinner, almost worn; or maybe it was because she had come to the table in a yellow sweater and a short skirt.

Mrs. Mayfield began to talk about a book she had just finished reading, she told about it firmly and clearly, and her brother listened with attention. No wonder, thought Maggie. She's got such an interesting way of telling about things, and she knows such a lot. Miss Dolly's very well educated and speaks French and all that, but she can't hold her own with those two. Not about books and things like that.

The rope of the dumb-waiter slapped gently against the wall; that was Mrs. Crabtree's signal that the entrée was coming up. Everything served just right, the leg of lamb carved in juicy slices, the vegetables in covered dishes, the plates warmed, the mint jelly solid.

I guess this is the last time, Maggie thought as she stood at the sideboard, and a curious pang of regret shot through her. It's *nice*, she thought, looking at the table with the candles and the red carnations. She knew every fork and spoon, every plate and glass; for six months she had been handling them with care and even affection. And I *like* to hear Mr. Camford and Mrs. Mayfield talk, she thought. I know they're mean to Miss Dolly, but they've got something.

"Maggie!" said Mr. Camford reproachfully. "*Water*, please!"

He felt strongly about having to ask for water. Mr. Camford liked observant service, Mrs. Mayfield had said. And he's right, Maggie thought, filling his glass and looking down at his bald head with new indulgence.

Well, I guess I'll never see him again.

She had her own dinner in the kitchen with Mrs. Crabtree, and it was cosy. Mrs. Crabtree was particular, too; they had a nice clean tablecloth and napkins, their plates were warmed, too. They ate just what the others did, only instead of coffee they had a big brown pot of tea.

"The grocer's boy had a late paper," said Mrs. Crabtree, "said he found it. He left it for me. He's a nice boy. There's more about that Mrs. Amber in it, and you can see it's the way I said. She brought it on herself. Divorced, she was, and living all by herself, except for this colored maid. And she had these cocktail parties that lasted half the night, and so on. A gay life, as they call it."

She washed the dishes, and Maggie dried them.

"Well ..." said Mrs. Crabtree after she had locked the iron gate to the area and seen to all the windows. "I'll leave the paper for you, Maggie. I'm off to bed."

"Good night, Mrs. Crabtree."

"Good night, Maggie."

I'm not going to read about Mrs. Amber, Maggie thought. I'm sick and tired of it. And I've got other things to think about.

She was supposed to remain on duty until ten o'clock in case the doorbell rang. Well, it was after nine now, and she thought she could well use the interval in planning what she should take. Her bag was small, and there was so little that could be got into it that her planning was soon done.

Then, to fill in the last few moments, she picked up Mrs. Crabtree's newspaper. Clubman Sought in Amber Slaying. And a picture of Mrs. Amber, smiling. She had been found dead, shot, lying on the floor of her bedroom, partially clad, the papers said. I'm sick of that case! Maggie cried to herself, and turned to the editorial page. She read the editorials every day, all of them, to improve herself.

Ten o'clock. She gave the neat cosy kitchen a last look, and turned out the light; she went upstairs to the parlor floor. Mr. Camford was in the drawing-room nearby, but the other rooms were empty; she went on up to the top floor and began to pack the little bag of imitation crocodile, very soft. She had decided to wear the black poplin dress she had on, and she packed her cap and little apron, and a clean morning uniform. Miss Dolly had said she was to be a secretary and not a maid, but there might be little things to do.

When the bag was packed, she sat down to read her book, *Anna Karenina*. It was one of the classics she was determined to read; it interested her and exasperated her. She left her door ajar, and at eleven o'clock she heard Mr. Camford mounting the stairs. The house was quiet now, very quiet.

Her heart beat fast, her hands were cold as ice. Oh, suppose I met Mr.

Camford or Mrs. Mayfield now? she thought. Sneaking downstairs with a bag.... Whatever could I say to them? Or suppose Mrs. Crabtree came out now to the bathroom and saw me? I don't think it can be *right,* to do anything that makes you feel so terrible.

So guilty. She put on the round felt hat and the grey coat, and bag in hand started down the stairs. What'll I say if anybody catches me? I ought to have something ready to say.... Well I can't. I won't. I'll say—I'm going away, that's all. Nobody can stop me.

Nobody tried to stop her. She went past the closed doors of the bedrooms and down to the lower hall where a dim light burned all night, down into the black basement, stuffy, filled with the warm, stale smells of cooking. She unlocked the door and stood in the little space between the door and the iron gate to the area. It was nice to be out in the air, nice to look out at the quiet upper East Side street with a light on the corner, and cars going by, and now and then someone on foot.

There was a man on the corner with his back to her, a stocky, broad-shouldered man in a brown pullover and dark trousers; the street light shone on his bare head that was silvery white. She looked at him idly, wondering what he was doing there, then she looked back over her shoulder, she listened for the sound of Miss Dolly's footsteps. A gust of wind blew through the barred gate, damp and chilly, there were no stars in the sky. Not much of a night for a drive, she thought. I hope it's not a long way.

The man was still standing there; what could he be doing? I wish I had a watch, Maggie thought. As soon as I can save up more, I'll get one. Whatever is that man doing? Could he be that *Othello?*

A sound behind her made her start; she saw the beam of an electric torch across the kitchen floor.

"Maggie!" said Miss Dolly's voice.

"I'm here, Miss Dolly."

Miss Dolly came to her side and set down her bag. "It weighs a ton," she said. "Oh, there's Neely! Open the gate, will you, Maggie?"

Maggie opened the gate, and Miss Dolly went out, leaving her bag behind her. Ah, well ... said Maggie, and picked up both the bags and followed her.

Miss Dolly and the silver-haired man had moved aside from the circle of light; they were going round the corner talking to each other, a queer couple, Maggie thought. The man was so kind of poor-looking, and Miss Dolly so stylish in her short fur jacket and her narrow black skirt, her black turban, her high-heeled shoes. The chauffeur, he must be.

There was a car drawn up to the curb, a big, old-fashioned car; the man got in behind the wheel, and Miss Dolly stood waiting for Maggie.

"Will you sit in the back, Maggie?" she said. "I want to talk to Neely."

There was a glass partition behind the front seat; Maggie, alone in the back, was shut off in silence and a moldy darkness. It's a funny feeling, not to know where you're going, she thought.

She looked at Miss Dolly and she was astonished. The light on the dashboard showed her face all alive and sparkling; she was smiling, talking to that driver, and he was talking to her. Not like a lady and a chauffeur. Well, maybe he wasn't a chauffeur, but the owner of the car, only he looked so sort of poor.

It came into her head then, that, after all, she knew very little about Miss Dolly, and nothing at all about her friends. A very funny feeling it was not to know where you were going, or who you were going with.

Chapter Three

They were out of the city, driving along a wide boulevard, when the rain began dashing against the window, drumming on the top of the car. The two straight rows of lights ahead twinkled through a veil of falling water, the flat countryside was blotted out, the cars and trucks that passed them went with a blurred rush.

Maggie leaned back in a corner, chilled and depressed. She was in the habit of going to bed early, and she closed her eyes and fell asleep now. But only for a little time; she waked with a start, and there was the rain and the black flat countryside, and Miss Dolly's vivid happy face turned again to the driver.

She dozed again, and waked when the car began to jolt over a road full of ruts. There were trees here and no lights, the car slipped and struggled in mud. It's just miserable not to know where you're going or where you are, she thought. If I even knew what time it was ... I wish I had a watch.

That bothered her more than anything, that feeling of blank and unlimited time. Suppose I've been asleep for hours? she thought. Suppose it's to-morrow night? Well, it isn't. I mustn't be silly. There's Miss Dolly right in front of me. She's somebody I *know*. There's nothing queer about her. She just wants to get away from that man, and get a little peace and quiet in the country. That's natural.

She's pretty friendly with that driver.... Maybe he's a friend of hers. He's got white hair, but he doesn't look old. He's got a hole in the elbow of his sweater. Well, that's nothing. Some people don't care. I've heard about millionaires that look like regular tramps.

She made an effort to go to sleep, she leaned back and closed her eyes. But the road was very bad now, she was jounced and shaken, she felt the car skid and slew around, she opened her eyes and the car stopped. The white-haired man was getting out.

There was nothing here, nothing but rain and the dark. She thought something must have gone wrong with the car, nothing serious because Miss Dolly sat smoking there, with no gesture of alarm or even curiosity. The rain dashed against the windows as if flung from a bucket; it was surprising to think of the white-haired man out in it without hat or coat.

And then a light sprang up and outlined a window, she could see the dark bulk of a house. In a moment the man came back, running, with a blanket held against his breast; he opened the door to the front seat, and Maggie saw Miss Dolly laugh, her teeth white against her rouged lips. She moved over, and the man put the blanket over her head and around her shoulders, he took her arm and helped her out.

Maggie sat close to the window; she saw them run along a path and up the steps of a little porch, the man opened the door and they went in.

Well, have they stopped in to visit somebody? Maggie thought. If I'm a secretary, it's a sort of funny way to treat me, going off and not saying a word. But I never really believed much in all that. She sat there waiting in drowsy discomfort, yawning in the close dampness. Then the door of the house opened and the man appeared in the light, waving his arm as if scooping something out of the air toward his face. She watched him for some time before it occurred to her that he was beckoning to her.

Well, that's not very polite, she thought, and taking up her little bag she opened the door and got out in the pelting rain. It was too dark and too slippery to run, she went cautiously along the path and up the steps.

"Look here!" said the man. "Get something for Miss Camford to eat, will you? Just a little snack—coffee—anything. Here's the kitchen. Take anything you see."

His hair was not white, but a pale blond; he was young, with a broad, strong-boned face, and pale eyes that rested on her for a moment with impersonal coolness.

"Here's the kitchen," he said again. "Call me if you want anything."

She went into the room he pointed at, a dim and dirty kitchen lit by a feeble bulb hanging from the ceiling, with a bare wooden floor, an oil-stove furry with grease, a narrow iron sink. She set down her bag and looked around her, and narrowed her eyes to keep from crying.

All right! she said to herself. All right! I was a fool to come. I might have known ... But here she was, and she accepted the consequences grimly. She opened her little bag and put on her apron, she looked around and she found a paper bag of coffee, she found a battered old aluminum coffee pot; there was a small wooden ice-box in a corner, and in it she found ham, and butter and eggs, and some ants running around. I wouldn't work for the woman who runs *this* house, thought Maggie, not for fifty dollars a week. I never saw—

"For God's sake ..." said a voice behind her, and she turned quickly. A man in a dressing-gown stood in the doorway, a big, sun-burned, grey-eyed man, staring at her, and yawning like a big cat. "For God's sake, who are you?" he asked.

"I'm—I came with Miss Camford," said Maggie briefly.

"Susanne," he said. "The dainty little French maid."

"I'm not French," said Maggie.

The man ran his fingers through his dark hair, and it stood out like feathers behind his ears; he leaned against the doorway, and Maggie noticed with disfavor that his feet were bare.

"You're pretty," he said earnestly. "You're the cutest little trick I *ever* saw. Red hair, too. Are you saucy?"

With all her heart she resented his words, his tone, the way he was staring at her. She went on with her work, trying to ignore him.

"I bet you slap people," he said. "Fresh guys. Piff. Paff. Pouff. Non?"

There was a loaf of bread on a shelf, not wrapped, just out there in the dust. It was stale, too, hard as a rock, she sawed away at it with a knife.

"You're pretty," he said, "but not very polite. After all, when a pretty little girl all dressed up like Susanne suddenly appears in my kitchen in the middle of the night, I think she ought to speak."

"Is it your kitchen?" said Maggie.

"Half of it's mine," he said. "It happens to be the half you're in now."

"Where do you want supper served, please?" asked Maggie.

"What supper?" he said. "The only thing is, you ought to wear silk stockings instead of cotton...."

She looked at him with scorn in her blue eyes.

"Aha!" he said. "I knew you were saucy."

This was too much for her.

"I'm not saucy," she said. "I'm here doing the work I'm paid to do—and minding my own business. If you feel like standing there and making fun of me, I can't stop you."

He straightened up.

"I wasn't making fun of you," he said. "That's just a cheap idiot way I have. Meant to be amusing ... Meant to hide my sensitive spirit. Cassidy is the name. Johnny Cassidy."

The kettle was boiling and she made the coffee; she began to butter the rock-like bread, and to make ham sandwiches. She was not a bit tired or confused now; she was deft and quick and perfectly sure of herself and she felt ready to go on working for hours in a sort of rage. I'd like to scrub the floor, she thought, and clean up this nasty dirty place. That man can stand there staring just as long as he likes. *I* don't care.

"Oh, Maggie!" said Miss Dolly's voice. "Oh, you *poor* child! What are you doing?"

"Getting some supper, Miss Dolly."

"But it's three o'clock, Maggie. You must be worn out."

"I'm not tired, Miss Dolly."

"You're not to do another thing," said Miss Dolly. "Come on, and I'll show you your room."

"I'll just finish—"

"You come along this minute," said Miss Dolly, and took her hand.

"May I ask for an introduction?" murmured Johnny Cassidy.

"This is my secretary, Miss MacGowan," said Miss Dolly, with more than a trace of curtness. "Do come along now, Maggie. What put it into your head to start all this at such an hour?"

"The—other gentleman asked me to," said Maggie.

"Neely?" said Miss Dolly. "Oh, he hasn't any sense of time at all. This way, Maggie."

Maggie picked up her bag from the corner, and Johnny Cassidy took it from her.

"No, thank you," she said. "I'd rather—"

But he went ahead of her out of the kitchen and up a steep and narrow stair; he mounted these, limber and nimble in his bare feet. He put the bag in a room and came out, and stood aside.

"Good night, Miss MacGowan," he said.

Miss Dolly closed the door and they both looked around them at the room. It was a big room, low-ceilinged, furnished with a big divan, a wicker chair, a bamboo table, some shelves of books, and a tall old-fashioned radio cabinet. Here too, the only light was from a bulb hung from the rafters; it was gloomy, shadowy, smelling of mold.

"We can fix it up to-morrow," said Miss Dolly. She crossed the room to the divan and pressed it with her hand. "It *seems* very comfortable," she said. "My room is just in here through this door, and the bathroom is just across the hall."

"Thank you, miss," said Maggie.

"Don't call me 'miss' any more. Call me Dolly, won't you, Maggie?"

"I'll try to," said Maggie.

"It's going to be nice here, don't you think, Maggie?"

"Well, it's hard to judge yet, Miss Dolly."

"Please call me Dolly! We're going to have a wonderful summer here, Maggie. We'll change things, and make the place charming."

"Excuse me, Miss Dolly, but—isn't there any—any lady of the house?"

"No," said Miss Dolly. "It's Neely's house. He's an artist, you know, and very talented. I didn't know Johnny Cassidy would be here. But I don't think he'll stay long. He never stays anywhere."

"There's just Mr. Cassidy and Mr. Neely?"

"Curtius. Cornelius Curtius. He's a Dutchman, Maggie, from Holland. You'll like him."

"Yes, miss."

"But you will call me Dolly, won't you? You've come here as my friend, Maggie."

"I'll try," said Maggie.

"Let's go to bed," said Miss Dolly. "We're both tired."

She smiled at Maggie a little anxiously, and after a moment she went off into the room that opened out of this big one. She came back almost at once.

"Maggie, could you possibly help me with the bed? It seems so queer."

There was nothing at all in the little room but a white iron double bed and a chest of drawers. And the bed was queer because the covers were not tucked in, but just folded on top of it. Maggie made it neatly while Miss Dolly began to undress.

"Now I'll go and wash," said Miss Dolly, "and then I won't have to disturb you by going through your room again."

She had left her things scattered all over, her lovely delicate underwear, her little gold watch and her sapphire bracelet tangled up in her stockings on the chest of drawers. Maggie made the room as neat as she could before Miss Dolly came back. She looked surprisingly pretty and glowing, in a white terry robe, her black hair loose about her olive-skinned face.

"It's going to be lovely here, Maggie!" she said.

"Yes, miss," said Maggie. "Good night!"

She went back to the big room, closing the door softly behind her. She was not going to take off even her apron when she went to the bathroom to wash, not she! Not when she and Miss Dolly were alone in this house with those two men. Queer men ...

She returned to the big room, and she wanted to lock the door. There was no key in the lock, no bolt. She fixed a chair under the knob, and took the faded green cover off the divan. Nothing under it but a mattress, no sheets, no blankets, nothing at all.

She did cry a little then, but while the tears ran down her freshly-scrubbed cheeks, she was busy. She put the green cover back, she fluffed up the pillows, she took off her apron, her black dress, her shoes, she put on her dark-blue dressing-gown and her felt slippers, she brushed her hair, one hundred strokes, and then she went to the shelves to get a book. For she had decided to sit up all night.

She found a novel that seemed nice, and she found a tabloid newspaper of yesterday's date. She sat down in a chair, determined to read, and the first thing she saw in the paper was a picture of the murdered Mrs. Amber, smiling, with her hair in a cloud about her face. Police of Two Cities Seek Clubman for Questioning, she read; and there was a picture of the Clubman, looking as he ought to look, dark and handsome, with a neat little moustache. Arthur Carran, Socialite and Sportsman, Evaded Police in New York and Boston To-day. Friends think he has gone to Florida to avoid publicity in connection with the death of Mrs. Sally Amber, found partially clad.

I'm sick and tired of that case, Maggie thought. She brought it on herself, Mrs. Crabtree said.... They all do, she said.... By getting mixed up with some man, one way or another.

And what's Miss Dolly doing?

Coming out here to this nasty dirty queer house with these two men in it. What kind of men *are* they, I'd like to know? They could be blackmailers—or anything. I don't believe Miss Dolly's any judge. She seems so happy ... I never saw her smiling and laughing before ... I suppose she thinks she's safe now.

Well, I don't. No key in the door. I hope to goodness there isn't any kind of balcony outside the window, she thought, and rose hastily. There were some french windows at one end of the room; they would be the dangerous ones. There was a key in the lock there, she tried it and pulled the window open. And there was a balcony; the light gleamed on wet planks.

She put on her shoes and threw her coat over her shoulders, because she wanted to see, she would see, what there was out there. The rain drove at her in a slanting sheet and she stepped carefully to the railing. She saw no lights, no trees, only the dark sky. She glanced down, and there, directly beneath her she saw a sheet of black water. She could hear it lapping against the wall underneath the planks where she stood.

A house—right *in* the water ... ? She leaned over the rail, staring, half-incredulous, but it was true; that was water, moving water. Something flounced in it, making a little curl of white; something alive.

She went back into the room and locked the window, and because everything was so dreadful and so miserable, she rebelled against it. Nothing to be afraid of, she told herself, sharply. She knelt down and said her prayers, and turned out the light.

The big room was black as the pit. Very well. Everybody goes to sleep in the dark except cowards. Still in her dressing-gown and slippers, she lay down on the divan. The wind came in gusts, the rain spattered against the windows, and when a little lull came, she could hear the water lapping against the wall.

All right. She wasn't afraid of water. If something flounced again, it was a fish. Natural for there to be fish in the water, and I suppose night is the same as day to them, she thought. It'll be morning pretty soon. I'll get some sleep, and the first thing it'll be light again.

She felt cold, and she curled herself up in her coat.

The wind blew and the rain poured down, and the dark water lapped, and she went to sleep.

Chapter Four

It's a miserable thing not to have a watch, thought Maggie. It was certainly day, but the rain still fell, a steady drizzle now from the grey sky; it might be early morning, and it might be late. Back in New York you could tell by the sounds from the street; here there were no sounds, not even the lapping of the water any more.

She put on her clean blue cotton dress to go to the bathroom; she took it off to wash and put it on again. She was not going to meet those men in any dressing-gown. Then when she was all neat and trim, she went down the narrow stairs, quietly but not timidly. She felt that she had been deceived and shabbily treated; 'put upon,' she called it in her mother's phrase, and that warmed her heart with a good, steady anger.

The nasty dirty house was chillier and mustier than ever; she went through the room at the foot of the stairs, glancing at it with scorn, a sort of dining-room it was with a cheap golden oak sideboard cluttered with unbelievable things; she saw a red satin slipper there, two empty brandy bottles, a dying purple flower in a pot, a blue lustre horse, an iron bank modelled after the Statue of Liberty. Plenty of other things too, but she did not trouble to examine them, she went on into the kitchen, and it was just as she had left it last night; no one had touched the coffee or the sandwiches, nothing had been put away.

She put on the kettle to make tea, and then she opened the back door. There was a little porch out there and a sort of wooden tunnel roofed over by the upper story of the house and filled with dark, lapping water. On one side a ramp led up to a steep bank, there was an iron stanchion there to which a rowboat was tied, and beside this was a little launch at anchor.

And through the tunnel she could see a path of water running through flat marshes; everything was flat and grey and empty. But the damp air was salty and good, she was glad to breathe it, she was glad to see a gull swoop low over the reeds. This was a place you could get out of, it was lonely enough, strange enough, but it was no longer a nightmare.

She left the door open while she ate her breakfast of tea and stale bread.

It did not seem to her proper to take any of the other food in the kitchen; only bread was always proper, it was what you had a right to take. Now then ... she thought. I don't know ... I'll wash the things I've used myself, of course; but I don't know if I'll clean up this nasty kitchen before I go, or not.

Go she would, as soon as Miss Dolly waked up, no matter how much she talked about being a secretary, and having a lovely summer. Of course I can't ever go back to Mrs. Mayfield now, after going away like that without a word, she thought, and maybe she won't even give me a reference. But I guess I can get another position like that in a *nice* house, and I've got twenty dollars saved up. I guess I could make out for two weeks if I have to.

The prospect did not daunt her in the least; she would have gone back to New York with a half, with a quarter as much money, and not been seriously worried. She *knew* she was a good worker, she knew she could do things people were glad to pay for; she was young, healthy, nimble, and she had great faith in herself. I'll walk to a railroad station if I have to, she thought; but this very day, back I go.

She looked at the sink, narrowing her eyes. Oh, well ... she thought. I will clean up everything. I've just got to, that's all. She filled the kettle again, and she had begun to rinse the dishes when there was a knock at the door. As a matter of course she dried her hands and went to open it.

A taxi was just driving away, and a man stood on the porch, a portly, clean-shaven, white-haired man with a square jaw and stern blue eyes.

"Will you kindly tell Miss Camford that Mr. Angel is here," he said.

"Miss Camford isn't up yet, sir," said Maggie.

"I'm sorry," he said, "but I'm afraid I shall have to disturb her. If you'll tell her that Mr. Angel is here—"

"Does she—excuse me, sir; but will she know the name?"

He smiled a little.

"Undoubtedly," he said. "I am Miss Camford's lawyer."

A fine looking man, and handsomely dressed, a man to be credited. "Will you step in, sir?" said Maggie. "This room isn't very tidy, sir, but we just got here."

Mr. Angel looked about him at the dining-room with a distaste that pleased Maggie, he took off his hat, and he was drawing off his grey gloves as she started up the stairs.

Miss Camford's lawyer? she thought. Well, somebody's found out where she is, and pretty quick, too. Well, it's a good thing. I hope they make her leave here. It's no place for her. She knocked on the door of Miss Dolly's room, and getting no answer, she opened the door. And she was somehow touched by the look of Miss Dolly asleep with her black hair spread out on the pillow, and her face so pretty and so serene.

"Miss Dolly! I'm sorry, but Mr. Angel's here, Miss Dolly!"

Miss Dolly opened her eyes and looked blankly up, at Maggie.

"What?" she said.

"Mr. Angel is here, Miss Dolly."

"Mr. Angel?" she repeated. "But, Maggie!" She sat up in her lovely ivory silk nightgown with a yoke of écru lace. "Mr. Angel? But he *couldn't* be!"

"Well, he is, Miss Dolly," said Maggie.

"But—where is he, Maggie?"

"He's in that dining-room, Miss Dolly."

"Maggie, are the boys with him?"

"The boys, miss?"

"Neely and Johnny. Are they talking to him?"

"No, miss. I don't think they're up yet. They didn't get any breakfast for themselves anyhow."

"Let me think a moment ..." said Miss Dolly. "Wait ... Maggie. Bring Mr. Angel upstairs."

"Up *here?*" said Maggie in stern astonishment.

"Yes. Up to the sitting-room. The room you slept in. Hurry up, Maggie! And don't tell the others he's here until I've had a chance to talk to him. Hurry up, Maggie!"

And why? thought Maggie. What's all this hurry and worry about, I'd like to know?

"Maggie, hurry!"

"Yes, ma'am," said Maggie without any expression. She closed the door as she went out, and she took time to tidy that room, to put everything belonging to her out of sight; then she went down to Mr. Angel. She found him standing with his hands behind him looking at the sideboard.

"I suppose you have a telephone here," he said.

"I don't know, sir," said Maggie.

"I hope so," he said. "I shall want it to send for a taxi presently. I'm obliged to be back in New York for an appointment. That's why I came at such an early hour. Miss Camford coming down soon?"

"She'd like you to come upstairs, please, sir."

"Upstairs?" he repeated, with a look that Maggie observed with understanding and sympathy. "Miss Camford—er—she's not feeling well?"

"There's a kind of sitting-room upstairs, sir," said Maggie. "This way, please."

She led him into that sitting-room, and knocked at the bedroom door.

"Maggie?" said Miss Dolly. "Come in!"

She was wearing a dark-red housecoat with a high collar, and her hair was tied back from her forehead with a ribbon to match; she looked wonderfully tired and gentle, and wonderfully young.

"Look, Maggie!" she said. "Here's a little note for Neely. His room is the first door on the right beside the stairs. I'm asking him to drive you down to the drug store right away to get this prescription filled."

"Miss Dolly ... If he could go by himself ... I haven't got the dishes washed yet."

"That doesn't matter. I'd rather you took the prescription for me, Maggie."

Well, if it's something sort of confidential ... thought Maggie. But how much she did not want to go knocking at that Neely's door! How much she hated all of this, the dirt, the disorder, the general queerness ... She knocked, and he called out at once. "Who is it?"

"It's—me," she answered.

He opened the door, and she was relieved to see that he was dressed. "Oh, it's you!" he said. "Miss—what is it?"

"MacGowan," said Maggie. "Here's a note for you from Miss Camford, Mr. Curtius."

He unfolded the piece of paper and read it. "All right!" he said. "Come along."

"I'll get my hat and coat, Mr. Curtius."

"Don't bother," he said impatiently.

"I won't be a minute," said she.

"Dolly wants the medicine at once," he said. "I'll wait for you outside in the car."

She knocked at the sitting-room door and there was no answer. She knocked again and waited, knocked louder. Well, for goodness sake, she thought. Has she gone and got him into the bedroom? She opened the door and entered and the room was empty. All right! she thought. It's none of my business. She got her hat and coat out of the closet, and then as she turned away, she saw Mr. Angel out on the balcony, standing by the rail. The rain had stopped, the grey sky was growing light. He had his hands clasped behind his back again, his white head was raised; he looked sort of noble, she thought, like a senator, or something.

She ran down the stairs and out of the house, and Neely was sitting at the wheel of the big car. For a moment, Maggie hesitated, but he did not open the door or suggest her sitting in front with him, so she got into the back seat. She could see now how isolated that queer house was, standing almost in that river that was not exactly a river but a slow current winding through the marshes.

They turned away from that and along a road slippery with mud, and lined with fields of grass yellow and stunted; no trees, no houses. But when the sun came out, this flat and empty world grew gay, there were dandelions and clover, there was a sweet freshness in the air. They came presently to a highway and filling stations, and diners and a little house here and there, and then they came to a street in a village, tree-shaded, tranquil, with a public library behind a grass lawn, a squat, white-pillared post office, a drug store on the corner. Neely stopped the car, and Maggie got out. I like it here, she thought. This is a nice place.

A thin man in his shirt-sleeves, with spectacles a little down from the bridge of his nose, took the prescription and studied it.

"Take me half an hour," he said. "D'you want to wait?"

"Yes, thank you," said Maggie. "Could I get a soda?"

"Yes," he said calmly.

Neely sat down beside her with his hands in his pockets.

"What's wrong with Dolly?" he asked.

"I don't know," said Maggie.

She did not care for Neely, she did not like the careless way he dressed, she did not like his rude, indifferent ways; she glanced at him and found his pale-blue eyes looking her up and down with no light in them.

"You have good bones," he said.

Well, if that's all he finds to admire in me ... thought Maggie. Bones ... The druggist had set the chocolate soda before her, and she began to drink it through a straw, giving it her whole attention.

"I'll come back for you," said Neely abruptly, and went out of the store; through the window she saw him get into the car and drive away.

Well, I don't know ... Maggie thought, sipping the soda. It's certainly not what I expected. I just hate that house, and I don't like these two men, but still ... It's experience, and if I help Miss Dolly with her book it'll be a reference, and I can get a really nice job. It's queer, and Miss Dolly's acting queer, I must say, getting so lively and cheerful all of a sudden. You'd think she'd forgotten all about that letter about the vitriol.... If Mr. Angel could find out so quickly where she had gone, that Othello man might find out too.... I don't know. There are lots of things I don't like, but I'll guess I'll stay.

"Here's your eye lotion, miss," said the druggist. "Forty-five cents, that'll be."

Maggie took the bottle and counted out the money. Eye lotion? she thought. Sending me off in such a hurry for *that?* I never heard her say anything about any trouble with her eyes. No ... It was just to get that Neely out of the house while Mr. Angel was there. And I suppose she wanted me to go with him to make it look more reasonable. Well, I don't wonder she didn't want Mr. Angel to see Neely. I don't know what Mrs. Mayfield and Mr. Camford would say if they knew she was living in this nasty dirty house with two men.

She finished the soda very leisurely, and she looked around for a clock, and saw none. "Excuse me," she said to the druggist, "but can you please tell me the time?"

He took a big watch out of his pocket. "It is now —" he said deliberately, "a—ten forty-five."

"Thank you!" said Maggie.

She was getting a little tired of looking out of the window; she got up and walked about the store looking at the soap and powders, she took up a booklet about kidney pills, and read the testimonial letters in it, she went back to the window and looked out at the street where two girls in summer dresses went by, arm-in-arm. Neely's taking a long time, it seems to me.

The time grew longer and longer, the sun grew hotter. She did not like to ask the druggist to look at his watch again; she sat on a stool, she got up and went to look at a case full of cigars, the box lids up, displaying colored pictures of Indians and beautiful girls in white robes with long black hair, reclining under palm trees. A whistle began to blow.

"Excuse me," she said to the druggist, "but is that for noon?"

"That is the noon whistle over to the mills," he said.

It's certainly time Neely came back, she thought. And what if he doesn't come at all? Why, I don't even know where the house is. I don't know where I'm living. She went out into the street then, and looked up and down; there was a stationer's nearby and she went there and bought a little magazine full of condensed articles. You get a lot of information from things like that, she thought, and if I'm going to be a secretary, I want to be able to talk about what's going on.

She went back to the druggist's and sat down again. The druggist went away, and a dark and gloomy boy in spectacles came to take his place. I'll read this one article about high-lighting your personality, thought Maggie, and then I'll find out how to get back by myself.

But Neely came just before she had finished. "You were certainly gone a long time," said Maggie.

"What of it?" said Neely. "There's no hurry."

"Speak for yourself," said Maggie. "I've got things to do."

"To wash dishes?"

"No," she said briefly, and they went out and got into the car.

"I don't know why she brought you here," said Neely.

It's none of your business, thought Maggie, and did not answer at all.

They drove the rest of the way in silence; when they reached the house he jumped out and ran up the steps and opened the door. Maggie followed with a proud lack of haste; she looked into the dining-room and the kitchen; nobody was there, she went up the stairs and found no one there either. She started to make Miss Dolly's bed when Neely called from below.

"Maggie, look here! Come here, will you?"

She went into the hall and leaned over the stair railing.

"What do you want?" she said, coldly.

"Can you row a boat?" asked Neely from the doorway.

"Yes," she answered.

"Then, will you row me somewhere?"

"I can't," she said, "I've got work to do."

"It won't take long," he said. "I've got to take a bundle somewhere."

"Take it in the car," she said.

"I'm out of gas," he said. "Come on, please. It's only a little way."

"My goodness!" said Maggie, unsteadily. "You people don't care—*what* you ask me to do."

"I don't know how to row," he said, as if that explained everything.

She had reached a stage in which she would have refused him flatly if it had not been for one thing. She had a passion for small boats. Her father had taught her to row and to paddle when she was a little girl; he had taught her a little about sailing, too, and she had taken to it with ecstasy. But he had died at sea, and there had been no more time or money for recreation.

"All right," she said, "if it's not far."

It was warm now in the afternoon sun and she did not bother with hat or coat. She went out with Neely to the ramp at the foot of which the rowboat lay.

"What's that?" she asked frowning.

"It's a mannikin," he said, "a dummy someone lent me to draw from, and I've got to take it back."

It looked like a body, she thought, that long thing stretched out on the bottom of the boat covered with a tarpaulin. It was queer, but everything these people did was queer. She went down the ramp and got into the boat, sure-footed and happy to feel the lift of it under her feet; she sat down and took the oars, and Neely got in awkwardly. She could look right into the kitchen window.

"I never saw a house so close to the water's edge before," she said.

"It used to be a boat-house," Neely said. "They fixed it up for the summer people."

"Which way do we go?"

"Left," he said, and she began to pull on the oars, easily and strongly, going through the dark tunnel out toward the bright glittering water. The last time I went out with Father ... she thought. We were so happy that day.... If I'd been a boy I'd have gone to sea. I'd have been a captain some day like Father.

They came out of the wooden tunnel, and turning left they came into a part of the river she had not seen from the house; it was far more like a real river here, with higher banks.

"The current is strong here," she said.

"It's tidal," said Neely. "The tide's running out now."

"Salt water?" she asked.

"Oh, yes," he said.

The sun was hot on her head and shoulders, the breeze was fresh against her face. Oh, this is lovely, she thought. Oh, if only I could make a living doing something like this! I'd never feel tired.

The banks were growing steeper, and now she saw a willow.

"Isn't that pretty!" she cried.

Neely did not answer; he was trying to light a cigarette, but the match blew out, and he threw it into the water. It was quiet here; the sky was so blue. The river made a turn, and the boathouse was lost to sight, there were more trees stirring in the wind. It's lovely! It's lovely! she kept saying to herself.

Neely was trying again to light a cigarette; he stood up straddling the bundle, he swayed clumsily.

"Sit down!" she said, sharply. "You'll tip the boat over."

He lost his footing and fell, grasping the side of the boat and capsizing it. Maggie was tumbled out on the surface of the water, the chill of it made her gasp. She swam a stroke or two, and put her hand on the drifting boat and looked for Neely. He was standing in water up to his waist, just standing.

"Catch those oars!" she shouted, but he did not stir. "Mr. Curtius!" she cried. "Help me to turn the boat over, or we'll lose it."

But he didn't do anything. She stood up then, and she shuddered a little to find thick soft mud under her feet. She struggled with the boat, but it was very heavy.

"Why don't you *help* me?" she cried.

With an effort she lifted the boat, but it came down into the water again. Then something drifted by her. It was Mr. Angel, floating on his back, going slowly down the stream; the current caught him, and his arms went back behind his white head as if he stretched and relaxed in great comfort, sinking a little below the surface.

Chapter Five

"Oh ... Stop him!" she cried.

Neely reached for one of the oars that was floating away; he waded a few steps to catch the other oar. But he didn't even look after Mr. Angel.

"Help me—to get him!" cried Maggie.

"No. He's dead," said Neely.

"He's going out to sea!" she said in horror, and turned to go after him. The mud was too thick; she lost one of her shoes, and the feel of the mud was sickening. She began to swim after Mr. Angel, and in spite of her clothes she went fast, helped by the tide. She came up with him and took hold of his sleeve. A matter of two or three strokes would bring her to the bank and she could get him out of the water.

But a rough hand had seized her by the shoulder and pulled her backward, so that Mr. Angel escaped and went on his way.

"Don't be a fool," said Neely, standing beside her waist-deep in the water. "He's dead."

"I know that," said Maggie. "But I want—"

"You can't do him any good," said Neely, "and you'll do Dolly—and all of us—a lot of harm. Yourself, too."

She was on her feet now in that thick hateful mud; she tried to free herself, but he held her fast.

"I won't *let* him go out to sea!" she said.

"Look here! He had a fit or a stroke or something like that. I found him in the boat dead, so I wanted to get rid of him."

"You ought to know better!" said Maggie. "Let me go! You'll get in a lot more trouble with the police, acting like this. Let me *go!* It's everybody's duty to tell the police—"

"Why?" he asked.

The boat was coming along, and he stopped it. "Let's go home and forget it," he said. "Nothing we can do."

"You're awful!" she said. "I won't do it. I'm going to get Mr. Angel—"

"Angel?" said Neely. "Is that his name? Really his name? Angel?" He grinned from ear to ear. "Angel's on his way to heaven," he said. "That's a good one."

"You ought to be ashamed of yourself! You let me go this minute. I'm going to get poor Mr. Angel out of the water, and then I'm going to tell the police."

"What makes you such a fool?" said Neely. "Let Dolly have her party, anyhow."

"Party! Her *party!*"

"It's important. She's got important people coming."

Maggie began to struggle in earnest to get away, but he was very strong.

"Stop!" he said, not much interested. "Let's turn the boat over and get into it. Silly to be standing here in the water. You look funny."

"You're not—human," said Maggie.

Mr. Angel was out of sight now; either he had disappeared around the bend of the river, or he had sunk to the bottom.

"Come on. Let's go home," said Neely.

"I'm going to find Mr. Angel," she said, "and you can't stop me."

"I will stop you," said Neely. "I don't want you to find him. I want to go home. I want you to row me back."

"I won't," said Maggie.

"Oh, you're a nuisance!" he said angrily.

He let the oars, which he had held under his arm, drop into the water, he gave the boat a shove, he let Maggie go, and he began to walk toward the bank. "If you tell the police," he called back, "you'll get yourself in a hell of a lot of trouble, and *I'll* say it's all a lie. I'm not going to get mixed up in this for any dead angels."

She stood there in the mud and the cold running water with the sun blazing down upon her, not a house, not a living thing in sight, except the broad-shouldered, sturdy figure of Neely making his way across the marsh. Her teeth were chattering with cold, she clenched them and began to swim after the boat. She reached it and went along beside it sometimes swimming and sometimes wading; she caught the oars and pulled them along with her.

She went round the bend of the river, and the boathouse was in sight. But not Mr. Angel. She could see a long way ahead of her, but not a sign of him. She was utterly alone in the empty, sunny world; she was so cold ... An idea began to come into her head. She tried to banish it, but in vain. If poor Mr. Angel had sunk to the bottom of the muddy water ...

She swam the rest of the way, juggling both the boat and the oars, shoving them ahead of her into the dark tunnel underneath the balcony. Even in here she could not, and would not set foot on the bottom. She took the painter of the boat in her teeth and scrambled up the ramp; she made the boat fast and took in the oars. And she did all this because it was not in her to waste or destroy anything, and because she had a particular respect for boats.

Shivering and dripping, limping with one shoe on, she went round to the back door. She took off her shoe then, and wrung out her skirts and went up the stairs to the big room. There was no hot water in the bathroom, and she could not face a cold bath; she scrubbed herself with soap and a damp towel, she put on clean underwear and her felt slippers and the black poplin dress. Now I'll call up the police, she told herself.

She looked upstairs and down for a telephone until there was only one place to look. She knocked at Neely's door.

"Come in!" he said, and she opened the door.

Barefoot and in singlet and dark trousers, he was standing at a high tilted board, drawing with a piece of charcoal.

"Well, did you find your angel?" he asked.

"I'm looking for a telephone," said Maggie, briefly.

He put down the charcoal, and thrust his hands into his pockets, frowning; she noticed that his thick lashes were silvery when the sun touched them.

"My God!" he said. "I think I have a hole in my pocket. I must have dropped that telephone in the water, maybe; isn't that too bad?"

"Do you think there's anything to be funny about?" asked Maggie.

"To cry about then?" he asked. "Too many people getting killed in the world now. If some old fellow has a fit and tumbles down dead in a rowboat, all right. He's lucky. He lived a good long time, and he died easy."

There was something foreign in his speech now, not an accent, but an inflection, a choice of words, he looked foreign, too.

He took up the charcoal and began to draw again, and Maggie left him. She was completely at a loss now. There was undoubtedly a telephone to be found somewhere along the highway; but that was a long long way to go in felt bedroom slippers. It would take a long time, too, and what would be happening to Mr. Angel in the meantime? She felt the sharpest distress to think of him, in all his dignity and decency, hurried off upon that shocking journey. He must be brought back, treated with respect and kindness.

Miss Dolly and that Mr. Cassidy will be back soon, she thought. I'll just have to wait for them, and then they can telephone. In the meantime she could get a little work done. She descended to that kitchen again, angry at it, yet with a certain grim enjoyment in the challenge it offered.

The doorbell rang—she dried her hands and took off her work apron, and went to answer it.

A very stout lady stood on the porch.

"Tell Miss Camford Miss Plummer is here," she said affably.

"I'm sorry, ma'am, but Miss Camford isn't in just now," said Maggie.

"She ought to be back by this time," said the other. "Well, I'll come in and wait."

She was a cheerful and amiable lady, dark-haired, in a gay print dress and a dark coat, and sensible low-heeled shoes, and a straw hat coming far down on her face. She looked funny, so stout and in such bright colors, but she looked, Maggie thought, like a lady.

"Miss Camford didn't leave any word for me?" she asked.

"No, ma'am," said Maggie, and Miss Plummer entered the house.

"Mon dieu!" she cried stopping in the doorway of the dining-room.

She turned to Maggie. "Do you know—?" she asked, "What they've done with all my things?"

"No, ma'am," Maggie answered. "I just came yesterday."

"What's your name, my dear?"

"It's Maggie, ma'am."

"Irish!" cried Miss Plummer.

"No, ma'am," said Maggie. "I'm Scotch. On both sides."

"Oh, dear ..." said Miss Plummer. "Edinburgh ... A magic city ... What can they have done with the faience hen, do you know, Maggie?"

"No, ma'am," said Maggie, and withdrew into the kitchen.

She was not sure that she had done the right thing. Perhaps she should have told Miss Plummer about Mr. Angel and asked her advice. Through the half-open door she could see her moving about, shaking her head in consternation; her house, it seemed to be.

A car was coming now, she heard footsteps on the porch, and before she could reach the door, Miss Dolly had come in followed by Mr. Cassidy with his arms full of packages.

"Oh, Mitzi, you darling!" cried Miss Dolly. "We're late, but we've bought fine things.... Excuse us one *minute*, will you?"

She caught sight of Maggie then, and she came toward her and prevented her getting back into the kitchen, and closed the door.

"Maggie," she said. "Come upstairs with me—"

"Miss Dolly, I've got something to tell you—"

"Tell me upstairs. *Please* come along, Maggie!"

Maggie followed her up the narrow stairway to the big room, and Miss Dolly went on into her bedroom.

"I've got a little dress here—" she said.

"Miss Dolly, something's happened."

"Well, what?" asked Miss Dolly bending over her suitcase that was open on the bed.

"Mr. Angel ... Mr. Angel—met with an accident," said Maggie.

"Oh dear!" said Miss Dolly. "The poor thing told me he wasn't feeling at all well when he was here. Maggie, look! Put this on."

She held up a dress, a new dress she had bought only a few days ago.

"Miss Dolly," said Maggie. "I'm sorry to tell you, but Mr. Angel is dead."

"Oh, heavens!" said Miss Dolly. "I suppose he had a heart attack. I'm terribly sorry. But I've got to speak to you now about this afternoon, Maggie. It's *terribly* important for me."

"Miss Dolly, we'll have to do something about Mr. Angel, first."

"Do something? But, if he's dead—"

"He was—in the river, Miss Dolly; floating away out to sea."

"Maggie! You mean, drowned?"

"No, Miss Dolly. Mr. Curtius found him in the rowboat, dead, and he tipped over the boat. I—think he did that on purpose. I'm quite sure he did. And he wouldn't help me to stop Mr. Angel."

"Stop him?"

"He was—going out to sea," said Maggie swallowing hard. "I went after him—but I couldn't find him. If we got the police—quick—they could drag the river—"

"Yes, we will," said Miss Dolly. "What a dreadful thing! But now, Maggie, put on this dress will you?"

"What for, Miss Dolly?"

"Maggie, I told you I wanted you here as my secretary. I want to introduce you to these people this afternoon. Put on the dress; it's brand new, and I think it will suit you."

"I'm sorry, Miss Dolly, but I just couldn't," she said.

"Maggie!" cried Miss Dolly. "You can't *possibly* refuse to help me!"

Can't I? thought Maggie.

"Maggie, this is a really important day for me," said Miss Dolly.

An important day for Mr. Angel, too, thought Maggie; but that doesn't seem to bother you much.

"Please remember," said Miss Dolly. "These people are coming here—and I can't let them get the impression that I'm staying alone in the house with two men."

"Well, they'll see me here, ma'am."

"But it isn't the *same,* Maggie! If you're—" She paused, and by the pause, the effort to put the matter tactfully, made it doubly offensive to Maggie. "Anyone can see what an absolutely honest, straightforward girl you are—and if people felt that we're friends—that—that we're confidential together …"

"That lady downstairs knows I'm a servant," said Maggie. "I let her in, and I told her my name was Maggie."

"Oh, she doesn't count," said Miss Dolly. "She doesn't notice anything. Oh Maggie, do please hurry up and get ready before the Gettys come!"

"Miss Dolly, something's got to be done about Mr. Angel."

"Of course! I know it. I'll send someone—I'll send Johnny Cassidy to telephone to the police."

"Right away, miss?"

"Yes. The moment I've got you ready."

"I don't need any getting ready, Miss Dolly."

"How *can* you be so stubborn?" said Miss Dolly. "I've tried to be nice to you, Maggie. I asked you to come as a secretary, and you agreed—"

"I can be a secretary, miss, without dressing up in somebody else's clothes—"

"The Gettys will think I'm a bitch," said Miss Dolly.

What a word to call your own self! thought Maggie. But it impressed her; she felt a reluctant sympathy for Miss Dolly in this dilemma. Nobody wanted to be talked about, she thought. I don't think she ever ought to have come here to this house; but here she is.

"I didn't understand what you meant," she said. "Or I'd never have come."

"But it's too late now for me to do anything. Maggie, please ... !"

"All right, miss," said Maggie. "This once."

It was a lovely dress; Maggie had seen it the day it came from the shop, and it cost *forty dollars* ... A sort of long-waisted effect, and a yoke over the hips and a pleated skirt.

"But my shoes, Miss Dolly. I lost a shoe in the mud—"

"Try these," said Miss Dolly.

Maggie tried on a patent leather pump.

"It's too big for me, miss," she said with quiet satisfaction.

"Well, it's a little too long," said Miss Dolly. "But it's not too wide. I have very narrow feet."

"Yes, miss," said Maggie. "So have I."

"Well, here, try this," said Miss Dolly, taking off her suède sandal.

"I guess I can make these do, miss," said Maggie, "if I fasten the straps in the very last holes."

"Please remember not to call me 'miss.' Call me Dolly."

"I couldn't, miss. I could say Miss Camford."

"All right!" said Miss Dolly with a sigh. "Now let's see ... Your hair's perfect. You have very nice hair, Maggie."

"It's naturally curly," said Maggie.

"Here! Here's a new lipstick, Maggie. I'm afraid it's a little dark, but try it, won't you?"

Maggie made no objection to this. She had never before used a lipstick, but the idea gave her a small thrill of pleasure.

"Put cold cream on first," said Miss Dolly. "Use plenty of lipstick, Maggie.... No, this way ..."

Maggie regarded herself in the mirror. She looked taller in this grey dress, and her face was different; the rich red lips made her eyes look bluer, and her fair skin, dusted with powder, seemed dazzlingly fair. I love it, she thought. I'm going to buy a lipstick for myself.

"Now, let's go down," said Miss Dolly. "And don't open the door, Maggie. Don't wait on people."

"Who *is* going to wait on the people, Miss Dolly?"

"Not Miss Dolly!"

"Miss Camford."

"We'll all wait on ourselves, Johnny'll mix the cocktails, and I brought along potato chips and popcorn. It's going to be very informal. Let's go down now, Maggie."

"But what about Mr. Angel?" said Maggie with a guilty start.

"Johnny Cassidy will go and telephone."

"But, Miss—Miss Camford, every minute counts."

"It can't if he's dead," said Miss Dolly. "But I'll send Johnny right away. The doorbell rang.

"Oh, there they are!" said Miss Dolly, catching Maggie by the wrist. "*Please* do the best you can ... "

She started down the narrow stairway, and Maggie followed her, suddenly sick with fear. Oh, don't let me make a fool of myself! she prayed in her heart.

Miss Mitzi Plummer had already opened the door, and a man and a woman had entered.

"Gabrielle's pretty shaky," said the man. "It was pretty ghastly. We came over in the launch, you know, and when we went down to the landing-stage, there was a body—a man, washed up on our beach."

It's Mr. Angel, Maggie said to herself. It's a judgment.

Chapter Six

"But, how horrible!" said Miss Dolly.

"Yes ..." said Gabrielle.

She was a blonde girl, very thin, with hollows under her cheekbones, and no figure. But she made an asset of her gauntness; she had style, distinction, the fluid grace of a cat, in her plain dark-blue linen dress.

"This is my secretary, Maggie MacGowan, Gabrielle. Maggie—Mrs. Getty. And Mr. Getty."

Maggie did not like the looks of Mr. Getty. He was handsome, in a way, but it was a way too male for her taste, too unromantic. He was dark, stalwart, heavy-shouldered, with a bluish jaw and a quick uncheerful smile.

"How do you do?" he said, appraising Maggie with a quick glance.

"Was it suicide, do you think?" said Miss Plummer.

"Could be, I suppose," said Getty. "But I didn't think of that. Well-dressed fellow, prosperous looking. I thought of murder."

"Murder ... ?" said Miss Plummer. "But why think of that, Hiram?"

"Well," said Getty, "he wasn't dressed for boating. Didn't look like anyone who'd fallen overboard from any kind of craft. Anyhow, people don't fall overboard in this kind of weather. And suicide didn't come into my head. He was too comfortable looking."

"Strange accidents happen," said Miss Plummer.

"You're right," said Getty. "Anyhow I called up Captain Hofer and he's on the job. We'll soon find out."

"He had white hair ..." said Gabrielle Getty, unsteadily. "He looked—"

"Take it easy, Gabrielle," said her husband. "Try to forget it. Have a drink."

He looked about the dining-room, and Miss Dolly gave a little start.

"Will you make the cocktails, Hiram?" she asked. "I'll show you where everything is."

He followed her into the kitchen, and Maggie was left alone with Miss Plummet and Mrs. Getty. She had grown accustomed to going out of a room when people like these began to talk; she wished with all her heart she could go out now. She sat in a chair, her eyes lowered, she listened to their talk in misery. They talked about art exhibitions, and artists, and people they knew; and what must they be thinking of this Miss MacGowan who had not a word to say for herself?

Johnny Cassidy came in then, and little as she liked him, she had a certain admiration for him, he was so easy, so amiable. He stood beside Miss Plummer, and Maggie heard snatches of this conversation.

"After all," said Johnny, "what is an artist? Dreamer—or maker?"

"A maker, surely," said Miss Plummer.

"But then what of the dreamer?" asked Johnny. "The man with a vision?"

"But the vision must be seized," said Miss Plummer. "As Ruskin says, fine art—Ah! Here are the cocktails!"

At the sight of Miss Dolly and Mr. Getty coming in, each with a tray, Maggie rose by impulse.

"Don't get up, Miss MacGowan," said Johnny, and she sat down again.

He came to her in a moment with a cocktail and a glass dish of popcorn.

"Well, thank you ..." she said. "Only—no, thank you."

He set the glass on the floor, and drew up a chair beside her.

"You ought to be pleased with yourself," he said.

"Why?" she asked, coldly.

"Because you're a very perfect little being," he said. "You always do the right thing."

"Well, I don't," she said.

"You're so nice and neat and pretty," he said. "All one piece. I'd like to be you."

"Well, you wouldn't," she said.

"You sit here," he went on, "despising me."

"I wasn't doing anything of the sort," she said. "I don't despise people, and anyhow I thought the way you were talking was interesting."

"Yes, it was," he said. "I'm a fine talker, very plausible. I can talk in foreign tongues, too. I wonder if you realize what an interesting and colorful personality I am. I've been around. I was in Spain for that show. Camera man. Worked in Paris. Went to Moscow. Do I interest you, Miss MacGowan?"

"Well, yes," said Maggie, considerably at a loss.

He sat down on the floor at her feet.

"I've been around," he said again. "Only now I'm not doing anything, and I don't want to do anything, and I don't like anything. Except you, of course."

He's not joking, exactly, she thought, glancing at his bony face. He looks—I don't know. Kind of queer. Kind of miserable. As if something had gone wrong with him. He's fresh, she thought, there's no doubt about that. But he's—very intelligent. I guess he's the most intelligent person I've ever met.

And here, in this room with Miss Dolly, Miss Plummer, and Mrs. Getty, Johnny Cassidy chose to sit beside Maggie MacGowan.

"Do you write, or anything?" she asked.

"No," he said, "I'm a photographer, same like I told you. I'm trying to get myself sent to China."

"China?" she said with respect.

He looked up at her, his hazel eyes vague and sad.

"Here you see me," he said, "an outcast, a ruined man. Shot to pieces. The Navy turned me down, and the Army. On account of how I've got a bullet in my shoulder."

"A bullet?" said Maggie. "Did you get it in a battle?"

"Oh, yes," he said. "I got it trying to run away from a battle." He rose. "I think I need another drink," he said, and went off to the kitchen.

She missed him. The party had become animated now. Hiram Getty sat on the arm of Miss Dolly's chair talking to her, Miss Plummer sat on the couch beside Mrs. Getty, and Neely, whose entrance she had not noticed, stood before them. Not one of them so much as glanced at Miss Mac-Gowan.

Well, she thought, here I am at a cocktail party. It was not the sort of cocktail party she had seen in the movies, with women in long dresses, and maids and butlers carrying around trays; the background, too, this dusty, untidy dining-room was very inferior. But still, it's interesting, she thought.

She glanced down at the glass that still stood on the floor beside her chair.

Well ... she thought, and picked it up. If I'm at a cocktail party, I'm going to try it.

It was nasty. But there must be something about it, she thought. It must make you feel different. Feel how? One drink couldn't do much harm, when even Miss Plummer had finished her second. I'd sort of like to say that I'd had a cocktail for once, Maggie thought, taking another swallow.

She drank it, all of it, and leaned back to see what would happen.

A car was coming along the road; it stopped, and heavy footsteps mounted to the porch; she rose and went to the door just as the bell rang. It was a square, burly man with a red face, in a uniform. A police uniform.

It's about Mr. Angel! she thought with something like terror. A dreadful, a shocking thing to be sitting here drinking, with Mr. Angel lying dead.

"Mr. Getty here?" asked the man.

"I'll see, sir," she answered. "What name will I say, please?"

He stared at her with his lips pursed, and she realized that Miss Mac-Gowan had spoken like Maggie. But it didn't matter.

"Tell him it's Captain Hofer," said the man, and she went back to the dining-room.

"Mr. Getty," she said, "Captain Hofer's here to see you."

"Come in, Captain!" called Mr. Getty, and rose. "He told me he'd let me know about this fellow we found on the beach," he explained to Dolly.

Captain Hofer entered and glanced about the room.

"Good evening, Mr. Getty," he said. "Miss Plummer— Well, it looks as if the summer had started now all right."

He looked extremely hot; he took out a handkerchief and wiped his red face. "Whew!" he said. "Now I wonder if anybody here knows of a Miss Camford —a Miss Dorothy Camford?"

"That's *meee!*" said Miss Dolly.

"You're Miss Camford ... ?" He stared at her, pursing his lips again. "I'm afraid I've got some bad news for you, Miss Camford. Try to take it easy. You know anybody by the name of Nicholas Angel?"

"Mr. Angel? Oh yes! He was here to see me this morning," she said.

"Now take it easy, Miss Camford," he said. "I'm sorry to tell you that Mr. Angel has had an accident."

"Oh, poor *thing!* But he told me he wasn't feeling well."

"How did he leave here, Miss Camford?"

"He said he wanted to walk to the station. He said he thought the exercise would help him. So he started off—"

"Did you notice which way he went?"

"Why no, I didn't," she said. "Is he ill, Captain Hofer?"

"Well ..." said Captain Hofer. "I'm afraid it's more serious than that, Miss Camford."

She looked up at him with her dark eyes wide.

"But not—? He's not *dead?*"

"Take it easy, Miss Camford."

Her eyes filled with tears.

"Oh ... He must have had some sort of heart attack," she said. "I shouldn't have let him walk."

"Well ... Maybe not...." said Captain Hofer.

Maggie observed this scene with stupefaction. However can Miss Dolly be so double-faced? she thought. Tears in her eyes and all that, when I *told* her long ago about Mr. Angel.... And she's lying. She's lying to the *police.* Well she won't get away with that. Because *I'm* not going to tell any lies.

The moment Captain Hofer asked her a question, she would tell him the truth. If that meant trouble for Miss Dolly and Neely, they deserved it.

"I'm sorry, Miss Camford," said Captain Hofer, "but I'm afraid I'll have to ask you to come with me, to identify."

"I can't!" she said.

"I'm sorry," he said again, "but I'm afraid you'll have to, Miss Camford."

"I'll go with you, Dolly," said Miss Plummer. "And we can all stop at my house afterwards for a little supper. That'll cheer you up."

"Oh, Captain Hofer, *must* I do this?" asked Miss Dolly.

"Sorry," he said, "just no way out of it, Miss Camford."

She rose and stood holding the back of a chair; Captain Hofer took one arm, and Miss Plummer the other.

"You people follow along," said Miss Plummer. "Somebody drive my car for me, while I go with Dolly. Johnny, won't you? Hiram and Gabrielle can take Neely with them."

She was arranging it all with great gaiety and spirit, making a party of it. "Come Dolly!" she said, and they started, Miss Dolly, white and dazed, like a prisoner between those two. And Maggie let them go. I've got to wait, she thought.

For what she had to tell Captain Hofer was no more or less than an accusation of Neely and of Miss Dolly, and it was impossible to make it publicly in front of all these people. And she did not want to ask Captain Hofer for a word in private either.

Her reluctance surprised her. It's the right thing, to tell him, she thought, and I'm certainly *going* to tell him; only I'd sort of like to warn Miss Dolly and Neely that I'm going to tell.... They did not deserve to be warned. The way they were behaving was altogether wrong, and she was certainly in the right about everything. But, standing aside ignored, while these other people made their plans, she felt like a little girl, and to tell Captain Hofer seemed very much like telling tales in school. That was something she never had done.

I'll wait, she thought, till Miss Dolly's identified Mr. Angel. When she comes back, I'll tell her, right out, that Captain Hofer's got to know the whole thing. They were all getting into the cars and driving away; when they had gone she went out on the little porch. A faint mist was rising from the marshes, like smoke; it was not dark yet, but there was no color anywhere. Sad, sort of, she thought.

That Miss Plummer *might* have asked me if I'd like to come to supper. I wouldn't have done it, but she might have asked me. Or Mr. Cassidy or Mr. Curtius might have said *something*, living right in the same house.... I must say it seems a pretty funny way to treat a secretary. A pretty rude way. Sort of—discouraging ...

A warm indignation began to rise in her, replacing the unwonted melancholy. They had all gone off to supper; let them go. She would get her own supper.

There was nothing to eat; nothing real, no potatoes or vegetables or meat; only a few silly things in cans, shad roe and turtle soup, and fruit salad. There was not even any bread except that rock-like loaf that now had green mould on it. She was hungry, and she was affronted by all of this, by the disorder, the carelessness, by the empty gin bottles and the dirty glasses, the cigarette ashes in the sink. And by this desertion. She went upstairs and it was dark now, she took off Miss Dolly's dress and put on her own black one, and the cap and apron, too. She went down and with tears of wrath, set about cleaning up the kitchen again.

She opened the can of shad roe and fried it, she made tea, and she sat down at the kitchen table and ate. I haven't had a decent meal since I left the city, she thought. I haven't any sheets and blankets, or anything. And then, on top of all *that*, Mr. Curtius has to go and get me to row that boat....

Tears ran down her cheeks. And a cocktail party! she thought. Right after I'd seen—poor Mr. Angel ... Who ever heard of such a job as this? And what kind of a way to live, with just Miss Dolly and me here with these two men....

The tea did her good, and she went upstairs to get a book. She poured herself out a second cup, good and hot and strong, and just as she prepared to enjoy it, she heard the sound of a motor-boat coming fast. She did not want anybody to see her at her supper in the kitchen; she whisked away her dishes, and stood drinking the hot tea as quickly as she could. The boat was coming into that wooden tunnel now, making waves that dashed against the house, and then the engine was shut off and it was quiet.

It was too quiet. This could not be the party that had left here. No sound of voices, nothing but the wavelets that still lapped against the house. But who would be out there in the dark, in a boat .. . ?

Oh ... she said to herself, and clapped her hand across her mouth. No!

she told herself. I don't believe in things like that. There *aren't*—any ghosts. No. A boat came, and there was—there was a person in it. There had to be. And where was the person now? Sitting out there in the dark? Or lying ... ?

I just never knew I was like this, she thought. Such a coward. At least I could look out the window ...

But it was not a sensible thing to go and stand in the lighted window when you did not know what might be outside. She stood very still listening for the sound of a stealthy step on the porch, for a splash in the water; she glanced over her shoulder. If anyone was watching out there in the dark, she must not look frightened, not even hurried.

She set down the teacup and went out of the kitchen, she turned on the light in the dining-room and looked at the stairs. It was dark up there. All right! The more you give in to it, the worse it is. I hate and despise being scared! she said to herself and she started up the stairs. Miss Dolly's sandals were loose on her heels so that they clattered, and if there was anybody else coming up the stairs behind her she could not hear it.

Don't run. And don't turn on the light. She stopped at the top of the stairs and looked down into the lighted hall. There was nothing there. She drew a good long breath and groped her way cautiously into the big sitting-room; she opened one of the windows and stepped out on the balcony.

It was better under the open sky. She stood still, and now she heard voices, low voices, but as she drew near the rail they were quite audible.

"But you can get a divorce from a swine like that," said a man's voice, deep, and a little unsteady.

"I know I could, Hiram," said a woman's voice. Miss Dolly's voice. "But—I don't know if I could ever explain—how it is ... "

"You mean you still care for him?" asked Getty.

"No ..." Miss Dolly said. "No, it isn't that. It's because he cares so very much for me."

"Is that your idea of 'caring?'" Getty asked. "This damn brute who's made you utterly miserable for years—"

"I knew I couldn't explain," she said with a sort of weariness. "It's really no use. Only, I never really did love him, and he knows that. And it hurts him.... I was so young—and so stupid for my age. I didn't know what love was."

"Do you—now?" Getty asked, his voice very unsteady.

"Hiram," she said. "I must go in now."

"No. Wait, Dolly," he said. "Dolly, look here ... You said ... You said—let's run away. You said let's go away from the others—"

"I know. It's been a rather dreadful day for me, Hiram, and to-morrow won't be very pleasant. I wanted to go home."

"And you didn't care who came along?" he said. "You didn't want me particularly?"

There was a silence.

"If I did," she said quietly, "it was because when I first met you, I thought you were—rather different from the other men I've met. I thought you'd understand me."

"I *do*," he said after a moment. "You can count on me, Dolly. Always."

So she's married, thought Maggie, overwhelmed.

Chapter Seven

Miss Dolly came up the stairs slowly; the damp air had made her hair curl at the temples, her damp lashes made her eyes starry. She looked pale, fatigued, very lovely.

"It was horrible, Maggie," she said. "I could never *tell* you how horrible.... I didn't like Mr. Angel, I couldn't. But to see him lying there ..."

She sat down on Maggie's couch, and put her hair back from her forehead. "It seems strange ..." she said. "I thought I could have a little peace—a little happiness.... I need it so.... Maggie, do you know why Mr. Angel came here?"

"No, ma'am."

"He came—he's dead now, and I don't want to be bitter—but he came here to ruin everything for me —if he could. You see, an uncle who was very fond of me died last month, and he left me some money; not very much, but enough to give me a little freedom. Mr. Angel was the executor. I asked him for just enough of that money—my own money—to let me get away. But he refused. He said I couldn't have anything for a year at least, until the estate was settled. I couldn't wait a year, Maggie, shut up in that miserable prison of a house."

"Well ..." said Maggie.

"I borrowed on it," Miss Dolly went on. "It wasn't a good way to do. I knew that well enough. I had to pay an exorbitant interest, and I had to get it from a rather queer man. He makes a business of doing that, advancing money on legacies."

"A *money-lender*, Miss Dolly?" Maggie asked, turning to look at her in dismay. "But, they're terrible! I've known people who got into their hands."

"I know—but I felt—oh, desperate, Maggie. I don't know how Mr. Angel found out about it. He said he was going to tell my uncle and that would have done me a great deal of harm. Maggie, isn't it a strange thing that there are so many people like that? People who can't bear to see anyone else happy."

"Well ... Yes, ma'am ..." said Maggie, very doubtfully.

She had been brought up with grave suspicion about happiness; it was a dangerous and frequently a discreditable thing. And to go to money-lenders in order to be happy ... That shocked Maggie.

What's more, she thought, I didn't hear anything in the beginning about her coming here to be *happy*.

She said it was to get away from that man, so that there would not be any scandal. She said it was to translate a book—and what about that? She hasn't been straightforward with me, and I don't like that.

"But, Miss Dolly, I thought you came here to get away from that man," she said.

"I'll never get away from him," said Miss Dolly with sombre despair.

"Well, but Miss Dolly ..." said Maggie. She paused, embarrassed but resolute. "I don't mean to be prying, but ... That letter you showed me ... I mean, it was signed Othello ... Well, that was Desdemona's husband, wasn't it?"

Miss Dolly glanced at her with dark, blank eyes. "Yes," she said. "He's my husband."

There was a silence.

"I'll tell you about it," Miss Dolly went on. "I trust you utterly, Maggie.... It was years ago in Paris. I went there after my parents died, and I was dreadfully lonely and unhappy. I met this man ... I needed somebody kind and generous and understanding, and I thought ... I won't go into all that. Even before we got back from our honeymoon I saw what a ghastly mistake I'd made. I left him and I came home. I didn't tell anyone."

"Not even your aunt and uncle, Miss Dolly?"

"They're the last ones I'd ever tell," she answered, and was silent again, looking down at her clasped hands. "They'd never understand." She glanced up. "I didn't know what he was like, what a reputation he had. They'd despise me, Maggie. They'd wash their hands of me. And after all— they're all I have. They mustn't know, ever."

She leaned back against the cushions, lost in some melancholy vision, and Maggie looked at her with an uneasy wonder. Here before her very eyes was a woman who had had the tragic experiences that make a heroine, an unhappy marriage, grief, disillusionment; she had lost her home and her money; she was threatened, in danger.

"I suppose this will get into the newspapers," Miss Dolly said. "About poor Mr. Angel. But nobody needs to know anything about the rest of it, anyhow. I mean about his being in the boat."

"But, Miss Dolly, I've got to tell—"

"But why?" asked Miss Dolly. "What earthly difference does it make? It will only make trouble for Neely, serious trouble. The police would *arrest* him, Maggie."

"They'd let him go again if he could prove—"

"There's no reason why he should have to go to court and prove things. He's a genius, *I* think. It's outrageous to think of his being bullied and tormented for nothing."

"Miss Dolly, I don't think Captain Hofer would bully anyone who was innocent."

"Well, he *isn't* innocent," said Miss Dolly. "I mean I'm perfectly sure it's against the law to move dead bodies. They might be able to send him to prison for having done that. You wouldn't want *that* to happen, would you?"

"Miss Dolly, *I'd* be breaking the law if I didn't tell the police."

"I don't think you would," said Miss Dolly. "I think it's only when you tell the police a lie."

"No, Miss Dolly," said Maggie flatly. "If you know something wrong has been done and you don't report it, that's obstructing the police, and it's being an accessory."

"How can you possibly know all these things?" Miss Dolly asked.

"Because a woman in our street did it. She saw this other woman she knew steal some silk stockings in a department store, and she didn't tell the police. And when they found out that she'd been right there, and must have seen what happened—"

"That's entirely different," said Miss Dolly. "Nobody's going to find out about this. And if anyone does—very well. Maggie, I'll take the whole responsibility. I'll say I told you not to mention it."

"*Nobody* could tell me what's right for me to do," said Maggie.

They looked at each other straight in the eyes, and they were equally baffled, and equally dismayed.

"You mean you *will* tell? You don't care what trouble and misery you cause for Neely who hasn't done anything wrong?"

"Well, you couldn't call it the right thing to do," said Maggie. "Poor Mr. Angel—"

"He was *dead!*" cried Miss Dolly.

"I know it," said Maggie. "But he shouldn't have been treated *that* way."

They were still looking at each other. Then Miss Dolly sighed.

"I can't argue with you," she said. "You're so obstinate. I'm going."

"Going where, Miss Dolly?"

"I don't know. I don't care. I can't stay here and face this scandal you're going to bring down on my head."

"Well, I can't see how it would be a scandal for you, Miss Dolly. You hadn't anything to do with it."

"Everybody will know why Neely did it. He did it to save me from being worried and harassed. And once that Hofer starts poking into Neely's affairs, he'll find out everything. He'll find out that I took the house for Neely and paid the month's rent."

"Miss Dolly!"

"It's one of the few things in my life I'm proud of," said Miss Dolly. "It's a privilege to help an artist like Neely. But I know very well what Hofer and everybody will make of it. I've been brought up among stuffy, spiteful, self-righteous people. I won't stay here one more minute."

"Miss Dolly! Please tell me where you're going!" Maggie cried.

"I don't know. I'll get a train somewhere. I've got eight hundred dollars in my purse. That'll be enough to take me somewhere—"

Maggie clasped her hands in an unconscious and ancient gesture of despair. She had never before been faced with a moral dilemma; she had not believed that such things existed. Right was right, and wrong was wrong. But not now.

It was plainly her duty to tell the police everything she knew about poor Mr. Angel. But it was her duty too, to protect another woman from scandal. A scandal it must be. Paying a man's rent was one of the most scandalous things you could do.

No. She could not let Miss Dolly go off alone at this hour of the night with eight hundred dollars in her purse.

"I—I'll try not to tell anyone," she said. "Only if I have to take an oath ..."

Miss Dolly sat down at the table and began to cry, with her shining dark head on her folded arms. Maggie stood looking down at her in miserable confusion; she had no rules for this. She had heard of, and even known, women who paid a man's rent, but they were not women like Miss Dolly, and they had not acted from any motive like hers. Oh, you wouldn't think that Mr. Curtius would let her! Maggie thought.

Artists are different from other people, so they say. But that Mr. Curtius was young and strong; he *ought* to pay his own rent some way. It isn't right! It isn't! she said to herself. And the way he talked about poor Mr. Angel was horrible, no matter what anyone says.

But she was very sorry for Miss Dolly. Miss Dolly was good in her own way, she had qualms and scruples about that husband of hers; she had spoken to Mr. Getty with an admirable dignity. She was reckless and foolish; but she's a *good woman*, Maggie thought.

And if she had not been a Good Woman in Maggie's own and definite sense, she would have got little sympathy from young Maggie.

Miss Dolly sat up and lit a cigarette; she was pale and tear-stained but calm now.

"It's a miserable beginning for our happy summer, isn't it, Maggie?" she asked.

"Well ..." said Maggie. She wanted to say that the one to feel sorry for was Mr. Angel, but she was afraid of starting those tears again. Of course, she thought, if Miss Dolly'd seen Mr. Angel the way I did, she'd feel different. That's something to cry about if you like.

Somebody was coming up the steps of the porch; there was the sound of a key in the lock, and in came Neely and Johnny Cassidy.

"The ladies—God bless them!" said Johnny. "And lookie lookie ... !"

He took a bottle of whiskey out of a paper bag he had brought in under his arm; he set it on the table and unscrewed the top.

"Glasses!" he said. "Glasses, Neely, for the two lovelies."

Neely shrugged his shoulders in a very foreign way and leaned back against the wall, folding his arms.

"Then I'll get them," said Johnny, moving toward the china closet.

He's drunk, Maggie thought. I hope Miss Dolly'll have the sense to stop him taking any more. But Miss Dolly only sighed.

"I'd be glad of a little drink," she said. "It's been a horrible day."

Maggie hated to see Johnny Cassidy like this, his eyes looking big and starry in his thin face, his dark hair rumpled, a sort of desperate eagerness about him. He doesn't know what he's doing, she thought. Miss Dolly ought to stop him.

"Let's go down to the kitchen, Dolly," he said. "I don't like this room. Let's pretend the kitchen's a bistro in Paris."

She rose, smiling at him. She shouldn't *do* that, Maggie thought. She shouldn't encourage him to drink any more. She hasn't got much sense, and that's a fact.

"Miss Dolly," she said, "I'm going to bed."

"Oh Maggie! It's early—"

"I'm tired, Miss Dolly. I'm going now. Could you please tell me where I can find some sheets and pillow-cases?"

"Oh, Neely knows," said Miss Dolly. "Tell Maggie, will you Neely?"

"Come!" he said. "Here, this way."

He went into the hall, and Miss Dolly and Johnny Cassidy went down the stairs. There was a narrow cupboard at the head of the stairs, and Neely tried to open it. But the door stuck; he pulled at it, his brows drawn together, a look of leonine ferocity on his face. He gave it a kick and tugged at it, and it came open.

"Take what you want," he said. "There isn't much. But I didn't know she was going to bring another woman."

"You didn't think Miss Dolly'd come here just with you, did you?" asked Maggie indignantly.

"Certainly I did," he said. "Why not?"

"You ought to know better," said Maggie.

"I *don't* know better," he said. "I suppose they wouldn't let her get away alone."

"Of course she could have come alone, if she wanted to," said Maggie, frowning more and more angrily at him. "But she didn't want to. She's not *like* that."

"Like what?" he demanded.

"You know perfectly well what I mean," said Maggie. "She's not *like* that."

"That's silly!" he said. "You talk like a child. How old are you anyhow?"

"That's my business," said Maggie. "Will you kindly move out of the way, and let me see what you've got in there?"

"You're silly!" he said. "You don't know anything of life."

He turned down the stairs, quick and noiseless in his tennis shoes. I could teach *you* a lesson, Maggie said to herself. You rude, nasty-minded beast! Her hands were unsteady with anger as she ransacked the shelves; there was plenty of linen there, or rather cotton, all of poor quality and much of it torn, but at least it seemed to be clean. She took what she needed and closed the cupboard door. Miss Dolly's laugh came to her, clear and gay, very sweet; she heard Cassidy give a shout, then she went into her room and closed the door.

Miss Dolly ought to know better, she thought, while she made up the divan. I'm—well, I'm disappointed in her. She ought to know better than to sit down there drinking whiskey with those two men. And she shouldn't have paid that Neely's rent. He's a sort of foreigner, and of course he takes it the wrong way. Well, if her husband was ever to find out about *this*, he'd have a right to feel jealous.

She turned out the light and lay down. She was tired, very tired, but to her distress, she was not at all sleepy. The water was lapping quietly against the walls, and now and then there was a splash; and what was it that splashed, that jumped out there in the dark?

She thought of Captain Hofer, she thought about Hiram Getty and his wife, about Miss Plummer; she thought about poor Mr. Angel. I just hope there are people who care about him, she thought, people who'll see he has a decent funeral and all.

She had dozed off when the banging of a door startled her wide awake again. I don't know what to make of these people, I really don't, she thought. I'm sorry Miss Dolly's down there drinking. But she's not like Neely thinks. The way she talked to that Mr. Getty was nice.

There had been dignity in that, something sad, and lovely. I liked that, Maggie thought.

Footsteps were coming up the stairs very slowly, they stopped outside her door.

"Good night!" Miss Dolly's voice said, low but always so clear.

A man's voice, utterly unintelligible, muttered something.

"Yes, I know that," she said. "I can't get away for ever—not until one of us is *dead*."

The door opened and closed, she crossed the room cautiously in the dark to her own little room, and shut herself in there. And Maggie lay wide awake in the dark for a long time. I suppose that's just a way of talking, she thought. It's hard to tell, with these people, whether they're joking or not.

Only that Neely didn't joke. I wonder, Maggie thought, which one of them she said that to? If Miss Dolly had said that to Johnny Cassidy, it needn't mean anything much. But if she had said it to Neely then it was sort of queer. Sort of worrying.

Chapter Eight

She waked early, as she had done all her nineteen years, and she got up promptly. And this morning she went to the bathroom in her dressing-gown, she didn't seem to care any more if she met anyone in the hall. She ran a bath, and she did not care whether the noise of the water disturbed anyone. If they waked up, they could go to sleep again. There were no settled hours here, no seemly, pleasant routine.

There was no hot water, and it had to be a bath so cold that it made her gasp. She took her cotton uniform, still wet and muddy from yesterday, down into the kitchen and washed it; in the broom closet she found a piece of rope and she rigged it up on the back porch for a clothes line. She made coffee and drank it, eating a whole box of Kocktail Kracker Bities. There was nothing else.

I'm *hungry*, she thought. The sun was up in the bright sky; it could not be so very early. She got out a broom and a duster, and started on the nasty dirty dining-room; and she felt better with that job of work to do.

The whiskey bottle was empty. Nasty stuff, she thought. Nasty dirty house, and what a way to live. All of them still sleeping, and no breakfast, no decent food ...

She had such a passion for neatness and cleanliness she was determined to get this disgraceful place in order. And she was determined not to think of anything else just now, not to make any plans, not to look at certain dark unstirring things that were in her mind. Not yet.

A car was coming along the road; she wondered if it could be anything so pleasant and normal as a baker or a grocer. But it was a taxi. It stopped before the house and for a long time she saw a pair of grey gloves moving inside the shadowy interior, then the door opened and Mr. Camford descended.

"What!" he said at the sight of Maggie on the porch.

The taxi drove away and he mounted the steps.

"Kindly tell Miss Camford I'm here," he said.

"Miss Camford's asleep, sir," said Maggie.

"I'm afraid I'll have to disturb her," he said.

He was an enemy. She was clear about that. He looked extraordinarily tall standing on the narrow little porch, he looked curiously distinguished in his grey suit and his grey felt hat, and his grey gloves, and he looked so disagreeable as to be almost funny. Sour-puss, she said to herself.

The miserable embarrassment and constraint she had used to feel in his presence had gone now; she was conscious of her youth, her energy, she felt independent. And she decided not to tell him anything.

He stood there drawing off his gloves and frowning petulantly.

"I've come all this way ..." he said. "What *is* this place?"

"It's a house, sir," said Maggie.

"Naturally," he said. "But *whose* house?"

"I don't know, sir."

"You must know who lives in it."

She said nothing.

"I don't understand this!" he said angrily. "I was informed last night of poor Angel's shocking accident. Some policeman had found letters addressed to me in his pocket. And this fellow told me that Angel had come out here to see my niece. Who does she know in this place?"

Maggie said nothing.

"I cannot understand this," he said. "Why did you go off like that, without a word to your mistress?"

I haven't any mistress, thought Maggie.

"What are you *doing* here?" he asked, angrier and angrier.

"I'm helping Miss D—Miss Camford," said Maggie.

Holding his grey gloves in one hand he switched at his leg with them.

"I've never heard of such a proceeding!" he said. "It's— What's that?"

It was a voice singing, a rich warm baritone, singing in French something very fancy. It was Mr. Cassidy, Maggie thought.

"What—is—that?" asked Mr. Camford.

"It sounds like the plumber," said Maggie, on the spur of the moment.

For she could not tell Mr. Camford—of all people—anything about this queer household. Miss Dolly could do her own explaining when she came down, and anyhow, thought Maggie, I can't see that it's *his* business. She's a grown woman, and it's her own money.

"Ouvre tes yeux bleus—" Johnny Cassidy sang.

"Oh shut up!" called Neely.

"What's the meaning of *that?*" asked Mr. Camford.

"I don't know," said Maggie.

"I intend to know," said Mr. Camford. "What's more, I intend to put a stop to all this. I intend to take my niece back to New York with me, immediately. Pack her things please, and your own."

"I'm sorry Mr. Camford, but I couldn't do that unless Miss Dolly told me to."

"Er—Annie—Jennie ..." he said. "You don't understand the situation. Your wages are paid by Mrs. Mayfield and myself, and not by Miss Camford. Miss Camford is not in a position to employ a servant. Now, kindly call Miss Camford, and as soon as she's ready I'll send for a taxi."

"There's no telephone here, Mr. Camford," said Maggie with quiet relish.

"Pshaw!" said he. "Then you can go to a neighbour's and telephone."

"There aren't any neighbours, Mr. Camford."

"Very well!" he said, almost shouting. "I'll get a taxi, somehow. But I want everything packed so that there'll be no delay. I can't afford to waste all day."

"It won't take me long to pack, sir," said Maggie, "if Miss Dolly wants me to do so."

She saw the veins swell in his temples, he slapped the palm of his hand with his gloves, looking at Maggie, and Maggie at him. *What* a temper, she thought, and her blue eyes were bright with an unholy exhilaration. People in rages made her feel like that. He won't get any change out of *me*, she thought. Let him try!

Then he sighed, and his anger was gone; he took off his hat and smiled ruefully.

"You're quite right," he said. "From your point of view. Naturally—you don't know—you've had no way of knowing, all the complications ... Suppose we sit down and talk it over?"

"Well ..." said Maggie.

"Come!" he said. "You sit there, opposite me, and let me explain things to you a little. I think you're going to help me when you understand what I'm trying to do, and that I'm here for no other reason but to help Miss Dolly."

She did sit down then, on the settee opposite him, and it came across her how strange this was. She, in her black dress and Miss Dolly's shoes, sitting here on the porch of a house in the country with Mr. Camford. And he wanted to explain things to her ... Honestly, she thought, truth is stranger than fiction.

"Miss Dolly's a very impulsive woman," he said. "I dare say you've noticed that. And she's extravagant. Perhaps you've noticed that, too? She's one of those people who have no money sense. It's understandable, heaven knows. She was an only child, you know, and her parents idolized her. Her father left her quite a snug little fortune, not a trust fund unfortunately, but in excellently placed and varied investments. Excellent. She'd have had an income for life, not a spectacular income, but more than adequate. As time goes on, I'm more and more impressed with my brother's good judgment in these investments."

He was silent for a moment, thinking gravely and sadly of those investments.

"It never occurred to me," he went on, "that Dolly would ever attempt to tamper with the financial arrangements her father had made for her. But she did! She went to her lawyer ... I blame him entirely. He should have let me know at once. But he was an elderly man, and she was an extremely pretty young girl of twenty-three or four."

He smiled, lifting his upper lip and showing a sort of triangle of big even teeth. "That's the way of the world, eh, Jennie?" he said. "He did protest, but not strongly enough. And she took these gilt-edged securities and sold them and bought—God knows what. She met some fellow who called himself an investment counsellor ... Well, the long and short of it was that in two or three years' time she didn't have a penny. She came back to us— naturally—and we did what we could to give her a pleasant and normal life. But ..."

He fell silent, and Maggie waited, a little impressed by this talk of gilt-edged securities and investments. Only I don't see why he's telling me all this, she thought.

"We did what we could," he said. "But—as you've seen for yourself, Jennie, we're quiet people, we live quietly, we like the old ways. Dolly wasn't happy. So that when her Aunt Emma left her a few thousands, and she wanted to travel, we offered no objection."

"Well, but—" Maggie began, and stopped abashed.

"Yes?" said Mr. Camford, encouragingly.

"Well, I only meant—nobody could have stopped her, could they, Mr. Camford? I mean, she was grown up and it was her own money ..."

"That's the crux of the whole matter," said Mr. Camford. "I'm going to explain it to you candidly, Jennie. Once you thoroughly understand the situation, you can be of great help to us—in helping Miss Dolly." He crossed his knees, and leaned his narrow bald head against the wall, looking thoughtfully before him. "You see," he said, "when Miss Dolly came to us after she'd squandered every penny of her inheritance, we found it was necessary to take steps to protect her from her own folly. We knew she'd be coming into more money, later on. So we insisted that everything we did for her was to be called a loan, and that she should sign a note for it. She—as you've no doubt noticed—spends a great deal of money on clothes. Fur coats."

That made him smile again, with that lifting of the lip that made him look rather like an intelligent rabbit.

"She went to Europe." he said. "She spent a year or so in Paris. And she came back penniless, and with a collection of highly undesirable people she called friends. Again she came back to us. Again we had a period of great resentment on her part, and a great many difficulties and sacrifices on our part. We all shared in the distribution of her Aunt Emma's estate, and poor Dolly took an apartment ..."

He shook his head slowly.

"We needn't go into the details," he said. "She came back again, and this time she was overwhelmed with debts. She'd even backed some sort of business venture in a shop to sell God knows what from Mexico. Mrs. Mayfield and I paid these debts, and we insisted upon a properly executed note. And now the situation is this. She owes us every penny of this new legacy from her Uncle Paul, and a great deal more.... We cannot permit her to squander this ... For her own sake—and I'll freely admit it—for ours also as well, we *must* put a stop to this."

This was very impressive. It was convincing, too. Everything that Miss Dolly had said and done fitted in with this account. Even the bottle of whiskey. Drink and debts and bad companions ...

But she was on Miss Dolly's side. She had to be. She had come here with Miss Dolly of her own free will, and she could not go over to Miss Dolly's enemies.

"If you'll go in and pack up her things and your own," said Mr. Camford, "then as soon as Dolly—Miss Dolly is ready, we'll make a start."

"I'll tell Miss Dolly, Mr. Camford," she said.

"Tell her she *must* come with me at once," said Mr. Camford. "Poor Nicholas Angel undoubtedly came out on the same mission—to persuade her to leave this place, whatever it is." He glanced at the front door with a slight frown of suspicion. "In a way," he said, "Dolly's responsible for poor Angel's death—"

"Oh, Mr. Camford!" said Maggie.

"But it's quite true," he said. "He wasn't a young man by any means. And the strain and worry of coming out here so early in the morning ... What's more, they may have had a stormy interview. No. It may not be pleasant, but it's more than probable that Dolly's directly responsible for Nicholas

Angel's death."

He mustn't go around saying that, thought Maggie. That could make things very bad for Miss Dolly.

"She didn't ask him to come, Mr. Camford," she said. "She—didn't want him to come."

"Nevertheless, she was the *cause* of his coming here, getting up early and possibly hurrying to catch a train on a hot morning. He was trying to protect her—as I am. She's very—"

He stopped at the sound of a step on the stairs, and in a moment Miss Dolly came into the dining-room in her wine-red housecoat.

"Uncle Giles!" she cried.

They stood looking at each other with something less than affection.

"Sit down, won't you, Uncle Giles?" she said. "I'll be with you in a moment. Maggie, will you come upstairs please. I want to speak to you."

They went up to Maggie's room.

"Maggie," said Miss Dolly, "has he seen either of the boys yet?"

"No, but he heard them."

"What did he say?"

"Well, when he heard Mr. Cassidy singing, I said it sounded like the plumber."

"Then Maggie, get them away. I'll take Uncle Giles out on the porch. Get them *out* of the house by the back door, and keep them away till he's gone."

"How can I, Miss Dolly? What will I tell them?"

"Oh Maggie, for heaven's sake be a little resourceful. Get them *away!* Maggie, do please try to help me. I've just been through a horrible ordeal— and now there's this other spiteful old killjoy. He's going to talk and talk about how I owe him a million dollars or something. He made me sign all sorts of papers ... Now hurry, please Maggie!

"But—" Maggie began, when Cassidy opened his door.

"Hello there!" said Cassidy gaily.

"Hush!" said Miss Dolly. "You must both of you get away from this house, this instant!"

"I want some coffee," said Neely from within.

"Oh, never mind now!" she said. "You'll have to go—"

"No," said Neely. "I want some coffee first. I'll stay in the kitchen with the door shut," he added.

"Johnny," said Miss Dolly, and went to his side. She spoke to him in a whisper, and he listened looking down into her anxious face with a wide grin. Then he beckoned to Maggie.

"Let's gang awa'" he said. "Oot the hoose. Come awa', Neely ma braw—"

"I'm going to make coffee," said Neely.

"All right!" said Johnny. "Come awa', bonnie wee wifie, and we'll find something to eat."

"Go *on*, Maggie!" said Miss Dolly.

"If we want to get away unmarked," said Johnny, "we'll have to go by water. In the rowboat—"

"Oh, no!"

"You can trust me," said Johnny. "I'm a regular little water-baby. Don't be afraid."

But she got into that rowboat with a heart like lead.

Chapter Nine

Johnny Cassidy rowed badly, in a one-sided way that made the boat slew round and graze the wall of the boathouse. They came out of that shadow into a steely dazzle, the water glinted everywhere, spread out over the marshes so that it seemed a primeval world without a foothold for a human creature.

He did not go up the creek as Maggie had gone with Neely; he went in the other direction where there were no banks, only the water running among the reeds. This was the route that Mr. Angel must have traveled.

"And that was Dolly's rich bad uncle," said Johnny.

"I wouldn't call him bad," said Maggie.

"All rich people are bad," said Johnny. "But I enjoyed hearing him talk."

"But did you hear him?"

"Every word," said Johnny. "Very interesting it was."

He ran the boat into a jutting clod of earth.

"Maybe I could help you," said Maggie. "I could look ahead and tell you when you're not in midstream."

"That's symbolic," he said. "That's what *you* do. You're always going to stay in midstream, and go right straight ahead. If you hear anyone calling from the rushes, you won't turn your head."

"What makes you think that?" she asked.

"Because you're a virtuous woman," he said, "and they're always deaf and blind. And maybe dumb. I yield to no one in my reverence for virtuous women, but I can't talk to them. Nobody can. Who, I ask you—or rather—to whom do men tell their secrets? They tell them to filles de joie, and to beautiful female spies. Only, not ever to good women in aprons."

The boat ran into the bank with a jar; he pulled away from it, frowning.

"I'll take a turn rowing now, if you like," said Maggie.

His blue shirt was damp with sweat, his hair was damp, his eyes were too brilliant. He's still under the influence of that whiskey, she thought, but not with anger or disgust. She was sorry for him.

"The reason I row like this," he said, "all crooked, is on account of my shoulder."

"Then maybe you shouldn't use it," she said.

"I want to," he said, and she let him alone.

They were coming now in sight of open water.

"Is that the ocean?" she asked.

"The Sound," he said. "There's a place along here where we can get a very fine little lunch. I'm hungry. I don't know why I stay in that damn house with that damn nuisance of a genius. I don't know why I do anything."

He rowed on faster and crookeder, talking in fits and starts, and she was very sorry for him. They came at last to a ramshackle wooden pier over the marsh, and at the end of the boardwalk there was a big wooden house ornamented with fretwork and a cupola. It was a hideous old house, but the scene in general enchanted Maggie; there was a willow tree beside a pond where a flock of ducklings swam, there was a big grey horse looking over a fence.

"It's a real farm," she said.

"You call *this* a farm?" said Johnny, surprised.

"Well, I haven't seen much of the country," said Maggie.

He seemed to know the place well, he led the way into the house to a room in the front shadowed by the verandah, dim and cool and quiet, with five or six little tables covered with white cloths. A stout woman in a very clean white dress, with grey hair screwed into a knob on top of her head, came in from the hall.

"Good morning, Mrs. Albee!" said Johnny.

"Good morning!" said she, severely.

"We'd like a fine fat roast duck—" he said.

"We don't serve dinner till six," said she.

"Make an exception," he said wheedlingly. "I've told Miss MacGowan about your duck dinners, and she's all agog."

"It'll take a good hour and a half," she said, "and it'll cost you a dollar twenty-five cents each."

"So be it," said Johnny.

"No ... Wait!" said Maggie. "I don't think I can stay so long."

"Sure you can," said Johnny. "It wouldn't matter if you didn't go back until dinner-time. Or ever. Just sit down and take it a little easy."

"You can sit out on the peeazzer," said Mrs. Albee.

There were some rocking chairs out there, and Johnny dragged one around the corner and set it facing the field where the grey horse stood patiently.

"Now!" he said. "Sit here and look at your farm. Too bad you don't smoke ... I'll be back presently."

What queer things happen! Maggie thought. If I'd got a job in an office, I'd never have had this experience.... Mother was certainly right. You certainly learn more about life this way.

She was glad to sit here and think things over for a while. But, to her distress, her mind was not working with the usual clear energy; a curious haziness had settled upon her. Maybe after a good square meal, she thought ... and she was shocked to find her mouth literally watering for the roast duck. She had meant to think about Mr. Angel, she tried to, but nothing came of it. Mr. Cassidy's been gone a long time, she remarked to herself.

The horse grazed for a time and then came back to the fence and stood looking at her; she was surprised to see that it had eyelashes, giving it so gentle a look. She could hear a sweet, excited peeping from the little ducks, and after another wait she strolled down to the pond where they went in a proud little flotilla. It was lovely here in the shade of the willow tree, a cat came along and stood for a moment at the edge of the water; then with an absent-minded air, it turned to Maggie and rubbed against her ankles, purring.

Johnny's been gone a *very* long time, Maggie thought. She went back to her rocking chair and waited and waited, and presently Mrs. Albee came out in an apron.

"It's ready," she said.

"Well ... Do you know where Mr. Cassidy is?" Maggie asked.

"I don't," said Mrs. Albee. "But it's ready, and you better eat."

"Well, I think I'll wait a little while," said Maggie.

She had brought no money with her, and she was not going to start on any dollar twenty-five meal. Where could he be? Mrs. Albee went back into the house, letting the screen door slam behind her; the willow tree rustled and the little ducks peeped.

Restless and growing uneasy now, Maggie went down the steps again. If the worst comes to the worst, she thought, I'll get in the boat and row home. A picture came into her mind of Mrs. Albee, outraged and justly so, coming after her, calling after her all along the boardwalk. As she set foot on it, she looked ahead to the pier where the boat was tied.

Where the boat had been tied. The boat was not there.

He's gone, she thought. It's one of his mean nasty jokes. He's gone. And she would have to face Mrs. Albee alone. She went back to the rocking chair, sick with dread and dismay. Well, shall I say I'll pay for the dinner later? she thought. Shall I ask her how I can walk home? I just never was in such a miserable position…. She'll ask me who I am and where I come from. Well, will I say I'm Miss Camford's secretary? Maybe everyone in the neighbourhood knows about Miss Dolly and me, living in that house with those two men. She'll think …

"Hello!" said Johnny coming around the corner.

"Wherever did you go to?" she cried. "Mrs. Albee's got the dinner ready, and I couldn't *find* you."

"I rowed up to the Point," he said, "to see if old Bascom had any clams. Sorry I kept you waiting."

He spoke civilly and nicely and she tried to master her burning desire to go on and on at him.

"I think …" she said unsteadily. "I thought—maybe it was a joke. That maybe you thought it was funny to go off and leave me …"

"The crazy drunken Irishman," he said.

"I don't mean that," she said. "It's just—"

"Let's eat, Maggie," he said. "You must be hungry, you poor little devil. You must be tired and worried and all upset. You want to go home. Have you got a home?"

"Yes," she answered proudly. "We've got a two-family house. Only my mother had to go away."

With his hand on her arm, he steered her toward the front door and into the dining-room. Mrs. Albee entered at once with the roast duck beautifully browned, apple sauce, peas, mashed potatoes, spiced peaches, celery.

It was not right to care this much about food.

"God!" said Johnny looking down at his plate.

"What is it?" she asked.

"Ghosts," he said. "Kids in Spain, and old women in China."

She liked him for that. They began to eat, and a strange friendliness was between them. After a while they began to talk, and it was easy to talk. She told him about her father and his ship; he told her about his father who had been a minister in Maine. They ate all Mrs. Albee had brought them, and when she returned with home-made strawberry shortcake, they ate that, too.

"It must be terribly late," said Maggie, her conscience beginning to work again. "Miss Camford will wonder where on earth I am."

"Why don't you leave here?" Johnny asked.

"Well, why should I?"

"I'd leave if I were you," he said. "I'd leave right now."

"Well, why?"

"Oh, there are things going on," he said. "Things are going to happen."

"What kind of things?"

"Things you won't like," he said.

"That can't be helped," said Maggie, and there was a silence between them.

"I'd like to row back," said Maggie presently, and Johnny consented.

He was peaceable now, he sat facing her, his big thin hands clasped between his knees, a mild and thoughtful look on his face. She felt peaceable too, and contented. The sun was low, and she took it easy, rowing with a leisurely rhythm against the current that was surprisingly strong.

"The tide's going out," she said.

"So it is," said Johnny. "Going fast. And the sands of life ... Oh Lord! If I could only get away. If I could only get back to a war!"

"I can't understand that," said Maggie with a certain severity.

"No," he said, "I don't think you could. That's because you have no craziness in you. I'll explain." He took out a cigarette and lit it. "War is the grand supreme simplification. You have the Good People banded together, all very cosy; and you have the Bad People. The Enemy. When I'm not in wars, I have a lot of trouble telling the good people from the bad. I have a lot of trouble knowing what to do. Or wanting to do anything. You don't have these worries in a war."

She had never before met anybody like Johnny Cassidy, and the people in the stories she had read, and the movies she had seen were not like this. Yet she felt curiously at ease with him. She could talk to him, perhaps because *he* could talk; he was able to say all the things that came into his head. He was silent now for a time and she wondered what he was thinking about, and what had happened to make him like this.

"I'd like to ask you a favor, Miss MacGowan," he said with courteous formality.

"Yes," she said seriously.

"If you didn't mind," he said, "I'd like to touch your hair when the sun shines on it. I'd like to lay my hand on it."

The color rose in her cheeks. She was profoundly embarrassed. He leaned forward and put his hand on the crown of her head for a moment and then sat back.

"It's warm!" he said. "It's alive. You're alive, you little healthy thing ..." He sighed. "You'll take my advice, won't you, Maggie and leave here? Go this afternoon."

"I couldn't leave Miss Dolly like that."

"If you're short of money—"

"I'm not, thank you."

"If you're worried about finding another job—"

"I'm not, thank you."

"Then why d'you stay?" he demanded. "There's nothing here for you. Go away, won't you Maggie? Please! I'll drive you to the station."

"I couldn't go like that," she said. "I'd have to talk it over with Miss Dolly."

"I tell you there's trouble coming."

"That's all the more reason why I couldn't just walk out on her," said Maggie briefly.

They had now reached the entrance to the boathouse, and she rowed into that darkness. Johnny Cassidy got out and held out both his hands to her; he made the boat fast, and they walked in silence to the door of the kitchen. There was a sound of voices, a man talking.

"My goodness!" said Maggie. "D'you suppose Mr. Camford's still here?"

"That's not Camford," said Johnny. "That's Hiram Getty."

He and Miss Dolly were in the dining-room, and the only way for Maggie to avoid them was to remain in the kitchen. And she wanted to avoid them, for some reason she did not trouble to analyse. She sat down in a chair and surveyed the kitchen.

It was like a nightmare. No matter what she did to it, no matter how she left it, it was always like this when she re-entered it; dirty dishes and glasses, and pots and pans, a demoralized look about it.

"Well ..." said Johnny and opened the door; he went into the dining-room and closed the door after him.

Of course, I'm not going to stay much longer anyhow, she thought. But I'll give Miss Dolly time to find somebody else, another secretary. She certainly couldn't stay in this house here with these two men. Well, maybe Mr. Camford persuaded her. Maybe she'll be going home herself. She ought to. She wouldn't have to be so miserable back in their house. She could have a nice life there. She could have nice friends. She could do something. She could do war work or something for a charity. If she owes all that money—

"Oh, Maggie," said Miss Dolly pushing open the door. "You're back ... ?"

"Yes, Miss Dolly. Is—Mr. Camford upstairs?"

"No, he's gone," said Miss Dolly. "Will you make cocktails please, Maggie?"

"I don't know anything about making cocktails, Miss Dolly," said Maggie.

"I'll teach you," said Getty, standing behind Miss Dolly.

Maggie was about to refuse to learn, but she changed her mind. It's just as well to know how to do things, she thought. You never know. So she listened to Hiram Getty with attention; under his direction she measured out gin and vermouth, bitters and lemon juice into a glass jug. She put in ice cubes and stirred it all with a wooden spoon.

She memorized the formula, and she felt a little pleased, a little proud;

it was, she thought, sort of sophisticated. But she would not take a drink, even a sip.

"No thank you, Mr. Getty."

"You've never tried one, Maggie," said Miss Dolly.

"Excuse me, but I have, Miss Camford," said Maggie.

Johnny was coming down the stairs now, his face bright at the sight of the jug on the dining-room table. Liquor's a *hateful* thing! Maggie thought, and went upstairs to get away from it.

The door of Neely's room was half open, and on the drawing-board she caught sight of a little landscape in watercolors, so vivid it looked, that she stopped, fascinated. The room was in wild disorder; on a deal table were paint and brushes and crayons. There were clothes all over the room, and there were two canvas cots unmade. I suppose Johnny sleeps in here too, she thought. There doesn't seem to be any other room.

She wanted a better look at the little picture, and she went in. It was just a bit of marsh, the green reeds and the brown creek; strange that he could so infuse it with light. He had made it *his* marsh, you recognized it, but only he could see it like this.

Maybe he was a genius. If so, she might make up his cot for him, and Johnny's, too. She turned to cross the room when she saw something that astounded her. On the seat of a chair she saw a wallet that she knew very well. It was a pigskin wallet with the initials G. C. C. in a corner. It was Mr. Camford's wallet, and it was soaking wet; there was a little pool of water under the chair.

She backed away from this and out of the room; she closed the door and leaned against the wall.

What does it mean ... ? What does it mean ... ? she said to herself.

She remembered Mr. Camford telephoning home once from his office, with orders for her to look under his pillow for that wallet. He thought a lot of it; he kept important things in it— What does this mean...

Chapter Ten

They were laughing downstairs, all very lively, Miss Dolly and those three men. Maggie stood at the head of the stairs, listening to them, and she was completely at a loss. Something had to be done about Mr. Camford's wallet; somebody had to be told. And there was nobody here that she trusted.

It startled her to realize that. Not one of them, she thought. Not the Gettys, and not Miss Plummer, certainly not Neely. And not even Miss Dolly. She doesn't tell the truth, and she's not sensible about things.

Well, Mr. Cassidy? she thought. She considered him for a moment, and then ruled him out. I don't really know how he feels about things, she thought. I wish I could have a talk with Mother. Or Mrs. Crabtree.

Mrs. Crabtree! She nearly said the name aloud. But that's the thing to do, she cried to herself. I'll call up Mrs. Crabtree, and find out if Mr. Camford's come home. If he has, then everything's all right. And if he hasn't, I'll tell *her* about the wallet, and she can tell Mrs. Mayfield.

She went down the stairs then greatly fortified by this plan of action. If there's been any monkey business, she thought, if anyone's tried to rob Mr. Camford, they're not going to get away with it.

She entered upon a strange and disturbing scene. Miss Dolly sat with her arms stretched out on the dining-room table, holding a glass; Hiram Getty stood beside her, and she was looking up at him with a sweet drowsy smile; Johnny Cassidy sat opposite her staring fixedly at her, Neely stood leaning against the wall with his arms folded. They didn't look like nice, well-bred people, any of them, in that dirty, disorderly room, they too looked disorderly and queer.

"Have a drink, my pretty pigeon," said Johnny Cassidy.

"No, thank you," said Maggie. "I don't drink."

"You can learn, dear, if you try," said Johnny gently.

Maggie did not answer. He's drunk, she thought. *He* couldn't drive me to where I could telephone to Mrs. Crabtree. He was the one she had meant to ask; now it would have to be either Hiram Getty or Neely. And it was hard to think of a way to approach either of them. I can't tell them what I want to do, she thought, because—

Because somebody in this room knew about the wallet; somebody had put it where she had found it. Maybe more than one person knew, maybe they all know. I don't really understand any of these people, she thought. I don't know what's going on.

Johnny sat down again and took up his glass.

"I died—three years ago—in Paris," he said in the same gentle tone, looking before him at nothing. "Did you know that, Getty?"

"No," said Getty, curtly.

"Now, you, for example," said Johnny, "you've never been alive at all. You—"

"Johnny, don't be silly," said Miss Dolly.

"Why not, dear?" he asked. "Here we are, all riding on a merry-go-round, on dragons and horses, and it's very silly. I thought once that I was riding on a horse with wings, but the wings fell off, and the horse never got anywhere. Just went round and round. We're all going round and round ... And there's good, good little Maggie watching us, all aflame with virtuous indignation."

"Johnny, you've had too much," said Miss Dolly.

"You're right, dear," he said. "I've had too much everything. Too much love, too much joy, and I am sick of an old pain. I have been faithful to thee—Cyn—"

"Hiram, let's go up and sit on the balcony," said Miss Dolly, rising.

"Whither thou goest, there go I," said Johnny, getting up, too. "And who knows? Maybe Getty and I, locked in a death-struggle, will both fall off into the water and drift away locked in each other's arms."

"Johnny, lie down and go to sleep for a while," said Miss Dolly.

"I might have a nightmare," he said.

"Come, Dolly!" said Getty, taking her arm. "This is—"

"Sickening," said Johnny. "Sickening."

He picked up the whiskey bottle by the neck and followed the other two out of the room; he began to sing in his fine tenor voice.

"Ridi! pagliacci ..."

Neely still leaned against the wall with his arms folded. Well, is he drunk, too? Maggie thought, and she decided to get him talking, so that she could find out about that. Only it's so difficult to begin.

"Why do you stay here?" he said so abruptly that she started.

"Because it suits me," she said.

"You don't like any of the people here," said Neely, "and they don't like you. Why don't you go away?"

"You're polite, aren't you?" said Maggie.

"I don't care about being polite," he said. "Why don't you go away and do something useful? Some war-work, go and do."

"Well, why don't *you*?" she said.

"I'm going all right," he said. "Once they make up their minds whether they'll take me in the Army or send me to Ellis Island as a dangerous enemy alien."

In spite of her indignation against his rudeness, she was interested.

"I thought Dutch people were all right," she said.

"Certainly they're all right," he said. "Only they can't make up their minds if I'm Dutch or not. I think I was born in Berlin."

"Don't you *know* where you were born?"

"No. Who does? You know that somebody tells you, that's all. Very well. I think my mother told me I was born in Berlin. I think she brought me to this country on the German quota. But I don't know what her name was."

"You don't know your own mother's name?"

"No," he said. "That's the way the Immigration people talk to me, and the Army people, and the police. Even someone from the F. B. I. They think I'm very fishy. Well, I don't care. In the meantime I can go on with my work."

"But I don't see how you can not know your mother's name," said Maggie.

"For this reason," he said, with an impatient frown. "My father was—I don't know—something bad. A drunkard maybe. Anyhow my mother left him, and she took back her maiden name. I don't know if she got a divorce, or if she just went away. Anyhow, she brought me over here. She said we would use the name of her family, Curtius, and what did I care? I was only a child. Well, I think we had a different name on the passport, and I don't remember what it was. So they can't find any record of how I got into this country, and that makes them mad. I don't care about that, either."

He was rude and curt, and queer, but she did not think he was drunk.

"Mr. Curtius," she said resolutely, "will you please drive me to some place where I can telephone?"

"Why?" he asked.

"Well, because I want to make a call," she said.

"Who is it you want to call?"

"Well, really ..." she said. "I think that's my own affair."

"I think I won't drive you anywhere," he said.

"But why?" she said, startled.

"Because you want to make trouble," he said. "Because you're a little spy."

"*What?*"

"That's it," he said. "I know—"

He stopped and turned his head, listening to a car that was coming up to the house.

"Now, if it's that damn policeman ..." he said. "I'll do the talking."

But it was Miss Mitzi Plummer.

"Neely-boy!" she cried.

"What do you want?" he said.

"But aren't you going to let me in, Neely?"

"I don't care if you come in or not," he said, and in a moment she appeared in the dining-room doorway.

"Oh, it's you?" she said, eagerly, glancing at Maggie. She sat down in a chair looking immense and curiously formal in a black silk dress and a silver turban. "Neely!" she said.

"*Yes?*" he shouted from outside.

"But come here, my child!" she said. "Willie Hofer's been at me and at me—about *you.*"

He came back into the dining-room.

"All right!" he said. "You don't know anything about me. Tell him that."

"He asked me," she said, and began to laugh, "he asked me what were the relations—between you and Dolly."

"Shut up!" said Neely, and turned on his heel and went away.

"Neely, come back!" she cried. "I won't tease you any more. I came to bring you home to dinner, Neely. I've got such a *nice* chicken—"

The screen door slammed and he was gone.

"He's a fascinating boy," said Miss Plummer. "But, of course, I'm quite definitely masochistic."

"What's that?" asked Maggie.

"I like to be ill-treated," said Miss Plummer. She smiled dreamily. "I'd love to be tortured," she said.

Maggie looked at her with disgust, and a dim fear. This was something new to her, and it was bad.

"Does that shock you?" asked Miss Plummer.

"Well ..." said Maggie.

"Tell me, child, where do you come from?"

"From Brooklyn," said Maggie.

It nettled her to see Miss Plummer laugh at that.

"Really," said Miss Plummer, "you're the most macabre little note, my dear, in a very gruesome set-up. This is my house, you know, and Dolly rented it from me for the summer—for a marvelous genius, she said. Of course I came to call on him the moment he arrived, and I adored him. There he was, painting away, with nothing to eat in the house. Can't you picture him jumping into the water and catching fish in his hands, and eating them raw?"

"No," said Maggie.

"I can. *I* think he's divinely savage. But then—along came Johnny, and I can't cope with him. I called up Dolly, and she told me to let him live in the house, too. That did seem unnecessarily depraved, but, after all, it's not *my* affair. Is it?"

"No ..." said Maggie trying to understand the implication of all this.

"Now, I'm simply waiting," said Miss Plummer. "It's fascinating. I'm simply waiting—for the murder."

"What murder?" said Maggie.

"I *hope* it will be Dolly," said Miss Plummer. "But maybe that's too obvious. Well ... !" She rose. "I'll be running along now. Would *you* like to come back to dinner with me, you quaint child?"

"No, thank you," said Maggie. "But—if you'd drive me some place where I could telephone, Miss Plummer—"

"Why not?" said Miss Plummer. "Come along!"

Maggie hesitated for a moment. She was not in the habit of walking out of a house without a word; her mother had always expected to be told where she was going and when she was coming back, and Mrs. Crabtree had been like that, too.

But no, she thought, I'm not going to tell Miss Dolly. I'll be back in time for dinner. I'm not going to be polite and considerate in *this* house.

It gave her a certain pleasure to walk off like this. Only I don't like Miss Plummer, she said to herself. I think she's awful. Is she crazy, I wonder? She glanced at Miss Plummer, starting her little car, at her face with the heavy-lidded eyes, the bold nose, the full lips, the double chin. You can't tell by looks. But the things she said ... Waiting for the murder ... ?

The sun was in the west, and the summer world was very tranquil. They left the house and the marshes behind and came to the highway where there were other cars and trucks, and a bus.

"If you'll just leave me at the nearest place where there's a telephone, please, Miss Plummer."

"Yes, yes," said Miss Plummer. "You know, I thought this Mr. Angel had been murdered, but Willie Hofer says definitely, no. Natural causes. A stroke of some sort. Willie's theory is that Mr. Angel was walking along by the creek, and fell in. He wasn't drowned; they can tell, you know. I said to Willie, but *why* should he be walking around alone in that godforsaken landscape? And Willie gave me a piercing, sleuthish look and said—how do you know he was alone? Willie's not stupid."

Well, if he wasn't drowned, and wasn't murdered, Maggie thought, it can't make any real difference for Captain Hofer not to know about Mr. Angel in the rowboat. But I wish he did know. I wish I'd told him right away. I think I made a mistake, not to tell him.

I think I made a mistake to come here at all. I think I've got into something that's sort of out of my depth ... I think ... The conclusion she was reaching was so novel, so very unpleasing that she balked at it. But in the end, she took the hurdle. I guess I'm not as smart as I thought I was, she said to herself.

"Well, here we are!" said Miss Plummer.

She stopped the car before a shabby little house with a garden surrounded by a picket fence, in a street of other little houses like it; as they got out, a train went roaring past along the tracks at the corner.

"My father's mill hands used to live here," said Miss Plummer. "I used to walk by here sometimes with my governess, and wonder what sort of animals they were. Now the wheel has turned, and here I am myself."

The door of the house was not locked, she opened it and Maggie followed her into a little hall where a large oil-painting hung, hot with color. "There's the telephone in the sitting-room," said Miss Plummer. "I'll go and get us a drink."

Maggie sat down at the desk and got long distance on the old-fashioned telephone; while she waited for the Camford number to answer, she looked about her, and she was impressed. It was a small room, crowded and dusty, but it was a room of great culture, bookshelves on three sides, paintings on the walls, and statues standing about. I'd like to know more about Art, she thought. I've got a lot to learn.

"Hello!" said a familiar voice that made her heart leap.

"Oh ... Mrs. Crabtree?" she said. "This is Maggie."

"*Well!*" said Mrs. Crabtree. "I must say I'm surprised to hear from *you.*"

"I know," said Maggie. "I'll explain it all some day, Mrs. Crabtree. Only just now, I'd like to know ... Mrs. Crabtree, is Mr. Camford home yet?"

"No," said Mrs. Crabtree, "he's not."

"Well ... Are you expecting him, Mrs. Crabtree?"

"No," said Mrs. Crabtree. "We are not."

"Mrs. Crabtree, I'm *worried* about Mr. Camford."

"*In*deed?" said Mrs. Crabtree.

"I am! Really I am! I can't tell you now—but I think I'd better speak to Mrs. Mayfield."

"If you're really worried," said Mrs. Crabtree, relenting a little, "then I don't mind telling you we had a wire from him not long ago. He's gone to Boston."

"A wire? A telegram? What did it say, Mrs. Crabtree?"

"It said he'd gone to Boston."

"But—"

Miss Plummer took the receiver out of her hand and pushed her aside so roughly that she nearly fell off the chair.

"Time's up," she said into the mouthpiece. "Good bye!"

She hung up, and turned to Maggie.

"What's all this about?" she asked.

"It's—a private call," said Maggie.

"You're trying to make trouble, you red-headed little hellion," said Miss Plummer. "Come on!"

"Come—where?"

"I'm going to take you back to the boathouse," said Miss Plummer. "And this time you'll stay there. Come on!"

"I'll go home by myself."

"Oh, no you won't. You're not going to go wandering around telephoning to people and making trouble. Who are you, anyhow, and where did Dolly pick you up? Come along!"

"I won't!" said Maggie.

"All right!" said Miss Plummer. "I'm not going to make a scene now in broad daylight and drag you out. You'll stay here then until it's dark."

"I won't!" said Maggie.

"Just try to leave," said Miss Plummer.

It was a well-populated street with houses on either side of this and all the windows were open, a cry for help would surely be heard. But you can't just begin to yell, Maggie thought, when you haven't been hurt or anything.

"You're a nasty little thing," said Miss Plummer. "I thought so the first time I saw you. A smug, self-righteous, common little thing ..."

Was that how she seemed to these people? Was that what she *was*?

No! she said to herself. And aloud, "I've got p-plenty to say for myself," she retorted.

"Then say it. Who were you telephoning to about a telegram?"

"That's my business," said Maggie.

"I'll find out," said Miss Plummer. "You don't imagine you're a match for *me*, do you, brat?"

Maggie did not answer. She stood looking down at the carpet that glowed in deep blue and ruby red in a bar of sunlight. She was wounded, stricken by these words. She thought of herself at the cocktail party in Miss Dolly's dress—and this was how she had seemed? She thought of the duck farm and the nice things Johnny Cassidy had said to her. I suppose he was sorry for me, she thought. I suppose that's how people felt about me when I was looking for a job.

"Come into the kitchen," said Miss Plummer. "I want a drink."

She was breathing faster, color had risen in her swarthy face, her mouth was set in an ugly line. She's working herself up into a regular rage, Maggie thought, alarmed.

"I *said*, come into the kitchen!" said Miss Plummer.

It's broad daylight and there are plenty of people around, Maggie thought. There isn't really anything to be frightened of.

But she was frightened. A train was thundering along, and the house shook, the windows rattled; the sunny little room seemed suddenly hot beyond bearing. I can just walk out, she told herself. But she did not believe that. She thought Miss Plummer would pounce on her like a cat if she moved. And Miss Plummer looked so big, so heavy, so powerful.

"No," said Maggie, "I won't go in the kitchen."

"You—" Miss Plummer began, her eyes narrowed.

The front door opened and Johnny's voice called.

"Whaur's ma wee lassie?"

Chapter Eleven

"Wait!" said Miss Plummer, and as he appeared in the doorway she put her hand against his chest, and pushed him out into the hall. They began to talk in low voices.

Maggie crossed the room to a mirror hanging against the wall. Well, anyhow, I look neat and clean, she said to herself with a sob rising in her throat. Anyhow, I don't drink and carry on like these people.

But this gave her little comfort. She had lost the regard of everyone, above all, of Mrs. Crabtree. If my mother were here, she thought, I'd go right straight back to her now. I'd learn more about life in a position like this, Mother said. Well, I certainly have. I've learned enough to last me for a long time....

Miss Plummer came back into the room now followed by Johnny.

"I came to take you home, dear," he said gently. "Ready?"

His eyes were soft and starry in his white face; he swayed on his feet as he spoke to her.

"But—you're not going to drive, are you Mr. Cassidy?" she asked.

"I can drive anything—any time," he said. "You're safe with me."

"Thank you, but—"

"Oh, go along!" said Miss Plummer. "You can't stay here."

"I can take a taxi."

"Come with me, Maggie," said Johnny.

"Don't be such a snivelling little coward," said Miss Plummer. "Go on! Get out of my house!"

She made a sort of rush at Maggie, and Maggie stepped back into the hall.

"Go on! Go on! Go on!" cried Miss Plummer, flapping her hands at Maggie. Johnny opened the front door and Maggie went out on the veranda.

"Go on! Go on!" cried Miss Plummer, coming out after her.

There was something so confusing, so alarming in the clamor she made, in her flapping hands, in her looks, so big in her black satin ... Maggie got into the car with Johnny.

"Drive fast!" screeched Miss Plummer from the top of the steps. "It's much easier that way, Johnny. Drive fast! Drive like hell!"

"Don't you do it," said Maggie. "She's—she's a dreadful woman."

"I'll be careful, dear," said Johnny.

He did better than she had expected; he drove steadily enough back to the highway and along it, and then he turned into a side road.

"Is this—? Are you sure this is the right way?" she asked.

"I'm headin' south," he said. "Let's get away from all this. I've *got* to get away. Let's go down to Mexico."

She felt like crying in her fatigue and wretchedness. But he would have to be managed.

"I've got to get my things first," she said. "Let's go back—"

"No going back," he said. "Time marches on. And you haven't any 'things,' poor pretty little Maggie. Just scraps and odds and ends."

She was crying now.

"They're things—I want, anyhow. Please let's go back."

"I'll buy you things," he said. "I'll pull myself together and start a new life, with you. I'll be good because you're so good."

"Please, Johnny ... I couldn't leave Miss Dolly like this—"

"*I* could," he said. "*She* thinks I can't get away. But she's wrong. She thinks she's put a spell on me. She thinks— Did you ever read about Paola and Francesca, Maggie machree?"

"No, I never did."

"They went round and round in hell, in each other's arms. Round and round and round—"

He ran the car up on a bank with a jolt that made her feel faint.

"I'm *sorry!*" he said seriously. "But now that we're here, let's stay. Will you let me sleep a little while with my head in your lap, my sweet? For I am weary and I fain would rest."

"Let's just stop at the house first, Johnny."

"You're a guileful little dove. Oh Maggie, Maggie! If I could sleep with your hand on my brow, I'd wake up cleansed and new."

He closed his eyes and held her hand against them.

"Johnny dear ..." she said. "I'm so tired—and my head aches. Will you *please*—take me home?"

"Oh God!" he said. "Poor little Maggie ..."

"*Come* on, Johnny. It's getting so late. Look at the sun ... Johnny, please ... "

She got him to start the car again but he would not turn back to the highway.

"Where does this road go?" she asked him.

"Who knows?" he said sadly.

It was little more than a lane, and completely deserted. He drove slowly, jolting over ruts and stones, there were fields on either side and the grain rustled in the light breeze. The sun was gone, leaving a light that was pallid and clear. Around a bend in the lane they came into woodland, and it was dark here, the trees almost meeting overhead, and the branches brushing lightly against the top.

Maggie was not frightened any more, not angry at Johnny, not even impatient. He's in a miserable state, she thought, and she meant that in more ways than one. She had always despised drunkenness, but she was not despising Johnny now. She was dreadfully, unbearably sorry for him. He's—sort of lost, she thought. What makes people do things like that? Things like drinking—or worse ... And then there are the other people like Father and Mother, like Mrs. Crabtree—they don't even *want* to do anything bad ...

He drove on and on along the winding lane under the shade of the trees. And she didn't care much any more where they were going. I'll telephone to Mrs. Crabtree again to-morrow, she thought. I'll find out where Mr. Camford went in Boston, and then I'll find out if he ever got there.

Ever got there ... ? That sounds—queer. He does go to Boston every now and then. He could have dropped his wallet somewhere and not missed it until he got on the train. Well, maybe he was in too much of a hurry to come back for it. Maybe there's nothing at all to worry about.

Anyhow, what *am* I worrying about? Mr. Angel had a stroke. Well, the same thing wouldn't happen to Mr. Camford, too. That would be too much of a coincidence. Nobody really did anything to Mr. Angel. There's no reason to think anything—anything terrible has happened to Mr. Camford.

Only I do feel worried. I do! If I only knew he was safe in Boston ... I'll have to find that out. I'll have to do something about it. And the definite purpose discouraged her. She did not feel smart and sure any more.

The moon was up and shining through a silver mist when they turned into the road that led to the boathouse. How lonely the lighted windows looked! How lonely the world was ... Johnny stopped the car and got out; he held out his hand to Maggie, and when she took it, it was cold and damp. Poor Johnny ...

He stumbled going up the steps, and fell, and she helped him up. "I'm sorry ..." he said.

"That's all right, Johnny," she said.

She opened the door, still holding his arm, and they entered the hall. He looked as white as a ghost, blinking his eyes in the light; he looked so forlorn.

"Need a drink," he said.

"No, you don't, Johnny," she said. "You'd better go right straight to bed."

"Maybe so," he said. "Good night, dear."

She stood watching him while he climbed the stairs, and then she turned toward the kitchen. I'll make a cup of tea, she thought. That'll do me good. I haven't had a bite since lunch. Lunch at the duck farm, and was that only to-day? I do wish I knew the time.

She pushed open the swing door, and stopped short, astounded at what she saw. Neely in singlet and flannel trousers, ironing. He had the folding board set up, he had a wicker basket of clothes on a chair beside him, and he was working in a methodical and matter-of-fact way.

"Hello!" he said, glancing at her.

"Hello!" she answered and drew nearer.

He stood the iron on end, and smiled at her. "Now will you finish this?" he asked.

"Finish your ironing?" she said. "And why should I?"

"You're a girl," he said. "You know about things like this."

"I'm going to make some tea," said Maggie. "I'm tired."

Neely sat down on the edge of the table and lit a cigarette.

"I never tried to iron before," he said. "Only if we're going away to-mor-row—"

"Who? Who's going where?"

"We're all going, you too, on Getty's yacht. We're going to take a little cruise up to Maine."

Maggie put on the kettle, and began to look for something to eat. *I'm not going on any yacht*, she said to herself. "You'd better disconnect that iron," she said. "It's just wasting current."

He rose at once, and unplugged it.

"I'll be glad to go on the cruise," he said. "See something new. Will you like it?"

"No," said Maggie, taking butter and two eggs out of the ice-box.

"You're quick," said Neely. "I like that. I think you're very clean, too."

"Certainly I am," said Maggie.

"Have you a lover?"

"What do you mean?"

"A lover—a sweetheart."

"No," said Maggie, "and I don't want one either."

"That's silly," said Neely. "When you've had your supper, will you fin-ish this ironing for me?"

"No," said Maggie again.

"I want to look nice," he said. "They're very rich, these Gettys. They could help me a lot."

She fried the eggs and made a pot of tea, and carried the tray into the din-ing-room.

"Why do you go away?" asked Neely coming after her.

"Because I don't want to quarrel with you," said Maggie.

"I don't mind if you quarrel with me," he said.

"Well, I do," she said, and he walked off to the kitchen.

When she had finished her inadequate supper, she left the dishes where they were; what did it matter in this house? She was tired, very tired, and she was going to bed. But when she opened the door of her room she found Miss Dolly in there, kneeling on the floor in her housecoat, packing a suitcase, a cigarette between her lips.

"Oh, Maggie!" she said. "I thought you'd *never* come."

"I'm sorry," said Maggie, unconvincingly.

"We're leaving to-morrow, Maggie—"

"Well, not me, Miss Dolly. I'm sorry, but I'm not going on this yacht."

Miss Dolly looked at her with dismay in her dark eyes.

"But Maggie, it's going to be lovely. A cruise—"

"I'm sorry, Miss Dolly. But I thought I was going to be your secretary—"

"But I'm going to begin working on the book, Maggie. I'll start when we get on the yacht."

"I just can't do it, Miss Dolly."

Maggie sat down on the bed, and Miss Dolly sat back on her heels.

"Miss Dolly," Maggie said, "I'm worried about Mr. Camford."

"Please!" said Miss Dolly. "Please don't *mention* him, Maggie. You don't *know* how horrible he was to me this morning."

"Well, I'm worried about him," said Maggie, doggedly.

"But why should you be? He's gone—"

"Miss Dolly, did he say where he was going?"

"He said something about going to Boston. But—we had a quarrel, Maggie. He was horrible to me—he said horrible things."

"Did he go away in a taxi, Miss Dolly?"

"Oh, I don't *know!* I left him. I went out of the house and left him here."

"Miss Dolly ..." Maggie paused a moment, curiously reluctant to go on. "Did you leave him alone in the house?"

"Yes," said Miss Dolly, her eyes fixed on Maggie's face. Then a change like a shadow came across her face. "Yes ... I think so ..." she said. "I'm pretty sure, Maggie. Why do you ask, Maggie?"

"I've got my reasons, Miss Dolly. I couldn't explain just now."

"Maggie, don't *talk* like that! You frighten me!"

"I can't help it, Miss Dolly. I'm worried."

"About Uncle Giles?" Miss Dolly crushed her cigarette against the top of the pale-grey suitcase, leaving a black mark on it. "He was all right when I left him."

"But you didn't see him leave then, Miss Dolly?"

"No. But—Maggie, I swear—I'd swear it on the Bible, if I had one here— I swear he was perfectly well and all right when I left him."

"I've got a Bible, Miss Dolly."

"Then bring it out, Maggie. I'll take an *oath* about Uncle Giles and then you won't worry any more."

Maggie did not move, did not stir. Nobody could do that, she thought. Nobody could swear on the Bible to a lie.

"But how did Mr. Camford think he was going to get away from here, Miss Dolly?" she said, after a moment. "When he couldn't telephone for a taxi?"

"I don't know. I didn't think about it. I was so upset, so miserable. If you could have heard the way he talked to me, Maggie ... ! I dare say I'm not very prudent or thrifty. I'm not pompous. I don't *care* about the things Uncle Giles and Aunt Emily think are so important. But I've never done anything wrong in my life, Maggie."

That's certainly a lot to say, thought Maggie.

"I may have been thoughtless. I may have been foolish. But I've never done *anything* ..." Miss Dolly paused. "Maggie, bring out the Bible."

Maggie took the little black Bible her father had given her out of her bag, and still kneeling on the floor, Miss Dolly laid her hand on it, her delicate narrow hand with the tinted nails.

"I swear I left Uncle Giles perfectly well and all right and ready to go off to Boston," she said, in a low, steady voice.

"And—Miss Dolly—you don't know where he did go, or what happened to him?"

"I swear on the Bible I don't know where he went after I left him."

"Or what happened to him?"

"Or what happened to him. But, Maggie, why do you think anything happened to him?"

"Because—" Maggie said slowly and reluctantly, "I found his wallet here in the house—all soaking wet."

Miss Dolly pitched forward on her face.

Chapter Twelve

Maggie had seen other people faint; she knew what was done. She bathed Miss Dolly's face and wrists with cold water, and presently she opened her eyes.

"Maggie ... I've got to *get away*—from this horrible house ..."

"You must rest now, Miss Dolly. I'll help you get into bed when you feel better."

"I've got to get *away*, Maggie ... Where did you find that wallet?"

"Well, that doesn't matter, Miss Dolly. Let's not talk about it any more."

Miss Dolly lay flat on the floor, her black hair damp about her white face, her thick curling lashes damp, her eyes wide.

"His wallet, Maggie ... What was *in* it?"

"I don't know. Let's not talk any more about it, Miss Dolly. I'll help you into bed."

"I'm frightened, Maggie."

"Don't be, Miss Dolly. I'm right here."

Miss Dolly lay there looking up at the ceiling; faint musky perfume came from her, she seemed piteously fragile and helpless and stricken.

"Maggie ... Mr. Angel ... "

"Yes, Miss Dolly?"

"I don't know—how he died, Maggie."

"It was a stroke, Miss Dolly."

"Are they sure?"

"So I heard, Miss Dolly."

"That horrible Hofer man asked me so many questions about him.... If he ever finds out about the rowboat—what will he think, Maggie?"

"He seems like a sensible kind of man, Miss Dolly."

"I'm so frightened, Maggie."

"You must get to bed, right away, Miss Dolly, and try to get some sleep."

"Yes, I will, Maggie. You're so kind to me."

Maggie helped her off with the housecoat, and put her into bed; she was cold, her lips pale, she was shivering. Maggie went downstairs; she found everything in darkness there, she turned on the kitchen light, and boiled a kettle of water and filled an empty whiskey bottle with hot water.

"Oh, Maggie, that feels so good!"

"You must try to get some sleep now, Miss Dolly."

"Get me a drink, please, Maggie. There's a flask in my suitcase."

"Miss Dolly—couldn't you sleep without?"

"I *couldn't*, Maggie."

Miss Dolly poured out her own drink, and Maggie was no judge as to whether or not it was a big one. She tidied the room and she turned out the light.

"Leave the door open, will you Maggie? I feel—so nervous."

"Yes, Miss Dolly. Good night!"

"Good night, Maggie! I don't know what I should do without you."

Maggie got into bed and put out her own light, but for all her weariness, she was not sleepy. I don't know how it is, she thought, but now I'm *sure* something's happened to Mr. Camford. And Miss Dolly thinks so, too. Maybe she's got some good reason to think so. Maybe she knows something—or anyhow suspects something. Or somebody.

There were two people you had to think about when you thought of that wallet. Johnny and Neely. Neely was here in the house when we left, she said to herself. And when you think about how he acted about Mr. Angel ... Mr. Angel was dead then, of course, but even at that how could he be so heartless about him ... ? He's so queer and hard—about everything ... And he was right *here*.

But Johnny went away from the duck farm in the rowboat. He was gone a long time, a very long time. It was sort of a queer thing for him to do. And I don't really know about him. I don't know about any of these people. About Miss Plummer or the Gettys, or any of them. Not even Miss Dolly. When we were in New York, she seemed so different. She seemed to belong to the Camford family. But now ... All this drinking and carrying on ... Oh, if I could have a talk with Mrs. Crabtree, just for half an hour....

A smug, self-righteous, common little thing ... I didn't mean to be like that. I meant—to be a good, valuable person. I meant—to improve myself, and read, and learn things.

She buried her head in the pillow and cried herself to sleep.

"A few routine questions ..." said Captain Hofer in a loud, serious voice.

There were footsteps on the porch, and a door closed. Maggie sat up in bed, filled with a sense of extreme urgency. Now it's begun, she thought. She got up and put on her dressing-gown and slippers, to go and wash in a hurry. But her door stuck; she tried the knob, she pulled and pushed it, and it would not come open.

I've got to get down to Captain Hofer, she thought. He'll have to ask me questions. The best thing is to get all dressed and then try the door again. If it won't open, I'll bang on it, she thought, and when she was dressed, she tried again. And she knocked at it; she rattled the knob and knocked louder.

Well, *that's* provoking, she thought. You'd think somebody'd hear me. She thought a minute and then went out on the balcony. It was a bright lovely day; a shaft of sun came into the tunnel and the water in its path was a warm brown, flecked with foam. The rowboat floated easily, and the little launch; a fresh, steady breeze was blowing. I wonder ... she thought. I wonder if I couldn't get in by some other window.

The floor of the balcony sagged under her feet, the railing was crumbling and broken away in one place. It's not *safe*, she thought, going cautiously close to the wall of the house. I'd hate to fall into that nasty dark water ... Here was another window, and facing it, sitting at a table, was Neely, drawing with a crayon.

She looked at him through the rusty screen. He's quite good-looking, in his way, she thought impersonally; then she scratched on the screen, and he glanced up with his clear pale eyes.

"Let me in, will you please?" she said. "My door is stuck. I can't get out."

"You can't come in here," said Neely. "Go back. I'll get it open presently."

"I just want to go through your room."

"You can't," said Neely.

"I'm in a hurry," said Maggie. "Just move your table and pull up the screen—"

"No," said Neely, and he began to draw again.

"Now, look here!" said Maggie. "I'm not going to stay shut up. I want to go downstairs *right now*."

He did not answer, and she moved along to the next window, beside him. He jumped up and slammed it down and locked it. She went back to the first one.

"I'll smash that other window if you don't let me in," she said.

"Try it, and see what happens," said Neely.

"Whatever is the matter with you?" said Maggie. "What makes you so mean and spiteful?"

He looked up at her again.

"I understand women very well," he said. "I understand *you*. I know what you're up to. You think, because you're pretty, you can make a fool of me. Well, you're wasting your time."

"What are you talking about?" cried Maggie.

"Women mean nothing to me," said Neely. "When I was twenty, I was a fool. I'm glad of that. It won't happen again. Now you can stand there and make big eyes as long as you like."

"I'm not making big eyes!" she said, scornfully.

"You're a hypocrite," said Neely. "You deceive other people, but not me. You and your little aprons and your dish-washing ... You—"

"Well ..." said Captain Hofer's voice from below. "Very much obliged, Miss Camford."

"Let me in!" cried Maggie.

"Not I," said Neely.

A car started and drove away, and Captain Hofer was gone.

"All right!" said Maggie. "I think I see now. You wanted to keep me from telling about Mr. Angel in the rowboat."

"And you wanted to tell about it," said Neely. "You wanted to see me in jail. I know why."

"Well, why?"

"Because I didn't make love to you," said Neely. "I didn't pay any attention to you, and for that reason—"

She turned her back on him and went into her own room again. Someone will have to let me out pretty soon, she thought. I guess Neely locked me in. Well, Miss Dolly or Johnny will let me out. There's nothing to worry about. Only—it makes you sort of nervous, to be shut in. I never knew there were such hateful people as Neely and that Miss Plummer.

She made her bed and tidied the room. When I do get out, she thought, I'm going to call up Mrs. Crabtree again. I'm going to ask her to speak to Mrs. Mayfield, and tell her to find out if Mr. Camford really is in Boston.

And if he wasn't? Miss Dolly was frightened when she heard about his wallet. Maybe she'll do something herself. Maybe she's spoken to Captain Hofer already. Maybe I needn't worry so ... She sat down on the bed, and she felt hungry. I wonder what time it is? It's not early; you can tell that by the sun. If only—

Somebody was trying the door-knob.

"Maggie, will you let me in, please?" called Miss Dolly.

"I can't get the door open, Miss Dolly."

Miss Dolly rattled the knob, and pulled and pushed.

"I'll get Johnny," she said.

And in a moment he came along the balcony and in through the long window; he dropped down into a wicker chair and lit a cigarette.

"Aren't you going to get the door open?" Maggie asked.

"I'll try," he said. "But I'd like to talk to you first. Getty'll be along any minute; there's not much time."

"I'm not going on that yacht," said Maggie.

"Dolly told me that," he said. "That's what I want to talk to you about, Maggie." He sat hunched forward in the chair, elbows on his knees; he looked strained and weary and bleak. "Do go, Maggie," he said. "It'll be only a week or ten days out of your life, and Dolly needs you."

"I'm sorry," Maggie said. "But I'm not going. I've got things of my own to look after."

"You're a kind kid," he said. "If I tell you Dolly's in a spot—"

"I'm sorry," Maggie said again, "but I just can't go on like this."

"Maggie, if Dolly goes off on Getty's yacht without you, it's the finish for her."

"Why don't you tell *her* that, Mr. Cassidy?"

"God ..." he said. "If you knew how I've tried to talk to her. She won't believe me. Gabrielle Getty isn't going along, you know. If Dolly goes alone with Getty and Neely ..."

"She ought to know better," said Maggie.

"Oh, yes," he said. "She ought to. Only she doesn't. She won't believe that Gabrielle hates her."

"Well, does she?"

"Why not?" he said. "Getty's infatuated with Dolly; he fell for her the moment he set eyes on her. *She* says it's just a beautiful friendship, and that

Getty understands her, that he knows she 'isn't like that.' Maybe, I don't know. But it doesn't look that way to Gabrielle. She'll bring suit for divorce, and name Dolly, and that'll be the pay-off. You can figure out for yourself what that'll do for Dolly."

"She ought to know better," said Maggie.

He sat forward, his hands clasped between his knees.

"Dolly has a theory," he said. "She says that if she doesn't do anything 'wrong,' nothing can happen to her. It's a dangerous theory, and it's got her into plenty of trouble before this. But you've seen quite a lot of her. I dare say you've got a fairly good idea by this time of her romantic temperament. Well ..." He sighed, staring down at the floor. "Well—I don't know any more to say. Maybe you're right, Maggie. Maybe you'd better look after yourself, and to hell with Dolly."

Smug and self-righteous? "I can't help it!" Maggie cried. "I *don't* want to be mixed up in things like this. I can't go on and *on*, trying to help Miss Dolly out of the mistakes she makes."

He rose.

"I can see how you feel," he said. "I'm sorry—I'm damn sorry, because I'm fond of Dolly. But I shouldn't have expected you to worry yourself about all this." He held out his hand. "Good-bye, Maggie!" he said, smiling down at her.

"But—are you going away?"

"Yes. I've got a job. I'm off to China."

She took his outstretched hand, and his fingers closed over hers; his eyes narrowed, as if in pain.

"You're a dear little kid," he said. "I wish ... Well, it doesn't matter. Very likely nothing matters."

He was the only one here who had never said anything mean to her; he had been kind to her, nice to her.

"I don't mean to be—self-righteous about Miss Dolly," she said unsteadily.

"I don't know ..." he said. "It must be a wonderful feeling."

"If I do go along with her—"

"I'd thank you to the end of my days," he said, and bending, he kissed her on the temple. "Don't mind," he said. "You wouldn't, if you knew ..."

He went out through the long window on to the balcony, and Maggie stood looking after him with tears in her eyes. Maybe I will go ... she thought.

Chapter Thirteen

There was a hammering outside the door, and a picking at the lock, and after a time, Miss Dolly came in through the window.

"They can't seem to get the door open," she said. "Something's happened to it. But it doesn't really matter. Will you get your things packed as quickly as you can, Maggie? The Gettys will be here any minute."

"Both of them?" asked Maggie.

"I don't know," said Miss Dolly.

"Miss Dolly, if I go with you, I've got to stop in the village, first."

"I can lend you anything you want, Maggie."

"I've got to get something in the drug store," said Maggie. "Some special medicine."

"Well, I'm sure we can arrange that," said Miss Dolly.

So Maggie began to pack her bag while Miss Dolly sat on the bed, smoking, scattering ashes on the floor. Maybe this isn't really so very queer, thought Maggie. I'll talk to Mrs. Crabtree from the drug store, and maybe Mr. Camford's home by this time. It's broad daylight, and people are coming and going. Captain Hofer came here. The door's stuck, but people can get in and out of the room.

Miss Dolly was foolish to think of going on that yacht without Mrs. Getty; she was foolish about everything, about coming to this nasty dirty house with two men living in it; she had been incredibly foolish to go to a money lender, and to sign papers. But being foolish isn't the worst thing in the world, Maggie thought. And if it's only for a week ... A yacht ... she thought. Me going off on a yacht ... There was something faintly immoral about yachts, but undoubtedly adventurous. I do love ships and boats, she thought. And it certainly will be an experience.

"Let's go downstairs," said Miss Dolly.

"I'll make some coffee, Miss Dolly."

"If there's time," said Miss Dolly. "But we'll have to start the moment the launch comes for us. It's something to do with the tide."

They climbed in at the window of Neely's room that was empty now; they found him in the kitchen standing at the stove.

"What are you doing?" Dolly asked.

"I'm making coffee," he said. "I'm hungry."

He looked very neat and clean in a blue suit, his light hair brushed down, a little damp on his head; he began to whistle as he measured out coffee from a can into the battered tin pot.

"That's too much," said Maggie.

"We can use it all up," he said. "We're never coming back here."

"Never?" she said. "And where do you think you're going?"

"Hiram's late," said Miss Dolly. "He said ten o'clock, and it's after eleven."

Neely went on whistling, pouring boiling water through the grounds.

"*Don't* whistle, Neely!" said Miss Dolly.

He looked sidelong at her and kept on; she frowned and went out to the little porch off the kitchen.

"She's nervous as a cat," said Neely. "She wants to get away from here."

He seemed in very good spirits, and Maggie contemplated him with great displeasure. He let Miss Dolly pay his rent, and now I suppose he's willing for the Gettys to do things for him. Johnny's got his faults, but he isn't like that. He's got a job anyhow. He's gone off to China and I don't suppose I'll ever see him again. He didn't say anything about seeing me again ...

Neely put his hands to his mouth and blew a bugle call piercingly loud.

"Oh, do stop!" cried Miss Dolly opening the screen door. "What can be keeping Hiram?"

Neely sat down and poured himself a cup of the strong brew he had made, and Maggie sat down opposite him.

"I hear a car coming!" cried Miss Dolly.

"Take it easy," said Neely stirring his coffee. But Miss Dolly had gone out into the hall, the front door opened and in a moment they heard her clear light voice.

"Why, Gabrielle ... !"

"Hiram thought I'd better come," said Gabrielle. "Something very horrible has happened."

There was a complete silence, Maggie pushed back her chair and rose; when she went into the hall she saw the two women standing on the porch; Miss Dolly, so dark, so curved and supple in her yellow sweater, Gabrielle so thin and slight in a brown linen dress and a big yellow hat.

"What ... ?" said Miss Dolly. "*What's* happened?"

"We found another body on our beach," said Gabrielle.

Miss Dolly sat down on one of the benches.

"What—what *kind* of body?" she asked.

"It's like a nightmare," said Gabrielle. "It was another elderly man, very well-dressed, very dignified."

Yes, Maggie thought. You could imagine how he would look, lying there on his back, tall, spare, infinitely distinguished. He had made the same journey Mr. Angel had made.

There was a curious swirling inside her head, filmy thoughts trailing round and round. But they were coming to rest in a dim pattern. The awful thing that had stirred in her when she saw the wallet dripping wet, took form now. Mr. Camford was murdered, she said to herself.

"How horrible for you!" said Miss Dolly.

"Yes ..." said Gabrielle. "Hiram sent for the police, and he thought I'd better come along and tell you—so that you wouldn't be waiting."

"Will it—will this delay our sailing?" Miss Dolly asked.

Gabrielle turned her head.

"We can't go *now*," she said. "They'll have to investigate this. Hiram and Captain Hofer will be here presently."

"Captain Hofer! Captain Hofer's coming here?"

"That's what he said," Gabrielle answered.

"Won't you come in?" said Miss Dolly with a sudden politeness and she held the screen door open for Gabrielle to enter. "Oh ... !" she said, "that's Captain Hofer now, I guess."

But it was Miss Mitzi Plummer.

She came in smiling, wearing a dress of flowered chiffon, black, with huge red roses, over a red taffeta slip; she wore a red straw hat untrimmed, tilted at the back of her head, she had lipstick smeared around her mouth.

"Bon jour, la compagnie!" she cried. "Let's have a drink!"

"Something's happened, Miss Plummer," said Maggie, sternly.

"T-tut-tut!" said Miss Plummer, laughing.

"The police are coming, Miss Plummer," said Maggie. "You don't want to meet them and answer a lot of questions."

"I *love* policemen!" said Miss Mitzi. "And why are they coming? A spy? I *know* it's a spy!"

"Don't you think you'd better start for home right away, Miss Plummer?" said Maggie.

For it seemed to her the last straw, the intolerable touch to this dreadful little scene, that a figure so grotesque should enter. There was no doubt that Miss Mitzi had been drinking; all these people drank in the very face of death. She wanted to get at least this one away; but it was too late, another car had stopped before the house, there was a knock at the door not like other knocks.

She opened the door, and it was Captain Hofer with Getty behind him. There was a policeman sitting at the wheel of Captain Hofer's little car, there was a battered old sedan that Miss Mitzi had come in, there was the big, old-fashioned car that Neely drove, and there was a beautiful little tan roadster that must be Mrs. Getty's. It looked strange to see all these cars standing before the little house in the sun, with nothing else in sight in the flat, empty country, it looked somehow ominous, this gathering of people.

"Well," said Captain Hofer looking down at her. "Mrs. Getty here?"

"Come in, sir," she said.

He went in with a heavy tread, and she closed the door.

"Good afternoon!" he said to everyone.

"Oh ... Sit down, Captain Hofer!" said Miss Dolly. "And you'll have a cocktail?"

"No, thank you," he said.

"Oh, do!" she entreated him.

And everything she said was wrong, and everything she did. She was much, much too airy and sweet. He did not even answer.

"Mrs. Getty," he said, "this is certainly bad luck for you. But of course, when the tide runs out, everything goes right along to the Point ... We got your report at the station, but if you'll just run over it again..."

"I went down to the beach," she said. "We were coming here in the launch. And I saw a man lying partly in the water. I pulled him on the beach, and I saw that—he was dead. So I went back to the house and told my husband."

"Was there anybody else on the beach, Mrs. Getty?"

"No," she said. "I was alone."

"Anyone in sight. Any boats, for instance?"

"No. Nothing," she said.

"You didn't recognize the man?"

"No," she said, "I'd never seen him before."

There was something clear as crystal about her, about her words, her voice, her blue-grey eyes; the outline of her thin, fine body was so definite, and the way her fair hair was shaped to her head. She made everyone else look a little blurred, a little clumsy.

"Well ..." said Captain Hofer. "No letters on him, no papers. Nothing to identify this time. I don't know if anyone here can help me?" He looked around. "Body of a man between sixty and sixty-five, height five foot eleven, weight about one hundred and fifty-five pounds. Bald. Wearing a grey suit."

Nobody said anything. Neely was leaning against the wall with his hands in his pockets, Miss Dolly was looking at Captain Hofer with her dark eyes wide. Maggie moistened her lips.

"That sounds like Mr. Camford to me," she said.

"Who's Mr. Camford?" he asked.

"But that's my uncle!" cried Miss Dolly. "And it couldn't *possibly* be!"

"I could identify Mr. Camford, sir," said Maggie. "I was right there in the house in New York with him for two months. If you'd like me to come with you—"

"We'll see," he said. "Miss Camford, when did you last see this uncle of yours?"

"Yesterday," she said. "He came here to see me yesterday morning."

"Yesterday morning?" said Captain Hofer. "And when did he leave?"

"I don't know. You see—we had a sort of—disagreement, and I went out. I went out and left him in the house ..."

"What time was this?"

"I don't know. I didn't look. But I went out and left him—in the house."

"I met Miss Camford walking along the road at about eleven-thirty," said Getty. "She told me she'd left her uncle in the house. I persuaded her to get into my car, and go along to the Country Club for a bite of lunch. We got there by twelve, or earlier. It will be easy to check."

"Where was your uncle when you left him, Miss Camford?"

"He was—upstairs."

"Was your uncle expecting you to come back, Miss Camford?"

"I—no, I don't think so."

"What was he doing in the house then?"

"He—he was—he had some papers he was looking through."

"When you left, did you expect to return, Miss Camford?"

"Oh, yes! Oh, of course!"

"Did you expect to find your uncle here when you returned?"

"Oh, no! He said he was going to Boston."

"How did you think he'd leave, Miss Camford? On foot?"

"I'm afraid—I—I *didn't* think ... I was—I was upset ... I just went away."

"Where were you going?"

"I don't know ... I was just—well—just walking..."

"Who else was in the house when you left?"

"Why, nobody," she said.

"Nobody," he repeated.

"Tut-tut!" said Miss Mitzi, suddenly, and he turned to look at her in severe surprise.

"What's that, Miss Mitzi?" he asked.

"Tut-tut!" she said with a giggle.

There was a silence.

"I'll just step upstairs and have a look around."

"This way, sir," said Maggie, and he followed her up the stairs to the floor above.

He stopped in the hall, looking around him.

"Was Mr. Camford drowned?" asked Maggie.

"I don't know anything about Mr. Camford yet," he said. "The body hasn't been identified."

"Was the man you found on the beach drowned?"

He straightened up and turned to her.

"And why do you want to know that?" he asked.

"It's natural to want to know," said Maggie.

"You seem to be mighty sure it was Mr. Camford."

"Yes," she said. "You described him."

"Where were *you* yesterday morning?"

"I went out to lunch with Mr. Cassidy. We went in the boat to a farm."

"No farms around here."

"The woman's name was Mrs. Albee."

"Well, yes ... They call it a duck farm. So you went there? What time?"

"I haven't any watch. I don't know."

"Mr. Camford here when you left?"

"Yes."

"Anybody else?"

"Yes, Miss Dolly Camford."

"Anybody else?"

You had to tell the truth and not think.

"Mr. Curtius."

"Mr. Curtius," he said. "Well, all right."

He started toward the french window.

"Captain Hofer," she said, "was Mr. Camford drowned?"

"I don't know if it is Mr. Camford."

"Was the man you found drowned?"

He made a wonderful face, his lips pursed, his forehead corrugated.

"You're in a hurry," he said. "These things take time, young lady. We have to have an autopsy before we can—"

"Oh!" she said.

"What's the matter?"

"It just seems sort of awful, when it's someone you know."

"By the way—" he said, "which is Cassidy's room?"

"Oh ..." she said again. "Oh, that's it."

He went to the open window and looked in. "Yes ..." he said. "Yes ... Now, what about Cassidy? What's your impression of him?"

"Well ... It's hard to say."

"Quarrelsome, isn't he? Heavy drinker?"

"Well ... I don't think he's quarrelsome."

"Oh, you don't? Drinker?"

"He drinks—sometimes."

"What is his relation to Miss Camford?"

"I don't know."

She stood before him, her eyes lowered, her heart racing. Two years ago she had gone with a neighbour to visit her son in prison, and she would never forget what that was like, or how she had felt. She had seen men arrested too, one of them fighting and shouting until he was knocked out. She profoundly respected Justice; she adored order and propriety. But an unsuspected and passionate rebellion rose in her against being the instrument of justice. It was not in her nature to be the instrument of anything.

Her Covenanting ancestors had made many a bargain with the Lord, and she now proposed a bargain to Captain Hofer, representing temporal power.

"I'll answer any questions you ask me," she said. "I'll tell the truth."

"Very good!" he said. "If you have any information relative to these two deaths, let's have it."

"Ask me questions and I'll answer them," said Maggie.

"*That* won't do," he said. "It's your duty to volunteer any information you may have."

"It's my duty to tell the truth," said Maggie.

"Now, see here!" he said. "It's a mighty serious thing to withhold evidence."

"I've answered every question asked me, so far," said Maggie, "and I'll keep right on."

"This," he said, "is a matter of life and death, young lady. You can't make a game out of it."

There she stood with her eyes lowered, a high colour in her cheeks, her hands like ice.

"If you'll just ask me questions ..." she said.

"Have you any information?"

There was a silence.

"You mean," he said, "that you've got information, and you're going to make me get it out of you word by word. All right. All right! I can do it."

She raised her eyes, and he was glowering.

"I treat everybody fairly and decently," he said. "I give everybody a break. *But—*" He paused. "If anybody gets tough with me, believe me, young lady, I can be plenty tough myself."

Pooh! thought Maggie. Captain Hofer failed to alarm her.

Chapter Fourteen

She followed Captain Hofer down to the dining-room where all the others were assembled, and she was startled to see Johnny there, sitting on the edge of the table. If he knows about the wallet, she thought, maybe he'll tell Captain Hofer now. I just don't feel like telling him yet.

No, I don't think Johnny's a murderer. He does drink too much. He does talk in a sort of reckless, wild way. But it seems to me there are some good things about him ...

"Miss Camford," said Captain Hofer, "I'm sorry, but I'll have to ask you to come with me—"

"Oh no!" she cried. "You can't … You can't—arrest me!"

"I'm not arresting you," he said, as if a little injured. "It's a question of identifying deceased—"

"I can't!" she said almost in a scream. "I *can't* go to that awful place again … I can't! I can't! I *can't do it!*"

"I'll go," said Maggie.

"We'd like to have a relative," he said. "It won't take you more—"

"I can't!" Miss Dolly cried. "I won't! I won't be dragged to that horrible place again … I won't! I don't know anything about what happened. I won't—"

"Take it a little easy, Dolly," said Johnny. "If this man isn't your uncle, well, there's an end of it."

Hiram Getty spoke to her in a voice too low for anyone else to hear; he stood beside her chair with his hand on the back, a broad strong hand with a ridge of black hair. She listened to him, she raised her eyes to his face with a dazed look; she listened to him.

"All right!" she said to Hofer, "I'll go. But I think it's—barbarous, to make me."

"Then we'll get going," said Captain Hofer. "In the meantime I'd like the rest of you kindly to remain where you are until we come back."

"Now, people!" said Miss Mitzi. "Let's get together and solve this case before Captain Hofer comes back."

Maggie went up the stairs. She got Miss Dolly's hat and purse from the bedroom, and as she started down the stairs again, she heard an argument going on between Captain Hofer and Johnny.

"Be reasonable," said Johnny. "Look at the telegram for yourself. I can't afford to miss this."

"Everyone's got to stay here," said Hofer. "For the time being."

"I'll come back," Johnny said. "But this is a guy I've been trying to see for weeks."

"Nobody's going to leave the house yet," said Hofer.

"Captain, dear," said Johnny. "I didn't did it. I wasn't here. You know Mrs. Albee. A fine honest woman, descendant of generations of clam diggers. Ask her. She'll tell you what time Miss MacGowan and I got to the duck farm."

"What time you got to the duck farm doesn't interest me," said Captain Hofer.

"But it's an alibi," said Johnny.

"Is it?" said Hofer. "How d'you know what time to have an alibi for?"

"But I've got an alibi for *all* times."

"All right. We'll take that up later. I'll be back before long—"

"Captain, dear, take me with you then, and let me call up New York. You wouldn't like to feel that you'd ruined my future, would you?"

"A few hours isn't going to make any difference."

"Ah! Look at that telegram! Contact me immediately at St. Pol. Lentz. See? Says immediately."

"No."

"Just let me telephone. Just take me along, and I'll sit in the car like a little mouse."

"Well ..." said Hofer, slowly. "All right! I'll do that."

He and Dolly and Johnny went out of the house, the policeman got out of the little car and came up on the porch and sat there.

"Now, people!" said Miss Mitzi. "Gather round! Let's solve this case! First, let's see about our alibis."

"No sense in this," said Getty. "We don't know who the dead man is."

"It's Dolly's uncle," said Miss Mitzi.

"We don't know that."

"*I* do," she said. "And if Dolly left him alive at eleven-thirty, all alone in the house—"

"I understood that he wasn't alone," said Getty.

"You think I was here?" said Neely.

"That's what I understood," said Getty.

They hated each other; you could see that in their faces.

"You're wrong," said Neely. "I was at Mitzi's, hours before that. I got to her house before eleven-thirty, and it's a good forty minutes' walk."

"That's true, Neely," said Miss Mitzi.

"Nobody knows when this man was killed," said Neely. "Only they found him on your beach."

"What do you mean by that?" said Getty.

"Me? I don't mean anything. I don't care anything about these dead men. Two men dead, well, what's that? Nothing. Only I'm not going to be bothered about them."

"No?" said Getty.

"No," said Neely.

Gabrielle Getty rose and went out of the dining-room; Maggie saw her standing in the little hall, looking about her with a sort of despair, and she went out after her.

"Is there anything you want, Mrs. Getty?" she asked.

"I thought perhaps I could find some place to go," said Gabrielle. "Some place where it's quieter."

"There's the porch," said Maggie, and they went out there together.

"It's a—queer house, isn't it?" said Gabrielle.

"Yes, it's very queer," said Maggie.

Gabrielle stood at the edge of the steps, tall and slight.

"I don't understand these people," she said in her clear, even voice. "I don't know anything about artistic people." She paused for a moment. "I don't like them," she said.

"Well ..." said Maggie. "I dare say that when you get to know them they're all right."

"I'd never like them," said Gabrielle. "I—I suppose I'm too conventional. I've been told so. I—" She paused again. "I think you understand," she said.

"Well, I guess I'm pretty conventional myself," Maggie said soberly.

She sat on the bench and Gabrielle stood motionless by the steps; they were both silent for a long time.

"I don't quite know what to do," said Gabrielle at last, and her clear voice was a little unsteady. "I got a letter this morning, an anonymous letter. I'd have destroyed it. I'd have—put it out of my mind, if it hadn't been for this—this new thing that's happened. But now ..."

She opened her big square purse and took out an envelope; there was a letter in it typed on cheap white paper; she handed it to Maggie.

Mrs. Getty. You are going to lose your husband if you don't look out. The Bitch in the Boathouse is after him. She is a man-eater. One man is dead and *there are going to be others*. Look out.

                                                                          A Friend.

Maggie read it twice.

"You'll show it to Captain Hofer, won't you, Mrs. Getty?" she asked.

"I don't want to," said Gabrielle. "It would only make trouble. I meant to show it to Miss Camford, but—I couldn't. I don't understand her. I'm sorry, but I don't like her. I think that perhaps if you showed her this letter, she'd go away."

"Well ..." said Maggie. "I'll show it to her, Mrs. Getty ..."

"I didn't want to take this cruise with her," said Gabrielle. "But I couldn't very well refuse. Hiram is so very generous and kind to anyone in trouble, and he thought it would help her ... I'll have to go—unless she gives up the idea. If you show her this letter, perhaps she'll go away. That's all I ask, for her to go away from here."

"Yes, I see," said Maggie.

Either Johnny Cassidy had lied about the cruise, or Gabrielle was lying. She did not think it was Gabrielle.

Gabrielle sat down; she sat where Mr. Camford had sat. And he's dead, Maggie thought. He came here like Mr. Angel. He came for the same reason, to get Miss Dolly to go home. And now he's dead. If nobody else tells about that wallet, I'll have to. *I'll have to.*

Only you don't like to tell when you don't know what's happened. Maybe Mr. Camford had an accident, too, and telling about the wallet might only make trouble for someone who hadn't done anything—really wrong . . I think Johnny told me a lie about Mrs. Getty. I don't think she's the kind to bring a divorce suit and make a dreadful scandal. I'm sorry he told me a lie. I'm sorry he drinks so much. I'm sorry—about—a lot of things ...

But if somebody killed Mr. Camford, if this is murder ... It was hot out here in the sun and the bench was narrow and hard. I wish I could take a walk, she thought, all by myself, and sort of think things out. Before I have to talk to Captain Hofer again. If only, only he'd heard about the wallet from somebody else before I see him ... I don't like to be the one to tell him....

A car came along the road now, a taxicab. You couldn't tell who it might be, or what was going to happen next. A dreadful thing had begun, and dreadful consequences would follow inexorably. The cab stopped and Johnny got out and held out his hand to Miss Dolly; she tottered and leaned on his arm; as the cab drove away, she leaned against him.

"Take it easy!" he said, and led her along the path to the steps. "Come on!" he said, gently. "Come in and have a drink, and you'll feel better."

Maggie followed them into the dining-room.

"Well!" cried Miss Plummer. "It was your uncle, wasn't it?"

"No," said Miss Dolly. "It was someone—I'd never seen. A stranger. But it was a horrible experience."

Chapter Fifteen

Miss Plummer had one of her unaccountable changes of mood; she became compassionate and almost affectionate toward Miss Dolly.

"Poor darling!" she said. "You must come home with me, and I'll cheer you up."

"We might all go somewhere," said Miss Dolly. "To Seaview Inn, perhaps—"

"Let's!" said Miss Plummer. "Music and bright lights. Let's go, good people!"

"I'm sorry," said Gabrielle distinctly, "but I'm going home. Are you coming with me, Hiram?"

He glanced at Dolly, and he might as well have spoken aloud to her, asking, shall I go with her, or stay with you. She lowered her eyes, and he turned to his wife.

"We can all start together," said Miss Plummer. "Neely, you're coming, of course? And Johnny?"

"Miss MacGowan," said Gabrielle, "won't you come home to dinner with me?"

That was the nicest thing, the kindest thing, the most courteous thing.

"Thank you," Maggie said, a little unsteadily, "but I—I've got things to do."

"Then will you have lunch with me to-morrow?"

"Thank you! Yes. Thank you."

"Then I'll send the car. At twelve?"

She held out her hand, and her thin fingers, cold as ice, closed on Maggie's. She's really a lady, Maggie thought. All the others are just—riff-raff. That's what they are.

"Come on, good people!" Miss Mitzi called out.

"Maggie," said Miss Dolly, very doubtfully, "would you like to come along?"

"No, I wouldn't!" said Maggie. "When will you be back, Miss Dolly?"

"Oh ... Pretty soon, Maggie."

"Late?"

"Oh, no, I'll be early, Maggie."

They all began to move toward the door, and Maggie watched them. Riff-raff, all of them. No exceptions. Even Johnny Cassidy who had once seemed the best of the lot. I don't believe that story he told me about Mrs. Getty and the divorce suit, she thought. I believe it was just to make me go on that yacht. And why ... ?

She sat down on the porch to think things over. It was very quiet here in the late afternoon sun, no sound but the insects chirping in the grass, the breeze was fresh against her face. I need this time, she said to herself. Because it's come now, the kind of crisis I felt was coming. I know it's Mr. Camford that they found on the beach.

Here's where he sat talking to me, and now he's dead. Neely tried to get Mr. Angel out of the way, just to dump him into the water and get him away from here. Now Miss Dolly's trying to do that to Mr. Camford. Just to get him out of the way.

Well, it *won't work*. Because I won't let it. Mr. Camford's going to have a decent funeral, in his own name. He's not going to be just shoved out of sight. I don't know how he died, but Captain Hofer will find out. And if it was murder ...

I think it was murder, she said to herself, curiously calm about it. She got up after a while and went into the kitchen to get some supper for herself.

But there was the kitchen in all the familiar disorder, the dirty glasses, the cigarette butts on the floor. She could not eat in such a place. She cleaned it up and put on the kettle, and now it was growing dark. She stood by the window waiting for the water to boil, and there was the rowboat floating on the darkening water. The rowboat Mr. Angel had been lying in, the rowboat Johnny had left the duck farm in for such a long time.

She was alone in this house without a telephone; there was no one anywhere who was concerned about her. Her mother would be thinking of her as safe and snug in the Camford house in New York. Mrs. Crabtree couldn't have any idea what sort of place she was in.

She turned on the kitchen light, and made tea, and ate some crackers. I'm going to bed now, she thought. There isn't anything I can do to-night. But to-morrow, somehow, I'm going to get to see Mr. Camford. And nobody can stop me.

She left a light in the hall, and she turned on the light in the upper hall. The door of her room was still shut, she had to go through Neely's and Johnny's room and out of their window, and along that balcony. I don't know, she said to herself, I feel sort of nervous. She went into Miss Dolly's little room, she looked in the closet and under the bed. Her own divan seemed a solid thing, but she got down on her knees, just to see. It was not solid; underneath it was a dark cavern where a lot of queer things lay.

She took down a shade on the roller, and poked out everything. There was an empty gin bottle, there was a book, there were empty cigarette packages, a pair of black socks, and there was a doughnut, green with mold, and gnawed. By rats?

She thought about water rats. Perhaps that was what she had heard flouncing in the water at night. Perhaps they could climb up and come in here, dripping wet ... All right, I am frightened. Mr. Angel, and maybe Mr. Camford came here—up in this room ... I am frightened.

She got up on the divan with the shade roller beside her, and she opened a book. Miss Dolly said she'd be back early, she thought. If I had a watch, I'd know when to expect her.

That bitch in the boathouse ... One man is dead already, and there will be others.

Others. Did the person who had written the letter think that Miss Dolly had already killed a man? No! Maggie said to herself. That's silly. Miss Dolly isn't a murderess.

And how do you know that?

Because anyone would know a murderer.

Mr. Camford? Did he know his murderer at first sight? And all the people you read about in the newspapers? Do they know, so that they scream and try to run away?

They don't know. It is someone who comes up behind them—in the dark. Or it's someone who comes in the broad daylight; someone familiar. Someone who smiles, maybe, and speaks in a voice you know ...

Have I spoken to the one who killed Mr. Camford? Have I seen—that one? I'm frightened, Maggie thought. I'm frightened ...

It was not fear of any danger to herself that made her shiver, that made her heart race. It was terror at the thought of seeing a face and hearing a voice, and *knowing*. And worst of all, she thought that she did know already, in some unconscious way, and that one word, one gesture would bring the horrible hidden knowledge into the light.

I wish I had a watch, she thought. Then I could know—how much longer the night will be. Shall I go down and lock the front door? I mean, would I rather let them get in by themselves when they come? Or would it be better to go down and open the door when they ring? Miss Dolly and Johnny Cassidy and Neely ... Which would come home first? And whom did she want to see first?

None of them. It was better, a thousand times better to be here alone, even with the water lapping against the walls, even with those things that jumped and splashed.

Someone was coming up the steps of the porch. Just one person, alone. Oh no! she said to herself, and cowered against the wall—if this is the one ...

Then she had a vision of herself cowering and trembling, and it made her furious. She jumped up and went along the balcony and into the bedroom. The door downstairs was opening.

"Who's that?" she called, louder than she had meant.

"Me," answered Neely. "Is Dolly home?"

"No," Maggie answered.

He closed the door and began to mount the stairs slowly as if he were weary. Half way up he raised his eyes, pale and clear, to her face.

"You're *lovely*," he said, as if surprised. "You look like a nymph of the forest. You are very delicately made, and your hair is quite marvellous. You're much younger and prettier than *she* is. Why does anybody look at *her*?"

I suppose he's drunk, Maggie thought. They're all drunk, all the time. But he did not look drunk; only very tired. He came up the stairs and into the bedroom.

"Don't go," he said, as Maggie put her knee on the window sill.

"I've got to," she said.

"I've got to talk," said Neely, simply.

"Then I'll come downstairs," said Maggie.

She was perfectly aware that he was unmanageable. Not violent, but blind and deaf to anyone else's wishes. He turned and went down the stairs docilely enough, he sat down in a straight-backed chair in the dining-room.

"You know," he said, "she's a fool."

Let him go on and talk.

"She's a fool," he said. "What does she want with Getty? She couldn't live his kind of life. She's a tramp, you know. She couldn't live that life comme il faut. You can see *her* giving a nice little dinner party? Oh yes! Oh my dear Madame Dulac! So glad to see you ... ! Then, if Monsieur Dulac is at all good-looking ... !"

He began to speak in a foreign language, but his pantomime was deadly true. He was Miss Dolly looking up into a man's face with one of her long, earnest looks, her lips parted.

"Don't!" said Maggie.

He snapped his fingers.

"Okay!" he said. "But she's a fool. You must talk to her. You must tell her that she has to marry me. She promised to marry me, and now she has to do it."

"It's not my business to talk to her," said Maggie.

"You're her friend," he said. "Or she thinks you are. She told me you were devoted to her. I don't believe that, though. No woman is ever really a friend to another woman."

"You've got some queer ideas," said Maggie.

"In the beginning," he said, "she was quite wonderful. Somebody brought her to the studio I had in New York to see my work and she was quite wonderful. She had respect for my work. I was having a lot of trouble then, bills, debts, and all that, and she helped me. I couldn't tell if she was in love with me or not. She'd come to the studio alone, you know, and she'd stay late. But if I tried to make love to her—nothing doing. She'd be sad about it—you know. Disappointed."

Maggie said nothing.

"Well, I got tired of that. She's not a young girl. She's a mature woman. She's independent, she has money. She can do as she pleases. I said, if you don't love me, don't come here any more. Then was when she said, let's get married."

He leaned his silvery-fair head against the back of the chair and stretched out his legs; in grey flannel trousers and tan shirt, he had the look of a day-labourer, strong, compact, wholly self-sufficient. Love? Maggie thought. He couldn't be in love with anyone.

He was without the slightest consideration for anyone else; he was ruthless, bleakly aloof. Yet she felt the strangest compassion for him. Does he think Miss Dolly's going to get a divorce? she wondered. Or doesn't he know about her husband?

"I'd like to get married," he went on, gazing up at the ceiling. "I'd like to have a home. I'd work better without all this moving around all the time, all this worry about money. She can buy this house. I like it. And you can cook and keep it clean."

"Suppose I don't want to?"

"Then she can find someone else," he said. "That big room upstairs, that's the room I want. She can have a skylight put in it. Only I don't want to wait. What *is* she waiting for, anyhow? Do you know?"

"I don't know anything about it," said Maggie.

"We can get a license in two or three days. I want to get married now. I want to get settled. I don't know why she keeps putting me off. If I thought it was Getty ..."

He shot out his arm and looked at the watch on his wrist.

"She told me she'd be home before this," he said. "I don't believe she is with the Plummer."

"But didn't you go with them?"

"I? No. I went to a diner and got something to eat, and then I walked back here."

"What time is it, please?" Maggie asked.

"Why d'you want to know?"

"I've been wanting to know the time all along. I haven't any watch."

"It's five to ten," he said, still looking at his watch. "If she's gone with Getty, there'll be hell to pay."

He spoke absently, almost carelessly; what he said was scarcely a threat, it was a statement. And the lack of violence made it shocking.

He lowered his arm. "You know," he said, "she told me Getty was going to do things for me. She said he was interested in art. But now that I've seen him, I don't believe that. Do you?"

"I don't know anything about it," Maggie said.

"Is she in love with me?"

"I don't *know*," Maggie said in a sort of despair. "It's no use talking to me about all this."

"I haven't anyone else to talk to," he said. "Cassidy's no good."

"I think I'll go out and take a stroll," said Maggie. "I want some fresh air before I go to bed."

"I want to talk to you."

"Well, later on," said Maggie. "I'm tired, and I feel sort of nervous. I'll take a walk and think things over, and then I'll come back."

"Don't be long," he said.

"I won't," she answered. "Have you got a flashlight?"

"Look in the top drawer of that thing," he said.

She opened the drawer of the sideboard and found an electric torch. She made herself go at a leisurely pace into the kitchen, and out of the side door.

But then she began to run, along by the wooden wall of the tunnel. Because she had heard the sound of a motor-boat, and she thought, what if it was Miss Dolly and Getty ... ?

Chapter Sixteen

Hell to pay ... she kept saying to herself in a queer anger. She stopped where the wooden wall ended and the water ran past the low bank. It was not a dark night, it was grey, with a faint mist from the marshes, like smoke; there was a rank swamp smell in the still air.

And the sound of the engine was growing louder and louder, a dreadful sound, inexorable, a machine rushing toward her. Hell to pay ... what does she *mean* by saying she'll marry Neely, when she's got a husband? And if she cares that much for Neely, what does she mean by leading Mr. Getty on? A married man ... No wonder somebody wrote an anonymous letter to Mrs. Getty.

She's killed one man ... But out under the open sky, the phrase had a different meaning. It doesn't mean murder, Maggie thought. It means destroying men's souls, and dragging them down. Like the woman I saw in the movie, the one who ruined the bull-fighter. Miss Dolly wouldn't kill anyone. She couldn't. But she's a liar. She's—a bitch.

That was the first time Maggie had used that word, even in her thoughts. But it was just the word she wanted. She stood, looking along the creek that was like a dark gleaming ribbon through the misty land; the noise of the engine was loud and dreadful but it seemed to come no nearer; there was nothing to be seen. I don't see how Neely can help hearing it, she thought. Maybe he'll come out to see ... All right! If there's hell to pay, it's her own fault. She brought it—

Oh ... ! she said half aloud. For now she remembered Mrs. Amber. They bring it on themselves, Mrs. Crabtree had said. They get mixed up, one way or another, with men. Like this. A tangle of lies and evasions, a net of jealousy and suspicion and bitter anger, until someone broke free from it, with violence.

Off in the marsh a green light showed, clear as an emerald: the boat was coming. The starboard light, she said to herself. Father taught me that when I was almost a baby. I've never seen another man like him. He was so—true ... She turned on the torch and swung it over her head in a half-circle.

If only they'll stop, she thought. Stop here and not go on into the boat-house. There's Neely sitting in there, thinking about her ... She promised him to come back early—but a promise doesn't mean anything to her. She's a bitch.

She swung the torch again.

"Ahoy there!" called Getty's voice.

Maggie did not answer; she did not want Neely to hear her. The engine was turned off, the boat came gliding along in a gentle swell that washed up on the bank where she stood; the light of a torch shone on her.

"Oh, it's *you*, Maggie," said Miss Dolly.

"And me," said Neely's voice beside her.

There was a silence.

"I was getting worried about you," Neely said.

"I couldn't get away from Mitzi," said Dolly. "You know how she is. And I didn't like the idea of her driving me home."

"Oh well!" said Neely with a curious heartiness, "here you are safe and sound. Are you coming in for a drink, Getty?"

"Thanks," said Getty, "but I'll have to be going along."

Neely held out both hands to Dolly and helped her out of the boat. The engine started.

"Good night!" said Getty, and the boat shot forward up the creek.

"And where's *he* going up there?" Neely said as if to himself.

There was no answer; they moved toward the house in silence. Neely pulled open the door and they entered.

"Well?" he said. "Shall we have a little talk, Dorothea, gift of God?"

"If you want," she said.

She looked beautiful and sorrowful and exhausted; her olive-skinned face was pale, her eyes were heavy; she raised her hand with that familiar gesture, and pushed her dark hair back from her forehead; her lovely narrow hand with scarlet nails. "I'll be down in a moment," she said and went up the stairs.

Neely leaned against the wall with his hands in his pockets; he looked, Maggie thought, more than ever like a workman, with the cool independence of a skilled artisan. She did not know what to do, she had no wish to stay here with Neely, but neither did she want to be with Miss Dolly just now. She went, with unhappy hesitation, into the kitchen.

Hell to pay ... But she doesn't care. I suppose she can explain and make everything right. But suppose she can't? If Neely ever finds out that she's got a husband ...

"Go up and tell her to hurry," said Neely from the doorway.

"You can call her," said Maggie, but it was a halfhearted rebellion. There was something about him that could not be denied, something savage, and something strangely touching. She got up and went toward the stairs. It's a mistake for her to keep him waiting, she thought. It'll make things worse.

She can't play with *him*.

She was startled to see Dolly standing motionless at the end of the hall upstairs, by the window.

"Miss Dolly ..." she said.

"Hush!" Miss Dolly said. "What do you want, Maggie?"

"Mr. Curtius says, will you please come down—"

"I'm coming," Miss Dolly said. "I'll just—is that a car coming, Maggie?"

"I don't hear anything."

"Get my red housecoat, will you, Maggie?" she said, standing near the door. And she was listening, you could tell that. Listening for what? What was it she expected? Maggie got the dark-red housecoat from the little room, and, standing in the hall, Dolly took off her skirt and yellow sweater. In her ivory satin slip with a yoke of écru lace she looked elegant as a princess, with her bare arms and shoulders, her full bosom, her small waist.

"Here's your housecoat, Miss Dolly," Maggie said. But Dolly did not answer or stir; she was listening. "Miss Dolly!" said Maggie, sharply, and she came to with a little start.

"Oh Maggie ..." she said. "Neely's so unreasonable, and so unkind."

"Unkind?" said Maggie.

"I've tried to help him every way I know. But it's not enough for him. Nothing you can do is ever enough for a man. What a man calls 'love' is a *horrible* thing."

Maggie was not touched.

"Hadn't you better put on your housecoat and go downstairs, Miss Dolly?" she said. "Mr. Curtius—"

"I *dread* trying to talk to him. He's—sometimes I'm afraid of him, Maggie."

I don't blame you, thought Maggie.

"If I could only—" Dolly began, and stopped. "Maggie! Isn't that a car coming?"

"Yes, it is," said Maggie.

"Will you go down, Maggie, and let—and open the door?"

She knows who it is, thought Maggie. It's someone she expected. Who could it be? I'd like it to be Johnny Cassidy. I wish it would be.

"Hurry up, Maggie!"

She went downstairs slowly, there was no reason to hurry; no one had knocked or rung the bell. Maybe the car had come this way by mistake and had turned back again. She hoped it was like that; an unreasonable dread had seized her at the thought of Miss Dolly's expected visitor. I'll just see ... she thought, and had her hand on the doorknob, when Neely spoke.

"Don't open the door," he said.

"I thought I heard a car ..."

"All right. Don't open the door."

"But it might be—Mr. Cassidy."

"I don't want anyone in here just now," he said. "Not until I've had my talk with Dolly. Get away from that door, will you?"

She looked back over her shoulder at him, and maybe he was worse than that unknown person outside.

"Get away from there!" he said and came along the hall toward her. She stepped back, and then someone knocked. Someone who must have been outside there for a long moment, very quiet. Neely beckoned to her by jerking back his head. But she was afraid to go to him.

There were three of them in the house, and somebody outside, and it was absolutely quiet ... Everybody was waiting. And then there was another knock.

"Open the door. It's the police."

"All right. Go ahead!" said Neely to Maggie.

It was Captain Hofer and he looked different. He came in and closed the door after him.

"Mr. Curtius," he said, "I'd like a few words with you."

"Here I am," said Neely.

They went into the dining-room. "Sit down," said Hofer, but Neely shook his head. "I've received information regarding you," said Hofer, "and I want an explanation. Now then, Mr. Curtius, when did you last see Mr. Angel?"

"I don't know," said Neely, "I didn't look at the time."

"When did you last see him?"

Neely was silent, with one hand resting on the table, and the overhead light shining on his fair head.

"What's this about?"

"I'm asking the questions here," said Hofer.

"I'm not answering them," said Neely, "until I know what it's about. This isn't a game. If you've got anything against me, you can tell me, and then we'll see."

"All right," said Captain Hofer after a moment. "I've received information that you attempted to dispose of Mr. Angel's body by overturning the boat in which the body was concealed."

"Yes," said Neely.

"How d'you mean, yes?"

"I mean, I did that," said Neely impatiently.

"Are you willing to make a statement to that effect?"

"I've just made a statement."

"A statement under oath—"

"Oaths ..." said Neely. "What damn nonsense the whole thing is."

"You think it's nonsense, do you?"

"That's what I think. Here's another statement for your collection. I didn't kill that man. I found him dead in the boat. I thought it would make a lot of fuss and bother if he was found here, and I tried to get rid of him."

"Did anyone assist you?"

"I suppose she told you," Neely said. "I got that girl there to row the boat. But she didn't know anything about Angel. She didn't like it when she found out."

Hofer glanced at Maggie, who stood in the hall near the doorway perfectly still. Neely smiled.

"I don't blame her for telling you," he said. "She's got a lot of fine old-fashioned sentiment about dead bodies. She's a *good* little wench."

He looked at her still smiling a little; the light shone on his thick fair lashes and gave him the look of a cat or a panther.

"Now what?" he said.

"Now you come along with me," said Hofer.

"Arrested?"

"Nope," said Hofer. "For questioning."

"God!" said Neely. "That's a bad word in Europe. All right. I'm ready."

"You'll remain here," said Hofer to Maggie.

They went out of the house and the door closed behind them. It was all very quiet and simple; just Neely walking off, hatless.

But it was horrible. He had been betrayed. He thinks I'm the one who told Captain Hofer, Maggie said to herself. But *she* did it. She wanted to get rid of him; and she's done it.

Chapter Seventeen

When she went up stairs, Maggie was startled to find the door of her own room open. Miss Dolly was standing in there lighting a cigarette.

"How did you get in?" Maggie asked.

"I found the key in Neely's room."

Maggie went into the room slowly.

"Miss Dolly—"

"I'm too tired to talk, Maggie, too miserable."

"Miss Dolly, we've got to talk. Miss Dolly, from the way Mrs. Getty described that man they found—"

"Oh, don't!"

"Miss Dolly I think that was Mr. Camford."

"*Don't!*"

"I'm going to ask Captain Hofer to let me see him. And if it is Mr. Camford, I'm going to tell the truth."

"Then wait, Maggie! Wait just *one* more day!"

"You mean it is Mr. Camford?"

"Yes," said Miss Dolly. "Yes, it is."

"Why didn't you say so?"

"He was—murdered," said Miss Dolly. Her mouth was oddly stretched and stiff, giving her face a piteous and almost ugly look. "They made me look at him—and his head—" She put her hand to her temple. "Here ... His *head* ... !

"Miss Dolly, don't scream like that," said Maggie, sharply.

"They made me look ... First Mr. Angel—and then Uncle Giles—both lying there in that place ..."

"Don't think about it, Miss Dolly."

"I can't help it! I can't help it! Oh God! I thought I was coming here—to be happy ... Just for a little little while ... But I never can be happy. I can't get free ..."

"You needn't work yourself up so, Miss Dolly. Because we've got to talk about this, and get this straight. Mr. Camford can't lie there, in the morgue."

"Stop it! If you knew what that place is like—"

"Well, I do," said Maggie. "I went to a morgue once with a woman who lived on our street, to identify her brother. And that's one more reason why I can't stand the idea of Mr. Camford's lying there."

"Maggie, wait one more day before you do anything. One more day can't make any difference to Uncle Giles."

"But it makes all the difference in the world to the police, in finding the murderer."

"That's what I want," said Miss Dolly, faintly. "I want him to get away."

"Oh ..." Maggie said.

It seemed to her that a sudden cool breeze came streaming in against the back of her neck; she looked quickly behind her. Nothing there, only the long window open on the balcony.

"Then you know—who it is, Miss Dolly?" she asked.

"*No!*" said Miss Dolly in a scream. "I *don't!* But I'm so afraid ... If it's—who I think—then whatever happens to him will happen to me. I can't ever, ever get away from him ... A woman told me that—a Frenchwoman ... It's in my stars—"

"Miss Dolly, don't talk so wildly. If you know who it is, you've just got to tell the police. They won't let anything happen to you."

"Give him one more day! One more day!"

No, Maggie thought, I can't. I won't. But it's no use trying to talk to her in the state she's in. "You'd better get to bed, Miss Dolly," she said with a certain compassion.

"Then promise, Maggie. Promise to wait just one more day."

"I'll think it over carefully, Miss Dolly, and we'll talk about it in the morning."

"Maggie, lock the doors downstairs, and all the windows."

"I will, Miss Dolly."

"And Maggie, here's the key for your door. You can lock it now. And put a chair against it, so that we could hear ..."

"All right, Miss Dolly."

She went downstairs to lock up everything, and she did it thoroughly, every door, every window. When she went up again, she found Miss Dolly closing the long window in the big room.

"Miss Dolly, we'd better have one of these open, to get a little air."

"No ... No, let's close them, Maggie."

In a bad state, Miss Dolly was. She made Maggie stay in the bathroom while she washed, and she would not put her light out after she had got into bed. Maggie lay down on the divan and pulled the sheet over her, and got ready to think.

It's her husband, she thought. Her husband killed Mr. Camford. Or anyhow, that's what she thinks. Then he must have been out here ... Has he been right in this house? She threw back the sheet because the room was so hot, so airless. It makes you restless, not to have fresh air ... The bar of light shining from Miss Dolly's open door bothered her, too. Her arms began to itch, she got a cramp in one foot, the pillow felt prickly under her cheek.

I want to lie quiet and think, she told herself. I've got to think things out before I see Captain Hofer to-morrow. Because I'm certainly going to see him. And tell him. In a way, I'm sorry for Miss Dolly. It's going to be pretty bad for her when all this comes out.

Her discomfort was becoming frantic. It's just no use! she said to herself. I can't rest, I can't even think unless I have some air. She got out of bed very quietly, and looked into the small bedroom. Miss Dolly was lying relaxed and quiet with her eyes closed, and after watching her face a moment, Maggie crossed the big room and opened one of the french windows, opened it wide.

The blessed air came flooding in, damp and fresh; she could hear the lapping of the water, she stood there breathing deeply, filled with an unreasonable sense of relief.

"Maggie?" said Miss Dolly's voice, drowsy and gentle.

Maggie ran nimbly back to her bed.

"Yes, Miss Dolly?"

"Maggie, do you know ... ? Maggie, can he swim?"

"Who, Miss Dolly?"

There was a minute's pause.

"Neely," said Miss Dolly. "Can he swim?"

"I—don't know," Maggie answered, sitting motionless, waiting for more. *What can she ever mean by* that?

"Maggie?"

"Yes, Miss Dolly?"

"You're sure the windows are all closed, Maggie. The windows on the balcony?"

"I'll take another look," said Maggie, springing up.

She closed the french window and turned the handle. Could Neely swim? What difference could that make? Nobody's going to be swimming now, at this time of night, out there in the dark. Unless there were water rats. I wish this couch was solid, she thought, returning to it, with no room under it —for anything ... I wish I knew the time.

But the morning will come, and then there'll be people about ... I wonder if Johnny Cassidy's ever coming back ... ? Neely will come back when they've finished asking him questions. Unless they keep him in jail. I'll be glad when the day comes and there are people around....

But the person she found waiting in the dining-room was Mrs. Crabtree, composed and friendly as ever. How did you get here, Mrs. Crabtree? Maggie asked. Why, I came in the rowboat, Mrs. Crabtree answered. All the way from New York? Maggie asked, and Mrs. Crabtree smiled, and Maggie was afraid of her.

The rowboat was in the kitchen covered over with a tarpaulin, and she thought she could see something moving feebly underneath it. What's that in there, Mrs. Crabtree? she asked. Oh, just a duck, Mrs. Crabtree said. But whatever it was, it made a sound, and she bent over. Tut-tut, it said. Tut-tut ...

She tried to rise, and could not stir, she tried to call for Captain Hofer, and her voice strangled in her throat. Help ... ! she began to scream. They've killed another one ... Help ... !

Mrs. Crabtree ran out on the porch, her footsteps making such a clatter ...

She opened her eyes, and it was day, and someone was knocking at the door. She got up staggering with sleep and hurried down the stairs, and there was another knock.

"Oh, hush up!" she said angrily. She opened the door, and Captain Hofer and two other men stood there.

"Miss Camford?" said Captain Hofer.

"She's not up yet."

"Well, ask her to get up then," said Captain Hofer.

They all came into the house unbidden, and it was plain they were taking charge.

"You tell Miss Camford that the District Attorney wants to see her in his office. And come down again yourself."

Miss Dolly was sound asleep, and the sun streaming into the room made it hot as an oven.

"Miss Dolly! Captain Hofer is here, Miss Dolly."

She did not answer; Maggie shook her and she did not stir. There she lay, so pretty, so comfortable.

"Wake up!" Maggie cried and lifted her hand. Miss Dolly opened her dark eyes.

"Captain Hofer is here. He wants to see you right away!"

"Oh," she said with a sigh. "Oh Maggie ... Will you get me a cup of coffee, Maggie. It's—"

"They won't wait for that, Miss Dolly. You'll have to go down right away."

"But Maggie, I took a sleeping pill ... I was so nervous and miserable. I can't just spring out of bed—"

"You don't want me to tell Captain Hofer *that*, do you?" Maggie demanded.

"Then if you'll get me a towel wrung out in cold water, Maggie, and a glass of water to drink ..."

Maggie brought them and then she began to dress in haste.

"Maggie ..." said Miss Dolly, still lying in bed, "don't put on that black dress again. I've got an extra skirt and blouse here—"

"No, thank you! I'd rather wear my own clothes."

"Maggie—it's *important*. You've *got* to look like my secretary. Maggie, *please* don't be so stubborn about every little thing. It's bad enough as it is."

"Oh, *all* right!" said Maggie. "You'd better get up, Miss Dolly."

"In the closet, Maggie. That skirt—no! On the right. And the lavender blouse."

"That's too fancy."

"No, it isn't. Please don't be obstinate! And *please*, Maggie, try to act like my friend. Things are bad enough—"

The black skirt was a little too loose at the waist, a little too short. And the blouse of lavender chiffon with amethyst buttons and long full sleeves was far too delicate and expensive and fancy. But after all, what did it matter?

"Miss Dolly, you honestly ought to get up!"

"I am getting up, Maggie. But these sleeping pills leave me so tired ..."

"I'll go down, Miss Dolly, and I'll tell him you're coming right away."

"Yes, and make me some coffee, please, Maggie."

Captain Hofer was standing at the foot of the stairs; very hot he looked, and angry.

"In there," he said. "In there," and pointed with his thumb toward the dining-room. "Now," he said, "the District Attorney's going to question you about this rowboat business. I suppose you know it's a serious thing for you."

"Well ..." said Maggie.

"You know as well as anybody else that it was your duty to tell the police—a thing like that. You've got yourself in a very bad spot, young lady."

"I'm sorry," Maggie said.

But she was not alarmed. She could not feel that she had done anything criminal, and she did not believe that Captain Hofer was hostile. He was cross, that was all.

"And now," he said, "I want the letter Mrs. Getty gave you."

"Oh ..." she said.

"That's just a little more evidence you were withholding from the police."

"I don't see how it could be evidence of anything. Just a spiteful anonymous letter."

"Oh you don't?" said he. "Well, let's have it."

She took it out of her purse with great reluctance; he glanced at it and put it into an envelope.

"I'm sorry," she said, politely.

"You're going to be still sorrier," said he. "Now, what's the matter with Miss Camford? Did you tell her I was waiting?"

"Yes, but she's not very quick," said Maggie. "Could I make some coffee?"

He gave her an outraged look.

"Do you realize," he said, "that the District Attorney is waiting to see you two?"

"Well, yes," said Maggie. "But it would only take a few minutes, and we could answer the questions *better* if we had some coffee."

He continued to look at her for a moment, and then he went into the hall.

"Miss Camford!" he called in a terrific voice.

"Oh, I'm coming!" cried Miss Dolly, and she came, wearing the yellow sweater again, looking pale, anxious and appealing. "I'll just swallow my coffee ..." she said.

"There's no coffee," he said.

Tears came into her eyes.

"Come, madam!" said he. "We've got to get going."

She was crying as they went out of the house.

To Maggie's surprise, there was a little crowd of people out there in the sun, and three cars. A man in a battered felt hat came up to her.

"Miss Camford," he said, "I represent the *Evening Standard.*"

"No time now, boys," said Captain Hofer.

"You any theory about this murder?" asked another man.

"Play fair now," said Captain Hofer. "You'll get your chance, boys."

He hurried Miss Dolly into the waiting sedan, Maggie got in after him, and he himself took the wheel. Looking back, Maggie saw the little crowd going up the steps of the porch and into the house.

"Are they allowed to go snooping into the house?" she demanded.

"Take it easy," said Captain Hofer. "I've got a couple of men in charge there."

He drove along the highway and into the pleasant tree-shaded village street; he stopped before a neat new building.

"Now!" he said. Miss Dolly gave a sob. She was still crying when Captain Hofer took her into an office, and Maggie was left in an anteroom.

There was a girl in spectacles who answered the telephone, and typed very fast; there was a man with his hat on sitting in a corner and smoking. Nobody spoke. The typewriter clattered, the telephone rang, the man in the corner struck a match, and Maggie waited and waited. If only I had a watch, she thought. If I only knew the time ...

She was strangely unable to think. Certainly she was not frightened, or even moved. The whole problem was out of her hands now, there were no decisions she could make, there was nothing for her to do. She was no longer independent, no longer free.

The typewriter clicked; what was the girl doing? Was she copying? Pages and pages about crime? The telephone rang and she answered it in a professional sort of voice, almost inaudible. Mr. Price is busy just now. The man in the corner lit another cigarette. I guess he's a detective, Maggie thought. A policeman in uniform came in, and went over to the girl in spectacles, he leaned both hands on her desk and they talked, very low. It was a long wait, very very long. It was so much quieter than you would expect.

And all this time it's going on, she thought. The law was moving in its course. Was Miss Dolly crying in there? It was a very long time ... She thought of a movie that she had seen, a beautiful girl sitting in a chair, while the District Attorney stood in front of her, pointing his finger at her, shouting at her; the girl's luminous tear-filled eyes grew wider and wider in horror ...

The door opened.

"Come in!" said Captain Hofer, and she rose and entered the inner office.

The District Attorney was a short dark man, with a long upper lip and dark hair combed up at the temples. He was a very quiet and serious man; he did not bark or snap or point his finger at her. But he disapproved of her.

He asked her question after question about the episode in the rowboat, and a young man sitting beside his desk took everything down in shorthand.

"I'd like to know the time, approximately, that Curtius asked you to go out in the boat with him," he said.

"I'm sorry," she said, "but, you see I haven't any watch."

He wanted to know—approximately—the time she had gone to the duck farm with Cassidy; the time—approximately—when she had left Mr. Camford in the house. He disapproved of her not knowing any times.

"You understand," he said, "that in withholding your information from the police you have made yourself liable to severe penalties?"

"Yes, sir," she said, "and there's another thing ..."

"Go on."

"The day that Mr. Camford came—when I got back to the house, I found Mr. Camford's wallet there."

"What was your object in withholding this information?"

"Well, you see sir, I didn't know then that anything had happened to Mr. Camford."

"And when did you first learn that anything had happened to Mr. Camford?"

"Well, I thought when I heard Mrs. Getty describe the man she found ... I called up his house to ask if he'd got home—"

He showed no serious interest in the wallet or her concern for Mr. Camford.

"This anonymous letter," he said, "where did you get it?"

He knew that already. "Mrs. Getty gave it to me."

"Have you seen any threatening letters addressed to Miss Camford?"

"Yes," she said after a moment.

"Describe these letters," he said, and with reluctance she told him.

"Have you any knowledge as to the identity of the writer signing himself 'Othello?'"

"No, sir."

That was the truth. She did not *know*. And I do hate to be the one to tell about Miss Dolly's marriage. I will, if I have to, but I *hope* I won't.

"When did you last see Miss Camford's husband?"

"I never saw him, sir."

"When did Miss Camford tell you about her marriage?"

"After we arrived here, sir."

"You were surprised?"

"Yes, sir, I was."

"You asked Miss Camford questions about her marriage?"

"No, sir, I didn't."

"What's your exact position in that household?"

"Well, I'm Miss Camford's secretary."

"You're paid to act in that capacity?"

"Well, yes."

"Have you any knowledge of any letters or telephone calls from Mr. Haverhill?"

"Mr. who, sir?"

"Haverhill."

"I don't remember that name," she said frowning a little.

"That is the name of Miss Camford's husband," he said, and he leaned forward in his chair.

"I want you to answer carefully and fully," he said. "Have you at any time seen any evidence that might lead you to think the boathouse had been entered or used by someone unknown to you?"

"Why, no!" she said, startled.

"You haven't seen any articles lying about that might have been left there by a stranger? Think carefully."

"No, sir," she said.

"Have you heard anything that might lead you to believe someone was concealed in or near the boathouse? Any unaccountable noises, for instance?"

"No, sir," she said.

"Would it be possible for anyone to be concealed in the house without your knowledge?"

"Well ... I don't know. Maybe it would be."

He went on for a long time about that, about doors and windows and where she slept, and what she could see when her door was open. It puzzled her. She had to admit that it was possible for someone to hide in the house, possible for someone to enter unnoticed by one of the three doors, or by a window. But she did not believe in it.

"Now," he said, "there's one more point. This Cassidy. What are the relations between Cassidy and Miss Camford?"

"Well, they seem to be friendly."

"Have you at any time heard Cassidy express hostility toward Miss Camford?"

"Why, no."

"Now, Miss MacGowan, I'm going to let you go," said he. "I'm going to accept your story of the disposal of Angel's body—temporarily. You did very wrong in withholding this information, and you rendered yourself liable to criminal prosecution. But you've given me a straightforward and credible account to-day, and I'm going to let you go. You'll remain in Miss Camford's house of course, and you'll hold yourself in readiness for further questioning at any time."

The look he gave her now was more like that of a District Attorney in the movies.

"Yes, sir," said Maggie.

"Have you anything more to say?" he asked.

"No, sir," she said. "Nothing that's—evidence."

He looked up at her with a nice little smile.

"You make a good witness," he said. "Just be straightforward and co-operative with us, and you'll have nothing to worry about."

It seemed to her a very unsatisfactory interview.

Chapter Eighteen

She went out of the office, not through the anteroom, but by a door that led direct into the corridor. There was a policeman there, and she spoke to him.

"Excuse me," she said, "but could you tell me how I'll find Miss Camford?"

"She's went," he answered. "The newspaper fellers was after her, and Mr. Getty, he took her somewheres in his car."

"Well ..." said Maggie. "Can I get a bus back to the boathouse?"

"You could," he said judicially. "Only the buses don't run more'n once every forty-five minutes and there's a long walk after you get out. If I was you, sister, I'd get me a taxi and I'd charge it up to the expense account."

He liked her. He thought she was pretty. You could tell.

"Thank you," she said, and rang for the elevator.

"It's nice weather," said the policeman.

"Yes, it's lovely," said Maggie.

The elevator door opened. "So long!" said the policeman.

"Good-bye!" said Maggie.

I've got to go back and stay with Miss Dolly now, whether I like it or not, she thought. But she's—the most selfish, thoughtless woman I ever heard of. She doesn't care how I get home. She'd go home and leave me on a desert island. She's like that to everyone. *Look* what she did to Neely ... !

She went out of the building into the quiet, tree-shaded street. There were five or six cars parked along the curb; two women went by, one of them pushing a baby-carriage, the other carrying a string bag with feathery carrot tops coming over the edge; a little boy was coming down the steps of the library across the square. This was everyday life, and she was shut away from it, imprisoned in a world where nothing was ordinary and peaceful and seemly.

"Maggie!" called a clear voice.

It was Gabrielle Getty, in a roadster. She opened the door and beckoned to Maggie to get in beside her. "They told me you were here," she said, "so I waited. You said you'd have lunch with me, you know."

"That's *very* nice of you, Mrs. Getty."

"Gabrielle," she said. "We must be about the same age, I think. I'm twenty-three."

She drove the car through the village and out on to a boulevard that ran along the shore; here was the open water, sparkling in the sun; the salt air was wonderfully fresh and stirring.

"You know," said Gabrielle, "I told Captain Hofer about Dolly Camford's husband. I thought about it last night for a long time. I believe he wrote that anonymous letter. I think he's dangerous."

"Do you know him?" Maggie asked.

"No, but she told Hiram about him, and Hiram told me. Dolly wanted it kept a secret, but that seemed to be altogether a mistake. She said the man was violent and threatening when he'd been drinking. Does he seem like that to you?"

"I've never seen him. I never heard of him till we came out here."

"He must have followed her here," said Gabrielle. "She told Hiram she'd seen him in the village."

"Oh ... !" Maggie said, startled. She reflected for a moment. "Well, do you think he's the one who—did away with Mr. Camford?"

"I don't know," said Gabrielle, in her clear, careful way. "I'm afraid I wasn't even thinking much about that. It was only that—" She was silent for a time, her steady grey eyes fixed on the long straight road ahead. "Hiram's very generous and impulsive," she said. "He's sorry for Dolly Camford and he might easily get into serious trouble, trying to help her." She paused again. "I'm not sorry for her," she said. "And I don't want to see Hiram in trouble—for her."

"No," said Maggie.

"I'm not sorry for her," Gabrielle said again.

The wind loosened her fair hair a little, and a strand light as a feather stirred against her temple; her face in profile was clear almost to sharpness. And it seemed to Maggie that her nature was like that, too; nothing cloudy or vague in it. She's unhappy, Maggie thought, but she can stand it.

The Gettys' place was breath-taking. This was an Estate. They drove in through a stone gateway, and the house was not even visible; they went along a road lined with noble trees, they rounded a corner and there it stood, on a gentle rise, a house of red brick with a white portico, neat, elegant, impressive.

As they mounted the steps to the terrace, an elderly man-servant opened the door.

"Any messages, Harolds?" Gabrielle asked.

"Mr. Getty will not be home to lunch, madam," he answered, gravely. "Mrs. Lawrence telephoned, and a lady from the China Relief, and they will both call again later. Are cocktails to be served, madam?"

She glanced at Maggie. "No, thanks, Harolds," she said. "We'll have lunch when it's ready."

She took Maggie up to her room, a cool and airy room done in white and grey, with two turquoise lamps, a single bed, no trace of Hiram Getty here. They went down to lunch and it was served by the man-servant, assisted by a young parlormaid who knew all the fine points of waiting on the table. Glazed sweetbreads, they had, with peas and mushrooms, and salad and strawberries and cream. It's a company lunch, Maggie thought. For me.

That pleased her and touched her so; everything she saw here made her like Gabrielle more and admire her more. She had those qualities Maggie valued most highly, she had self-control and dignity and grace.

Conversation was a little difficult at first. But Maggie knew her duty as a guest.

"I was reading a very good book before I came here," she said. "I'm sorry I didn't bring it along. *Anna Karenina*, it was. I guess you've read it, haven't you?"

That turned out to be an excellent subject. Ever since she had begun reading it, Maggie had wanted to discuss that book with someone. She had tried telling Mrs. Crabtree about it, but Mrs. Crabtree had said she did not care much for foreigners, and that if a woman had a husband and a child and a good home, and still couldn't behave herself, she for one didn't want to read about her.

"There really are women like that," said Maggie. "My father had a friend—another captain—and his wife was like that. They lived on the same street as us in Brooklyn. She lost her head over a Purser in the company and she ran away with him and left her husband and her two little girls. The Purser lost his job over that, and they lived in a miserable poor way for a year or two, and then she came back. And her husband let her stay. He forgave her. I suppose that's the right thing to do."

"I don't think it's a question of forgiving," said Gabrielle. "You can forgive anyone for doing you an injury, but you can't forgive anyone for—just not loving you enough."

All her life Maggie had longed for conversation like this, about books and ethical problems; her heart kindled, the color rose in her cheeks, words came to her that she had never used before, her thoughts took form; she savored the delight of creation.

"I've been to Russia," Gabrielle told her. "My father was sent there as a Naval Attaché when I was a little girl and we lived there nearly a year." He was plainly her idol. "I don't know where he is now," she said. Now she was alone. You could tell that.

They had coffee on the terrace and Gabrielle smoked a cigarette. I wouldn't mind learning to smoke, Maggie thought. Oh, this is like something in a dream! I'm so glad there really are people like this.

Harolds came round the corner of the house, dressed now in a chauffeur's uniform of grey gaberdine; he got into the car and drove off.

"He's gone to get us an evening paper," said Gabrielle. "We'll see if there's any news."

"Oh, what time is it, please?" asked Maggie.

It was half-past three.

"I'll have to go," said Maggie, conscience-stricken. "The District Attorney told me to stay there in the boathouse. And Miss Dolly won't know where I am."

"Harolds can drive you home, then, if you have to go," said Gabrielle. "But—isn't it a little horrible there?"

"Yes, it is," said Maggie.

There was a silence.

"Have you a theory about—what's happened?" asked Gabrielle. "Or would you rather not talk about it?"

"I don't mind talking about it," said Maggie, and looked out over the green lawn. "Only it's confusing ..."

"I hope Dolly's husband did it," said Gabrielle.

"You hope—?"

"Well, you see," Gabrielle said, "he's someone I don't know, someone I've never seen."

"Yes," Maggie said, "that's better, of course."

So very much better if the murderer was someone you had never seen.

"It's logical, too," she said, with a sort of vehemence. "That husband's the logical one."

"If he wrote that anonymous letter—"

"I hadn't thought of that," said Maggie. "That makes it more logical."

"Dolly told Hiram her husband was insanely jealous. Well, he might not have known who Mr. Camford was and he might have been jealous of him."

It was difficult to imagine anyone feeling insanely jealous of Mr. Camford, but it was possible.

"Especially if he'd been drinking a lot," said Maggie. Why *shouldn't* it be Miss Dolly's husband? she asked herself, with that same vehemence. Miss Dolly thinks so, and she knows what he's like.

"Here's Harolds with the paper!" said Gabrielle.

She beckoned to Harolds, but he pretended not to see the gesture. He went round the corner of the house.

"He's so stubborn about bringing things on trays," said Gabrielle.

He wants to do things the right way, thought Maggie.

In a moment he came out of the front door with the newspaper on a salver which he proffered to Gabrielle.

She unfolded it and sat down on the arm of Maggie's chair. "Look!" she said.

Maggie looked.

POLICE SEEK CLUBMAN IN SLAYING

Police of New York City and Long Island are searching to-day for the clubman husband of socialite Dorothea Camford—

"But—!" said Maggie. "That can't be!"

"What can't?" asked Gabrielle.

Maggie did not answer; she went on reading.

Miss Dorothea Camford, an attractive brunette who gave her age as thirty, told reporters this morning of her marriage, some years ago in Paris, to Ewan Haverhill, wealthy clubman prominent in European café society. Because of the fact that Haverhill had recently been divorced by his first wife, Miss Camford decided to keep this marriage a secret from her aristocratic old Knickerbocker family.

"I intended, of course, to tell them later," Miss Camford said. "After they had met Mr. Haverhill. I thought it would be better to arrange it that way. But before I returned to the United States I realized that we were not suited to each other."

Jealousy, Miss Camford told reporters, was the cause of the marital shipwreck. "Even during our honeymoon," she said, "Mr. Haverhill showed an uncontrollable jealousy which had no foundation in fact."

"They make her talk like a servant girl, don't they?" said Gabrielle.

"Yes ..." said Maggie.

Miss Camford stated that, although there was no legal separation, she and her husband had come to a definite understanding before she left him in Paris. "There was no question of any financial arrangement," she said. "I only wanted to live in peace."

Six months ago, Miss Camford said, she began getting letters and telephone messages from Ewan Haverhill, demanding to see her. She was at that time occupying an apartment in the exclusive lower Fifth Avenue section, but these messages so alarmed her that she returned to live with her aunt and uncle, Mrs. Calhoun Mayfield and the late Mr. Giles Camford. "No," she said, "I didn't tell them even then of my marriage. I didn't want to involve them in any sordid publicity."

In order to avoid the possibility of an encounter with Haverhill, Miss Camford rented a house in Sayresville, Long Island, and left New York without informing her aunt and uncle of her destination. "It was foolish," Miss Camford said, "but I suppose I was a little panic-stricken, and my chief thought was not to involve my family."

Miss Camford arrived in Sayresville accompanied by her secretary, Miss Margaret Gower, aged twenty-seven—

"Twenty-seven!" Maggie said aloud. But, after all, that did not matter.

"The morning after my arrival in Sayresville," Miss Camford said, "I saw Mr. Haverhill drive past the house, very slowly, in a car." Miss Camford told reporters that she had not mentioned her husband's appearance in Sayresville until she informed District Attorney Morgan Price this morning. Asked if she had any theory in respect to the slaying of her uncle Giles Camford, who had come to Sayresville to see her, Miss Camford became very much agitated. "I have no theory," she said. "I am entirely satisfied to leave everything in the hands of Captain Hofer. I have perfect confidence in his ability."

The police of New York and Sayresville are now seeking information in regard to Ewan Haverhill, described by Miss Camford as a man of forty-five, five feet eleven in height, and weighing approximately one hundred and seventy-five pounds, with dark hair and a small dark moustache. When last seen by Miss Camford he was wearing a light-grey suit and a Panama hat.

Maggie looked up from the newspaper with a blank gaze. But don't they realize ... ? she thought.

"They're sure to get him soon, I should think," said Gabrielle.

"Well, I— If you don't mind, Mrs. Getty, I think I ought to go home now."

Gabrielle sent for Harolds and he stood by the door of the car.

"I've had a lovely time," said Maggie, gravely.

A feeling of complete unreality possessed her; she went down the steps of this princely house, to the car that waited for her, and she felt like a figure in a dream. But hasn't anyone else noticed ... ? she thought.

For the description of Miss Dolly's husband was identical with the description of Mrs. Amber's Clubman, hat and all.

I don't believe there's any such person as Mr. Haverhill, she thought.

Chapter Nineteen

As they turned into the road that led through the fields, a taxi was stopping in front of the boat house, and a woman got out of it.

"Why, that's Mrs. Mayfield!" Maggie said, aloud.

Harolds drove steadfastly on, making no comment. The taxi turned back, and passed them, in a little cloud of dust.

"Thank you," Maggie said to Harolds as he held open the door of the car.

He bent his head with dignity, and stood beside the car while she went up on the porch where Mrs. Mayfield still stood, ringing the doorbell.

"Maggie," she said, "there doesn't seem to be anyone at home."

"I don't think the door's locked, ma'am," said Maggie, and it was not. She opened it and they entered.

"What a peculiar little house!" said Mrs. Mayfield, looking about her at the dining-room.

"Yes, ma'am," said Maggie.

"This is—" Mrs. Mayfield's cultured voice was unsteady. "This is the most shocking tragedy, Maggie ..."

She was in mourning, black dress and coat, black stockings, and an unexpectedly stylish hat, pulled too far over one eye. Her face had a bleak and ravaged look, and it occurred to Maggie for the first time that Giles Camford's death was a personal grief to his sister.

She remained standing, holding her purse in her black-gloved hands. "Miss Dolly, Maggie?" she asked.

"She's out, ma'am."

"The police, I suppose," said Mrs. Mayfield, and Maggie saw no necessity for telling her otherwise.

"I came alone," Mrs. Mayfield went on. "I didn't want anyone with

me—until I'd seen Dolly ... And on the train—I bought an evening paper—
and I saw this other thing.... Maggie, did you know about this? This marriage?"

"Not till I came out here, ma'am."

"It was such a shock ..." said Mrs. Mayfield. "And coming on top of the
dreadful news—about my brother ... I don't see how Dolly can endure
this."

"Yes, ma'am," said Maggie.

"Ewan Haverhill ..." said Mrs. Mayfield. "There's no doubt, I suppose,
that he killed—my brother. And Dolly will have to see her husband
tried—for the murder of her uncle. Oh, Maggie!"

"Yes, ma'am."

"I'm sorry for her," said Mrs. Mayfield. "I am indeed. It was wrong of
her—very wrong—to tell us nothing at all. To come running out here ...
But what a frightful price she is paying now!"

"Can I get you a glass of water, ma'am?"

"No, thank you, Maggie. I've come to take Miss Dolly home—and the
sooner we can go the better."

Like Mr. Angel. Like Mr. Camford. That was what they had come here
to do.

"Mrs. Mayfield," said Maggie, "I'm sure the police wouldn't let Miss
Dolly go away from here just yet. Mrs. Mayfield, I'll stay right here with
her till she goes. Mrs. Mayfield, we can walk to the main road and you
can take a bus—or maybe we might find a taxi."

"The police won't allow her to leave. Of course. I hadn't thought of that,"
said Mrs. Mayfield. "Then I suppose I'll have to stay here for a day or so."

"Oh, no, Mrs. Mayfield! You wouldn't like it here. It's—you wouldn't
be comfortable. I'll look after things here if you'll go back to New York
now."

"Maggie," said Mrs. Mayfield, with severity, "what is going on here?"

"Well, nothing, Mrs. Mayfield."

It's only that Mr. Angel came here to take Miss Dolly home. And Mr.
Camford, too. And now you're here—and I *won't let you stay.*

"You have some reason for not wanting me to stay here," said Mrs. Mayfield. "You're not being candid with me, Maggie. I'm disappointed in you.
I had such confidence in you, and so did Mrs. Crabtree. We both felt that
you weren't to blame for this foolish and—disastrous running away in the
middle of the night. I know that Miss Dolly can be very persuasive, when
she's set her heart on anything. But I should think you'd have realized by
this time what all this secrecy and deception— What's that?"

They both looked up at the ceiling. Somebody was walking overhead.

"I—I'm not quite sure, Mrs. Mayfield."

"Maggie, when I got here, I rang and rang, and nobody came. Was there somebody in the house all the time?"

"I—don't exactly know, Mrs. Mayfield."

"Maggie, who lives in this house?"

"Well ..."

"Your common sense must tell you, child, that I'm certain to find out, sooner or later. You might just as well tell me now."

Maggie did not want poor Mrs. Mayfield to hear any more distressing facts just now.

"Well, there were some other people when we first got here, but—I think they've gone now."

Leisurely footsteps moved across a creaking board. The sun was shining into the dining-room through the grimy windows; the room was hot with it. The house was quiet now.

"Maggie, what's the matter with you? Are you frightened?"

Yes! Maggie thought. Yes, I am. Johnny's gone off to China, and Captain Hofer took Neely away and I don't know who's up there.

"I shall go up and see," said Mrs. Mayfield.

"Oh, it must be the plumber!" cried Maggie. "I'd forgotten. I'll just speak to him ..."

She went running up the stairs. It was better to run and not to think. As she reached the top of the stairs Neely came to the doorway of his room.

"Oh, you?" he said.

She put her finger to her lips and came toward him.

"Let me in," she whispered and he moved aside to let her pass. She closed the door. "Miss Dolly's aunt is here," she said. "There's no use in upsetting her—"

Then she looked at Neely and her heart failed her. There was a dark bruise on his jaw bone and his mouth was cut; his pale eyes seemed blazing in his white face.

"What's happened to you, Neely?" she asked.

"I hit one of those policemen," he said. "And then they hit me."

She leaned against the door, overwhelmed by a feeling of helplessness, of utter inadequacy. "What are you going to do now, Neely?" she asked.

"Now?" he said. "I'm packing up my things to get out of *her* house. But I'm coming back. Later."

"Neely—"

"She asked the police to lock me up. I know that. Because she was afraid of me. Before that, she talked and talked about getting married. I was to have a fine studio and meet all her rich friends and they would buy my work. I told her I didn't love her at all. Oh, what's love, Neely? she said. I don't think any more about love. My life's been so wasted, Neely, so sad and lonely. I only want to help you, Neely, for your good work. Fine."

"Neely—"

"Why do you keep on saying Neely, Neely? Are you afraid of me, too? The policemen, they thought I was a mad dog. Hey, you! Where's your papers? What are you doing, running around loose? They locked me in a cell. All right, I went to sleep. And as soon as I was asleep, they came in again. This time they brought a doctor—I think some psychiatrist, maybe. He put on a smooth, wise face. Ha! Now let's see ..."

His curious power of mimicry evoked for her the image of a doctor, bland and superior.

"You don't consider human life very important, do you? he asked me. The war has changed your ideas, maybe? With so many people getting killed, one more doesn't seem to matter much, eh? And all the time what he really is talking about is a dead body—the dead Angel. Then he went on. In a time of such tension we find alcohol a relief, eh? Or perhaps a drug? That made me angry. I shouted at him and when the policeman told me to stop I yelled at him."

"Neely—"

"Neely, Neely, my dear sweet Neely, please be good. Go away now and don't bother me, Maggie. I want to leave before she comes back. I have something to do before I see *her* again. Go away. And you can tell her I said nothing at all about our fine marriage we were going to have. Maybe she meant to have two husbands together."

He took up a drawing from the table and put it carefully into a portfolio that he tied up with tape; he picked up a queer little black satchel. "Now I'm going," he said.

"Miss Dolly's aunt is downstairs," said Maggie. "She's—so nice ... Please don't—please don't say anything to her."

"A nice aunt," he said. "A nice uncle, too, she had."

He looked at her and his bruised mouth widened in a smile. He put his hand on her shoulder and moved her aside; he went past her down the stairs, and she followed him. Mrs. Mayfield was standing in the hall.

"Good-afternoon, madam," he said.

"Good-afternoon," said Mrs. Mayfield, politely, and he went on, and out of the front door.

"Maggie, who was that?"

"A workman, Mrs. Mayfield. He came to fix something."

"Maggie, he looked—"

"There's a car coming, Mrs. Mayfield. Maybe that's Miss Dolly."

They went out together on the little porch and Neely was walking off across the fields with the satchel in his hand and the portfolio under his arm, his hair shining like silver in the sun. Where was he going, so direct and unhurried?

It was Miss Plummer's car and Miss Dolly was sitting beside her. They both got out, and Mrs. Mayfield stood waiting in her long black coat, the stylish black hat over one eye giving her long face a sort of pathetic look, Maggie thought, like the pirate in that movie, with a black patch. She's nice. She's good.

"Oh, Aunt Emily!" Dolly cried and caught Mrs. Mayfield in her arms.

Mrs. Mayfield stood motionless, her head rising stiffly above her niece's shoulder.

"I thought you might like me to come," she said.

That was the best she could do. She would help Dolly, she would stand by her, but she could not make even a pretence of affection. Dolly, aware of the stony quiet, drew away.

"I *couldn't* call you up," she said. "I didn't know how to tell you, Aunt Emily."

"I see.... The police called me up, and I came. I thought you might want me."

"Aunt Emily, sit down, dear. And Maggie will make us some tea."

"And I'll go into the kitchen and talk to Maggie," said Miss Plummer.

"Aunt Emily, this is Mitzi Plummer. She's been very kind to me."

"Miss Plummer...." said Mrs. Mayfield, bending her head. "Maggie, don't make the tea too strong, child."

Miss Plummer entered the kitchen in a gust of perfume. She was wearing a dress of dark-green linen with a great deal of eyelet work and she had a green silk scarf tied across her forehead, the fringed ends hanging down to her shoulders. Obese, flaunting, gypsy-like; she was a dreadful woman, Maggie thought, remembering that scene in Miss Plummer's house.

But Miss Plummer seemed to have no memory of it; she was quite affable.

"Is there a little drop of something anywhere around?" she asked, in a low voice.

"I don't know what there is, Miss Plummer," said Maggie.

"All this upsets me," said Miss Plummer, looking around. "Have you seen Neely?"

"He's not here, Miss Plummer."

"They let him out this morning," she said. She opened the china closet and found a bottle. "I *need* a tiny swig," she said. "Morgan Price—what did you think of Morgan Price?"

"I thought he was all right," said Maggie.

"I knew him when," said Miss Plummer. "A pompous little monkey he was, and is. He tried to trap me about Neely's alibi, but I could see at once what he was driving at. The moment he said what *time* did Mr. Curtius come to your house that morning, I knew. I was plausible beyond words. I told Morgan the cuckoo clock was just striking eleven as Neely came up the steps.”

She threw back her head and laughed.

“It was striking, too,” she said. “But God knows what. It’s crazy. It’s a monstrosity we bought years ago in the Schwartzenwald, and one night when we had a party for some opera singers, we kept setting it at twelve and shooting darts at the wretched bird. It’s never been the same since. But, my dear, what is time?”

Then you don’t really know what time Neely came to your house? thought Maggie. Nobody here ever knows the time. And time is so terribly important in—all this. I know that. I’ve felt that right along. If I’d had a watch ...

“Of course, now that this husband of Dolly’s has materialized,” Miss Plummer went on, “they won’t bother poor Neely any more. Why anybody ever did think he had anything to do with killing all these people, God only knows. Except that the boy’s an artist, and people like Willie Hofer and Morgan Price are naturally hostile to artists. He’s a genius, that boy is.”

The kettle was boiling; Maggie scalded the teapot and measured out the tea carefully. I don’t know whether Neely’s a genius or not, she thought. I wouldn’t be able to tell. But I do know that he’s—different. He’s got a different point of view—and it’s a pretty awful one. Heartless.

“Isn’t this aunt of Dolly’s piquant?” Miss Plummer went on. “I mean, the idea of Dolly’s having these aunts and uncles and all this background of the utmost propriety when she’s—what she is. The B. B., I call her. But I’m not going to tell you what that means!”

I know what that means, Maggie thought. The bitch in the boathouse. Miss Plummer wrote that letter. I’m sure of it. She found a loaf of bread in the bag Miss Dolly had brought in with her; she made nice little bread and butter sandwiches, and set a tray.

“Will you have some tea, Miss Plummer?” she asked.

“No, I won’t!” said Miss Plummer. “I’m going home.”

“But—I thought you’d wait a little while and see if Mrs. Mayfield wanted to go to the station—”

“No! I don’t feel one bit like taxi-ing Dolly’s aunts and uncles all over the country. She made that poor besotted Hiram Getty drive her to my house after lunch and then she begged me to drive her home. Because it looks so much better to come here with poor old Mitzi, doesn’t it? So *much* more respectable.”

Her dark face flushed; she stared down at her empty glass and then flung it at the sink, and it smashed.

"*That's* how I feel!" she said. "And let me tell you this. If I chose to go on a diet ... I'm not one day older than Dolly Camford, and I—"

"Excuse me," said Mrs. Mayfield from the doorway. "Miss Plummer, I'm sorry to ask such a favour. If I'd known there was no telephone, I'd have asked the taxi to wait. But, as it is, if you'd have the kindness to drive me to the nearest bus stop—"

Miss Plummer drew herself up haughtily. "No!" she said.

Then, as she looked at Mrs. Mayfield, she raised her eyebrows and then frowned.

"I should be pleased," she said, with great dignity. "I'll drive you wherever you wish to go. I recognize a *lady* when I see one."

"Thank you," said Mrs. Mayfield.

She looked ill, Maggie thought, and she looked strange; her rather prominent brown eyes had a look of painful anxiety.

"If you don't mind," she said, "if it's quite convenient for you, I'd very much like to start as soon as possible."

"Certainly!" said Miss Plummer.

"And, Maggie," said Mrs. Mayfield, "I'd like you to come with me, please."

"Yes, Mrs. Mayfield. But—"

"I'd like to speak to Maggie for a moment, Aunt Emily," said Miss Dolly, standing behind her, and they went into the hall together. "Maggie," she said, very low, "please come back. As soon as you can get away from Aunt Emily without her knowing, come back."

"Well, why, please?" Maggie asked, curtly.

"I'll tell you later. I'll tell you *everything*, Maggie. After to-night everything will be all right, Maggie. We'll go away somewhere and forget all this dreadful time. We'll be happy—"

"I just don't care about being happy," said Maggie. "But there's one thing you'd better know, Miss Dolly. Neely says he's coming back, and he—well, he's dangerous."

"I can manage him, Maggie."

"Well, I don't think you can."

"I know I can. Only I've got to get Aunt Emily and that horrible Mitzi out of the house. You will come back, won't you, Maggie?"

"Miss Dolly," said Maggie, slowly, "I don't think I will."

Miss Dolly's eyes widened; she caught Maggie's wrist.

"But, Maggie, please! Maggie, I need you!"

"Waiting! Waiting, good people!" sang out Miss Plummer.

"I've got to go," said Maggie.

"Oh, Maggie, come back!" Miss Dolly implored her. "I don't know what I'll do without you, Maggie. *I need you.*"

"I'm sorry," said Maggie. "I've got to go now."

Miss Plummer was sitting in her little car when Mrs. Mayfield and Maggie came out of the house. "And now," she said, suddenly in great good humour, "now whither, prithee?"

"The nearest bus stop, if you please," said Mrs. Mayfield.

"Oh, no!" said Miss Plummer. "You want to go to the station, don't you?"

"Thank you, no. I have some little errands to do in the village."

"But I'll take you anywhere the bus could take you, and it's so much, much comfier. Just say where you want to go."

"The bus stop will do nicely, thank you."

"I just won't let you," said Miss Plummer. "Just won't let you take a nasty smelly ole bus when I've got my car."

"You're very kind, Miss Plummer," said Mrs. Mayfield, "but I'd really rather take the bus."

That ended the battle; Miss Plummer stopped her car on the highway and they sat in it until a bus appeared. Thank you very much, Miss Plummer, and you're very welcome, Mrs. Mayfield.

The bus was nearly empty; they sat down near the back where there was no one to hear them.

"Maggie," said Mrs. Mayfield, "I know I can trust you. Even Miss Dolly has nothing but praise for you. It's a terrible situation, Maggie. We shall have to stand by Miss Dolly. You see—" She paused a moment. "No matter what Ewan Haverhill may have done, he's still her husband."

"Yes, ma'am," said Maggie. If there ever was any such person, she thought.

"Miss Dolly is going to help him get away, Maggie."

"Yes, ma'am."

"It's a problem," Mrs. Mayfield went on, "a very dreadful problem. Whether or not she ought to shield him. I don't know, Maggie, what I should do in such a case. I don't know."

"No, ma'am," said Maggie.

It was difficult for her to say anything at all, so great was her resentment against Miss Dolly for this new and shameless deception. As if poor Mrs. Mayfield didn't have enough grief and trouble without that made-up husband getting into it.

"She wanted to get everyone out of the house, Maggie, because he's coming back. I can understand that she didn't want—she *couldn't* turn him over to the police. Her own husband ... But, Maggie, I'm alarmed, I'm seriously alarmed at leaving her alone in the house with that man."

"Miss Dolly will know how to manage him, ma'am."

"I'm not at all sure of that, Maggie. She's not—very prudent, not very wise. And you read such horrible things in the newspapers. There's been a case, just recently ..."

Mrs. Amber, thought Maggie. *She* wasn't very prudent or very wise. I dare say she was quite a lot like Miss Dolly.

"It's such an isolated house," said Mrs. Mayfield. "No telephone, no one near her. I was very much opposed to leaving her there alone—yet I understood how she felt."

"I guess Miss Dolly knows what she's doing, Mrs. Mayfield."

"I wish I were sure of that, Maggie," said Mrs. Mayfield.

They were silent for a time. The bus was spinning along the highway that was lined with woodland, the trees were quiet against the bright sky. They passed a little lake of shining water and as Maggie looked back for another glimpse of that charming scene she saw Miss Mitzi Plummer driving along behind the bus. Following us? she thought.

"Mrs. Mayfield," she said, "excuse me, but how long did Miss Dolly think it would take to—get Mr. Haverhill away?"

"She couldn't be sure," Mrs. Mayfield answered. "There's a great deal to be arranged between them, of course, and she thought he might need a few hours' sleep. But she said we might come back as early in the morning as we liked."

"All the way from New York, Mrs. Mayfield?"

"I'm not going home, Maggie. I'm going to stay here in Sayresville. There's an inn Dolly told me about and I shall stay there to-night. And you too, Maggie."

"Yes, ma'am."

"It may be very wrong of me," said Mrs. Mayfield. "But I do think that Giles himself ..." Her lip trembled. "I do think that Giles himself would feel as I do. I can't help hoping with all my heart that Ewan Haverhill escapes. Not only for Dolly's sake—but when I think of his poor mother—"

"His mother, Mrs. Mayfield?"

"She's over eighty, Maggie, and she's a very conservative woman."

"But, Mrs. Mayfield ... But, do you *know* her?"

"Not very well," Mrs. Mayfield answered. "We were on a committee together once, years ago, in the other war. I saw Ewan once or twice when he was a boy—"

"You *saw* him, Mrs. Mayfield?"

"My dear child," said Mrs. Mayfield, "why not?"

"I just didn't know you'd—seen Mr. Haverhill," said Maggie.

"I suppose," said Mrs. Mayfield, "that at your age the things you read in the newspapers don't seem quite real. But they are real, Maggie. Unfortunately."

"Yes, ma'am," said Maggie.

Chapter Twenty

They got out of the bus in the square before the Post Office. There was an arcade here and in it was a stylish little shop, The Fifth Avenue Maison. Mrs. Mayfield bought two nightgowns and two pairs of stockings, two cotton kimonas, two pairs of slippers; what she bought for Maggie was just as good as what she got for herself.

"And a hat," she said. "You must have a hat, Maggie."

"I don't really need one, Mrs. Mayfield."

"You came away without any, the moment I asked you to, and it's only right that you should have a new one, Maggie."

She saw one that accorded with her taste. "Try this one on!" she said.

It was a triangular hat of rough and shiny black straw, with a rosette of green ribbon straight in the middle of the front, a hat that perched on top of Maggie's bright curly hair with a curious effect.

"Very nice!" said Mrs. Mayfield. "Don't you think so, Maggie?"

"Yes, ma'am," said Maggie.

She liked Mrs. Mayfield so much, she was so sorry for her that she would have agreed to worse than this. Five dollars, this hat was.

They went then to a drug store where Mrs. Mayfield bought soap and washcloths and toothbrushes and toothpaste, all the decent and ladylike things without which she could not envisage going to bed. They came out into the street and in a shop window Maggie had a glimpse of them, the tall gaunt Mrs. Mayfield all in black, and herself in Miss Dolly's elegant lavender chiffon blouse and her new hat, walking along this village street. The strangeness of life ... ! They turned a corner and there Maggie caught sight of Miss Plummer in her little car, creeping along by the curb. Following them?

She hates Miss Dolly, Maggie thought. She wrote that horrible letter. I dare say plenty of other people hate Miss Dolly, too, and you can hardly blame them. But I don't want her to be murdered.

That was what was in her mind now.

On a corner opposite the tidy little railroad station stood a hotel, the Lord Sayres Arms; they went into a pleasant little lounge, and Mrs. Mayfield, with a paper package under her arm, approached the desk and engaged two connecting rooms and bath. She was an unknown woman here, with no luggage except that parcel, but that made no difference to her, or to anyone else; her Mrs. Mayfield quality was beyond question.

"And please send up a menu," she said. "We'll have our dinner upstairs."

She took trouble in ordering for Maggie, suggesting things she thought the girl would like.

"You're *very* kind to me, Mrs. Mayfield," Maggie said.

"You're a comfort to me, Maggie. I feel—" She paused. "I feel very lonely," she said, with simplicity.

She could not eat, poor woman. She was half ill with grief and shock and anxiety.

"I cannot help worrying about Dolly," she said. "She's the last of the family left now. Her father was my older brother, you know."

It was still light when they finished their early dinner; they sat in Mrs. Mayfield's room, and she talked a little about her brothers, her young days. Maggie was touched; she would have been glad to listen as long as Mrs. Mayfield chose to talk, if it had not been for her desperate impatience to get on with her own thinking. The sky paled, the dusk came, and deepened; the lights of the station shone in at the window against the white wall; a little breeze blew in from the dusty street.

"You look tired, Maggie," said Mrs. Mayfield. "Go to bed and get a good night's sleep, my dear."

She had a book and a magazine that she had brought to read on the train, a Bostonian magazine and a book about World Conditions. She won't get much sleep, poor thing, Maggie thought. She'll be worrying and worrying about Miss Dolly. Well, it's something to worry about.

"Good-night, Maggie."

"Good-night, Mrs. Mayfield."

This was the first time Maggie had ever occupied a hotel room, and it impressed her. The bed was turned down and a lighted lamp stood on the table beside it; there was a nice little pink armchair, there was the bathroom, glittering with white tiles and nickel. She wandered about for a moment, looking at everything.

This is an experience, she thought. This is something new. My own telephone; someone to turn down my bed. This is a place you could really call your own, so neat and quiet. So—private. Nobody's going to come knocking at the door and asking you to do things. It must make people different, to live like this, in this peace and quiet. I've been so sort of busy, all my life.

A busy little girl, hurrying off to school, hurrying home to help her mother, growing up busy, and proud of it. In nineteen years this, she thought, was the first time she had really felt alone.

And she would have to think things out alone, and act alone.

She sat down in the pink armchair. So Miss Dolly's husband is real, she thought. Mrs. Mayfield's seen him. But how can he look just exactly like Mrs. Amber's Clubman? I don't see …

Unless he's the same man.

That was a thought that made her catch her breath in a faint gasp. The same man ... ? I'd better go right to Captain Hofer and tell him.... But I can't. Mrs. Mayfield trusted me not to tell. The same man ... ? Mrs. Amber had been pretty and dark, lively, too. The colored maid had come in and found her lying dead on the floor, partially clad. Police Seek Wealthy Clubman.

He had a different name, but that didn't count. They bring it on themselves ... Mrs. Amber and her gay parties. Miss Dolly and her relentless search for happiness. This man must have a way with him. Something about him that women liked and trusted. When he rang the bell, Mrs. Amber opened the door and let him in, and he murdered her. Maybe she had been waiting for him. As Miss Dolly was waiting now.

I need you, Maggie, she had said. But what can *I* do? If he came in with a gun ... Why does she need me? If she's afraid of him, why does she wait there for him, all alone? It's—silly!

But she is silly. Maybe Mrs. Amber was like that, too. A little bit scared—but not scared enough. Only, Miss Dolly knows her husband's a murderer. But I suppose she thinks he wouldn't hurt *her*, no matter what he's done. Yet she can't be too sure. Come back, she said. I need you. After to-night, she said, everything's going to be all right. That's because she thinks she's going to get rid of her husband to-night.

She rose and went to the window, and stood looking out at the lights of the little station and down at the street, that was curiously alive in the dim-out. A moving throng of people went by; soldiers and sailors and girls; such a lot of couples.

I'm sort of sorry Johnny Cassidy's gone away, she thought. You could talk to him. I suppose you can know a man isn't much good and still—sort of like him.... A train went hurtling past the station, and whistled, that long-drawn, wild and melancholy sound that evokes all partings and lonely journeys. It made tears come into her eyes. I'm getting to understand more about human nature, she thought. Ah, well ... !

She sighed, and her mind was made up, almost of its own accord. I'll go back to the boathouse, she thought.

But she was not going to take any foolish chances. She was not going to be stranded out there with Miss Dolly and a murderer. The thing was going to be thought out and done sensibly. She was ready to help Miss Dolly just once more, but she was not going to be foolhardy.

It would be nice to have a friend, an ally, someone to talk to; it would, she thought with unwonted humility, be nice to ask somebody's advice. It would not be Mrs. Mayfield she would have chosen for a counsellor. She admired and respected Mrs. Mayfield; in a way, she quite loved her. But Mrs. Mayfield was too much concerned with dread of family scandal, and she didn't, Maggie thought, know very much about life. Not nearly so much as Mrs. Crabtree and Johnny Cassidy.

But Mrs. Crabtree and Johnny Cassidy were out of reach and Mrs. Mayfield was right here. There was a small writing-desk in a corner and in the drawer she found envelopes and writing paper with a crest and a Latin motto.

Dear Mrs. Mayfield: I have gone back to the boathouse because I am rather worried about Miss Dolly. I hope to be back pretty soon but if I am not, I hope you will excuse me for going away without telling you, and I wanted you to know where I had gone.

Yours very truly,
Maggie MacGowan.

She addressed this to Mrs. Mayfield and then she put on that new hat. After this is all over, she thought, I'm going to have a different way of dressing. More stylish. I'm going to buy a lipstick and I'm going to be more up-to-date.

But when it was time to leave her room, new and disturbing worries came to her. She did not know how things were done in a hotel and the possibility of doing something conspicuous or laughable dismayed her. The best she could do was, to carry it off with a high hand, and when she went out to the elevator she had a look of cold disdain. She went down to the lobby and approached the desk, still with cold disdain.

"Good evening!" said the clerk, with a smile that she thought condescending.

"I wish to have a note delivered to Mrs. Mayfield in two hours," said Maggie.

"Certainly," said he, "if you'll give it to me."

"Well ... you'd better make a note about the time and all," said Maggie.

"Oh, *I* won't forget," said he, and he was undoubtedly condescending.

"It's important," said Maggie.

"*I* see," he said.

He was a tall and willowy young man with wavy black hair, and she did not like him.

"If there's any charge—" she said.

"Charge?" he said, as if astonished. "Oh, no. No, indeed. Mrs.—" He glanced at a typed list lying near him. "Miss MacGowan," he said, "don't worry. We manage to deliver a good many important notes, Miss Mae-

Gowan. Mrs. Mayfield will get hers safely."

"Well ..." said Maggie. She could think of nothing else to say, nothing to impress this young man. "Well, I hope she does," she said, with an almost sinister look at him.

She went out with the idea of crossing the street to the station, where she had seen a taxi waiting. But there was a taxi now in front of the hotel, with the driver reading a newspaper.

"Do you know where the boathouse is?" she asked.

"Miss Plummer's?" said he. "Yep. I know."

"I want to go there," said Maggie. "And I want you to wait—for quite a long while."

"Why not?" said he.

He was a stolid young man in his shirtsleeves, with a pale face and heavy-lidded eyes and a lock of black hair flattened against his forehead; he had a calmness that was reassuring to her. She got into the cab, and they set off along the village street.

"There is certainly some peculiar things happening out there," the driver observed. "I took out two other people for the papers this afternoon. What I think is, you people on the papers know more than the cops. I'll tell you why I think like that."

He told her a story, a long story about a murder, which he said, had been solved by his favourite New York newspaper. "The cops was stuck," he said, "and I'll tell you why. The cops are okay—up to a certain point. They got organization, some of them have good brains. Some, not all. Where they fall down is, they don't dee-duce. Now, take for instance how these newspaper babies are talking right in my cab this afternoon. This first guy that died. The doctors say he didn't die easy. It took him twenty minutes, they say, before he died, according to what the doctors say. He got a crack on the back of the head when he fell in the rowboat, and he's lying in that boat there, bleeding, kind of feebly moving—"

"Don't!" said Maggie. "I don't like to hear about it."

"Well, but facts has got to be faced," said the driver, aggrieved. "And I'll tell you why. Now las' year this guy I know, a truck runs over him. The way he was marked—!"

"I don't *want* to hear about things like that!" cried Maggie.

"*All* right! *All* right!" said the driver. "If you don't want to face facts, all right, don't face them. I got an interest in this case, and I'll tell you why. I like to exercise my brains. You got to exercise your brains just like you exercise your body. I figured out how it could be with this other baby, the one that's her uncle."

It was shocking to hear Mr. Camford spoken of like that. "He was a very fine man," said Maggie.

"Maybe," said the driver, "and maybe not. The interest I got in this case is, who is guilty. Now, from what I read in the papers, they all of them got alibis for the time he was bumped off. The artist, he's got an alibi that he was at Miss Plummer's. The noospaper guy, he was to Albee's farm with the secretary. Miss Camford, as they call her, she was to the Country Club with Mr. Getty. Maybe. Maybe not."

"People saw her there," said Maggie, interested in spite of herself.

"Maybe," said the driver. "And maybe people just *think* they seen her. Now, there's been many cases I've heard of where there was a double. She could for instance have a twin sister that was impoisonating her."

"If she'd had a twin sister, it would have come out before this," said Maggie, disappointed.

"That's not necessarily the case," said he. "Those things get hushed up. Now, you take for instance Hitler. He's got a double. Why the people in Goimany, they never see Hitler. They think they do, but all they see is his double. Same with the movie stars. They all got doubles. They never let on that Ardila Nynn was dead for one *year*. They took and put her in a special kind of tomb they got out there in Hollywood, and her double went right on acting in pictures for one year."

"I don't believe it," said Maggie.

"You don't have to," said he. "And it would still be true. There's more impoisonating done than you'd ever think. Now take Miss Camford's husband, for instance. *He* could have a double that's impoisonating him, and that could be why she don't know he's dead."

"Who's dead?" asked Maggie.

"Why, her husband, of course," said the driver. "These other newspaper babies knew *that*, all right. One of them said he called up his mother—"

"Whose mother?"

"Why, the husband's mother."

"Mrs. Haverhill?"

"That's it. Mr. Haverhill's mother was who he called up. She is very wealthy, and she says her son died four years ago in Paris."

"No," said Maggie. "It would have been in the newspapers."

"Well, it's going to be in the papers to-morrow, how he died four years ago. But *she* don't know it, see? And I'll tell you why. It's been someone impoisonating him."

"You're sure they said that?"

"Absolutely," said the driver. "The guy that was talking was the one that rung up the mother himself. Very wealthy, she is, and she told him her son was dead and buried four years ago over in Paris. What's more, Captain Hofer said all right, they could print it. Yep! He's been dead four long years now, in Paris."

"Captain Hofer knows that?" Maggie asked. "Captain Hofer said that?"

"Yep," said the driver. "I know him. I knew him when he was just a cop. Just a cop."

"But—hasn't he arrested anybody?"

"Somethin' cookin'," said the driver. "He's got somebody down to the station house right now, grilling them."

"Who?"

"I wouldn't know," he said. "It's only what I hoid."

He turned off now from the main road into the dusty road that ran through the fields. There were lights in the boathouse, looking unbelievably far away in the faint mist that was rising again from the marshes. There was that rank swamp smell again, and that sense of desolate space, no time, nothing.

"It's a lonely place," said the driver. "Nothing but frogs. I got no use for frogs."

He stopped the cab before the house, and reached back to open the door.

"Wait!" said a man's voice. "Who is it?"

"It's me, Mr. Getty," answered Maggie.

"Well, Miss Camford doesn't want to be disturbed just now," he said. "Come back in the morning."

"I live here," said Maggie.

"You can come back in the morning," said Getty, "but Miss Camford doesn't want you now."

"I want to see Miss Dolly, please," said Maggie. "She wants me."

"Not now," he said.

"Well ... !" said the taxi driver, deeply shocked. "If she lives here, she got a right to go in."

"I want to see Miss Dolly," said Maggie doggedly.

It had come into her head that the lighted house was empty. Nobody in it ... Only Hiram Getty prowling around in the dark.

"I want to see Miss Dolly," she said more loudly.

"I'll tell her then," said Getty, and went up the steps.

"That's Mr. Getty," said the driver in a low and confidential tone. "He lives out over to the Point. Very wealthy."

"Is he?" said Maggie. She got out but she stood close to the cab. She liked the driver now, she was glad of his company, very glad.

"All right!" said Getty from the porch. "You can come in."

"Well ... You'll wait, won't you?" said Maggie to the driver.

"Why, certainly," he said, aggrieved again. "Anyways I haven't got paid yet."

Miss Dolly was in the dining-room sitting at the table under the harsh overhead light that hung from the ceiling.

"Maggie, I'm so glad you came. I was afraid you wouldn't come, Maggie," Miss Dolly said in a sombre monotone. "I thought I'd have to go through this—alone."

Her dark eyes looked past Maggie at nothing; she was very pale and so tense that her rouged lips seemed stretched.

"I've come to the end," she said. "I—"

"Oh, the cab!" cried Maggie. "The taxi's going away!"

She ran to the door and opened it. The cab was driving away through the fields.

"Driver!" she called.

"Stop that!" said Getty. "I paid him—"

"Dri—" she began again, when Getty put his hand over her mouth, a strong, hot smothering hand. She tried to pull it away, and the ridge of hair on the back of it was damp, and she lost consciousness standing on her feet with her eyes open.

But only for the space of a long breath. He took his hand away.

"I'm sorry," he said. "But this—this is serious. We can't have that fellow around."

The tail light of the cab looked blurred and far away in the smoky mist.

"Dolly told me you understood the situation," said Getty. "You must realize ... We're waiting for the fellow—and he won't come, of course, if he thinks there's anyone around."

"What—fellow?" asked Maggie.

"But—don't you know?" Getty demanded. "That fellow Haverhill."

Waiting for him, were they? With the house brightly lit in the empty fields and the misty marshes; they were waiting for a man dead and buried four years ago, three thousand miles away.

Chapter Twenty-One

The ancient fear stirs readily. In the beginning of things, men in dark forests and on windy plains shook with fear of the dead. They piled great stones on them to keep them still, made chants to soothe the restless spirits, slit living throats to placate those in their graves.

No! Maggie said to herself. I don't believe in things like that. If Mr. Haverhill is dead, they can wait forever and he won't come back.

The tail-light of the taxi twinkled in the haze and vanished, and she was aware of the chorus of insects and the frogs. Well, she said to herself, I am stranded here, after all.

A queer grim resignation began to rise in her. She could not imagine what these two were waiting for, she could not imagine what was going to happen. But she could stand sturdy and undismayed against it, whatever it might be.

She went into the dining-room where Miss Dolly sat smoking with her elbows on the table.

"I feel so cold, Maggie."

"Shall I make you a cup of tea, Miss Dolly? Or coffee?"

"No, thank you, Maggie. I feel so cold—and dreadful."

"That's too bad, Miss Dolly," said Maggie, affably, and sat down across the table.

"Why should anyone want to harm *me*, Maggie? All I want—all I've *ever* wanted, Maggie, was to be let alone, to be happy in my own way."

"Well, that's quite a lot to want, it seems to me," said Maggie.

For the relation between them was wholly changed now. Miss Dolly no longer seemed the sophisticated woman of the world; Maggie no longer felt like the ambitious and eager young creature who could learn so much from her. It seemed to her that Miss Dolly was lost and drifting, and that she herself had found her feet.

"It seems to me so little, Maggie. I never *wanted* to hurt anyone."

Well, you have hurt people. People much better than yourself.

"You don't think I'm horrible, do you, Maggie?"

I don't know what I think of you. Only if there wasn't something bad in you, something very bad, you couldn't look like this. So pale and desperate. So—guilty.

"Maggie, can't you say anything?"

"I'm trying to think things out, Miss Dolly."

"Maggie, if I hear him coming ... Maggie, I don't know how I can stand it."

"Hear who coming, Miss Dolly?"

"My husband."

"You won't hear him, Miss Dolly."

"But he said he'd come."

"Miss Dolly," said Maggie, "he's dead and buried."

There was a silence between them. The full tide, flowing in, lapped against the walls, and hearing that you had to think of the creek that ran through the marshes to the sea.

"I wanted you with me, Maggie," said Miss Dolly. "You can see that I'm just sitting here waiting—in dread."

"You mean I'm a witness?" said Maggie. "Who is it you're waiting for, Miss Dolly?"

"I told you."

"And why is Mr. Getty here, Miss Dolly?"

"Because he's my friend. Because he's kind to me. Kinder than *you*."

Someone moved past the lighted window. It's only Mr. Getty, Maggie told herself. He's waiting out there—for somebody. The lapping of the water seemed very loud, the rowboat was bumping against the wall.

"Miss Dolly," said Maggie, "let's go upstairs."

Because someone was trying to open the back door with a key, and that wouldn't be Mr. Getty. That must be—someone else.

"Maggie!" said Miss Dolly, in a whisper. "Maggie, do you hear?"

"Yes, I do. Come upstairs, Miss Dolly."

Dolly sat rigid in her chair. Maggie rose and took her hand and tried to draw her to her feet. Then a shot came, frightfully loud, echoing and trembling in the air. Maggie's hand flew to her heart that seemed to check as if the sound had struck it.

"Hiram's killed him...." said Miss Dolly, faintly, and her breast rose in a long sigh.

It was a sigh of relief; the look of terror had gone from her eyes.

"You meant this to happen!" Maggie cried. That was plain to her now. That was what Hiram Getty was here for, to kill someone. "*Who is it?*"

"It's all over now," said Miss Dolly.

There was the sound of a key in the lock again, and they both faced the swing door. The back door had opened now, footsteps were crossing the kitchen. The swing door was pushing open. Miss Dolly gave a scream; she rose and rushed toward the stairs; she ran up them, stumbling.

It was Johnny Cassidy, with a streak of blood across his mouth and a gun in his hand.

"Oh, you're here?" he said, casually.

Maggie could not speak. He looked, she thought, like a wild beast just come from the kill. As he approached her, she backed away from him.

"What's—happened?" she said.

"Funny things," he said, and drew his hand across his forehead, leaving a streak of blood there. "Getty shot at me, and I jumped him and took away his gun."

"Did you—?"

"Did I kill him?" said Johnny. "No. He's out, but he isn't dead. Now I want to see Dolly."

That must not happen. If only somebody would come.... If only Captain Hofer would come....

"She did this, you know," said Johnny. "She gave me the key to the back door this morning and she told me to come back at ten-thirty. She said she'd arrange to be alone. She said she'd have eight hundred dollars for me, so that I could get away. Then she must have had some fine tale for Getty. She must have told him to shoot anyone he saw trying to come in by the back door. Maybe he knew who I was; maybe he didn't. Anyhow, it didn't work right. None of her plans have worked right. She's finished now."

"You mustn't blame her for what Mr. Getty did..."

"Mr. Getty did as he was told," said Johnny, in the same casual, offhand tone. "I know she wanted to get rid of me. She had to. But I didn't think she'd try this. It isn't like her. She's not usually so direct. Do you know, I can find it in my heart—to be sorry she did this."

"Yes," said Maggie, seizing on this. "She didn't mean this—"

"Oh, she meant it, all right," he said. "For years and years she's wanted to get rid of me. I've wanted to get free from her, too. But we never could. There was a bond between us—the damnedest bond.... I've been black-mailing her for years, off and on. You wouldn't think *that* would make a bond, would you? But it did. When I was broke, or in trouble, I'd make her give me money. But, by God, when she needed money, she didn't mind asking me for it. And I'd give it to her—if I had any. Queer situation ... Maybe we hated each other. But we've had some damn good times together, here, and in Paris. We've laughed together a lot."

There was one clear idea in Maggie's mind, to keep him from going up those stairs. He was quiet enough, almost mild, but it was the quiet of some-one who had come to the very end. Why didn't somebody come ... ?

"Johnny," she said, "she hasn't done anything—"

He smiled.

"You're right," he said. "You couldn't have put it better. She hasn't done anything. She's never done anything. She's *never* hated anyone and never loved anyone. She's the supreme catalyst. She causes things to happen and then shuts her eyes. She never had a husband, you know, never had a lover. She couldn't care that much for anyone. She'd lead a man on, and then she'd run away from him, in a panic. That's what she'd have done with Getty."

He sat down on the table, holding the gun loosely in his hand.

"You've got blood on your face," said Maggie. "I'll get a towel—"

"Stay where you are," he said. "It's too bad she got you into this, you poor little kid. Take it easy now. You can't stop what's going to happen. You've been in all of it, haven't you? Even the Angel episode. That was pure accident, you know. He had some sort of stroke and he fell through the rotten railing and landed in the rowboat, pretty hard. But he wasn't dead. She didn't kill him. All she did was to let him die there. She even cried, sit-ting inside the house with me. He was a killjoy, come here to spoil her fun."

He looked down at the gun and Maggie looked too. Blood was running along his thin hand and dripping on to the floor.

"You're hurt," she said. "Let me tie up your arm."

"It doesn't matter," he said. "She didn't kill her uncle, either. Not she! She only whispered to me that if somebody didn't stop him, he'd take away the last bit of money she had, or ever would have. Of course, she did know I happened to need money badly, very badly just then. She did happen to mention that he was leaving her something handsome in his will—if he didn't alter it. She just said she'd leave him alone in the house, and maybe I'd come back—and see if I couldn't plead with him. And I came back."

"You ... ?"

"Me," he said. "It was a bad thing to do. I didn't have *that* clear in my mind when I left you at Mrs. Albee's. I had some fine schemes for persuading him to let Dolly keep her money. Fine schemes. I've talked a good many people into a good many things. But I don't know. Maybe I knew all the time what it would lead to."

"While we—were there ... ?"

"Right while we were together," he said. "But it was a lovely day. You're such a good little kid, and I felt good myself. But he played into my hands. I don't think I'd have been able to walk up to him and smash him on the head with a stick. It's easier than you'd think to kill someone who's running away from you, or someone who's attacking you. But in cold blood, as they say ..."

He took a cigarette out of his pocket; he looked at it and put it back.

"But he started right in at me. You, sir, I've heard of you, sir. A common swindler, sir. Leave this house, sir. So I stopped having cold blood, and I could do it. I tied some stones to his arms and I thought he'd stay put. But I evidently didn't do it the right way. He came out. And then Dolly lost her head. If she'd shut up, there needn't have been much trouble. I'd sent that telegram, saying he was going to Boston. Nobody could prove anything. I was arrested in Spain by the Franco outfit, and I talked myself out of that. I've been arrested other times, and I got out of it. But the great stark fact of death was too much for Dolly. She panicked. First she tried to put it all off on Neely—which was childish. He didn't have anything to do with anything. Then she thought up this husband, and that made things worse."

He rose.

"Where—are you going?" Maggie asked.

"Upstairs," he said. "To get that eight hundred dollars. Don't you think I've earned it?"

"Don't," she said. "Please don't. I'll go up and get the money for you."

"No," he said. "It's too late, Maggie."

"You can—get away."

"Not now," he said. "It's too late. This is the payoff, Maggie."

"Please!" she said. "You can't go up like that—with blood on your face. Please ... I'll help you to get away—"

He was moving toward the stairs.

"Miss Dolly!" she called with all her might. "Miss Dolly, lock your door!"

"That won't help," said Johnny.

"Dolly! Dolly!" she cried. But there was no answer and no sound from overhead.

"She's probably taken some of her little pills," said Johnny. "That's another way she has to escape annoyance."

Maggie ran in front of him and spread out her arms.

"Stop! Oh, stop! Think what you're doing—"

"I'm sorry about you," he said. "I could have been very fond of you— ten years ago."

He put her aside and started up the stairs. Everything vital and quick and strong in her fused into one passionate resolution. He was going slowly, with one hand on the rail; she stooped and darted under his arm and ran frantically up the stairs ahead of him. She was too breathless to call again; she ran through the big room to the bedroom; the door was open and the light was on, and Miss Dolly lay in bed with her eyes closed.

"Miss Dolly ..." said Maggie, in a faint, breathless voice. "Wake up! Wake up!"

Miss Dolly's shoulder as she grasped it was warm and smooth; she was breathing. But she did not open her eyes. And Johnny Cassidy was coming through the other room.

"Wake up!" said Maggie and scratched that smooth shoulder.

"Don't ... !" Dolly murmured, fretfully, and opened her eyes.

"Wake up! Johnny's here!"

"Johnny's here," he repeated from the doorway. Her eyes were wide wide open now; she lay flat on her pillow, looking up at him.

"Go away, Maggie," he said.

"No," said Maggie.

She sat down, suddenly and heavily, on the bed and stretched her arm across Miss Dolly.

"You'll have to go," said Johnny.

Miss Dolly said nothing and did not stir.

He took Maggie's wrist and pulled her to her feet. She tried to hang back but he slung her around behind him; he pushed her out into the big room and closed the door. She opened it.

"No!" she said, in a hoarse loud voice. She was not afraid of Johnny Cassidy, not afraid for herself. There was nothing left in her but that one clear fierce passion to defend the woman lying there.

"Look here! Get out!" said Johnny.

"No!"

He looked at her, a look almost sorrowful.

"Like a damn little Scotch terrier," he said. "But you've got to get out."

"No!" she cried, in a shout. "Miss Dolly, get up! He'll kill you!"

"Maggie ..." came Miss Dolly's voice in a faint wail.

Maggie tried to rush past him but he stopped her. He threw the gun down on the couch and picked her up and carried her out on the balcony. She struggled desperately and silently, but he moved his shoulders, swinging her a little, like a bundle, and he threw her off, down into that water.

Chapter Twenty-Two

It was cold as death, closing over her head. But she came up at once and began to swim automatically. Her hand struck against the rowboat and she held to that for a moment. Then she edged hand over hand to the ramp and crawled up it on her hands and knees. Then she had to rest.

She was crying and sobbing, lying on the damp salty grass. She was crying because she could not get up. She tried, but she could not remember how to move her feet and her wet skirts twisted around her. She was defeated now.

A car was coming; a great blinding light shone on her as she raised her head. She heard a shot.

"Help!" she called. But she was not sure if she made any sound. She got up on her knees, with a dreadful effort.

"Maggie?" said Neely's voice. "Is that you?"

"Miss Dolly!" she said. "Go in quick—and see—"

"Hofer and the others are in the house," he said.

"What are you doing here?"

He laid his hand on her head. "You're wet," he said. "Soaking." He helped her to her feet and put his arm around her. "Better come into the house," he said.

She wanted to go in there, she had to go in there. Two cars were standing before the house and there was a man standing on the porch.

"Who's this?" he asked.

"She lives here," said Neely, and the man let them pass.

There was nobody there. The lights were on, very bright, and there were footsteps overhead.

"I want to go upstairs," she said.

"They wouldn't let you," he said. "Here—"

He took the cover off the couch in the dining-room and wrapped it around her. "Sit down," he said, "and I'll get you a drink of whiskey."

"No ..." she said, her teeth chattering. "N-never ..."

"Then I'll make you some coffee," he said.

He pushed her into the shabby armchair and went into the kitchen; he was back again in a moment. "Why are you so wet?" he asked. He had a dish towel in his hand and he began to dry her hair.

"Don't—bother ..." she said.

The boards overhead creaked under a heavy tread. "Please find out ..." she said. "Please—right away."

"All right!" he said, and went running lightly up the stairs.

He was gone so long and she was so cold. The couch-cover was wet now, and it was dirty; a moldy smell came from it. She took it off and stood up as Neely came down the stairs again.

"It's all over," he said. "Don't worry any more."

"What—?" she said. "What—happened?"

"Both dead," said Neely. "You'd better sit down again. You look quite sick and funny."

"How—dead?" she asked.

"Johnny shot himself," said Neely. "Only first he smothered her with a pillow."

"Othello!" she cried.

He pushed her down into the chair again. "I wish there was a blanket," he said. "And your shoes—"

"Look here!" she said, trying to steady her voice. "Don't you—*care*—one bit?"

He shook his head.

"You don't care—about Miss Dolly being—murdered?"

"No. Why should I? At first I liked her, but I stopped. She got me locked up in jail. She made a big fool of me."

She leaned her head against the back of the chair and looked up at him.

"You're just not human!" she said.

"What's the matter with you?" he asked, angrily. "You told me that before. What have I done that's so wrong? Nothing at all. I work very hard and I mind my own business. I don't drink—"

"You don't?"

"No, never. I don't tell lies, either. Yet it's always me you go for. I'm the one that's not human. And why?" He spoke with a sort of severe wonder. "Because I put a dead old man in the water? Because I don't shed crocodile tears for those two upstairs? I'd like to know what I've done you think is so bad."

"I don't know," she said.

Maybe Neely is good. And Johnny was bad—so bad.... Maybe I'm unjust—and mean. Maybe I'm a hypocrite, Maggie thought, with tears run-

ning down her face. Maybe I don't know *anything*—about human nature....

"Here," said Neely. "Here's a present I bought for you. Now I'm going away."

He tossed a little box into her lap and went out into the hall; the front door closed after him. She waited a moment and then she took off the lid. There was a wrist-watch there, quite a nice little silver watch.

Oh, dear! she cried to herself. Oh, dear ... !

"Now!" said Captain Hofer, grimly. "Now, then, young lady, what have you got to say for yourself?"

He was angry at her; perhaps he suspected her of all sorts of things. He had a right to be angry; she had not co-operated with him.

"I don't know ..." she said.

"You're all dripping wet," he said, with a scowl on his scarlet face. "What's happened to you?"

"I—don't know ..." she said again. That was so silly, but she couldn't help it.

"This won't do," he said. "No use your getting pneumonia. Come along now. I'll take you back to Mrs. Mayfield at the hotel and you can have a hot bath and get to bed. You can talk to-morrow."

"And Mr. Getty?" she asked.

"He'll be all right," said Captain Hofer.

He wasn't angry or mean. He was kind. Oh, dear! Oh, dear! How could you ever figure things out?

"Come now," he said. "Don't take this so hard. You're young and you'll get over it." He pursed his lips and shook his head. "Very young," he said.

THE END

The Virgin Huntress

By Elisabeth Sanxay Holding

Chapter One

At six o'clock Montford Duchesne left the shipyard and wheeled out his bicycle, to ride home. A stream of cars went flowing out and he stood waiting to let them pass, slender and tall, a handsome young fellow, very dark, with black hair and an olive skin, and thick long black lashes that gave a look of gentleness to his narrow face.

He watched the cars with somber interest; he was tired and depressed and he thought, with a sigh, of the cars he had driven, and owned, not so long ago. Now it's a bicycle, and the shipyard—and the Gettys, he thought. God, what a life! His room would be hot as an oven from the afternoon sun when he got back, and not clean, either; it never got a good cleaning. The little house would stink, he thought, of Mrs. Getty's awful cooking, of cabbage, onions, and always something getting burned.

The stream of cars was thinning out now, and he mounted his bicycle and set off along the shore road. I've lost out, he thought; lost everything. My friends, all the chances I had to meet people and get somewhere in the world, a decent way of living, everything.

He turned off into Brighton Avenue, and it was cooler there, and shady under the old trees; quieter, too, with little traffic. He began to feel better. After all, he thought, I'm only twenty-eight. I needn't feel as if life was over. There could be, probably there are a lot better things ahead of me than I ever had in the past. And there's that money in the bank; I never had that much money before. No.... When the war's over, I can go places. To South America.

His pay in the shipyard was more than double, twice as much as he had ever got in former jobs, and, for the first time, he had saved; every payday for over three years he had put most of his money in the bank. I haven't bought any new clothes, he thought; no place to wear them. I haven't had the upkeep of a car, haven't gone to a show, or a good restaurant, since I don't know when. It's cheap, boarding at the Gettys', and God knows I haven't spent much on Gwen.

He smiled a little, thinking of Gwen Getty. She's a pretty kid, he thought, and she's smart, too. She's fun. Of course, she's a menace, she and her mother, but I can cope with that.

They wanted to make him marry Gwen. All right! Let them keep right on trying. He wasn't doing any marrying just now, and if he ever did, it wouldn't be anyone like Gwen. I ought to be more careful, he thought, uneasiness stirring in him. I've been—well, sort of reckless.

He turned the corner of the long street, lined with shabby wooden houses, and there was here the same atmosphere that had surrounded him all day in the shipyard, that tension, that solemn excitement. Men in undershirts or shirt-sleeves were sitting together on front steps, groups of women in aprons were talking, children ran screaming up and down, and above everything rose the preposterous noise of the radios, a great, dull roar of frantic voices. President Truman is still closeted. The Washington correspondents are still ...We bring you the latest news from the nation's capital. Roar, roar, roar and yap, yap.

Silly fools! he thought, frowning. The war won't be over for another year, or more.

He wheeled his bicycle up the little gravel path and left it leaning against the side of the house. He mounted the steps, and Gwen came out onto the front porch.

"Monty!" she said. "Isn't it *won*-derful? The war's going to end!"

"Nothing but rumors," he said.

"It's the real thing, this time, Monty," she said. "I just know it."

She was pretty, very pretty, dainty and little, with blue eyes and chestnut hair and a sweet color in her cheeks. Her haircut was wrong, too much hair; it made her head look too big. Her dress was wrong, a black dress with a powder-blue yoke, a fussy draping to the skirt. But, just the same, she had a certain style of her own; she was proud of her littleness, and superbly self-assured.

"Monty, *be* a little bit excited!" she said, coaxingly.

"Sorry," he said. "I'm not. I want to wash up and change, Gwen."

"Is poor li'l Monty tired?"

"Yes," he said.

He remembered other times when she had said that, sitting beside him on the sofa in the parlor. Poor li'l Monty tired? Put your head on Mamma's shoulder. There! She was pretty expert at lovemaking, but she was prudish, too. Here, now! You behave yourself, Monty!

He glanced at her sidelong, and she gave him back a steady look; they were both remembering those evenings on the sofa. She's cute, he thought.

"Mummy's gone absolutely crazy," she said. "Goodness knows when she'll have dinner ready. She's just hanging on the radio. But I'll go see if I can do anything, while you wash up, Monty."

He went into the mean little hall with the elaborate hat-stand; he went up the stairs to his own room. It was very neat, because he left it so, but it was not clean, and it was uglier than any other place he could remember, brown walls, a threadbare green carpet, grimy curtains before grimy windows, everything gritty with dust.

I wasn't brought up to do housework, Mrs. Getty often said. People of our class in England don't *do* it, you know. My people always kept two servants, and there was a woman who Came In. I'm not used to it.

She had lived in the United States for thirty years, without growing used to anything much. Mind you, I like it here, she would say. But you must admit you can't get things. That cherry toothpaste, we never used anything else. And the cough syrup.... Unheard of here.

Her cooking, she said, was English. Monty found it very distasteful, and so did Gwen, but nothing deflected Mrs. Getty. She kept on putting before them the dishes they detested; they were both young and healthy, and they ate her shepherd's pie, the toad-in-the-hole, the liquid custards, because it was that or nothing. You see! she would say, once you're used to it, there's nothing like it.

Gwen could not cook at all. I daresay I could pick it up in a week, if ever I had to, she had told Monty. But I don't expect I ever will. She did nothing in the house, didn't even make her own bed, as Monty did, and this seemed quite right and proper to her and to her mother. If Mr. Getty had lived, Mrs. Getty would explain, you'd never have seen Gwen going off to work in an office, day in and day out. A tragedy, *I* call it.

Gwen did not think her life was tragic. Monty was sure that she lied about her job; he did not believe she was private secretary to a big shot in the company where she worked. She hasn't got what it takes, he thought. Probably a typist. But whatever it was, she liked it, she liked going to New York every morning, she liked eating her lunch in a restaurant, and, war or no war, she found men to take her out.

She had a great number of girl friends; they telephoned to her, they sent her post cards when they were away on vacation, she went to weddings, showers, engagement lunches. But she never invited anyone, male or female, to the house. She's probably fixed herself a wonderful build-up, Monty thought. Aristocratic mother, old family butler, all that. Well, you can't blame her. That English accent goes over big—when she remembers it.

He rather liked the English accent himself; he himself was sometimes impressed by her dainty audaciousness. He *knew* she was common, and her mother still more so, and God knew what the late Mr. Getty had been. But sometimes, when he took her out to a restaurant, he was a little surprised by her air of well-bred sophistication. And it pleased him to notice the interest other men showed in her.

She intended to marry him: he knew that, and he knew he had to be careful. She was a smart kid, and she had her mother there to help her. With a set-up like that, he thought, you could get yourself in a hell of a jam, if you didn't watch your step. He had thought of telling her that he was already married, and separated from his wife. She's a strict Catholic, he was going to say, and she'll never give me a divorce. But if Gwen believed that, she would never let him make love to her, and he *wanted* to make love to her.

Sometimes, in the middle of his work, he would think of her. Maybe this evening ... he would think. Maybe this evening Mrs. Getty would go up to her room, or go out to visit, and he and Gwen would sit side by side on the couch in the living room; he would put his arm around her and she would nestle against him; she would close her eyes when he kissed her, and then open them slowly, her lashes brushing against his face. A pretty kid, and ardent, too. But she managed her ardor; she could, when she pleased, turn it off, like a light. That'll do now, she would say, suddenly cool.

He could do that. He would go out for a walk and a couple of beers, and he would feel a sort of hatred toward her. Damn little teaser, he called her to himself, and he would feel a furious wish to conquer her, master her, and then leave her. But he always banished that wish; it was dangerous. Just asking for trouble, he told himself.

He went upstairs to the bathroom and took a shower and put on his cherished dressing-gown. Olga had given it to him, a black Shantung kimono that came a little below the knees, with a broad belt to tie around his narrow waist. With his black hair and his olive skin, he looked exotic. You look *lovely*, Olga had said. They had gone to Atlantic City for a week, and they had never met again. He had called her up, but she was not at home; he had written once, but she had not answered. All right. Let her go.

The memory of her stirred other memories. Sitting on the edge of the bed, he looked at his dusty, dirty room, and that pain came back. He thought of other rooms, in hotels, tranquil in lamplight; he thought of the sitting room in Flora's apartment, white flowers in a blue bowl, the etchings on the ivory-colored walls. Well, is that *all* gone? he thought. Gone forever? Is this the best I'm ever going to get?

No, he told himself. It is not. I'm saving money now, for the first time in my life. I've got quite a lot. And if this war lasts another year, I'll have enough to go to South America.

This was the persisting dream in his life. He did not remember when it had begun, only it was long ago, when he had been a schoolboy. He had read some story, or seen some movie, that had given him this great hope and desire. Even in those days, he had believed that if he could get to some Latin, tropical country, he would be completely happy, completely successful.

He believed it now. He imagined a little house, a bungalow, a big room, dim, with the Venetian blinds down. He would be stretched out in a chaise longue, in a white suit, and a native boy would bring him whiskey and soda on a tray. And presently she would come, that beautiful girl, thin and blonde, with a cool insolence to hide her secret misery. She was in great trouble, and he would help her. She would have no one but him; they would have only each other.

"Will you have a drink?" he asked.

"I'd like something to eat first," she said. "I'm hungry. Does that surprise you?"

He clapped his hands for the boy, and asked her what she wanted.

"I'd like roast beef," she said. "Or two or three hot dogs, with lots of mustard, and a big, cold glass of milk."

"Afraid there's nothing like that in the house," he said, looking down at her as she lay back in his chair.

"Then I'll settle for—a slice of bread," she said.

She smiled, and then she fell sideways, and he caught her as she fainted. They called her a bad girl, but he knew better. She was lonely and lost, that was all. She had lost faith in love.

There was a knock at the door, and the waking dream dissolved.

"It's me, Monty," said Gwen's voice.

"Oh, come in!" he said, rising.

She entered, in a sheer dress of lilac color.

"This darn zipper is stuck," she said. "Will you help me?"

The side of her dress was unfastened, showing a pink satin slip; there was a delicate perfume about her. A little warm, alive thing....

He pulled up the slide fastener with no difficulty. Nothing wrong with it.

"Now, why couldn't *I* do that?" she asked.

Their eyes met; he grinned, and she lowered her lashes. He put his arm around her and drew her against him.

"Mummy's back," she said. "She told me dinner in five minutes, Monty."

"Is she going out this evening?"

"Oh, sure to! She's too jittery to stay home. She has the radio in the kitchen with her."

"But we'll stay home."

"I don't know," she said. "I might feel like going out."

"You won't," he said, with his face in her thick, soft hair.

"I don't know," she said. "You go out whenever you feel like it—and yet you always think I'll stay home whenever you want."

"It isn't that," he said, with his cheek against hers. "I go out because I can't stand being here alone with you. All you do is tease, and then walk out on me."

"Certainly!" she said, coldly. "I wouldn't let you, or any other man, get too fresh with me." She looked straight at him. "Unless it was the man I was going to marry," she said.

It was the first time she had spoken of marriage, and it gave him a slight shock. But, after all, it was not unexpected; he recovered himself quickly.

"You're making a big mistake," he said.

"How d' you mean?"

"It's a mistake to marry a man when you don't know about him."

"How ... ? Oh, you mean *that?*" she said.

"You ought to know first if a man's a good lover."

"I've heard that tale before," she said.

"I wouldn't marry a girl who held out on me till she'd got me married," he said.

"Well, *that's* a nice way to talk!" she cried. "I'm no fool. *I* know how men are, thank you. If a girl gives in to them, they throw her aside like an old glove."

She stood away from him, but she left her hand in his; she looked sidelong at him, angry and troubled.

"Who told you that, babe?" he asked, gently.

"Everybody knows it."

"It isn't true," he said. "A lot of the married people I know—the happiest ones—lived together before they were married."

"I don't believe it," she said. "And anyhow, it's supposed to be wrong, in all religions."

"No," he said. "There's nothing in the Bible against it."

"There is, too! There's a commandment."

"That's adultery," he said. "That means one of them is married. It doesn't say a thing against it, if both of them are unmarried."

"I don't believe it," she said, again.

But she wasn't so sure, and neither was he. Only he saw that he had made an impression, and he had to follow it up.

"I grant you it's considered a sin, in all the great world religions, to have anything to do with anyone who's married," he said, gravely, even sternly. "I agree with that. But when two people are free, they have the right to love."

"Yes, and the right to quit and just walk out," she said. "I'm no fool."

"D' you call it being a fool, to be generous and—?"

He stopped short. O God! he cried to himself. That's—what I said to Nellie. And now, after all these months and months of rigid forgetting, of blocking out her image, back it comes, the tall, full-bosomed girl, always a little sloppy in her dress, but with the careless grace of a big cat. The first time he had met her she had been wearing a black skirt and a white blouse with blue dots, and the blouse kept pulling out over her waistband.

"I never wear any girdles or a bra, or anything," she had told him. "They just bother me."

"Monty!" said Gwen sharply. "What's the matter with you?"

"Nothing ..." he answered.

"You look—queer," she said.

"You can make a man feel 'queer,' babe," he said.

That pleased her.

"Well ..." she said, and touched her hair daintily with two fingers.

"I talk too much," he said. "I—don't mean everything I say, Gwen. I want things to be—*your* way. The way *you* want it to be. But—I'm only human, you know. I can't help trying—to get my own way."

That stopped her, all right.

"Well ..." she said, again.

"Get going, babe," he said. "I'm not responsible, if you stay around in my room."

"You're a funny kind of boy, Monty," she said.

Smiling down at her, he took her by the shoulders and pushed her out into the hall; he closed his door and locked it.

I've got to—to get hold of myself, he thought. I mean—those are the things I said to Nellie. I mean—about the great world religions—and being generous in loving.... And look—how it came out....

His knees felt weak; he sat down in the rickety little chair by the open window. No! he told himself. I don't *know* how it came out. Probably all right. Probably Nellie's having a hell of a good time, this moment, going out with some other fellow.

With a painful, a dreadful effort of his imagination, he could see her walking along a country lane, with her slouching, graceful gait, and a man beside her. A man in uniform, a soldier. She *told* me herself what a hit she makes with the G.I.'s, he thought. She's all right. Maybe she's married now.

I know I said I'd marry her. But I couldn't, I mean—we wouldn't have been happy. I wasn't the first man she'd had, she might have known ... And that baby ...? I bet there wasn't any baby. She was too smart for that. No.... She was probably plenty mad when she found out in the morning that I'd cleared out. But I left two tens in her pocketbook. No.... She's all right. She's having a hell of a good time this moment, the way she always did.

But he knew now that he was going to remember—the other part of it. He had kept it out of his thoughts, and out of his dreams. It had not come back to him even once, in all these months. But it was coming now.

The radios along the street were still blaring; a hot little breeze blew the grimy curtain against his face, and he pushed the chair back. He remembered. He had put his arms around her shoulders, to raise her up.

"I found a doctor, honey, and he'll be in later. But he gave me this for you to take now. He said it would stop your headache."

"God, it's got a nasty taste ..." she had said.

She was lying on the narrow white iron bed, in her pink pajamas that had a design of blue sea-horses; her thick chestnut hair was loose on her shoulders.

"Come on! Drink it, honey," he had said.

She had drained the glass, and lay back on the pillow. He had lit a cigarette, and waited. She had talked for a while, more and more languidly; then her eyes had closed.

"I feel—sort of sleepy, Duke," she had said, in a blurred voice.

"Do you good," he had assured her. "Sleep well, babe."

I *meant* that! he cried to himself. I just wanted to keep her quiet till I could get away. I didn't want ... Now, this stuff isn't candy, the druggist had said. Not more than three capsules, in any circumstances. Understand?"

He had emptied four capsules into a glass of water. Or maybe five. Or six. Or more?

I don't know! he cried to himself. I don't remember.... I only wanted to keep her quiet. That's all. I didn't mean ...

Maybe she was still quiet. Very quiet. He didn't know. He had heard nothing, and there was no one he dared ask a single question. Nearly two years ago....

"Mon-*lee*!" called Mrs. Getty. "Din-nah!"

Chapter Two

"It's coming," said Mrs. Getty. "*Any minute.*"

She had propped open the swing door to the kitchen, and the special smell of her cooking floated into the dining room, a flat, moldy smell. She went hurrying in and out, a woman considerably taller than her small daughter, with a fine large bosom, and below it a cylindrical body without waist or hips, ending in thin legs and long, thin feet, giving her somewhat the look of a prehistoric bird. She had a fine, fair skin and an abundance of light-brown hair, but her face, as she herself said, was not her fortune, little, peering gray eyes, a long, sharp nose, no chin.

She had been crying; her cheeks were stained by tears, her lids reddened.

"Any minute the peace'll come," she said, setting a dish down on the table.

"Oh, Mums, do give over!" said Gwen, exasperated.

"Well, when you've got a son over there ..." said Mrs. Getty. "I keep thinking of Charley...."

"We haven't any knives and forks," said Gwen.

"I'll get them," said Monty, rising.

It was his nature to help women, any women; he felt that way about them.

"Monty," said Gwen, "let Mums do things. It's good for her. Takes her mind off Charley."

But he went into the kitchen, where the little radio was babbling frantically. We give you our latest report from the nation's capital.... President Truman is still closeted ... The press representatives are still . . .

Mrs. Getty was bringing an enamel dish out of the oven, and Monty took it from her, with a dishtowel in his hand.

"Ladies' cabbage," she explained. "Mr. Getty *did* enjoy it. And nourishing, too, with an egg and a drop of milk."

I feel sick, Monty thought. I think I'm going to heave. Maybe it was the smell of the cabbage, which he detested; maybe it was the crazy babbling of the radio. Or maybe it was that other thing—about Nellie. He had felt, from the start, that his safety lay in not thinking and not remembering, and he had been able to do that. When you think about a thing, he had told himself, you're apt to give yourself away.

But now it had all come back, all the fear, the feeling of panic. If only I hadn't done that, he thought. Hadn't lost my head.... I could have got away from her, without doing that, taking that risk. If only I *knew*.... Maybe there's nothing to worry about.

But he did not know. Probably Nellie just slept late the next morning, and waked up all right, he told himself. She'd be mad at me for walking out on her, mad as hell. But she didn't know my name, or where I lived. She couldn't find me. But there's one thing certain. I'm not going to stay here alone with Gwen. Not this evening, or any other evening. No more monkey business. So help me God, I'll never get in a mess like that again.

Mrs. Getty stood in the doorway.

"We could bring the radio in the dining room," she said.

"Oh, for heaven's sake!" cried Gwen. "I couldn't stand it!"

"Well ..." said Mrs. Getty, and sat down at the table, to serve the pallid stew she had made. "If we don't get the news by the time I've washed up, I said we'd go over to the Matsons'. Their radio's so much bigger than ours."

"Not me," said Gwen. "I don't want to go over there."

And not me, thought Monty. He had spent two evenings at the Matsons', and that was plenty. Mr. Matson was a postman, a lean, middle-aged man with a gray mustache; his wife was much larger, very stout, with staring, anxious blue eyes. Their house was a miracle of neatness and cleanness, and they were proud and happy to entertain in it; they took guests into their golden-oak parlor and tried to make them comfortable and happy. They could not talk much, but they smiled; they brought in bottles of ice-cold beer, and sandwiches, and with them a little glass bowl filled with red, green, and yellow toothpicks, and small paper napkins on which was printed "Harry n' Ella."

I don't want to go there, Monty thought. But I'm not going to stay here alone with Gwen. He glanced across the table at her and, to his discomfort, their eyes met. She looked doubtful, still troubled; her air of saucy assurance had gone. His words had made an impression upon her; she was, he thought, making up her mind about him. All right. He didn't want to hear her decision. No more of that monkey business. Never again.

Mrs. Getty pushed back her chair, and rose.

"Nobody's eating much," she said. "Well, I've got a nice lemon jelly, nice and cold."

She pushed open the swing door and the radio was going on and on in the kitchen.

"What's at the Regal?" Monty asked.

"I don't know," Gwen answered. "I don't know if I feel like going to the movies, anyhow. Monty, when you said—"

"It's *here!*" cried Mrs. Getty. "It's peace! The war's over!"

She leaned against the door, holding it open, and they both rose and moved toward her, to hear.

"The Japanese have accepted our terms of unconditional surrender...."

A wild little piping began in the street outside, a small boy playing the Marines' Hymn on a mouth-organ. Then the ships began to blow, a deep, dull buzz that was like the sound of the ocean itself.

There goes my job, thought Monty.

"I feel—so queer," said Mrs. Getty.

"Sit down, Mummy! Monty, get her some water."

"I could do with a drop of Scotch," said Mrs. Getty, leaning back in her chair. "This is the worst time of all.... How do I know something didn't happen to Charley, even half an hour ago?"

"Oh, Mums, do give over!" cried Gwen. She poured some whiskey into a little glass. "Here! Drink this, and try to be a little cheerful. Just listen to those whistles and all, and think how happy everyone is."

"They didn't ought to be," said Mrs. Getty, weeping. "They don't know if their sons are alive this minute or not."

Her mouth was trembling, her hands were trembling; she looked strange and wild.

"Look, Mums!" said Gwen. "Put some powder on your nose, and let's go out, you and me and Monty. See what's going on." She put her arm around her mother's shoulders, glancing sidelong at Monty. "You'll feel better if you get out where other people are, won't she, Monty?"

"Sure to," he said, very sorry for Mrs. Getty. He knew how she felt, because he too felt like that.

"That atom bomb ..." said Mrs. Getty, still weeping.

You don't know *what's* going to happen, and whatever did happen would be entirely outside your control. You couldn't run your own life, you couldn't make any plans. Every payday, when he got his money, he had thought maybe this is the last. Maybe this is the last. Maybe they'll cut down on pay. Maybe it'll get like Russia, and you'll have to work wherever they send you, for anything they feel like giving you. Maybe the draft board will send for me again, and this time they won't care about that knee of mine. They'll be taking everybody. Everything familiar, everything you knew and liked, might end any day. And now it had ended. The great vibration of the whistles was the sound of a new world.

"*Come* on, Mums!" said Gwen, drying her mother's tears with a handkerchief. "Monty and I'll take you out somewhere, and you'll feel fine."

"I've got to run down to Oak Street first," said Monty. "There's a fellow there I made a bet with. He bet me twenty-five bucks the war would last another year, and I bet it would end this month. He said if I won I could collect from him inside of half an hour after the news before he got too tight."

"But couldn't you wait?" Gwen asked.

"I guess I could use twenty-five bucks tonight," said Monty, with a half-smile.

"Well, hurry back, won't you, Monty?" she said. "We ought to get out, and see what's doing."

She was honestly concerned for her mother, but she wanted to get out for her own sake, too; she was excited, the soft color in her cheeks had deepened, her eyes were brilliant.

"Gosh! I'm glad we can all spend this evening together?" she said.

Monty ran upstairs to his room, and got out sixty dollars he had hidden in a bureau drawer until he got a chance to take it to the bank. He glanced in the mirror, and saw that he looked as he wished to look, very neat, dark, handsome and quiet. He went downstairs, and out of the house.

He had no definite plan. He thought, vaguely, that he might find some other people he knew to join them for the evening; anybody would do. I don't want this to be like a family party, he thought. And above all he wanted to make sure that he was not left alone with Gwen. It was Gwen he was afraid of now, and no one else; Gwen was a danger to him. I must have been crazy, he thought, talking to her like that. She's pretty and all that, but she's common, and she's damn willful. If you got mixed up with her, it wouldn't be any easy matter to get out.

Well, my job's gone, he thought, with a sigh. No use going back there just to be fired. I'll have to start looking for another. If I could get away ... South America—or how about Mexico?

He turned into Oak Street, for no reason except that he had spoken of it. He knew no one who lived there. Only, if Gwen checked on him, it would be a good thing if he really had gone to Oak Street. And women do check on things; he knew that, all right.

It was a mean street, like the one on which the Gettys lived; there was a drugstore on the corner, and near it was standing a car that instantly attracted him. It was an English car, an old model, but of a make that could afford to be old, the car that was a synonym for aristocratic excellence. He went a little faster, along the empty street, wanting a good look at that car before it should drive off.

A sailor stood with one foot on the running-board, leaning toward the open window.

"Give me a kiss, and I'll go," he said.

"No," said a woman's voice from inside the car. "Please don't be troublesome."

"Lady, the war's over," said the sailor. "I was out there three years, and I thought I'd have to go back. You ought to be *glad* to give me a kiss."

Monty gave the sailor a thoughtful glance of male appraisal. Heavier than me, he thought, and stronger. He's drunk, and sometimes that makes them tougher to handle. But generally not.

The idea of avoiding an encounter never came into his head; indeed, he walked straight toward it. If he knew that a woman was watching him, he grew reckless; he could do anything.

The car stood under a leafy tree, and in the gathering dusk the interior was dark; he could not see the woman in there. But it didn't matter; the woman who watched him did not need to be young or beautiful.

"Excuse me," he said. "Is this man annoying you?"

"Oh, sweetheart!" said the sailor, in falsetto voice. "Oh, say not so!"

"Don't bother, please!" said the woman inside the car, and she had a lovely voice, low and warm. "I'm sure he'll go away now."

"Hey, look!" said the sailor to Monty. "You and me, we both get in the car with the girls, see? I got plenty money—and the war's over. Yippee-ee!"

His voice rang out, young and strong and somehow a little touching in the empty street.

"Sorry," said Monty, "but we're picking up some other people. This lady is a friend of mine."

"Friend of mine, too," said the sailor. "*All* girls are friends of mine. How's about it? Let's go!"

"Sorry," said Monty, "but I'm afraid you'd better shove off now."

"Says who?" the sailor demanded, in a sudden rage. "Says a sweet-smellin' Four-F to *me?*"

He stood on the curb, facing Monty, and without warning he hit at him.

It was a hard blow, but ill-directed; it caught Monty on the shoulder and sent him stumbling back, into the arms of someone behind him.

"Here, now!" said the newcomer, pushing him away. "Will I get the police, madam?"

"No," said the voice from the car. "He's going."

The sailor was walking off down the street, talking loudly.

"Sure!" he said. "Sure! Didn't we fight the war so's the sweet-smellin' Four-F's could stay home and get all the girls? Sure!" He began to sing, in a very good tenor. "Don't sit under the apple tree, With anybody else but me…. Oh, who the hell cares?" he cried, and turned the corner, out of sight.

The man who had caught Monty got into the driver's seat, with a glass partition behind him. Monty went to the window.

"You're all right now?" he asked, in his gentle voice.

"Oh, yes, thank you! Thank you so much. Please let us give you a lift, won't you?"

"Thank you," he said, "but I don't want to trouble you."

"It's no trouble at all," said she, earnestly. "Well, which way are you going?"

"We're going to the ferry, but we can perfectly well stop anywhere you like. Do, please …!"

"I'm going to the ferry myself," said Monty. "If you're sure it won't bother you—?"

She opened the door, and he got into the car. There was a faint and exquisite perfume here in the darkness, a perfume aristocratic and luxurious, reminding him of everything he most cherished. A great happiness filled him. The heavy car moved as if floating; it seemed to him as if he were rising, smoothly and easily, out of the Getty world and into that other world which he knew so much better, which was, to him, not at all a dream, but a reality he had seen through a half-open door. The woman beside him might be beautiful, but whether she was or not, she was lovely. He knew that, from her voice, from her perfume, by his own happiness.

Chapter Three

"I think we ought to go to Times Square," said the woman who sat next to Monty. "Just to see …"

She had a charming voice, low in pitch, with an appealing eagerness in it. The other woman's voice was nice enough, well-bred, but a little curt.

"You know how you hate crowds," she said.

"We needn't get out of the car," said the first one. "We can just *look*. We really ought to."

"It might be a very rough crowd," said the curter one. "You wouldn't like that."

"Well, Nichols can use his judgment," said the eager one.

"But you know he won't," said the curter one. "He'll do what you tell him."

These were the right people, Monty thought, the sort of people he was always longing for; easy and sure, without pretense, at home in the world, able to understand anything. He could not lose them.

"If I could be of any help ...?" he said. "I was going to Times Square myself, to see what was doing."

There was a silence, and his heart sank like lead. I've gone too far, he thought. I shouldn't have said that. It sounded cheap. As if I were trying to force myself on them. I should have waited for them to say something. I—

"That would be *very* nice," said the eager one. "We'll just *look*...."

His happiness came back, in a flood. Should I thank her? he asked himself. I mean, say thank you for the privilege. Or would that be flowery? Olga had used to laugh at him for being flowery. Don Juan Tenorio, she called him. He wouldn't ask her what that meant; she knew too damn much, anyhow, but he had guessed at the meaning.

"You know," said the eager voice beside him, "I didn't really believe the war would ever end. I don't believe it now." She paused for a moment. "What can be wrong with me? I'm not happy, not thankful. My heart is— hard as a stone!"

"Darling ...," said the curt one, with affectionate irony.

"It's true! Those men in the hospital ..."

"We've just been to Halloran Hospital," said the curt one, trying, Monty thought, to cover the other's agitation. "We went to see a boy who used to work for us. It's the first time we've been on Staten Island. It's a curious sort of place, isn't it? Not exactly a suburb, and not country, either."

"It's unique," said Monty. "I've been here for two years, working in the Maitland shipyard, and I've never got used to the island. Of course, there are some nice people, some nice old houses. There's a good golf course."

"Oh, is there?" she said, politely.

She was nice; he liked her. But it was the other one, the eager one, who drew him. He could see her only dimly, in a dark dress and hat; it was she who wore the delicate and aristocratic perfume. He looked forward to seeing her, but not too impatiently; this moment itself was perfect. She's not a kid, he thought; she has too much poise, and a sort of dignity. A married woman, maybe?

She must like me, more or less, he thought. I mean, she's not the sort who'd let just anybody come along with her. She must have seen me; it wasn't really dark in the street. So she can't mind my looks. All right. It's up to me to keep up the good impression.

"Maybe I'd better introduce myself," he said. "Montford Duchesne—at your service."

"You're French?" said the eager one. "I thought so, as soon as I saw you. Latin, I thought."

"Well, not French," he said. "My mother's a South American."

"No! From what country?"

"Venezuela," he said, and she spoke to him quickly and more eagerly than ever in a language he recognized as Spanish.

"I'm sorry," he said, "but I hardly know a word of Spanish. My mother had some trouble with her family."

They had stopped, in a long line of vehicles waiting to board the ferry; the line moved, and they with it; the heavy black car was next to the last one on board.

"Let's get out," said the eager one. "I hate these fumes, don't you?"

Monty stood ready to help her out, and as she descended, in the harsh light from overhead he saw her face, a pale oval, with great dark eyes raised to his. Here was beauty, delicate, elusive, infinitely appealing.

He scarcely saw the other woman as he helped her out; they crossed to the after-deck outside the Ladies' Cabin. It was crowded there, and dimly lit, but he could see her, his eager one.

She was a woman in her middle years, and grown a little stout, but she carried herself superbly, fine bosom outthrust. She was all in black, dress, gloves, hat; and her hair was black and shining as the wing of a bird; she wore no make-up except a dusting of powder that accentuated her natural pallor; no ornament but a wedding ring. In mourning? he thought. A widow?

No matter. She was a queen. He was entranced and humble before her dignity, her grace. Her dark eyes moved very quickly, glancing at him, looking out over the water, watching the people around her; it was as if she were a little alarmed, ready to flee.

"Oh ..." she said, suddenly. "We haven't introduced ourselves. I'm Luisa Brown, and this is my niece Rose Brown."

This Rose was a handsome girl; but in no way like her aunt. She was a little thing, straight and slim, with brown hair and long dark-blue eyes under straight brows, a sidelong look that was almost insolent, an underlip a little outthrust. She wore a dark-brown dress with a peplum, a brown and yellow turban, a yellow necklace like a wreath of flowers; she had style. But she had none of the other's touching charm; she was, he thought, a pretty, self-confident kid.

"How do you do?" she said, without a smile.

She doesn't like me, Monty thought, and it troubled him.

A few whistles still blew, but the great wild symphony was over; ships lay all about them, dark, the riding-light glowing; a light breeze blew. Why doesn't Rose like me? he thought.

"I haven't been to New York for weeks," he said. "We've been having a lot of overtime in the shipyard."

"You must feel proud now," said Mrs. Brown, "that you helped so much to bring this victory."

"It's pretty hard to feel proud, at my age, when you're not in uniform," he said. "People say things...."

"That's very cruel and stupid," said Rose. "When there's a draft, people ought to know that when a young man isn't in uniform, it's because he shouldn't be."

It was a right thing to say, a nice thing, but, he thought, it was impersonal, said from a sense of justice, and not to please or comfort him.

"Now Leon can come up here...." she went on, half to herself.

"That is Rose's little brother," Mrs. Brown explained. "My brother-in-law wants him to go to school here, but his mother could not endure to let him travel while the war was going on. The submarines, you know."

"You're—not from New York, Mrs. Brown?" he asked.

He was sure she was not; her appearance, her gestures, her very slight accent told him that.

"No," she answered. "From Argentina."

That was the last touch needed to make her wholly perfect. It did not matter to him that she was older than he. For him she had no more age than a gracious and lovely image in a church. Her charm for him was absolute; he was delighted by every word she spoke, by every gesture, the quick glancing of her dark eyes, the way she lifted her hand.

They got back into the car, and went off the ferry, slowly, behind a line of trucks. They drove through the empty downtown streets, up to the strange bazaar-like brightness of Fourteenth Street, where there was loud music, from God knew where, and up Fifth Avenue. The traffic was slow; the crowds moving along the pavements seemed to Monty strangely quiet and purposeful, as if they had something definite in mind.

"It isn't—*right*, is it?" said Mrs. Brown. "It isn't gay."

"It's convalescent," said Rose.

Times Square was strange, too; the huge, dim mob seemed as if struggling. The chauffeur pushed back the glass slide.

"Can't get through here, madam," he said. "Can't get any nearer."

There was a silence.

"We could drive uptown," Rose said, doubtfully.

"If you'd care to get out," said Monty, "we could walk a little."

"I don't know where I could park, madam," said Nichols, disapproving.

"Let's go back to the hotel," said Mrs. Brown. "Let's have champagne. Then perhaps it will be *right*. Will you have a glass of champagne with us, Mr. Duchesne?"

"Thank you," said Monty. "There's nothing I'd like better."

Thank God I've got sixty dollars with me, he thought. It certainly isn't much, for a big night like this, but it's something. And maybe I could get a check cashed, somewhere.

The car stopped before the Hotel St. Pol. My God! he said to himself. For in all the city there was no other place that had the same meaning for him. It was, comparatively, an old hotel, unostentatious, a little dowdy, but illustrious; a hotel for the best people. Before the war, he had taken a girl here to tea, one Sunday afternoon, and it had given him a sort of heartache, the polite little orchestra playing exactly the right tea-music, the well-bred voices, the formidable dowagers. The girl with him hadn't got the atmosphere at all; she had not liked it.

"No dancing?" she had said. "I thought we were going to dance, Monty."

They entered the enchanted lobby, rather somberly lit by gold-shaded lamps; they went through it, to the bar. It was crowded in there, not a table empty, not even standing room at the bar.

"We could squeeze in," said Mrs. Brown. "Oh ... Those people are singing!"

A party of six at a table, three men and three women, were singing the "Marseillaise," remembering or knowing only a few French words here and there, but earnest and passionate about it. Allons, enfants de la pa-ha-trie, ta-*ta*-ta-taaa tatata. A man waiting to get up to the bar reached out and took Rose's hand.

"Handsome ..." he said. "Have a drink with me. Been *looking* for you all m' life."

"Later, thanks," she said, and drew away her hand.

"Promise?" asked the man.

"Keep watching for me," said Rose, amiably.

But Mrs. Brown did not like this.

"We'll go up to the suite," she said.

They got into the elevator and rose to an upper floor; the corridor was carpeted in gray, mildly lit by little gold-shaded lamps, and it was entirely quiet except for a radio behind some closed door, playing "Anchors Aweigh." Rose opened a door with a key, and they entered a room that, like the other details of this magic night, was perfect—long, cool, and tranquil, filled with flowers that were, he thought, more delicate than any others he had seen, pink, lavender, white, stirring in the breeze of an electric fan.

"If you'll telephone for champagne?" said Mrs. Brown, and she and her niece went off into another room, closing the door after them.

Left alone, he was in a nervous haste to do this ordering before they returned, so that they should not overhear any mistakes. He telephoned to the bar.

"You might send up a bottle of Veuve Cliquot," he said. That was the only brand he could remember hearing mentioned. "What vintage have you got?"

"Very sorry, sir," said an English voice, "but we have no imported champagne left. We have some excellent domestic brands, though."

"I don't know them," said Monty. "What do you recommend?"

The man gave him two names, which he did not understand.

"Now, between the two ..." he said. "Which do you recommend? Which is the drier?"

"The Ste. Claire, sir. Excellent."

"Well, we'll try it," said Monty. "Send it up to room—" He glanced at the telephone. "Twelve-twelve."

I was right about asking for the driest, he thought. That's the sophisticated one.

"They haven't anything left but domestic champagne," he said. "I suppose we'll have to make it do."

"I *like* California champagne," said Mrs. Brown. "Have you tried any of the white wine from Chile?"

"I think so ..." said Monty, frowning. "Yes, I think so."

"Isn't it good?"

"Very!" said Monty.

He was far from happy now. He did not know whether the champagne was going to be Californian or not; he did not know what it would cost, or what tip he should give. Do I have to pour it out? he thought. Maybe I ought to give a toast. To peace, will I say? Or could I say something about the Argentine? Only, I think the Argentine's sort of in bad, just now. Fascist, or something. O God! Why do I have to be so *ignorant?* Such an oaf?

His mother had done that to him. If his mother had behaved differently, he would have known about champagne, about tips, about toasts, all the ritual of this world. *She* knew about it, all right. She had been born into it, she could have stayed in it, and kept a place for her son in it.

Anyhow, here he was, in a suite at the St. Pol, accepted as an equal by these two ladies. Or was he? Or was it just that this was V-J night, and the bars were down? He didn't know.

The waiter opened the champagne, and poured it; that was one worry settled. Monty picked up the check.

"No, please!" said Mrs. Brown.

"I'd like to—" he said.

"No, please!" she said, and her tone was not to be misunderstood.

She gave the waiter some money, and Monty had had no chance to see what the check was; he did not know what tip she gave. He wanted, he needed to know things like this.

I ought to propose a toast, he thought. Well, light—or should it be sort of serious?

"Peace—and good will!" said Mrs. Brown, raising her glass.

There were tears in her dark eyes, and she looked lovelier than ever. She took off her hat and laid it on the table; she pushed her hair back from her forehead, magnificent hair, thick, black and lustrous. She looked tired, Monty thought, and, in a rush, love and compassion came over him. There was grief in her heart; he knew that. He knew everything about her, how sensitive and gentle she was, and how generous.

She sipped the champagne. "What a good choice you made!" she said. "I've never—"

The telephone rang, and Rose went to answer it.

"Yes ..." she said. "Yes, it's I.... Oh, Juan ...? Yes?"

She stood, straight and slim, holding the instrument against her ear; her face in profile was clear and very fine, fine, thin lips, dark, delicate brows that slanted downward to a fine narrow nose. She was, after her fashion, beautiful, but it was a beauty that did not appeal to Monty. She's cold, he thought.

He finished his glass of champagne, and he wanted more, at once. He very seldom took a drink, or even thought of it; he cared little for it, and he knew, from experience, that he had a poor head for it. But if he took one drink, he always wanted more; he was always in a hurry to reach the level upon which he saw other people standing, poised and sure.

"May I pour you some more, Mrs. Brown?" he asked.

"Not yet, thank you," she answered, her almost full glass in her hand. "Please help yourself."

He did so, in haste, wanting to refill his glass before Rose turned back to them.

"It was Juan," she said. "He thinks we ought to go to Tia Clara's."

"It would be kind ..." said Mrs. Brown.

"Yes ..." said Rose, and was silent for a moment. "Juan's stopping for me in a few minutes. I told him you were very sorry, but you couldn't come. I said you had guests."

"Don't let me keep you, please!" cried Monty, rising. "I'll be getting along—"

"Sit down, please," said Mrs. Brown. "Rose doesn't want me to go with her."

"Because it would upset you so, Tia Luisa."

"You're right, my dear," said Mrs. Brown.

"And Ramon will certainly be here very soon."

"Very well," Mrs. Brown agreed. "If Mr. Duchesne will pour me a little more wine ...?"

He rose at once, and when he had filled her glass, he filled his own, too.

"I think I will have another glass, after all," said Rose.

Monty was sure he knew why she said that. She's afraid I'll take too much, he thought. She doesn't trust me. A stranger they picked up in the street. On Staten Island. She was hard, that girl was, hard as nails.

She went into another room, and she took her glass with her. She came back again, very soon, with the glass empty. But he had got another one while she was gone. Champagne was supposed to make you feel gay, but it didn't do that for him. He felt dull and miserable.

She had changed into a black dress and a smart little hat.

"I think I'll wait for them in the lobby," she said. "So that they won't have to come up."

So that they won't see me, Monty thought. Well, why don't I get out?

"I'll come back as early as I can, Doña Luisa," she said. "I hate to leave you, this special evening, but I suppose ... Good night, Mr. Duchesne! It's been so nice...."

She held out her hand, and he took it, not smiling. She was making it clear that she did not expect to see him again. Ever.

She kissed her aunt, and went away, and they were alone, in the softly lit room filled with flowers. This was the loveliest, the most lovable woman he had ever met, but he had nothing to say to her. The champagne had not made him gay, had not made him eloquent. The bottle was empty, and it had not helped him.

"I'll order another bottle," he said, rising.

"Oh, we couldn't possibly manage another!" she protested.

He tried to remember other times when he had had champagne. Or people in books or plays. What was the right thing?

"I'll order two brandies," he said, and went to the telephone.

This time he paid, this time he tipped, lavishly. Maybe she was noticing. After all, he thought, I'm *not* an oaf. Not a hick. My father's people ... I went to a really good school.

Yes, he thought. For just two years. Otherwise, nothing but public schools. I lost everything.

She stirred a little, and he thought, in a panic, that she was growing bored with him, so speechless. Maybe it was late, and she wanted him to go. He glanced at his wrist-watch, and he could not see the hands; there was only a blur. What's the matter with me? he thought.

She took a cigarette from a lucite box on the table, and he rose, to light it for her. And as soon as he was on his feet, he knew that he would stagger if he moved. This was so awful he could scarcely believe it. He sat down again, but even then he was aware of the weakness in his knees.

It's the worst thing that ever happened to me in my life, he thought. I didn't think I'd had too much. It hasn't gone to my head. My head's perfectly clear. But if she sees me staggering ... I've got to get away.

She was sipping her brandy. He had not touched his yet. I can't, he thought. I don't dare. But when she sees I'm not drinking it, she'll think ... I ordered it. It was my idea. At first I wanted to order another bottle of champagne. Another quart. She'll think I'm a fool. A common, ignorant fool—who doesn't know how to drink like a gentleman.

I'll knock over my glass, he thought. But then she'd expect me to order another one. O God! I don't know what to do.

"I think—I'd better be getting along ..." he said.

"Oh, must you?" she said. The worst thing to say. "I'm sure it will be harder than ever to get a taxi tonight," she said. "Perhaps you could telephone the desk and see if they'll get you one."

She wanted to get rid of him, and no wonder. He had been sitting here for God knew how long, without a word. Maybe he looked queer. Looked drunk, fishy-eyed, comic. Perhaps the brandy would help me, he thought. Perhaps that's why people order it, after a dinner with wine.

All right, it's damn well going to help me! He thought. I'm going to get hold of myself. I can.

He swallowed the brandy in three fiery gulps.

"Can I—?" he said. "May I—see you again?"

"Oh, yes! Call me up sometime," she said.

That meant never. He had ruined everything. He had made a fool and a beast of himself, and she wanted to get rid of him.

He waited a moment, summoning all his will power. I can walk all right, he told himself. I can get out of here without disgracing myself.

"Well, thanks," he said. "I will call up—about a taxi."

He rose, tall and straight, and moved toward the foyer. But he did stagger; he stumbled against the chair by the telephone and sat down on it with a thud. Sweating in shame and misery, he took up the instrument.

"Give me the hotel, please," he said. "I mean, the desk. The desk."

"Order, please!" said a clear voice.

"I want to see about getting a taxi—"

"Your order, please!" said the clear voice.

He could do no more. He hung up the telephone, clumsily, and sat where he was, in absolute despair. This was the worst thing that had ever happened in his life. And it was irrevocable. She would never let him see her again. She wanted to be rid of him, and he *couldn't* go. He couldn't even get up from this chair.

"Mr. Duchesne ..." she said.

She was standing beside him.

"I'm—so sorry ..." he said. "I didn't realize ..."

"Of course, you didn't," she said. "It's all the excitement."

"I'll go—in a moment," he said. "I'll be all right—in a moment. I'm—so sorry...."

"I don't think you'd better try to go home tonight," she said. "There'll be such crowds everywhere. I think you'd better stay here."

"*Here?*"

"My brother's away. You can use his room for the night. I really think you'd better."

"I can't," he said. "I can't—even get there."

"Oh, yes, you can!" she said. "I'll help you."

"No, please!" he cried. "Couldn't you please just leave me here? Couldn't you—go away, and leave me—just for a few moments?"

"No, I won't," she said. "Come! It's just down the hall. I'll help you."

She took his hand and pulled at it gently. He raised her hand and laid it against his cheek, and he wished he were dead.

"Come, you poor boy!" she said.

"I'm not a boy," he said. "I'll be twenty-eight next month."

"Will you really?" she said. "I'd never have thought it."

"I'm a man," he said. "I've had a man's life. I've been married. And it's been hell, all of it. All of it."

"Come," she said. "I'll help you."

She had her arm around his waist, walking down the gray-carpeted corridor; he walked, leaning against the wall.

"Shall I telephone for you?" she asked. "To your family? Your friends? Tell them you're stopping here overnight?"

"No, thank you," he said. "There isn't—anyone."

Chapter Four

The alarm clock was ringing and ringing; he stretched out his hand to stop it, and it wasn't there. Because it was a telephone. Always answer the telephone. Because you never know who's there in that booth, calling you up. Cops, maybe, motorcycle cops; three or four of them, jammed in there.

A light from somewhere was shining on the visors of their caps, and their eyes were shining.

Cops? You're crazy. You can see who's in there, the light shining on her long, glistening hair; she was holding the baby in her arms, and they were both grinning like gnomes. "Mr. Duchesne?" she asked.

"No!" he cried. "Don't let her give her name! Don't let her say her name!"

"But it's only—" a man's voice was saying.

"No!" Monty said, and jerked at the cord, letting the telephone go clattering off the table. But her name came roaring into the room, like an express train. It's Nellie! It's *Nellie!* Nellie Dover! Nellie Dover is calling you, Monty!

The telephone had stopped, and he went to sleep again. When he opened his eyes, there was a faint mauve twilight in the room; he knew, perhaps by the sounds in the street outside, that it was not evening, but before dawn.

She found me, he thought. O God! She was in that booth, shouting out her name. A queer booth, so very tall and narrow.... *Was* it a booth she was calling from—or something else? A coffin?

His jaw began to shake. All right! he told himself. She can't do it again. I knocked that telephone off the table. It can't even ring. I stopped her.

He turned his head to look at the dismantled telephone. But it was not dangling off the table; it was in correct position.

A dream, he told himself, and fell asleep again.

When he waked again, he came fully awake. He was wearing superb pajamas of heavy tan silk; he remembered nothing about them; he remembered nothing after the walk down the corridor. He didn't try to, either. He went into the bathroom and took a cold shower, a long one. The thing was, to be fit, ready for whatever was going to happen. He felt fit enough now, and regarding himself in the long mirror, he thought he looked all right; his narrow, olive-skinned face looked innocent and boyish as ever.

There were two razors in the bathroom cabinet; he used one of them, and cleaned it carefully. He wiped out the bathtub with a towel, so that there should be no ring. Her brother's room, he thought. Suppose her brother walked in now?

He had forgotten nothing about her. He remembered her arm about his waist, the clasp of her hand, her perfume; he remembered her lovely voice, her lovely dark eyes. She was all he wanted in the world, and he had lost her. I'll get out, he thought. I'll go—I don't know where. I don't care.

He began to dress, quickly, but with all his usual care. He was disturbed because he could not find a clothesbrush, and as he looked for one, he thought of Olga. You are like the little ermine, she had said to him, lying in bed and watching him brush his jacket.

"How's that?" he had asked.

"The little ermine dies," she had said. "His heart breaks, if there is one spot on his white fur." Amused, she had been; there had been too much of that. She had gone altogether too far, that week-end. Why the hell do I have to think of that? he asked himself, angrily. Now, of all times.

Only, he kept remembering things she had said. "Ach, you're sweet, Monty. Sweet. *But that's all.* There is no force in you. You should fall in love with some girl, very innocent, very domestic. Not a wild tiger like me."

Never came into her head that maybe it was *her* fault, he thought. She never imagined that *I* could be disappointed in her. I was. She was damn coarse. Lazy, too. I hope to God she stays in Poland, or wherever it is she went. I hope to God she never comes back here.

He was knotting his tie when someone knocked at the door. He stood absolutely still, with his heart pounding. Her brother? he thought. Someone from the hotel? Another knock, and then the doorknob began to turn. He had somehow taken it for granted that the door was locked, but it wasn't. It was opening now, and Rose Brown spoke.

"Mr. Duchesne?"

"Oh, yes!" he said.

He went over to the partly open door, and she was standing in the hall. She was wearing a thin black-and-white striped dress with long, full sleeves, but she had spoiled the effect of flowing grace by adding a black moire vest fitted tightly at the waist and fastened up the front with silver buttons, giving her that look of severity and primness.

"My aunt sent me to ask you to lunch with her," she said. "It's suite twelve-twelve."

"Yes, I remember. That's—very kind of her. But—"

"She'd like you to call her up in about an hour and let her know. And in the meantime, may I talk to you for a few moments?"

"Certainly. You mean—down in the lobby?"

"Why not here?" she asked.

"Well ..." he said, and held the door wide.

If she preferred it here, in a man's hotel room, with the bed still unmade, all right. She went over to the window and looped back the curtains before she sat down in an armchair. He resented that; she was, he thought, making herself too damn much at home.

She took a pack of cigarettes out of her purse, and he moved forward to give her a light. He didn't want a smoke himself; he felt sick; he felt queer.

"If I sound rather hard-boiled about all this," she said, "I'm sorry."

He had known from the start that this was going to be unpleasant, and now he felt a sort of fear.

"My aunt sent for the hotel manager," she went on. "She told him you were to keep this room as long as you wanted. Ramon and I begged her not to do it, but she would."

He was angry at this, and hurt, and still a little frightened.

"Mind telling me why you object to my staying here? If I do stay, for a little while, I'll pay. You needn't worry about that."

"You can't. My uncle's already paid for the room in advance."

"I'll send him a check."

"He wouldn't accept it. I only wish he was here.... Anyhow, what I came for was to ask what you'd take to go away—now—at once. And stay away."

"Take?"

"How much money. Ramon and I will do the best we can—"

He rose, and stood looking down at her, and she looked up him, steadily. God, I'd like to kill her! he thought.

"What d' you think I am?" he asked.

They were still looking steadily at each other.

"My aunt told the hotel manager," she said, "to let you sign for meals, drinks, cigarettes, anything you wanted, and she'd guarantee the bills."

He was startled, shocked. Doña Luisa had been beyond measure kind and sympathetic to him, but this...

"Well ..." he said. "That's very good of her. But I can pay my own bills. D' you think I'd *let* her—do that?"

"I don't know," said Rose.

"You mean to say you think—"

"Look!" she said, still with her steady glance on his face. "I'm not going to fence with you. I think—and so does Ramon—that you asked her to do that."

"That's a damn lie!"

"She was upset last night, about the war's ending. I shouldn't have left her alone with *you*—"

"Me? Especially me?"

"That's it. You. I suppose she brought out the photographs, and talked to you about Jo-jo. You do look rather like him."

"Jo-jo?" he repeated.

Maybe Doña Luisa had spoken of someone called Jo-jo. He could not remember it, but he could not trust his memory of the champagne-colored evening.

"If you'll go *away*," she said, "go now, at once, Ramon and I will give you as much as we can."

"And if I don't go? And don't want your money?"

"All right," she said. "Then I'll find out the truth about you."

He wished, with all his heart, that he could smash his fist down on her upturned face. But then the thing happened in his mind that had happened all his life. He could, he had hit people, and very effectively, but many times, when he had wanted to do that, he had seen, in a flash, that it would be a mistake, and, in a flash, he had brought out his other, his chief weapon. His charm.

He sat down and lit a cigarette.

"That's not very complicated," he said. "Maybe I can tell you what you want to know."

"Well, who *are* you?"

"That's a hard one, all right," he said, smiling faintly. "If I could say I was the Duke of Windsor, or Joe DiMaggio, something like that ... But I'm just a guy called—believe it or not—Montford Duchesne. Born in Pelham, aged twenty-seven. Occupation, any job I can get. I went to a good prep school, but I didn't make college, because my mother and father had broken up then, and there didn't seem to be any money. No police record."

I'm not getting it across, he thought. Not with that damn little prig.

"Where did you come from?" she asked.

"I thought I told you I was born in Pelham Manor—"

"I don't mean that. We picked you up in the street, and you came along with us. That wouldn't have seemed so queer, in all the excitement of its being V-J Day, and even your staying here, overnight, when you were drunk. But you just seem to be settled down here. You don't say anything about going home, even to get your things. You must have lived *somewhere*. You must have *some* belongings, somewhere."

"Naturally," he said. "I was living in a second-rate sort of boardinghouse on Staten Island. I'd paid a week in advance, and nobody there is going to bother about when or if I ever come back. I'm in no hurry. It was a ghastly place. Anything else you'd like to know about me?"

"I don't know anything about you yet. I don't know what you told Tia Luisa—"

"Look here! Don't you think your aunt is capable of judging character for herself?"

"No," Rose answered promptly. "She has this theory that people who look alike must be alike. She believes that you see people's character—natures—in their faces. We met a general in Washington, and just because he *looked* like Mussolini, she couldn't endure him. And now, because you look or she imagines you look like Jo-jo, she's sure you are alike. 'Poetic,' she said. 'Sensitive. But fiery.' Of course, I don't believe she really remembers much about Jo-jo."

"I'd be interested to know who Jo-jo is."

"He died—I don't know—before I was born. Twenty-six or seven years ago. Tia Luisa was engaged to him when she was just seventeen, and her people were always so hidebound, I'm sure she never saw him alone even once. Anyhow, he was killed, playing polo, and a year and a half later she married Uncle Edward Brown."

My—God! thought Monty. It was the sort of thing you could hardly believe, it was better than any of the daydreams he had invented. That a woman like Doña Luisa could think him like her lost fiancé ... 'Poetic' ...

"Was her marriage happy?" he asked.

"*What?*" said Rose, in such a tone, with such a look of incredulous disdain, that he instantly realized his shocking lapse in taste.

"Any other questions you'd like to ask?" he said, and tried to seem amused.

"I'd like to meet some people who know you, your family, your friends."

"I haven't any family but my mother, and she's away, just now."

"Friends, then," she said.

"I haven't any."

"But why?"

"Maybe nobody likes me," he said, with a faint smile.

"Maybe," she said. "But there could be other reasons."

"I've lost track of all the people I used to know," he said.

"You have?"

He could go on from here, all right. He could tell Rose, as he had told Gwen Getty, and Olga, and others; and would have told Doña Luisa herself.

"When my father died, my mother was left destitute. He'd been paying her alimony, and an allowance for me until I was twenty-one, and I traveled with a crowd that didn't bother much about jobs, or earning a living. When things got so bad with us, I just dropped out, that's all. And since then—well, in the kind of jobs I could get, I didn't meet anyone I could pal up with."

"You worked in a shipyard, didn't you?"

"Yes. After the draft board turned me down. About three years ago."

"How many people did they employ?" she asked.

"Around twenty-five hundred."

"And there wasn't one person—among twenty-five hundred—you wanted for a friend?"

He resented that. Just like Olga, he thought. His glance narrowed a little, and he smiled.

"Mean, did I think I was too good for them?" he asked. "It wasn't quite that. Maybe I was the unwanted one."

She was silent for a moment.

"My aunt tells me you said you'd been married," she went on, presently.

"Yes," he answered, courteously. "I was."

"But you're not now?"

"We're divorced."

Again she was silent for a time.

"Is your wife's name Nellie?" she asked.

"Nellie ...?" he repeated, blankly.

It was like a double-take. He looked at her in frowning surprise; then something caught him by the neck; he felt a curious tingling in his face and hands, a quickening of his heart.

"No," he said. "It's Flora. But why? I mean, why did you—ask that?"

He wanted her to answer at once, and when she did not, anger rose in him.

"Why did you ask that?" he demanded. "What business is it of yours what my ex-wife's name is?"

"I'm making this whole thing my business," she answered, unruffled. "When my cousin Ramon got here last night, Aunt Luisa sent him to see if you were all right. He said you'd just thrown yourself down on the bed, shoes and all, and Ramon managed to get you up and help you to undress. And he said you began talking in a very excited way about someone called Nellie. You said she was after you, trying to get you on the telephone." She paused; not with any trace of hesitation. "Ramon said you seemed very much afraid of this Nellie." This—is it! Monty thought, and he rallied to the danger almost automatically, almost without thought.

"Well, your cousin Ramon is mistaken," he said. "There's nobody I'm afraid of, and I don't know anyone called Nellie."

By these words, he thought, he had somehow finished Nellie, buried her. He felt no alarm now, only a sort of scorn for these people who were trying to trap him. They couldn't do it.

"I was drunk," he said. "I can't remember what I said. But it couldn't have been about any Nellie."

"Ramon is sure you talked about Nellie. You said a last name, too, but he can't remember that."

Nobody knows about her, Monty thought. Nobody ever will. She's gone, and the whole thing is over and forgotten.

"Look here!" said Rose. "Will you go away?"

"But—what d' you mean?"

"Will you go back to—wherever you came from? If Ramon and I get together some money? A thousand dollars?"

"I don't know what you mean."

"Will you *not* have lunch with Aunt Luisa? Not see her again, if we give you a thousand dollars?"

It was a body blow. He had had plenty of insults and wounds in his life, but never one that gave him such intolerable pain. He had never hated anyone as he did this girl.

"No," he said. "*No!* I'll see Doña Luisa whenever she cares to see me."

"All right!" said Rose. "We thought it would be this way. Then you'll have to let me find out about you."

"I don't have to."

"All right! Then we'll get a private detective."

"For God's sake, *why?* Why are you hounding me like this?"

"It's either a private agency—or you'll cooperate with me."

"But what d' you want me to *do?*"

There she sat, beside the curtains she had rumpled back, a pretty girl, even a beautiful girl, but completely without interest in him as a young and handsome man. She was, he thought, like some old-time Spanish Infanta, obliged to talk to a footman.

"I'd like to begin by seeing your former wife," she said.

"Mean you want to go to Flora, and tell her you're 'investigating' me?"

"I shouldn't put it like that. I'd say it was about a job."

"She's married again, and she has a baby. Very happy, from what I've heard. I don't see any reason why she should be dragged into this thing—whatever it is."

"She's not going to be 'dragged into' anything. I'd just like to hear how she speaks of you. Because she must know you, better than anyone."

Well, she doesn't, he thought. Flora never knew anything about me—or anyone else. She's stupid as an owl. But she's very decent, always. She'd never say a word against me to this damn gadfly of a girl. No.... After all, why not?

"I don't like it," he said. "But if that's going to make you a little less—hysterical about me and my past, very well. She works for Parini. It's—in the telephone book, and you can probably get her between three and four."

She rose.

"Thank you," she said, and her tone was a little changed, a little less arrogant.

"Her name is Mrs. Adamson," he said.

"Thank you," Rose said, again.

He opened the door for her and watched her down the corridor, straight as an arrow, so sure of herself, safe and protected in her own magic world. He hated her.

He closed the door and went to the telephone; he dialed Parini's number, and he got Mrs. Adamson without any trouble.

"Flora, it's Monty," he said.

"Oh ..." Flora answered, with a little gasp.

"May I come and see you this evening, Flora? It's about a job. It's—very important to me."

"But—couldn't we have lunch, instead, Monty?"

"Sorry, but I can't. I'll only stay a few moments, Flora. And I think you know I wouldn't bother you, if I could manage without."

"Well ... All right, Monty," she said.

He knew Rose couldn't get hold of her between three and four, when she had her daily conferences with Percy Parini. As long as I can see Flora first ... he thought.

Chapter Five

Then he called Doña Luisa, and the sound of her warm, cordial voice was hope and consolation for him.

"I'd like you to come to lunch, Monty," she said. "I think I have something to interest you."

"Thank you," he said. "I was going to write you a note—about last night. To ask if you could forgive me."

"That? Don't think of it. One o'clock, then?"

"Where shall I meet you?"

"Oh, here, if you don't mind," she said. "I don't like *lunch* in restaurants, do you? Sometimes I think I'm not really awake until five or six in the afternoon."

There was no one like her, he thought; no one. She could, in a moment, in a dozen words, give him the feeling of being an accepted friend. She'd understand anything, he thought. You could tell her anything. Even if Rose does try to undermine, it won't work. Anyhow, what could Rose tell her? Only that when I was drunk I talked about someone....

He ordered coffee and orange juice sent up, and a bottle of aspirin. I don't feel any too good, he thought, and I've got Rose to thank for that. What the hell business is it of hers, hounding me like this? If her aunt wants to know anything about me, she'll ask me, and I'll tell her.

Then he felt a stir of fear again. What if *she* asks me about—that? If Doña Luisa asked him, outright, if he knew a girl called Nellie?

All right! I don't, he told himself. I haven't heard a word from her, or about her, for nearly two years. All right! I fixed it so she couldn't get hold of me. She didn't know my right name, or where I lived, or where I worked. We met in that lousy little bar where I'd never been before—and I never went back to it. All the love-making we did was down on the beach, and those four or five nights in that little hotel away uptown in New York.

She told me about that hotel. She knew her way around, all right. She didn't have to get pregnant, if she didn't want to. She did it to make me marry her. If it was true. And I don't believe it was true. God, but she was hell-bent on marrying me! Made me take her to see some stinking little house, over in Jersey...

Now, for the first time in all these months, her image came clearly before him. She had taken his arm as they stood before one of those little houses; a tallish girl, with a lithe and beautiful body; a handsome face, too, fine-featured and arrogant. She had been wearing a thin summer dress that Sunday, white, with a design of big scarlet flowers, a wide black straw hat.

"God, Duke, couldn't we be happy here, you and me—and the kid?" she had said.

Happy? On that street, of cheap little houses, getting to know all the neighbors, going to the movies once in a while. Mowing the lawn on Sunday, drying the dishes after dinner.

"I'm a swell cook, Duke."

"I bet you are, sugar."

She had come from a small town in Kansas, and she had taken a correspondence course in How to Be a Model.

"I was such a hick then," she had told him, laughing.

And she never stopped being a hick, he thought. She had acquired a certain style; she really had done a little modeling for a dress manufacturer.

"And was he ever a heel!" she had said.

He had been her first man, Monty thought. After that, there had been other jobs, and other men, all the jobs had been no good, jobs in department stores, jobs as a "hostess" in second-rate restaurants; all the men had been "heels." At twenty-four she was growing frightened; she had had too many failures; there had been too many men, some of them lavish for a time, some of them dazzling to her, but not one who had not left her. She had never told Monty all this in so many words, but he could piece it together from what she did say, even her lies.

I bet she always tipped her hand, he thought. She'd be fool enough to start this getting married business to any man who was out for a good time. I bet she tried that baby racket on plenty of other fellows. All right. I hope she caught some sucker. Or maybe she went home to Kansas. If she—if anything had happened to her, I'd have heard, somewhere; read something in the papers.

Anyhow, she's out of my life, and that was how he felt, since that talk with Rose. I had to get away from her, that's all. She didn't want to let me out of her sight. Pretty soon she'd have found out where I lived, or where I worked; she was getting close, too, trying to trip me up with questions, trying to snoop in my pockets for letters. I had to get away from her, and I did.

At five minutes to one, he left his room and went down the corridor. Anybody else would have been disgusted with me last night, he thought. Only she wasn't. There's no one like her.

He rang the bell, and she opened the door promptly; a stream of air from the fan made her light-gray dress flutter like the petals of the flowers that stood all about the room.

"Come in!" she said, holding out her hand and smiling. "I've had a menu sent up. If you'll look at it ...?"

"We're going to have lunch here?"

"Oh, would you rather go down to the restaurant?"

"No, no!" he said. "I'd much rather be here."

He had had plenty of meals in hotel rooms before, but always in bedrooms, often with the beds unmade, clothes lying here and there, something stale and weary in the air.

He looked at the very large menu.

"I'll take whatever you're having, please," he said.

"But I haven't decided yet. Choose, please, Monty."

"I can't," he said.

"You have no appetite?" she asked, with courteous concern.

"It's not that," he said. "I don't know what to order. I'm—too ignorant."

"Ignorant?" she repeated, in surprise.

"You must have noticed it. I—don't know how to behave."

"But you have charming manners!" she protested.

"I don't know anything," he said. "When I'm with you, I realize it all right."

"But have I done anything? Said anything?"

"No, no! You've only been kind and wonderful. Only—I want *you* to know what I'm like."

That was the truth. To everyone else, he wanted to boast a little, he had a build-up for himself. But not for her. He wanted her to see, her alone, that he was hurt, and unhappy, and unsure.

"But I think—" she began, when the telephone rang, and she went to answer it, the menu in her hand. He rose, so that he could see her there in the foyer; she was speaking in Spanish, quick, warm and eager. Doña Luisa.

Directly she finished that conversation, she called room service and ordered lunch; then she came back to him.

"Now I'll make cocktails," she said.

"Well, but after last night ..." he said. "I guess I shouldn't."

"You mustn't think so much of that," she said. "If you'd really been a drinker, it wouldn't have happened. A nice little Martini will do you good."

He would do anything she wanted. Whatever she said was right. She opened a door, and beyond it he saw a little kitchenette, all shining white.

"May I help you?" he asked.

"No, thanks," she answered. "My brother's taught me to be quite good at it. You'll see!"

He watched her as she moved about in the kitchenette, getting out ice cubes, reaching down glasses. She had for all her plumpness an effortless grace; there was not a thread of gray in her shining black hair; her ankles were delicate, her feet narrow in her high-heeled sandals.

She brought in the cocktails on a tray, and they were cold and smooth and perfect. Everything was perfect, and that was unbearable. It was like a glimpse of paradise, through an iron gate. He found here everything he longed for, everything he most loved and admired. But he didn't belong here; he had got into this world only by chance, and he would have to leave it. And maybe never get back, he thought.

"Now!" she said, sitting down on the sofa. "Let's talk a little, before Ramon comes."

"Ramon?" he cried, dismayed.

"He's really like a nephew to me," she explained. "His mother was a cousin of mine, and we grew up like two sisters. After she died, he used to spend his holidays with us, unless he went to Paris. He's a charming boy, and very clever, too. And I have a special reason for your meeting. You won't mind my asking this.... But do you really *like* your position on Staten Island?"

"It was in the shipyard," he said. "It's finished now."

"Is that a worry for you?"

It would be, when he thought about it, when he faced it. And yet, he had no intention of returning to the shipyard. He had convinced himself that they would fire him. When he had left Flora, just before the war began, he had gone to employment agencies; he had filled out blanks, he had had "personal interviews." Education? He always brought up the prep school where he had been. A graduate? Well, no.... College? Well, no college. In the end, he had to clarify himself as the graduate of a public high school. What could he do? Bookkeeping? Typing? No? Clerical work? What experience? Well, Flora had got him a job in a department store, selling furniture. Olga had got him a job in a publishing house, where he had been called somebody's "assistant," and done the work of an office boy. Run down and get some cokes, will you, Monty?

"No ..." he answered. "I'll find something else."

"Because, you see," she said, "I know Ramon is looking for two or three men—young men—the right type, for a new thing he's opening in Venezuela. You'd like that, wouldn't you?"

"Oh, yes!" Monty answered.

Oh, yes. And a fine chance I've got that this Ramon finds me the "right type." After last night. I wish to God I didn't have to see him.

"You'll excuse me if I leave pretty early, won't you?" he said. "I want to look for a room."

"Don't worry about that," she said. "Everything's so frightfully crowded now. It may take you days. But in the meanwhile, do use my brother's room. He won't be back for two weeks at least."

"But I—"

"I'll tell the desk to give you the key," she said.

The lunch arrived on a wheeled table, and just behind it came a young man.

"Ramon!" cried Doña Luisa, holding out both her hands. "Ramon, Montford Duchesne. Monty, Ramon Viceni."

Looking at the newcomer, Monty felt a chill dismay. It seemed to him that there was a likeness between them; they were both tall, broad-shouldered, slender; the same olive skin, the smooth black hair, the narrow skull. And whatever likeness there was only accented the difference between them. Ramon, Monty thought, was the real thing, the poised and charming young man of the world, with money, with a standing that was never questioned; and he felt himself to be no more than a shabby imitation.

"No lunch for me, darling," Ramon said. "Only coffee, please. I've just finished breakfast."

But he sat at the table with them, and he ruined everything for Monty; he poisoned everything. He was civil to Monty, and amiable. That's how he'd be to anyone, Monty thought. To any tramp, any bum he found in Doña Luisa's place. Being charming, showing his perfect manners. God, but I hate him.

"And why did you breakfast so late, Ramon?" asked Doña Luisa, with severity. "Where did you go last night?"

"I? I don't know. I think maybe I was in a little car hanging from a giant Ferris wheel, spinning round and round, and I could see all New York below me, all the lights sparkling, music always playing—"

"And in the little car with you ...? A pretty girl?"

"A different girl, every time the wheel made a full turn. And all of them beautiful."

"Ramon! Keep these fancies for one of your poems. You took Rose to Tia Clara's and then, she tells me, you disappeared. The chauffeur brought her home."

"She made me disappear. She gave me looks that were like needles. When I sat down beside her, she gave a loud, loud sigh. I was frightened. I said, do I bore you, Rosita? And she said, you make me sad. You make me nervous, being so gay. Look at the people here who have suffered."

"Who *was* there?"

"Women," he said. "All in black, like a flock of crows."

"Ramon! Don't talk like that."

"Forgive me!" he said, and taking her hand, he bent his head over it.

God, but I hate that damn—gigolo! thought Monty.

Doña Luisa relented, and gave him a smile.

"Now I'm going in my own room to make a telephone call," she said. "You can tell Monty about your new enterprise in Venezuela."

The two men rose as she did, and Monty remained standing when she had gone, closing the door after her. Ramon sat down again, and lit a cigarette.

"I'm sorry about last night," Monty said. "Miss Brown told me about it. Sorry if I gave you any trouble."

"It was nothing," said Ramon. "Nothing at all. When I got home, I was in a worse state than that. And think of the others like us, everywhere, in Paris, in London, in Buenos Aires—everywhere, all drowning the war, for one night, anyhow."

Being cosmopolitan, Monty thought. Damn show-off.

"I hear that I had some sort of delusion about getting a telephone call ..." he said, carefully, watching the other's face.

"The telephone did ring, all right," said Ramon. "But when you answered it, I don't think you even heard whoever was speaking." He laughed a little, showing his white teeth. "You were so worried about your little friend Nellie Something, I was sorry for you. I thought to myself, the poor devil has some petite amie he's trying to escape from. We all know how that is. You feel so angry and annoyed at a woman who won't let you go, and at the same time, you feel so guilty—"

"Sorry," said Monty, curtly. "But I don't feel guilty."

"Never?" said Ramon, laughing again. "Then you're one of the lucky ones. I remember a girl in Paris, a North American, she was, not very pretty, but she seemed so bold and brave. She said she believed love should always be left free; no chains. But—"

The door opened, and Doña Luisa re-entered. "You've been talking about your new enterprise, Ramon?" she asked.

"That?" he said. "It's really nothing to talk about, just now. No. We were talking about beautiful ladies."

Ah, yes, indeed! Monty said to himself. Yes, indeed. The old brusharoo.... God, but I hate that fellow!

"You'll excuse me, won't you, if I leave now?" he said to Doña Luisa.

"If you must," she said. "But don't worry too much about finding a room. You're welcome to stay here, you know, and everything is so crowded."

"Oh, you're moving?" asked Ramon. "You don't like the room you have now? In New York, is it? Because I have a friend who's looking everywhere for a decent room."

"This room isn't—available," said Monty. "It's needed, for one of the family. That's why I had to give it up."

He had felt, from the beginning of their talk, that Ramon was trying to draw him out about Nellie, trying to trap him. He felt certain now that Ramon was as much his enemy as Rose was, as determined as she was to find out all he was concealing. When he was back in his room, he lit a cigarette, and was alarmed to find his hands trembling. That won't do, he told himself. I can't afford to lose my nerve.

But it's a damned unpleasant feeling, to know that people are—hunting you....

Chapter Six

Later in the afternoon, he took a taxi to the Grand Central, and he found that there would be a train in forty minutes. He went to a cafeteria for a sandwich and a cup of coffee. Funny, to be seeing Flora again, he thought. And it was still funnier that he was rather pleased by the prospect. Well, after all, he thought, two years together ... And Flora has a great many good qualities. A great many.

One of the best things about her was that you could always talk to her. She was never inaccessible, never aloof, never in the least hysterical. In that last talk she had cried, but it had been very quiet crying.

"Very well, Monty," she had said. "If that's the way you feel ... Certainly I'll give you your freedom, if that's the way you feel."

He boarded the train and sat in the smoker, remembering that talk. It had been horrible to him, to hurt her like that. She had hurt him enough, she had humiliated him time after time, but she had never meant to, never had known when she did so. That time, at somebody's cocktail party, in a penthouse, when he had said something about Hoya's paintings.

"It's Goya, Monty," Flora had said.

"The Spanish pronounce G like H," he had said. "Like Don Juan."

"But that's a J, Monty!" she had said, laughing. And then she had said to the people standing near them: "Monty's so crazy about anything Spanish. I do hope he'll get to *one* Spanish-speaking country, sometime in his life."

Of course, Flora couldn't know what I'd been saying to that blonde girl, he thought. I shouldn't have talked that way, anyhow, telling her I'd been in Mexico, and all that. Bitterness and resentment were not natural to him;

what he had felt was a passionate longing to get away from Flora.

He remembered the first cocktail party they had given, in the apartment near Washington Square; he would remember that as long as he remembered anything. Flora had invited forty people, and he had asked two, just two fellows from the office. That was a bad start, and it had kept on being bad. Flora's people all knew one another well; they were all department store and display people, not interested in Flora's husband. His two guests had found themselves pretty and ultra-stylish girls to talk to, and he had moved about, trying his best to be a zealous host, but miserably unhappy.

There had been plenty of other things, humiliating and depressing enough. Well, Flora never meant it to be like that, he thought. She's dumb, that's all. She's so darned insensitive herself that she can't imagine anyone who isn't like that. She was very fond of me. She was very nice to me, in her way. It wasn't my way, that's all.

She had never noticed his increasing restless unhappiness. She had never noticed how negligent and rude her friends were to him, how scornful was her family. The third time he had lost his job, she had had a serious talk with him; indeed, all her talks were serious.

"I can get you a job in Price & Wykoff, Monty," she had said. "There'd be a good future there. But I shouldn't want to recommend you, Monty, unless I really thought you'd make good. Unless you'd really feel a sense of responsibility, dear."

That was when he had made up his mind that he couldn't stand any more, and a few days later he had begun that talk.

It was another woman, he had told Flora. He wanted to marry her. He knew Flora's principles about things like that; she had told him, even before they were married.

"I think a marriage should last just as long as *both* the partners are happy," she had said. "If either of them wants to be free, that ought to be enough."

She had taken his news gallantly, but she had been stricken.

"If it's been my fault—in any way," she had said. "If there's anything I can do—to change things ..."

She had made one more attempt.

"Monty," she had said, "you have a perfect right to your freedom. Only—don't you think that sometimes a—passing infatuation can—mislead you? Don't you think that perhaps if you waited a while ...?"

This girl, he had told her, would be mortally wounded by such a suggestion. She was very young, a debutante, a Junior Leaguer; she was ready to give up all that for him, and naturally she expected *something* from him.

So Flora had gone to Reno, and it was finished. The ardent debutante had never existed; he had invented her because he could not bring himself to tell Flora that all he wanted was to be free from her.

He got out of the train, and took a taxi. Very likely Flora would ask him why he hadn't married the debutante. She died? No.... Her family had wanted to break it up, and they had taken her to South America. No. I mustn't get South America into every damn thing. To Europe. They worked on her. They got her married off to an Italian count. Do they have counts in Italy? Maybe a French count. Then the war came, and he didn't know what had become of her.

It was a large and handsome house that Flora lived in. He told the taxi driver to wait, and mounted the steps; he rang the bell, and the door was opened by a maid in black and white uniform. He was impressed by this, and by the look of things, the prosperity, the order.

"Mrs. Adamson will be down in a moment, sir," said the maid, and left him in a fine drawing room; the furniture was good, all of it, solid and honest, but not modern. He stood there waiting, and now he was nervous, wondering how Flora would receive him. Will she bring her husband with her? he thought.

He heard footsteps in the hall, and he braced himself.

"Hello, Monty!" she said, in exactly her old way, unsmiling but friendly.

She had grown a little stouter, and it suited her. She was a handsome girl, very tall, with fine dark eyes; she looked queenly now, so straight, her bosom much fuller. She was wearing lounging pajamas of black silk, narrow trousers, a sort of Chinese tunic with a high collar, very stylish. All her clothes were in the best of style, and always somehow incongruous. It was her duty, her job, to be stylish, but at heart she cared nothing about it.

"Sit down, Monty!" she said. "Will you smoke?"

"Thank you. Can I give you a cigarette?"

"No, thanks, not just now," she said. "Will you have a drink, Monty? Scotch? Gin?"

"If you're having one ..."

"No, thanks. But that needn't stop you."

"No, thanks."

He saw now that she was nervous, too, and it surprised him. It disconcerted him. What did *she* have to be nervous about?

"How is everything, Flora?" he asked.

"Fine, thanks. I have two children—"

"Yes, I heard."

"They're rather nice," she said. "A boy—he's two—and a little girl six months old."

"I'd like to see your children someday, Flora," he said.

He meant it. It seemed to him somehow touching that Flora should have children; he was sure she was a very good and loving mother.

"I've changed," she said. "But not you. We're the same age, but now you look lots younger than me."

That depressed him a little.

"Well, God knows I ought to look older ..." he said.

There was a silence; glancing at Flora, he found her looking at him, and there was no doubt that he was nervous. But why? he thought.

"Have you got a nice job, Monty?" she asked.

"I haven't any job, just at the moment. I was working in a shipyard, but that's finished now."

"I'm afraid there isn't anything open at Price & Wykoff just now, Monty," she said, frowning anxiously.

"Oh, I'll find a job, all right," he said.

"I've got everything pretty well tied up in War Bonds just now, Monty...."

"Did you think I came to borrow money?" he sked.

Her cheeks grew scarlet.

"Well, I'd be very glad to help you, Monty—" he said.

"I'm sorry you thought that," he said.

He was cruelly hurt. But not angry at Flora; he new her too well.

"I've got plenty of money, thanks," he said.

"Well, you see, you said a business matter. I'm sorry, Monty."

There was another silence.

"No ..." he said. "It's this. I've met some South American people, and there's a chance of my getting a job down there."

She smiled a little, indulgently.

"That's always been your dream, hasn't it?" she said.

"I'm very anxious to get this," he went on. "But—well, you know how South Americans are."

"No, I don't, Monty," she said, and there was in her tone something very familiar to him, and very unwelcome. She was saying, in effect, no, I don't know how South Americans are—and *neither do you*. She had a boring passion for accuracy. If you tried to tell some little personal experience in an amusing way, she would be disturbed if you pointed it up a little.

"They're pretty personal about things," he proceeded. "I mean, business references aren't enough. They want to know about my—private life. I mentioned, of course, that I'd been married and—the thing is, would you have any objection if one of them came to see you, Flora?"

"Why, no. Certainly not."

"I told them that the break-up was my fault entirely."

"It wasn't, Monty. When I look back on it, I see lots of things I did that were all wrong."

"No," he said. "It was my fault, all of it. I was a fool—and worse. I couldn't tell you how I've regretted it. I'll go on regretting it, as long as I live."

"Monty, you mustn't. We were young when we married. We didn't know how to make allowances. And when I look back on it, I can see that I wasn't the right person for you. I was too—well—humdrum."

"You were the right person for me," he said. "And I threw away all that."

This distressed her very much.

"But, Monty, weren't you happy in your second marriage?" she asked.

"There never was any second marriage, Flora."

"But, Monty—"

"It never came off. I got over that—insanity, almost as soon as I'd lost you."

"But, Monty ... *Enid* met her."

"Met—who?" he asked.

"It was at a huge cocktail party in Baltimore—"

"What was Enid doing in Baltimore?" he cried.

"Oh, visiting someone. She met this girl, Monty. She was introduced to her. Dukie's wife."

O God! he thought. That was the party I couldn't get to till late. And Enid was there. Enid —met Nellie. O God!

"Enid said she was very pretty," Flora went on.

"Yes ..." he said. "We never were married, Flora."

"But you wouldn't introduce her to people like the Josephsons as your wife if you weren't really married to her!"

She was shocked, and that made him furious at her. Sweat had come out on his forehead, his hands were damp. O God! he thought. What'll I do? What'll I *say?*

"Enid, naturally, took it in good faith. She never dreamed—"

Enid was Flora's younger sister, and, he had always felt, his enemy from their first meeting.

"Naturally," he interrupted. "Look here, Flora! I didn't do that, introduce her as my wife. I couldn't get to the cocktail party until very late, so she—this girl—went on there alone. *She* told everyone she was Mrs. Montford Duchesne. When I got there, almost everyone had gone. Enid had gone, too. And when Mrs. Josephson and some of the others began to talk about what a charming wife I had, I realized what had happened. Very well. What would you have wanted me to do? Make a little speech, explain that I wasn't married to the girl, and never would be?"

"Oh, I see now ...!" said Flora. "What a miserable position for you, Monty. What did you do about it?"

The thing had happened as he had described it to Flora. He had stayed at the party for only a few moments, making so great an effort at polite affability that he had felt physically sick. He had been tired of Nellie for months before that, bored and irritated by her, and very much worried as to how he could get away from her. But that evening he had hated her.

"You haven't any decency," he had told her, when they were out in the street. "No self-respect. Calling yourself my wife—"

"Look here, fella!" she had said. "*You* started it. You used to call me your 'little wife.' You used to talk a lot about us getting married. You said you'd thought you wouldn't ever want to marry again, after the hell you went through, the first time. But you said you felt different now. All right! How's about it? Do we get married—and I mean *now*—or don't we?"

"I certainly don't feel in any hurry just now," he had answered. "Not after that damn common, underhand trick you played on me today."

They had walked on in silence along the dark street; a sea wind was blowing, steady and warm.

"Well ..." she had said, "I just sort of felt I had to—force your hand, Monty. I mean, you were just stalling—and I thought that once you quit that, and made up your mind, you'd be—such a lot better off.

"Once we're married, you'll be happy, Monty, *honestly* you will. I know how to keep a nice house, and cook nice meals." She had taken his arm and pressed closer to him. "And I know how to keep a man, Monty. Don't I? *Don't* I, Monty?"

He had drawn her nearer, but without speaking. When they reached the boardinghouse, where they were registered as Mr. and Mrs. Duke, he went up the steps to the door with her, and kissed her cheek.

"Good night, dear," he had said.

"But, Monty! Aren't you coming ...?"

"Not now," he had said. "I want to do some thinking, by myself."

She had entreated him, cajoled him, reasoned with him. He had been gentle, and sad, and he was sure she did not suspect then, or any other time, that he hated her.

"I can't come with you now," he had said, again and again. "Don't ask me, Nellie."

As soon as he had left her, he had gone to the railway station, and taken the first train back to New York. He had known she would come after him; he had, in fact, made no effort to hide from her. It would mean giving up his job, and the little hotel room he liked. *And,* he had thought, if she comes running after me, that puts her in a spot. If she starts to make a scene, I'll tell her that's just what I can't and won't put up with. Vulgar, I'll say it is.

She had come after him, and there had been a scene. She had started out with one of her poses he especially disliked, a little air of cool amusement; she would thrust her tongue in her cheek, and look at him sidelong, with her brows raised.

"Running out on me?" she had asked, sitting down on the bed in his very small room.

"I didn't run," he had said. "Just walked. I knew you could find me—if you wanted. But I hoped you wouldn't want to."

"*Why* not, angel?"

"I thought," he had said, "that you might have a little pride."

"I've got a different variety," she had said. "I don't let any man make a fool of me, and then go off and leave me flat. If I did say I was Mrs. Duke—"

"What?" he had cried.

"What?" she had repeated. "Well, isn't that what all this is about? Because I said I was your wife—Mrs. Duke."

He had felt a relief so great that what she went on to say did not trouble him.

"I'm going to have a baby," she had said. "Your baby."

He had not believed her; he had heard too many tales about girls working that racket just to get a man roped and tied. The miraculous thing was, that she had not found out his name. Duke, Dukie, Monty, that was all she knew.

Flora's voice brought him back to the present.

"Did you tell the Josephsons later that you weren't married?"

"No. I just cleared out of Baltimore, that very night. I never saw the girl again, and I didn't want to see the Josephsons, either. It was—the whole thing was too humiliating."

"Do you want Enid to tell them, Monty?"

"No, thanks. Better not. I had no business to let her go to this party, anyhow. She was a little tramp. I'm—not proud of the episode."

"I wish you could find the right girl, Monty."

"I did," he said.

"But you say you *didn't* marry her."

"I did—marry the right girl."

She looked up at him, troubled, honestly concerned about him, and a great affection for her rose and rose in him. He could trust her, always; she was so honest, so generous. They had been married, they had started to build a life together, and he had spoiled it all.

"You're happy, aren't you, Flora?"

"Well ... yes," she answered.

He understood the chivalrous reluctance she felt, sitting here in her solid, handsome home, with her husband, her babies, her family, her friends, her place in the world of dignity and honor, to speak about her happiness to him, who was alone in the world, with no home, no job, no record of any success in his past. The realization of his loneliness and his failure came over him like a physical pain. Why the hell did I ever leave Flora? he asked himself. She's got everything, the best sort of background; she's handsome; she's kind, generous, absolutely trustworthy. I don't know....

"Then you won't mind if one of the South Americans comes to you to ask you some questions about me?"

"But, Monty, if it's about—financial things and your—relations—"

"It won't be. It'll be character. Did I drink too much, take drugs, steal, forge, was I cruel to animals—"

"If it's about your character, I'll have plenty of nice things to tell them," she said, earnestly. I wonder ... he thought. I wonder what she thinks my character is like? Well, after all, what is it like? *I* don't know.

He rose and held out his hand; she took it in a warm clasp, and rose, too, almost as tall as he. "Monty, I hope you'll get this job that you want," she said. "I hope you'll be very happy, Monty."

"Thank you, Flora. Good night, dear Flora."

Chapter Seven

He had a long time to wait for a train, and he walked up and down the platform, walked fast. To hear Nellie's name again had agitated him, but not too badly, when it came from Flora. She was completely to be trusted; she was the most honest person he had ever known. And she was kind, too.

But the thing is, he thought, I can't seem to get *away* from Nellie. Maybe it was she who called me up. Maybe she's—well, somewhere around here. Maybe I'll see her, sometime.

Any time, anywhere. On this train he heard whistling along in the summer night. She'll know, he thought. She'll know I gave her something. And she won't keep quiet about it. Maybe she's been looking for me, all this time. She never knew my right name, or that address on Staten Island, but she might be able to find me, somehow. And if she does ... She could probably get me arrested, sent to jail....

I wish she would, he thought, and the thought astonished and terrified him. He tried to deny it to himself, but it was like something written in his brain. It's—the not knowing that's so bad, he thought. If I just knew whether she's alive now—or not.

When I gave her those pills, I didn't mean ... I only wanted to keep her quiet till I got away. I didn't mean—

I didn't care. That's the truth. I didn't know what they'd do to her, and I didn't care. But if only I knew now.... God, if I only knew she was alive.... But with this hanging over me—all the time.... All the time.... And her name coming up....

When he got back to the St. Pol, he went into the bar and ordered a whiskey. He hoped it might fortify him, yet he was afraid of it. I wish to God I *could* drink, he thought. A lot of people get help from it; they can forget their troubles.

He had a second drink and then went quickly up to his room, afraid that he might become dizzy, might stumble, might even fail down. He undressed, and got into bed, and fell asleep at once; when he waked, early in the morning, his trembling dread was gone. He thought about Doña Luisa. I can't expect her to call me up every day, he thought. Maybe I could call her ...?

And say what? Could I ask her out to dinner? Well, no, he thought. I don't know why, but somehow it wouldn't be right.... And she wouldn't accept. Flowers! he thought, suddenly.

He dressed, with his neat carefulness, and went downstairs. Breakfast here would cost too much, he thought. And there's nothing coming in now. I've got to remember that. I'll have to start looking for another job, in case this Venezuela thing is off. It's off already, if it depends entirely on that gigolo Ramon. But maybe she'll persuade him.... She wants me to get that job. She likes me.

He went into a drugstore and sat down at the counter.

"Coffee and Danish," he said.

"*What?* Danish?" asked a voice beside him, and he turned, to see a saucy, pretty blonde on the next stool.

"Well ... Sort of like coffee-ring," he answered.

"I don't know what 'coffee-ring' is," she said. "I'm just a little mountain girl—from ole Kaintucky."

This was a game he knew very well. In every little love-affair he had had, the girl, or the woman, had always begun it. Sometimes he had accepted, gladly, but many times he had slid away. He had never started to pursue any woman; from the time he was sixteen, they had gone after him.

A few, a very few, Olga for instance, had left him. But for the most part, he had left them. There was a possessive instinct in women that disgusted and frightened him. He would have chosen, like Ramon, to stand under a balcony, sing his song. But he did not want to be dragged into the house, to meet the family.

"Going....?" said the pretty blonde.

"Sugar," he said, "I have to make a living."

"Don't we all?" she said. "Well, maybe I'll run across you here again."

"Could be," he said.

There was a florist's shop in the lobby of the St. Pol, but he was not going there. It looks too easy, he said. As if I hadn't taken enough trouble for her. He walked over to Madison Avenue, to a florist's he had seen advertised, and on the way he tried to plan the note he would send her. It was so difficult that he grew angry. "Only to say thank you." No! That's as if I were trying to pay her back. "I think you like flowers." No! "Flowers for a most gracious lady." That's better, a little better. But I don't want that damn gigolo to read it.... No. "For Doña Luisa." But I don't know how that's spelt in Spanish. No! Damn it, I'll just write "With all best wishes— or good wishes...." From—well, Monty?

He picked out the flowers with the utmost care, and he enjoyed that. A spray of tiny orchids, six delicate yellow roses, six white carnations. "Send them to Mrs. Brown, at the St. Pol," he said. "Initials? Mrs. L. Brown. And before lunch, please."

He did not want to return to the hotel until the flowers had reached her, so he went on a little shopping tour; two new shirts, socks, a dressing-gown, other things he needed, and a suitcase to carry them. I've left a lot of really good stuff down there on Staten Island, he thought. Well, it'll just have to wait for a while.

For he certainly was not going to enter the Gettys' home. Not just now. They would be mad as hell, he thought, with me walking out on them like that. Well, they'd get over it. Gwen will find a new boy friend; I think she's got a couple on ice, anyhow. And later on, if I do have to go, I can say ... He reflected. I'll say that the excitement gave me amnesia. I went to New York, couldn't remember where I came from, where I was going. I got knocked down by a car, and I've been in the hospital.

He ate lunch in a cheap little place, and then he went back to the St. Pol, carrying the new suitcase. When he got into the elevator, there was Rose.

"Hello!" she said. "Going away?"

"No. Not just now."

"Could I come along to your room and talk to you?" she asked.

"Enchanted!" he said.

He felt far from pleased. That girl's just bad news, he thought. There'll be another cross-examination. Or maybe she's found out something.... No, she couldn't have.

He opened the door with his key and they entered. It looked very neat, very bare; it's not mine, he thought. Rose sat down on the arm of a chair, and he was obliged to admit that she was very pretty, very attractive, in a canary-yellow blouse, sheer, with long, full sleeves, and a hat that was little more than a saucy bow of black ribbon.

"I've been to see your wife," she said. "I mean, your ex-wife."

"Oh, *you* went, yourself?"

"Yes. She's *very* nice. *Very* nice."

"She is."

"She's handsome, too, and so well-bred."

"I wonder," Monty said, "what sort of girl you imagined I'd married?

A waitress? Or some cheap little nobody?"

"I didn't mean it that way," she said, apologetically. "I only mean I liked her so much. And she thinks a lot of you, Monty. Friendly toward you."

"I'm glad you're so satisfied," he said, with a faint, ironic smile. "Does it make you any less suspicious of me?"

"Tia Luisa is trying her best to make Ramon give you that Venezuela job."

"But he won't. He doesn't like me."

"Oh, it's not so personal as that," she protested. "He just feels that we— well, it's true, isn't it? We really don't know anything about you."

"He could get my record from the shipyard."

"I know. But, you see, that's not exactly business experience. And there must have been other jobs before that."

"He didn't ask me for business references." He paused. "I haven't any good ones, anyhow," he said, sure that any leads he gave would be investigated. "I never stole, or got drunk, or made any serious mistakes. I never got fired, either. It was simply that I'd never had any sort of training; there wasn't anything much I could do. Any job I got was third-rate, and I'd quit it for another I hoped would be more promising."

"There are lots of good courses in night schools," she said.

"Quite!" he said, again with that faint smile. "But I'll admit I didn't feel like working in a department store all day and then going to a night school."

"What did you want to be, Monty?"

"Me? Dick Tracy, Superman," he answered, still smiling to hide his resentment. Damn school-ma'am, he thought.

"We'd like to meet your mother," she said.

"What!" he cried.

"Perhaps she'd have lunch with me."

"Thanks," he said, "but it's very unlikely. She doesn't care about going out. And if you did meet her, you wouldn't know what to make of her. She's a very unusual woman."

"I like meeting unusual people," said Rose.

"I don't see what my mother's got to do with any of this," he said, sharply. "Or why she should be dragged into it."

"I'll tell you why," said Rose. "If you're going to stay here, going to keep on seeing Doña Luisa, I'd like to know more—quite a lot more about your background."

"Why don't you leave that to her?" he demanded. "She's a woman of the world; she's certainly capable of making her own judgments. Why do you think *you* have to hound me like this?"

"Because you're—mysterious. You're not candid."

"*You* are," he said.

"Those flowers ..." she said. "I didn't like them."

Their hostility was in the open now.

"Too bad," he said. "But, y' see, I didn't get them to please you."

"They're so expensive!" she cried. "So ostentatious."

She could not have said anything that hurt him more. Ostentatious, vulgar. He felt his face grow hot, and he turned away from her.

"I'm sorry I said that. Only ... She, well, let's drop it. If you'll just call up your mother and ask her what day she'd have lunch with me, or tea, anything she wants."

"*Why?* What reason am I supposed to give her?"

"Can't you just say there's a girl you'd like her to meet?"

"No. If it was that way, I'd naturally bring the girl to see my mother."

"You refuse to let me meet your mother, then?"

He did not know how he felt about his mother, what he thought of her. He never had known. Since childhood, she had irritated and exasperated him; she had neglected him; after his father died, she had done nothing, taken no interest in his education. The way she lived now was shameful. But, at the same time, he was not ashamed of her, and, in spite of all the long catalogue of her offenses against him, he had a curious trust in her, an angry affection, even love for her.

I don't see what harm she can do me, he thought. Certainly she would never want to do him any harm; she would, as always, be very willing to help. But if I let Rose get the idea that I'm ashamed of her ...

"I'll call her up," he said. "I'll ask her when she wants to see you. I'll tell her that someone in your family is considering me for a job and that you've taken it on yourself to find out more about me."

"All right!" said Rose. "Let me know, will you?"

"Naturally," he said.

"Thank you, Monty!" she said, and smiled.

That's it, he thought. Just let her have her own way, always, about everything, and she's a very nice girl. But I'm not such a nice boy. Not such a quick forgetter. He opened the door for her, and closed it again. *Ostentatious* ... he said to himself. Is that how they look to Doña Luisa?

She'll do something about them, though, he told himself. She'll thank me for them, some way. I'll have to wait, of course. He sighed. Well! he thought. I might as well go to see Mother.

She lived far uptown, and a taxi would be expensive. But he got into one. I feel like it, that's why, he told himself. I've got about a thousand in the bank, and a stack of Government Bonds. I needn't worry about money. If I don't get that job in Venezuela, I'll find something else.

Not another job with the pay he had got in the shipyard. Maybe never.

I'm damn glad I saved the way I did. He sighed again as the taxi came out of the north end of the Park and into the streets he knew and hated so well. His mother lived in a dingy old apartment house on a side street off Riverside Drive, a steep street, noisy with yelling children, radios, a street jaded and sweltering in the sun.

She had rented the apartment, furnished, for a month, and she had stayed in it for seven years. He had lived in it with her, for weeks at a time, and he had always been urging her to move. Oh, it's such a *terrible* bore to move, she would say. And it's really quite comfortable here. So it was. She knew how to make it so.

The card under her bell in the lobby read Mrs. Annabel Lacey, but she was not Mrs. Lacey, and never had been, and did not want to be. Why don't you and your shamus get married? Monty had demanded, again and again. Too silly, Annabel always told him. And too boring. We've both been married before, and that's enough.

He rang the bell, and when the latch clicked, he pushed open the door and entered the house. There were all the smells he remembered, onions frying, sauerkraut, smells of dust and mildew and insecticide. He went up the three flights of stairs with a slowness not natural to him. I'm so damn tired ... he thought.

His mother stood in the open doorway, and at the sight of him, she gave her beautiful smile of welcome.

"Monty, *dear* ...!"

She was, as usual, wildly untidy. She never had an apron, or a housedress, or anything clean and crisp; she wore one of the cheap, shoddy dresses she bought on Fourteenth Street, wore it until the seams burst, the buttons fell off; he noticed that today the neck of her crumpled gray rayon dress was fastened with a safety pin. But, for some reason he could not figure out, she had distinction. She was tall, lithe, and slender, her black hair glossy, her blue eyes clear and merry under her dark brows.

"Come in, my darling pet!" she said. "It's—been a long time...."

The sitting room was in wilder disorder, papers and magazines on the floor, an opened package of laundry on a chair, a dingy little flowered hat perched on a lampshade; the furniture was of cheap varnished oak, the paint was peeling off the walls, the rug was worn thin as paper. But the place had a smell of fresh air; in all its untidiness, it seemed somehow clean, as she herself always was, with her fair skin, her shining hair, a faint fragrance about her.

"This is a hell of a place," Monty said.

"I don't know ..." she said. "I've got rather fond of it."

Here she lived with a retired police sergeant, Jimmy Lacey, and they were both very contented. Annabel had long ago deserted everyone she had known in other days; she had no friends, and wanted none. She was on excellent terms with the tradespeople, with neighbors, with anyone; she was polite, cheerful, attractive. "You make people think you like them," Monty had told her, "but you really wouldn't care if they dropped dead in front of you."

"Well, as long as they don't suspect it ..." she had said, amused.

But how will she seem to Rose? he thought. She can make herself look nice enough, when she takes the trouble, she speaks very well, she has good manners; she went to one of the best finishing schools; her parents took her to Europe three or four times. She's had all the things, the advantages I never got.

In a way, he trusted her completely. She would never mention her policeman to Rose, never say anything tactless, anything that would show her son in a poor light.

"Jimmy home?" he asked.

"Yes. He's reading," she answered.

They never went out, except to buy something. Never. They never went to a movie, never went visiting, never ate a meal in a restaurant. They had a massive television and radio cabinet, which they never turned on at random, but only for programs they had discussed and carefully selected; but for the most part, they sat reading, always in the diningroom, at the far end of the old-fashioned railroad flat. They read everything, old classics, new books, magazines. "I had a poor education," Lacey had told Monty. "In the old days, when I joined the Force, there was not so much required as in these days. But now ... Your mother's the finest teacher ever lived. She's the one tells me what to read. *Robinson Crusoe*, and Plato's *Dialogues*, *Tom Sawyer*, Shakespeare, all that."

"Jimmy's got a very good mind," Annabel told her son. They had a great respect for each other, great affection. Sometimes, when he had been staying for any length of time, Monty would almost forget the fantastic and discreditable situation, and see them as they appeared to their neighbors, a model couple, good, honest, respectable people.

"Look, Mother ... he said. "This happens to be very important to me. I've met these South American people—"

"Darling, you always *wanted* to meet South Americans."

"There's a chance that they might give me a job—but you know how they are."

"Darling, I *don't* know how they are."

"I mean—" he said, "they want to know more about—well—my background."

"Oh, *me?*"

"Yes. This girl, Rose ... She wants to meet you."

"A girl, Monty? Are you in love with her?"

"I am not," he said, curtly.

"I wish you'd marry again," said Annabel. "It's the only way to live, darling."

"You're a fine one to talk," he said, with a faint smile.

"Oh, well—" she said, and her smile was wide and gay. "Same thing, Monty. But why should a girl be doing this?"

"She's taken it on herself," he said. "She thinks I'm—a phony, a crook—God knows what. She's trying to find out something about me that will discredit me."

"But why, darling?"

That was a hard one to answer. He was silent for a time, sitting on the arm of a most hideous chair.

"Well ..." he said, at last. "Her aunt's interested in me. Her aunt—she's the most remarkable woman.... She ..."

"I see ...!" she said, and was silent for a moment. "Do you want me to call on these people, dear?"

"No, no. The girl wants to have lunch with you somewhere, tea, whatever you like. She'll call you up, when I give her the number."

"You're not coming with us?"

"No. She wants you alone—to see if she can't get something out of you—to discredit me."

"But, Monty ... What a queer idea! Your own mother—"

"She's hounding me, all the time."

"But, Monty—" she began, and stopped. "I'll be glad to see her, darling," she said. "What happened to that other one?"

"What other one?"

"The one you brought to see the television show. Nellie, that was her name. Nellie."

Sit still! he told himself. Don't let your hands shake.

"I don't know," he answered. "I haven't seen her for—a long time."

"She rather terrified me," said Annabel.

"Why?"

"I thought she was the type you'd have all the trouble in the world to get rid of," said Annabel.

He licked his lips.

"No," he said.

"I was afraid she'd get you," Annabel went on. "She was so possessive, and—I can only think of one word. Perky. A common, perky kind of girl."

She wade Nellie come alive, before his eyes, slender, trim, with slanting black brows and a big, ugly mouth plastered by crimson lipstick into a great oval. Alive ... She's alive, somewhere, he told himself.

"Sure you don't want a drink, Monty? Or a nice hot cup of coffee?"

"No, thanks."

"You look—tired," she said.

"I'm fine," he said, curtly. "Mother, if Rose asks you about Father, I'd rather you didn't tell her."

"But tell what, Monty? There wasn't anything queer about him."

"I mean, the way he treated me. I was eight when you got your divorce. And he never saw me again. Never wanted to. Never wrote to me."

"But, darling, it's nothing against *you*, if he—"

"I'm ashamed of it," he said, vehemently. "I always have been. I used to tell other kids that he was dead. I never let anyone know that he—simply hadn't any use for me. He didn't die until more than twelve years later—and he never wanted to see me."

"I didn't know you were so unhappy about it, Monty dear. I didn't even think you missed him particularly."

"It's not *that!*" he said, angrily. "It's not grief. It's—I'm *ashamed* of it."

"But, darling, he was like that, about everything. Really implacable. He told his sister, the nice one—remember Aunt Mimi? He told her that if she ever came to see me, or wrote to me, he'd never speak to her again. He told people we'd both known that they'd have to 'choose' whether they'd keep on seeing me, or him. He said it was going to be a 'clean break.' He liked that expression. He'd had a 'clean break' with his brother, years before, and he wanted to have a 'clean break' with business people and so on."

"Well, don't tell Rose about that."

"I won't," she said.

"And—" He licked his lips again. "Don't mention—that girl."

"Nellie? I wouldn't *dream* of it, darling! Why should I? I don't know why I happened to think of her, especially. Except that for a while I really was worried. I wondered how you'd ever get rid of her—"

Chapter Eight

He walked downtown, along the side of the Park. Nothing's happened to Nellie, he thought. She's too damn tough. *She's* all right. I might see her, any day, any minute. God, I hate her! "Perky" ... That's a good word for her. But I can think of better ones.

He remembered a dark-blue suit she had had, with a short jacket that stuck out in back like a robin's tail. That was perky, all right, he thought. I hated that suit. I hated the new way she started doing her hair. Her head was too big, anyway. She—

He saw her, waiting at the next corner to cross the street. He stopped, rigid with horror. There she was, and in an instant she would turn her head and see him. She would come straight up to him, look up into his face with her chin in the air, and that one-sided smile like a sneer. Oh, no, you don't, Monty! You don't get away *this* time. God, I hate her so much I could ...

She turned her head, and it was not Nellie, not anyone at all like her. I can't go on this way, he told himself. That was—almost crazy. If I don't do something about it, it might happen again. I might start thinking I saw her all the time. No, I've got to find out. Find out if she's in New York, or—

All right. Find out if she's dead or alive. That's what I mean.

And which would be worse? If she's alive, she'll find me, somehow, and that'll finish me with Doña Luisa, forever. Maybe it was true about the baby. Maybe she had one, and maybe it's mine. Looks like me.

He had a mental vision of a thin and foreign-looking little boy in a sailor suit, with a face unmistakably resembling his own. Hey, Poppa! it would yell, in a common nasal voice. No! That's crazy. If she did have that baby, it must be a year old, or less....

And if she—isn't alive? No! Let her be alive. Not lying there, in that bed, in that place.... She drank the stuff I gave her. She never thought ... I didn't want to do her any real harm. I swear I didn't! I just wanted to keep her quiet while I got away. Let her be alive.

Let him see her, alive, when he turned the next corner. Then he would never again have that other image in his mind, of her lying in that bed, in that place.

He stopped a taxi and got into it, overcome by that strange weakness. I'll think of a way to find out about her, he told himself. Only forget it now. Because to think of it was a mortal danger; he was convinced of that. If he thought about it, he would give himself away, somehow; there would be a look in his eyes, perhaps.... The mark of Cain ... he thought. What was it? A mark on his forehead, wasn't it? How did they know it meant that he'd—done that? Did it come suddenly? There were two mirrors in the cab, but they were strangely blurred; he could not see his image in them.

I will not! he cried to himself. I will not be such a fool. Such a craven. But he had to do it, had to push back his hat and draw his hand back and forth across his forehead. Damn nonsense! Look at the pictures of all other men who—are on trial. No marks on them.

He got out before the St. Pol, and there was Ramon, turning away from the desk, with a sheaf of letters in his hand. I don't get any mail, Monty thought. That must look queer.... But, anyhow, I can't stay here, using her brother's room.

"Duchesne!" said Ramon, with his vivid smile. "Let's go into the bar and have a drink, yes?"

"Well, thanks!" Monty answered, and at once regretted it. I shouldn't have said "thanks," he thought. As if I took it for granted he was going to pay for me. As if it was a treat. "Just a moment," he said, and wrote on a card the clerk gave him. "This is my mother's telephone number, as you requested. M. D."

"Put it in Miss Brown's box, please," he said.

The cocktail lounge was almost empty, a dim room with a blurred look, curtains of cotton tapestry in dull browns and blues, a dull-blue carpet; the bar had no mirror behind it. Along the walls were small tables, and chairs with tapestry-covered seats; all dull and dim, yet in no way depressing; it had some charm of its own. They sat down at a corner table, and a waiter came immediately, stood before them, his gray head a little bent, an expression of pleasant patience on his face.

"A rum collins, please," Ramon said.

"The same," said Monty.

I've never tasted rum, he thought. Maybe I won't like it, but what do I care?

"I needed this," Ramon said. "I have to go up to Tia Luisa, you know, with a full report about Tia Clara."

"Something—gone wrong?"

"With her? With Doña Clara? Everything is wrong. She is Doña Luisa's aunt, you know; she is growing old now, nearly sixty. But she's talking now about getting married again."

Monty glanced at him sidelong.

"She's a widow?" he asked.

"Once. Then there was another marriage; that was annulled. A miserable thing that was; she married a fellow young enough to be her son. She gave him everything, lavished money on him. And, well, the usual thing happened."

"What's the usual thing?" Monty asked.

He knew now why Ramon had asked him in here for a drink, and Ramon was well aware that he knew.

"A young fellow who marries a much older woman for her money's not a very strong character, no? That one was fickle; he began to look for young, pretty girls. In the end, Doña Clara caught him with her maid. This new one will be worse, because the poor woman is older now, and stout, you know, and I've heard he already has a girl he's keeping."

"Too bad," said Monty. "If you'll excuse me, I've got to get along. Waiter! Check, please."

He was a little surprised that Ramon let him pay for the two drinks without protest. It's his damned tact, his damn beautiful manners. They went up in the elevator together, they got out at the same floor, Ramon, who was the real thing, easy, handsome, rich, going to Doña Luisa, while Monty, the imitation, went down the corridor to the room that did not belong to him.

All right. I quit, he told himself. The flowers were "ostentatious." I'm a gigolo, just trying for Doña Luisa's money. Maybe they've made her believe that now. All right. I'll get out of here tomorrow morning. I'd go now, only I'm—I don't know ... Tired. I don't want any dinner.

It had been this way with him before, this utter depletion of body and mind; days when he *could not* go to work; days in his boyhood when he could not get up and go to school. He would lie stretched out in bed for a whole day and night, not asleep, except for a doze now and then, but not quite awake, either.

He unlocked the door, and turned on the switch, and there he saw a card that must have been pushed under the door.

MRS. EMILIO JOSE BROWN

"Dear Monty," she had written on it. "Your flowers! So lovely—and I have arranged them in the most artistic way. Won't you come in for a cocktail at half-past five, and see for yourself?

Luisa Brown"

No! he thought. I can't do it. Not with that fellow there, I can't. I couldn't talk to her, with him there. No, I quit. He sat down in an armchair by the window, almost fell into it. His knees were like water, his hands trembled, and worst of all, he could not think. I've lost everything, he said to himself. Everything's gone. I wish I was dead.

The sun came in at the open window; he could hear the sounds from the street below, trucks, taxis, the siren of an ambulance. What time is it? he thought. What day is it?

It was an effort to look at his wrist-watch. Quarter past five. I don't want to see her, and then go away, and never see her again. I don't know where to go. Where to look for a job.

He had been holding her card in his hand; it fell to the floor, and he stooped to pick it up, and was struck with the sharpest pain. I can't go like this. Just walk off, when she's written so sweetly. They haven't turned her against me yet, and maybe they never can. I can tell her anything, and she'd understand.

He got himself ready, with his usual extreme neatness, put on a new and expensive necktie. The miserable fatigue still weighed upon him, but he felt that he need make no particular effort. Not with her. He could sit there for a while, and watch her, and sometimes they would smile at each other.

He knocked at the door, and Ramon opened it.

"Ah!" he said. "Here we are again, yes?"

For a moment it seemed to Monty that he saw Doña Luisa enshrined, in a chapel, haloed in gold, surrounded by flowers. She was smiling at him, such a smile as he had never seen, so benign, so lovely.... She held out her hand, and he bent over it, raised it to his lips. He had never done that before, but it seemed natural now.

"Look!" she said. "Look at my flowers!"

She had indeed arranged them to make a fine display. But on the window sill he saw a pretty little wicker basket filled with tiny pink roses and sweet alyssum; he saw another vase of flowers he did not know. From other people ... he thought. Well, why not? She's—she's like a queen.

Ramon came out of the serving-pantry with a tray of cocktails; he held out his cigarette case to Doña Luisa, and then to Monty; very polite, he was. Maybe he'll go pretty soon, Monty thought. They all sat, smoking, sipping their cocktails, and the golden halo was sinking, below Doña Luisa's shoulders.

"Now we shall be hearing from Billy," she said. "But I suppose it will be—oh, months before they let him come home from Japan."

"Rita is quite mad," Ramon said. "She rang up her hairdresser at once. Billy might come by plane, she said. He might come any *minute*. I *must* get my hair done, and a manicure."

From time to time, Doña Luisa tried to include Monty in some sort of conversation, but it was too difficult. They had a world of their own, and he could not enter it. The golden sun went lower; the perfume of the flowers was too strong; Monty refused another cocktail, and rose.

"Thank you," he said.

"But thank you!" she said.

If she would only say, I'll be seeing you soon. If she would say—call me up tomorrow. He went back to his room and sat down again beside the window, limp, his mind blank. He dropped asleep, and when he started up, hearing the knock on the door, the room was filled with a dusk like smoke.

It was Rose.

"If I could speak to you for just a moment ...?" she asked. "Doña Luisa's ordered dinner already so I won't bother you for long."

"Sit down, please!" he said.

He offered her a cigarette, and lit it for her. But he did not turn on any of the lights.

"Found out something new against me?" he asked.

She did not answer that.

"I saw your mother this afternoon," she said. "She's a charming person."

"Where did you meet?"

"I went to her apartment."

My God! he thought, angrily. "My mother's not much of a housekeeper," he said, aloud. "I wish you'd met somewhere else."

"Well, I really preferred going there. And your mother was glad. She says she doesn't like to go out. She really is charming, Monty."

"Nice of you to say so."

"I don't say things if I don't mean them."

"I've noticed that," he said.

There was a silence between them. Her face looked white in the dusk; "implacable," he thought, remembering the word his mother had used about his father. She hasn't finished with me yet.

"Monty," she began. "I don't want to seem unkind, or suspicious. But—well, you can see, can't you? You just appeared, out of nowhere. You didn't seem to live any place, or have friends coming to see you. Or any plans. And Tia Luisa is so very—"

"So very what?"

"She's such a darling, unreasonable creature. She makes these snap judgments, all the time. Either she likes people at once, at first sight, or she takes a dislike to them. And you can't imagine how hard it is to convince her when she's wrong. She had a half-Indian boy for a gardener once, and nothing could make her believe, for ages, what a horrible sort of person he was."

"I see!" said Monty. "And now you feel you have to make her see that I'm something horrible?"

"It's not that, Monty. It's just that—I want to know about you. You see, you're staying here—"

"No, I'm leaving tomorrow.

"Oh, are you? Have you found a nice place?"

He had been very much offended, nettled by that reference to the half-Indian gardener, but, in spite of that, he was obliged to recognize that the girl was more considerate toward him, altogether nicer than she had ever been before. Flora had helped, he thought, and now his mother.

"Who's Mrs. Getty, Monty?" she asked.

He sat very still.

"Getty?" he said, as if wondering. "Getty?"

"She telephoned your mother while I was there, Monty, and I couldn't help hearing. Your mother has a lovely voice, and very clear. She said, 'Mrs. Getty? I'm sorry, but I don't remember ... Oh, my son stayed with you? On Staten Island? I see!' Then she seemed terribly startled. 'His effects?' she said. 'Oh, *no!* He's not dead, Mrs. Getty. No. There wasn't any accident. He's quite well.'

"Then, you know how some people's voices come right out of the telephone.... Mrs. Getty was in such a fury she was almost screaming, in a high, cockney voice. I couldn't hear all she said, only a bit here and there. 'As good as engaged to my daughter, 'e was,' she said. 'And 'e walked off, without so much as kiss me 'and. Not a word. Left all his things here.'"

She paused, obviously waiting.

"Anything to say about the Gettys?" she asked, after a moment.

"Not a thing."

"Nothing about being as 'good as engaged' to that girl?"

"I wasn't. That's all."

"Did you really just walk out on them?"

"I'd paid my board a week in advance just the day before. Is it criminal to leave a boardinghouse if you feel like it?"

"But—why did you leave your things there? Why didn't you tell them you were leaving?"

"Because I knew there'd be a hell of a scene, that's why. Both Mrs. Getty and Gwen were trying to trap me into marrying that girl."

"Without any encouragement from you?"

"Look here!" said Monty, in a tone of weary exasperation. "You've never known people like the Gettys. I don't think you've seen much of life, anyhow."

"Well ..." she said, surprised and a little abashed. "I think I have."

She stubbed out her cigarette in a tray on the table beside her, and with a painful effort, Monty rose, gave her another and lit it.

"I suppose you'll go and see the Gettys," he said. "The way you did Flora, and my mother. Well, if you do, you'll get something satisfactory, at last. *They*'ll tell you God knows what about me. They'll make up all sorts of vicious lies, and you'll believe them, of course. All right! I'm—I'm tired."

"There's only one thing more," she said, almost gently. "I told you I couldn't help hearing Mrs. Getty. She told your mother that when she was packing up what she called your 'effects,' she came across a receipted bill from a motel in Bagleyville. It was for a cabin for Mr. and Mrs. Monty Duke. She was sure it was you, and that you'd married again, under a false name. While you were courting her daughter."

This is it, he thought.

"Are you married now?" she asked.

"No," he said. "Let me alone. I'm—tired."

"Did you go to that place, that motel with a woman you pretended was your wife?"

"Let me alone," he said.

"Gladly!" she cried. "If you'll go away tonight, and promise not to see my aunt again, or call her up, or write to her."

"Tomorrow."

"Tonight," she said. "*I* don't care what you've done in the past, how many nasty, sordid love-affairs you've had. I just want you out of Doña Luisa's life. It's—can't you *see* how it looks? You're staying here—free—in my uncle's room. You haven't any job. You're—just queer and mysterious. Your mother's a charming person, but—she's mysterious, too. Go away *now*."

"Tomorrow," he said, again.

He was too ill, too exhausted to hold his own. The room had grown darker, and he was glad of that. She can't see me, he thought, and he was obliged to raise his hand and feel his forehead.

The telephone rang, and rang, and rang.

"Do you want me to answer it?" she said.

"No," he said.

He got up and crossed the twilit room, sat down on the bed and took up the receiver.

"Monty?" asked Doña Luisa's voice.

I love you! he thought. I love you so. I need you so.

"Monty?"

"Yes, Doña Luisa."

"Is my naughty Rose there with you?"

"Yes."

"Ramon and I are waiting for her, to eat our dinner. Will you tell her, please?"

"Yes, Doña Luisa."

"Monty, if you're not engaged, why don't you come, too? I'd be very pleased."

"Thank you," he said, "but I'm sorry. I—can't. I'm sorry. I—thank you."

"Well, soon, then," she said.

He hung up the telephone and sat where he was.

"Your aunt's waiting for you," he said.

"Will you go away tonight?" she asked.

"No."

"Then I shall tell her."

"You haven't anything to tell," he said.

"Will you promise to leave early tomorrow morning, without—?"

"No," he said. "I'm not going to promise you anything. Ever."

She rose, and went to the door; when she opened it, the light in the hall shone on her; he had a glimpse of her in a long dinner dress fitted smoothly to her fine, straight body, her hair was dressed high on her proud head. She looked taller; she looked stately. Like—who was it? he thought. That goddess that was always hunting.... Diana, was it? She's hunting me.

But she won't catch me. And she won't drive me away from here, he thought. Doña Luisa's voice had done that for him; it seemed to him as if she had brought him back from death. His despair had gone, and his horrible exhaustion.

He went out and ate dinner in a little restaurant, and all the time he was thinking of what he would have to do, to evade his huntress.

Chapter Nine

For God's sake, why did I keep that bill? he thought. I don't know.... These things just happen. You put a bill or a letter, or a card, in one of your pockets, or in some book you're reading, and you forget all about it. It just happens, that's all.

Or was it fate?

There's no such thing as "fate," he told himself. He had waked early, too early; the room was as it had been when Rose was here. When Rose had said "Bagleyville." She'll find out where it is, and she'll go there. She knows that Mr. Duke was me, and she'll ask ...

Well, if—nothing happened to Nellie, if she just waked up in the morning, she'd have been mad as hell when she found I'd got away from her, and she'd probably talk. Talk plenty to the woman who ran the place. What was her name? He thought for a moment, and then he remembered how it had been printed on the bill. *Turn in at Turner's.* If Rose finds Mrs. Turner, she'll probably hear the whole thing. How I'd given Nellie some sleeping medicine, and driven away.

All right. I can say I didn't give her any medicine, and why isn't my word as good as hers? I'll say we had a fight, and when I left, she took the stuff herself. It wasn't anything I was proud of, but it was just—an escapade. I mean, I never pretended I was a saint....

And if she—all right. If she didn't wake up, if she died, it's the same story. We had a fight, and after I'd left, she committed suicide. That's how it must have to look to everyone, anyhow. Because if there'd been any suspicion that it—wasn't suicide, it would have got in the newspapers. I watched the papers.... Just a suicide of a cheap little nobody, in an out-of-the-way place like that, wouldn't get in the New York papers, but if they thought it was ... All right! If the police thought it was murder, the tabloids would have played it up. Pictures, everything. They'd have found me, long ago. I can say I didn't know she'd died....

But I've got to know. It's—been preying on my mind too much, lately. I mean—I've got to know if Nellie's still around, or not. I'm going out to

Bagleyville this morning. I'll see Mrs. Turner. I'll tell her I've never heard a word from—I'll call her "Mrs. Duke" since we took that cabin, and I'll ask her if she knows where Mrs. Duke went.

Why not? I'll find out what story Rose would have heard, and maybe I can get it changed. I don't remember what Mrs. Turner looked like. Young, or old? Some of the people that run those places are pretty tough babies. Anything goes. You don't have to have any luggage, don't even have to have a wedding ring. You can come as often as you like with a different "wife," as long as you pay in advance. Maybe if I paid her something ...?

No! She would keep after you, blackmail you the rest of your life. Just try to—win her over. God! he said to himself, in surprise and a certain dismay. What a lot of that I've done! Winning people over ... It's—I don't know why I do it. Flora, he thought, and Gwen, and a lot of others. A lot. Only not Olga. She walked out on me.

It gave him comfort to think of Olga. They had had a date to meet at a certain restaurant they liked, and it was a thing taken for granted that he would go back with her, to spend the night in her apartment. But early that morning, he had got a note, delivered by messenger. "I am so sorry, my dear little pretty Ermino, but I have grown tired of this. I'm sorry, but that is my nature. Very quickly I grow tired of a job, a place, even, alas, of persons. I think we don't have fun together any more. Anyhow, I am off to California this morning, by plane. Then when the war is over, I shall go somewhere else. I am not too sad, because you will very soon find another sweetheart."

There had been more, but he couldn't remember it. Anyhow, she walked out on me, he thought, with satisfaction. *I* certainly wasn't "too sad" about it. I didn't like her very much. She was too cynical.

But the others? Flora—all the others that he had grown tired of? He had read articles, and a few popular books on psychiatry, and they had greatly appealed to him. They pointed out how things were not your own fault. Somebody had done something to you when you were a kid, your parents, usually.

That's it, he thought. It was Father. He let me know he had no use for me, so I had to try to make other people like me. It was all subconscious. I couldn't help it.

He fell asleep then, and when he waked, it was eight o'clock. He got up at once, to take a shower and shave and dress. He was out of the hotel well before nine, and he went to a garage he had found in the Red Book. He wanted to hire a U-Drive-It car, as he had before, but they wanted a bigger deposit, and they would not take a check. He called up Penn Station and asked about trains to Bagleyville, and there was one at ten-twenty.

So he had time to get breakfast; three cups of coffee would help him, he thought, but as he walked to the station, his sense of urgency, of haste, had increased. He sat down by a window in the smoker, and lit a cigarette. Take it easy! he told himself. Take it easy! Doña Luisa will listen to me, she'll give me a chance, no matter what Rose tells her. An escapade, that's all....

Then he thought, suppose Rose is on this very train? Suppose we get out together ...? She wouldn't let me go to see Mrs. Turner without her.... Damn her! Why does she hound me like this? She probably has a lot of money; she probably paid someone in the hotel to let her know when I went out. She's hired someone to follow me.

Stop it! he told himself. That's crazy. Nobody's following me. I mean— if you get thinking things like that, it's—what do they call it? Persecution mania, or something.

Yet when he got out at Bagleyville, he looked quickly up and down the platform; he stood there until the train pulled out and he was certain no one else would descend.

It was a miserable little wooden station, standing among flat fields, parched in the hot sun. There were no other passengers, no coming and going, no activity; it was as still as if under a spell. It was the sort of country, the sort of scene, he most disliked; sometimes in a nightmare he would be in such a place, and he would have to start running, desperately, from someone or something in pursuit of him. He would run and run, in this flat world; there were no houses, not a tree, not a big rock, nothing ahead but flat road and flat earth. If there would be one single human figure, one building, house, barn, shed ...

Nothing had ever happened in these nightmares; whatever pursued him never had caught up with him, yet he would wake from them in a sweat of terror; he would turn on the light, and see four solid walls around him. If he were lucky, there would be a sleeping girl there, and all terror dissolved at once. If he were alone, it took longer, but the comfort always came. There were other people, lights, voices, telephones; there was human life.

He went into the waiting room, and found it almost incredible. There were three rows of slatted benches, all empty, and all broken in one way or another; there were two brass spittoons from another era. The ticket-seller's wicket was pulled down, there was nobody here. He did not know what to say. "Hey!" he said, and then "Hiyah!" No answer. He saw a door leading somewhere else; he opened it, and there was another platform, deserted, except for a sagging old car with a card in the window. *Taxi service.*

The driver was beyond belief; he was something out of a comic. He was reading a comic book, too, with a straw in the corner of his enormous mouth; he had a thatch of corn-colored hair, and the face of an idiot.

"I want to go to Turner's Motel," Monty said.

The yokel turned upon him eyes of cornflower blue.

"What?"

"Isn't there a motel here?"

"Motel ...? Now, let's see.... Is that a kind of an auto court, like? Little cabins, and all?"

"That's it. Take me there."

The yokel started his car, which was an old two-door sedan.

"United Nations Auto-Court, they call it," he said. "Jeeze, I wish them United Nations would get together quick—before I get called up. *I* don't want to fight in no wars."

"Mrs. Turner still running the place?"

"She—is—not," answered the yokel, with emphasis. "They was a suicide there, a while ago, and Mrs. Turner, she thought it was bad luck, and she sold the place to these two guys. They—"

"Hold on!" said Monty. "I don't want to go there if Mrs. Turner's left."

No, he thought. I can go home. The whole thing's finished. Rose can't find out anything from these new people that run the motel. I can go home.

But then he thought that Rose wouldn't give up so easily. She would find other people to question; she would want to find Mrs. Turner.

"D' you know where Mrs. Turner's gone?" he asked.

"Gone?" said the yokel. "Hasn't gone nowhere. Lives right near here."

"Drive me there, will you?"

"Sure will. If you ask me, those guys she sold her place to, they're a couple of crooks, gangsters. They got a *motorboat.*"

"What's about a motorboat?" asked Monty.

"Well," the yokel said, "that's what they use for crimes, you know. For people they get wrapped up in cement, and for smuggling and gambling, and all. *I* wouldn't set foot in the place."

"I'll see Mrs. Turner instead," said Monty. "You *do* know where she lives?"

"Sure," said the yokel. "They tell me she made good money out of the place when she run it, and she got a price when she sold to them gangsters. Gee-ee-whizzz ..." he said, slowly. "I don't know why the cops don't crack down on them gangsters. One thing is they sell liquor, and they haven't got no license, see? But another thing that's worse, they got white slaves there."

Monty was bored with this talk; he said nothing.

"White slaves," the yokel went on, with relish. "They get 'em, you know, young ones, real innocent. They take all their clothes away—"

He went on and on, and Monty looked out at the flat fields.

"Crime," said the yokel. "Why, there's crime all the time. And what do the cops do? What does the President of the United States do? Nothing. They don't stop crime."

They had come now into the main street of a very small village. There was a tavern on the corner, then a stationer, a grocer, an empty store, a shop window with women's hats displayed on stands, all of them crooked, one of them half fallen off, with a blue quill upright, like a flag; on the other corner, a druggist. Did I come this way before? Monty asked himself. Did I see this before?

He could remember nothing of his drive out here with Nellie, not the flat meadows, not the village street. Not how he had felt, not what was in his mind. But it wasn't—that, he thought. I never—planned anything like that.

But he could remember how Nellie had talked. "What'll we call him, Monty?" she had asked.

"Call who?"

"Our baby. You know, Monty, lots of girls I know are scared stiff about having a baby. But not me! I'm crazy about kids. Are you?"

"I wouldn't know. I've never had anything to do with them."

"Just wait till you see your own. I bet you'll be crazy about him. Could we buy a house, Monty?"

"No," he had told her. "I haven't got that kind of money."

"Then we could rent one. A nice yard, for the kiddies, and we could get to know the neighbors, and you could teach me to play bridge, and all."

It was as if he could hear her voice now, close to him. She had kept on, painting a picture of that life she thought would charm him. Suburban life, at its cheapest, among *her* sort of people.

"We could ask your mother to come and visit us," she had said. "And maybe we could ask my brother and his wife, next time they hit New York, and my sister." She had laughed. "But not for long, will we, Monty? We're not going to have any in-law troubles, are we?"

He had never spoken to her of marriage. But she had thought the best way was to pretend to take it for granted.

"I wrote and told my folks I was going to get married," she had said. "I told the gang in the office I was going to get married."

She knew damn well I didn't want to marry her, he thought. I don't know why she was so hell-bent on getting me. Unless she really was going to have a baby, and she felt she had to marry somebody. Anybody. Maybe she knew from the start that it wasn't my kid. She never made any secret about the other men she'd had, ever since she came to New York at eighteen. Only she lied about this, the way she lied about everything. A bank president, she had told him, a famous actor; a likely tale.

They had turned into a wide boulevard, lined with woodlands. I think I remember this, he said to himself. Only, there are such a lot of places like this. Maybe he had driven along here, with Nellie beside him, talking about the cheap, mean little life they were going to have together.

I was trying to think of some way to tell her we weren't going to get married, he thought. Karky, in the shipyard, gave me the name and address of a doctor who'd fix her up. When we got to this motel, I meant to talk to her.

Yeah? And you had that envelope full of pills in your pocket?

It was like another speaking, and, as if in concert, he heard the yokel still talking.

"Crime," he was saying. "First thing they had ought to do is round up all them bad women. They're the *cause* of crime, is what I say. These gangsters, they hold people up, rob banks, shoot people, so they can give money to those dolls. If we can get rid of those women—"

Again Monty stopped listening; he lit a cigarette and leaned back, looking out the window. And there it was, a big signboard at the entrance to a lane. "Turn in Here to Turner's. Cabins. Daily or Weekly Rent. Breakfast Served."

They turned a corner, into a tidy, tree-lined street, with old-fashioned wooden houses on both sides. The cab stopped before one of them.

"Here's where Mrs. Turner lives," said the yokel. "Will I wait?"

"No, thanks," said Monty. "It can't be more than a mile to the station."

"'Tain't even that," said the yokel. "Three-quarters of a mile is all."

He was pleased with the tip he got.

"If you ever come out here again," he said, "if you want a taxi, just ask for Noah Anderson. Which is me. I'm in the phone book, and—"

"Thanks," Monty said, and started up the short path that led to the house. Mrs. Turner, I've come to ask if you can tell me anything about a Mrs. Duke who stayed in one of your cabins, nearly two years ago. *Suicide?* My God! I've been waiting and waiting to hear from her; I've asked everybody, written to everyone....

There was a placard in a front window. "Sylvianna Dobber. Fine Dressmaking. Renovating. Original Designs." Mrs. Turner can't be so well off, if she rents her front room, he thought. Or maybe she's a miser.

He rang the bell, and waited. He heard light, quick steps pattering inside, and after a moment the door was opened by a dwarf, a tiny little woman, scarcely four feet high, neatly dressed in a black skirt and a black sateen blouse with many pins sticking in it. She had a thick mop of gray hair, and sharp, gray eyes behind her pince-nez; she cocked her head to one side and looked up at him, in a challenging way.

"Mrs. Turner?" he asked, although he thought that he would have remembered if Mrs. Turner had been a dwarf.

"No!" she said. "What d' you want?"

"I'd like to see Mrs. Turner, please."

"She's just going out," said the dwarf. "She's going to the dentist, and she won't have any time to talk. You trying to sell something?"

Someone was coming down the stairs now, a stout woman in a flowered dress and a wide-brimmed black hat.

"Mrs. Turner?" Monty asked. "Can you spare me just a few moments?"

"Oh, dear!" she said. "I'm afraid not. I'm going to the dentist's—and it makes me so nervous.... Was it anything special?"

"I wanted very much to ask you about a Mrs. Duke—"

"Oh, *dear!*" cried Mrs. Turner. "That was just the saddest thing.... I was a nervous wreck.... But Miss Dobber can tell you all about it. Better than me. That poor Mrs. Duke was her own sister."

Chapter Ten

Mrs. Turner had hurried off, closing the door behind her, and Monty stood in the little hall, with the dwarf staring up at him.

"I don't see why I *should* tell you anything," she said. "*I* don't know you, or anything about you."

"I'm from a life-insurance company," said Monty, by inspiration. "Mrs. Duke had a small policy with us, and I'm making an investigation."

"Show me your badge," said she.

"We don't carry badges, Miss Dobber," he said, with a certain sternness.

"Then a card."

"I have no business cards with me. If you're—so suspicious of me, perhaps I'd better wait out on the porch until Mrs. Turner comes back." He put his hand on the doorknob. "If you are Mrs. Duke's sister," he said, "you're a beneficiary under this policy—"

"Don't need it," she said. "Don't want it. And her name wasn't 'Mrs. Duke.' Her name was Anella Dobber."

"Dover," she had called herself.

"Then I'll wait—" he began, but she interrupted him.

"I certainly am suspicious of strange men," she said. "'Specially if it's a smoothie. And it's too bad other girls aren't like me, the things you read in the papers. It's too bad Nellie wasn't like me. If she had been, she'd never have got herself murdered."

"*What?*" he cried.

"*Murdered!*" she shouted back at him. "That's what I say, and I'll say it to my dying day. Nellie was *murdered.*"

He felt the sweat come out on his forehead, but he dared not wipe it away.

"I was—given to understand—it was suicide."

"Bosh!" she screamed. "That's what they all said, the police, everybody.

May Turner believes it to this moment. But *I* know it wasn't."

"Have you told the police—"

"Have I told the police!" she cried. "Over and over and over. But nobody'll believe me. They found a letter from me in her purse, and the police, way out in Omaha City, they got notified, and they said for me to come here and identify her. I had to come in an airy plane, and I never was so scared. They'd cut her all up, I know very well, but I knew her all right."

"But—why do you think it was—not suicide?"

"Now, look," she said. "I knew Nellie ever since she was born. I'll tell you here and now, she wasn't the kind that could ever do that. And the last letter I got from her, she was as happy as a lark. Going to be married, she said. To this fellow called Duke. Why would she want to kill herself?"

"Maybe something went wrong. Maybe they—they quarreled."

"Well, my *goodness!*" cried Miss Dobber. "Nellie got engaged, I don't remember how many times. Sometimes she broke it off; sometimes the man walked out on her. She'd be upset, for a while, but she wasn't the kind to kill herself. I guess I knew her better than anybody else in the world, and I can tell you that."

"Did you tell the police what you thought?"

"I didn't 'think' it," she said. "I *knew* it. I told the police, time after time. I told everybody. I told 'em Nellie wasn't the kind to kill herself, and she wouldn't ever have had any sleeping pills or any of that nastiness."

She looked him up and down.

"I guess you can come in and sit down," she said. "This way."

She gestured with her thumb over her shoulder at the open doorway behind her, and he went past her into what had no doubt been the parlor, a large room with a dark-red carpet, wallpaper of white and dim gold stripes, and above the molding, a dado of dark red with a design of gold birds. There was an upright piano, and in a row stood three black dress forms, one of them wearing half a jacket; there was a sewing machine and a long table where some pale material lay, partly cut, with big shears beside it.

Miss Dobber let the window-shades fly up to the rollers; she drew back the curtains and fastened them with cords.

"Now!" she said. "There are plenty of people going up and down the street, and cars, too. You can be *seen*, any minute, so don't try any monkey business."

"That's ridiculous," said Monty, losing his temper.

"*Is* it?" said she. "Don't you ever read the papers? Don't you know what happens to girls that let in strange men when they're all alone?"

"Girl"? he thought, looking at her gray hair, the lines on her forehead.

"What's your name?" she asked.

"Decker," he said, at random.

She sat down in an armchair by the window, and Monty took a plain chair, opposite her. They were in plain view from the street, and, Monty thought, it must look comic.

"Well, Mr. Decker," she said. "I must say your company took plenty of time before they got around to Mrs. Turner. And me."

"Nobody came forward with any claim," said Monty. "We weren't notified of her death. We only heard of it by chance, a few days ago."

"Well, now, isn't that funny?" she said.

"Not necessarily. If you didn't come across the policy among her effects."

She was staring at him all the time, and he felt obliged to glance at her, too often. Her pale, flabby face was repulsive to him, and her habit of curling her upper lip away from her strong big teeth.

"Here's how it was," she said. "Here's what you can tell your life-insurance company. Nellie came to Mrs. Turner's place with a man, and they took a cabin for overnight. Mr. and Mrs. Duke, they signed. Well, *her* name wasn't Mrs. Duke, and I don't guess he was Mr. Duke, either."

"Those things happen ..." said Monty, soberly.

"I know," she said. "I used to be terrible hard on Nellie, for things like that. Why, I just about hated her, when we were going to high school. She was so popular, and I—well, you can see for yourself. I never had a beau. Even that letter from me that the police found in her purse, it was mean. I said if you ever do manage to get married, I hope you'll behave yourself. Things like that."

"D' you mind if I smoke?" asked Monty.

"Yes, I do!" she said. "It makes me cough."

Why does she stare at me so? he thought. Is she crazy?

"I hated her," said Miss Dobber, "and that's a sin. When I came here, and saw her in her coffin ... And they told me she would've had a baby...."

"They did?"

"Yes. When they cut her all up. I hated her worse than ever, because I couldn't have a baby. But I prayed a lot, and I got to see that if a girl's attractive—"

She was crying; she took off the pince-nez, and wiped them with a paper handkerchief. Monty looked out of the window; he saw a haughty-looking blonde girl holding a leash, and watching, with parted lips, while her little dog performed one of his natural functions. She had a look of desperate interest.

"It was a sin," Miss Dobber said. "It was Envy. The Lord made me—like this, like I am, and He had some good reason. Anyhow, I got no reason to hate—" She had to stop, to take off her glasses and dry them. "God made Nellie different. If I'd been like Nellie ... Well, how do I know how I'd have acted? Worse than her, maybe...."

Monty turned away again, from that white, flabby face, the curled upper lip. Now he saw two young mothers with baby carriages, going along side by side, talking. And it seemed to him that they looked so bad-tempered, unhappy, evil—like everyone else. Only not Doña Luisa. All peace, all happiness, all dignity lay with her. Let me get back! he cried, to himself. Let me get back to her—just once more.

"It was poor Mrs. Turner that found her," Miss Dobber went on. "In the morning, she saw the car was gone, and she thought the both of them was gone. After a while, she went down to their cabin, to fix it up for the next ones that came, and then she found Nellie. First, she thought she was asleep, and she let her be. Then she came back, later, and she got sort of worried. She tried to wake Nellie up, and when she couldn't, she sent for a doctor. He said she was stone dead.

"Well, Mrs. Turner was just wild. They took Nellie off to the hospital, to cut her all up and see what killed her, and next day I came, on that airy plane. I said yes, it's my sister all right. But poor Mrs. Turner, she couldn't remember a thing about what the man was like. There was so many coming and going, she said, and she's terrible nearsighted, anyway. She's kind of dumb," Miss Dobber added. "But, anyhow, her and I got to be good friends. I told her I was going to stay right here till I found out who the man was that killed her. The way I'd envied her, and sort of hated her, it was the least I could do."

"Why?" Monty asked. "It won't help your sister."

"I don't know about that," said the dwarf, frowning. "Maybe she's still around, only we can't see her."

"Well, if you believe that—" Monty said.

"I said 'maybe,'" Miss Dobber retorted, sharply. "*I* don't know, and *you* don't know. Some very smart people think that when you're dead, you kind of hover around, maybe for a long time. 'Specially if you think you haven't got justice done you."

He had nothing to say to that. He looked out of the window again, and this time he saw Nichols, driving Doña Luisa's car.

That was real. That was true. The huntress was after him. She would find out where Mrs. Turner lived; she would come here. She would hear this talk about murder....

"And they said she was going to have a *baby*," said the dwarf. "Oh, God, if she'd only had it.... I'd have taken it. I'd have worked for it, given it everything."

She was crying, and it was intolerable; it was disgusting to him.

"That's—very sad," he said.

"Sad?" she said. "It's a lot more than that. If I could just find that Monty—"

"Who? What?"

"That's what she called him. Monty. He killed her. He murdered her. I came on here, to identify her, and I made up my mind I'd stay right here till I found him."

"But why? He couldn't help now."

"I want to see justice done," she said, and then was silent, staring at him in that queer and disconcerting way. She said, "Decker, you said your name was?"

"Yes."

"What's your first name?"

"Miss Dobber," he said, "I don't like this. I came here, for your benefit, and I—"

"You wait a minute," said she, and rose. She went out of the room, and he saw her climbing up the stairs.

Rose will come here, he thought. She'll find out where Mrs. Turner lives, and she'll come. They drove past the house but they'll come back. She'll tell this—this damn harpy that *I'm* "Mr. Decker." She'll hear all this talk about—murder. About the baby....

I'm finished. Rose will find out that Nellie—died. She'll hear all this talk—about murder, about the baby, and all.... I'm finished.

No, I'm not. I'm going to fight this. No. The Gettys have that bill that says Mr. and Mrs. Duke. All right. Duke was a friend of mine. From Canada. He must have left the bill in my room, dropped it, probably. I don't know his address, see. Only, he told me he'd been having himself a time with a girl. Y' see? Mrs. Turner didn't recognize me. Nobody else saw me. No proof that I *was* Mr. Duke. Even if I was Mr. Duke, there's nothing against me.

Except that I'd look like the worst kind of heel. I walk out on a girl who's going to have a baby, and she kills herself. All right. I'm not Mr. Duke.

The dwarf was coming down the stairs now, and he rose. I'm going to get out, he thought. I don't want Rose to come and find me here.

Miss Dobber came into the room and stood before him, her head cocked to one side.

"Yes ..." she said. "Yes. I sort of thought so...."

"I'll have to be going now, Miss Dobber. I have a lot of other calls to make."

"Oh, no!" she said. "Oh, no, you're not. You'll leave, when the police come and get you—"

"What are you talking about?"

"They tried to find this Mr. Duke, when Nellie died. Mrs. Turner, she's terrible nearsighted, and she's kind of absent-minded. There were other people that night, renting cabins, and she couldn't remember anything about

Mr. Duke. If he was old or young, or anything. I showed 'em this, but she couldn't say if it was Mr. Duke."

"Showed them what?"

"This!" she cried, in triumph, and held up a snapshot.

It was a picture of himself and Nellie, one he had never seen before. They were standing on a beach, their bodies locked in a passionate embrace, their faces smiling at each other, he in trunks, she in her black bathing suit with a bare midriff. He put out his hand for it, but she drew back; she turned the picture over, for him to see what was written on the back of it.

"Here's my hubby-to-be. Isn't he a dream-boat!"

"She sent it to me," Miss Dobber went on. "She wrote that someone from her office happened to be at that beach where you were, and he came around a big rock, and found you like that, and he took a snap, just to tease Nellie."

"That's not me," he said.

"It's you, all right. When you first came in, I had a funny sort of feeling, like I'd seen you before. But, of course, you look so different, all dressed up, and your hair all neat, and everything. But it's you, all right."

She turned away.

"Where are you going?" he asked.

"I'm going to call the police," she said.

"The police have nothing against me."

"I'll just tell 'em somebody came here, calling himself Mr. Decker. From a life-insurance company. I'll tell 'em you're a phony. I'll show 'em this snap. And maybe they won't ask you a few questions."

"Listen," he said. "There would be some money coming to you—from that policy."

"All right. It'll come."

"Not without my say-so."

"Oh, so that's it?" she said. "You want to pay me to shut up?"

Rose mustn't see that picture, he thought. And she mustn't hear there was a baby coming. Miss Dobber was walking away.

"Come back here!" he said. "For God's sake, have a little sense."

She looked at him over her shoulder, with a sneer, a snarl like an animal.

"You can do your talking to the police," she said.

"You damn fool!" he cried. "I'll simply walk out of the house—"

"You won't get far," she said.

He was trembling, sick with rage and terror. Rose might come any minute.

"Look here!" he said. "What'll you take for that picture?"

"Oh ... Ten thousand dollars," she said, airily.

"Talk sense. I haven't got that much. But I'll give you what I can."

"About fifty cents," she said, looking him up and down. "That's about what *you're* worth."

She turned away again, toward the next room. He moved himself, and in the dining room there was a telephone on a stand.

"Give me that picture," he said.

She did not answer; she ran to the telephone and took up the receiver. He snatched it out of her hand, and let it dangle on the cord.

"Help!" she screamed.

"Shut up! Nobody's hurting you. I want that picture, that's all."

"Help!" she screamed, again.

He had to stop that. He put both hands round her neck; she clawed at him, but he held her tight. She was making some sort of noise in her throat, but it was not loud; she was glaring at him. The picture fell from her hand, but he did not pick it up. If I let her go, he thought, she'll scream again. I've got to go on, until she'll keep quiet....

What are you doing? something inside him demanded.

I've got to get *away*, he explained. If she screams any more, people will come.... She had stopped the clawing at his hands now; she was still glaring up at him, with her mouth open.

"Will you keep quiet, if I let you go?" he asked.

She stuck out her tongue, and that astonished him. She looked—queer; she looked awful. Suddenly she sagged downward; only his hands supported her.

He let her go, and she fell; she lay crumpled on the floor. O God! O God! O God! O God! he said to himself. He picked up the snapshot, and took it to the sideboard. It was spotted with blood. But how ...? The blood came from his own scratched hands.

He put the picture in his pocket. Then he remembered the drawn-back curtains and loosened them, so that he would not be visible from the street. And while he was doing this, he saw the car stop; he saw Nichols jump down and open the door for Rose; he saw her start up the path.

It seemed to him that this was a picture he had seen before, time and again. Or perhaps it was a dream, very clear and bright, Rose coming up the path, in the sunshine, toward the trap that had closed fast upon him.

He leaned against the wall, limp, without power, without volition.

All right! he said to himself. It's finished. I quit.

Chapter Eleven

The sound of the doorbell terrified him, so that he started violently, and nearly fell. You say I quit, as if that was going to make everything stop. As if it were going to make you dead. Only it doesn't. Even a rabbit doesn't quit, *can't* quit until the hounds are on him.

You can't quit. You can't make yourself dead. The bell rang again, and again it sent a current through him. Run, run, run! Hide! There was a door in the hall; he opened it, and inside was a closet, with coats on hangers. He stepped into it, leaving the door ajar, and he was breathing fast, almost in gasps, as if he had arrived here by an exhausting effort.

The bell rang again. Now, look! he said to himself, still panting. Nobody's going to let her in. *You* know that.

But she was going to get in; he knew that.

I'm a damn fool! he cried to himself. I ought to put *her* in here. Lock her in, out of sight. He could reach the dwarf's body from where he stood; he bent over and took hold of her black skirt. He pulled, hard, and she slid a little nearer to him. There was another ring of the bell, and he felt obliged to look at the front door. The handle was turning.

He drew back and shut himself into the closet. If the latch is off the front door, he thought, she can walk in. She's going to walk in. And when she sees that damn dwarf on the floor ...? She'll go out to Nichols. She'll either send him for the police, or she'll make him wait here, and she'll drive the car. That's the *one moment* I'll have, while she's going down the path to the car.

And if she doesn't? Suppose she faints? All right. That'll give me time to get out by the back way. I don't know what's out there, whether there's any place to hide. All right. But I won't be caught here.

Or suppose she just opens the door and yells for Nichols? I don't think she'd do that, but if she does, I can sneak out of here, quietly, behind her back.

The closet was black as the pit, and no air in it, only a smell of mothballs and brass polish, and the wintergreen smell of mice. It was awful, being shut in here, in the dark, with no air. Those coats hung all round him, brushing his face, ruffling his hair, tapping him on the shoulder. That Nellie's coat? he thought. That plaid coat?

I'm—going to die, he said to himself, and that was what he wanted. But then he remembered the other times when he had felt that he was going to die, and he had not died. He had said "I quit," and he had not, and could not quit. You *can't*. These coats were smothering him, but when he pushed them aside, the wire hangers made a horrible noise. Shut up! he told them.

He remembered a time when he was a kid, and he had, or thought he had, killed and squashed a cockroach with a fly-swatter. But two legs, or feelers, or whatever they were, came out, waving. Suppose you *couldn't* die….? He reached out to support himself, and there was a row of shelves on one side of his stifling prison. He touched something; he picked it up; it was a brass candlestick, he thought, and a heavy one. And he knew, at that moment, what was in his heart.

He heard the front door open, and close. He heard her footsteps in the hall.

"*Oh !*" she cried.

Then there was a silence that was almost beyond bearing for him. She had, of course, seen the dwarf lying on the floor; perhaps she was bending over her, to see ... And suppose the dwarf was *not* dead ... ?

She'll go out to get Nichols, he told himself. And then I can get away. Oh, God! I can't breathe in this place. Hurry up!

What was she doing? he thought. Bending down, looking at the dwarf? Hurry up! I can't breathe in here. He stood close to the door, waiting to hear her footsteps again. And he heard the click of the telephone dial.

"Operator?" she said. "Get me—"

She got no further than that. He hit her under the ear with the brass candlestick, and she slumped sideways in the chair by the telephone stand. As he replaced the instrument, he saw her slide down to the floor. Now hurry....

Behind the dressmaking parlor there was a dining room, with a swing door that led to the kitchen. And here was the back door, and a little porch, and a little yard of yellowish grass, with four clothes poles. A straggling, unpruned hedge separated it from another seedy back yard, belonging to the house on the next street. No cover here, no exit. If I go through anyone else's back yard, he thought, I'm almost sure to be seen, and maybe stopped. I can't go round to the front of the house, because Nichols would see me.

He stood in the neat, sunny little kitchen, tense, desperate. I've got to try it, he thought. I've got to get out of this house.

The scrawny little hedge was so low that he could step over it with no trouble. The back door of the house that faced him was opened, and a stout colored woman appeared.

"Telephone man," Monty said.

That seemed to satisfy her completely, and she retreated into her kitchen. He walked round the house, to the street, and it was, he thought, a street he had known all his life, a tree-lined street of shabby little wooden houses. A dog ran at him, barking, and that belonged in the picture. Then, rushing at him, came a tow-headed little boy, furiously pedaling a tin automobile. He squeezed a horn, that gave a puny honk.

"Get out! Get out! Get outa my way!" he screamed.

Monty stood squarely in front of him.

"Get out! Get *away!*" the child screamed.

"Not me," said Monty.

"I'll run over you ...!"

He was, Monty thought, the most horrible child he had ever seen, with his thatch of yellow hair, his nose with flaring nostrils, his bad, mean little eyes.

"*Get* out of my way!" the child screeched.

I'd like to kick your teeth in, Monty thought. I'd like to pull you round by the back of your neck, and then stamp all over your tin automobile. I'd like—

The child began pedaling backward, and there was a look on his face that gave Monty a queer icy tingle up his spine. The child kept on pedaling backward. Getting away ... Getting away, in a panic.

Is it—the Mark? Monty thought. He turned his back on the child, and, walking away, he drew his hand across his forehead. And, looking at it, his hand was bloody.

O God! O God! he cried to himself. It's there. He took out his handkerchief and wiped his forehead, and there was no blood. Only on both his hands, where she had clawed him.

What else could I do? he thought. I had to get that picture. I knew Rose would be coming, and I couldn't let her see that. I can't let anybody see it. It ties me right up with Nellie.... Never mind Nellie. I had to do that to Rose. She'll get over it, all right. I had to do it, so I could get away. I only knocked her out. She's young and healthy. She'll get over it.

And then he thought, perhaps she's over it *now*. Perhaps she's in the car, with Nichols, and they'll see me.... He did not know where he was; all sense of direction had left him. He was here, in this street that seemed somehow so familiar to him, and yet was utterly unknown. I've got to hurry.

He was going to Doña Luisa; there was no doubt in his mind about that. She was the only refuge, the only solace in the world. I've got to hurry, he told himself, over and over, but he did not know which way to go, and there was no one in sight to ask. He heard a car coming, and he stood still, rigid with fear. It's Rose, he thought.

But it was a little sedan, and it went past him. And now a woman came round the corner toward him; a pale and dumpy woman with black hair straggling wildly from under a big, crooked straw hat. She was holding a tiny girl by the hand, and though she walked slowly, the child lagged behind; they had a curious air of indifference, as if they were unaware of each other.

"Excuse me," Monty said, raising his hat. "Can you tell me the way to the railway station?"

"What?" she asked, in a loud, flat voice.

"The station. The railroad station."

"Oh, the *station!*" she said, staring at him. "Go straight along Lawrence, and you'll see it."

"But—what's Lawrence?"

This seemed to offend her.

"Why, it's right where you *come* from!" she said, sharply.

"Hey, Momma! *Momma!*" cried the child. "I gotta go—"

"Hush up!" screamed the mother.

"Naaah ...!" screamed the child.

"Thank you," said Monty, and started to go past them.

"*That's* not the way to Lawrence!" the woman called to him.

"Oh, I have to stop somewhere first, thanks," he said.

For he could not go back, past that house. And if that's the road to the station, he thought, Nichols would see me. I've got to find some other way. He went forward, in a daze, in a strange world; he was soaked with sweat; he was walking fast.

He spoke to the next person he saw, a thin elderly man in overalls.

"The dee-po ...?" he said. "Now, you turn around and go back to Lawrence Avenue—"

"I don't—I don't want to go that way," said Monty. "Isn't there some other way?"

"Why? What's the matter with Lawrence Avenue, hey?" The old man waited. "I *say*, what's the matter with Lawrence Avenue?"

"Well, thanks," said Monty. "Never mind."

"Nutty," said the old man, half aloud. "Just as nutty as kin be."

A strange world, filled with pale, hostile strangers. He kept on walking, he kept on asking directions; he was in a hurry, but only to get back to New York. Fear had left him, and the dread of being pursued. Rose didn't see me, he thought, and none of the people who did see me know my name. There's nothing to tie me up with—whatever happened.

Only, I'm so tired, he thought. It's hard to think, when you're as tired as this.

Chapter Twelve

He sat in the smoker, relaxed and exhausted. I've got to think things out, he told himself. But after all, there did not seem very much to be thought out. He wanted an alibi, in case Rose began questioning him, but he knew, without any thinking, who would provide that for him. His mother, of course, and she would do it well; she would be plausible, amiable, unshakable. All he would have to tell her was that he had got into a little trouble, and she would cover for him.

"Say!" said the man in the seat beside him. "You look like you bin mixing it with a wildcat."

"What d' you mean?"

"Why, your hands. Couple of scratches on your chin, too." The man chuckled. "Or maybe it was just the girl friend."

Monty did not speak, did not smile, but the other was not disheartened. He was tall, lanky, a man of middle age, deeply tanned; he went on, in a drawling voice, to tell of adventures or experiences he had had with wildcats, mountain lions, bears.

"Now, that was the damnedest thing I ever *did* see...."

Monty fell suddenly asleep and did not wake until the other man shook him by the shoulder.

"We're here, Mac," he said. "Right here in New York City."

Monty opened his eyes and looked at the other. But still he did not speak or smile. It seemed to him almost impossible to rise, to go into the aisle, to descend from the train. I want to go to sleep again, he thought. Only he knew he could not. He knew that he was in danger, and must be awake and alert.

He stepped out onto the platform, and it was strange and terrifying; it seemed to have no end. A mob of people went marching along it, under pale, ghastly lights, and he had to go tramping along with them. Then there was a flight of stone stairs to climb, and there was the enormous, gigantic rotunda, and mad voices roaring. *Two-thirty express for Baltimore track number sixteen two-thirty Buffalo track ...*

He remembered a drugstore alongside the ramp leading to the street; he remembered, too, the caffeine tablets some of the men in the shipyard had used if there were a lot of overtime and they felt sleepy. He bought a box of those and swallowed two or three with a glass of ginger ale at the counter.

I'd do better to take a cab up there and talk to Mother about it, he thought. But damn it, I'm too tired. So he went into a booth and telephoned. She listened patiently.

"No matter who asks you, you'll stick to that, won't you?" he said.

"Of course, dear," she answered. "You came up here about half-past nine this morning, is that it? And did you stay to lunch?"

"Lunch? I'd forgotten about that. Yes. I had lunch with you. I just left your place half an hour ago. Sure you've got it straight?"

"I'm sure. You said you were tired, and you just sat here quietly and read some magazine."

"I wish to God you had a cat!" he said angrily.

"A *cat*, dear? But d' you want a cat? Because the grocer—"

"*No!*"

"Don't shout so, dear. You must be nervous. I hope you haven't got yourself into any sort of really troublesome mix-up, Monty. Remember that if you have, Jimmy'll always be glad to give you the very best advice. What was *that*, dear?"

"I just smothered a sneeze," he said.

But it had been a laugh that he had choked off. A policeman ... Just the one I want, to give me advice....

"And if you did forget your lunch, eat something now. A nice sandwich and a cup of coffee."

"Yes, yes."

"You don't sound like yourself, Monty."

"Maybe I'm not," he said, and this time he let himself laugh.

"Call me soon, dear. Come and see me."

"You bet!" he said.

When he came out of the booth, he felt very much better. Maybe those tablets have bucked me up already, he thought. Or maybe it was because I was able to laugh, about Jimmy....

God knows there's nothing funny about—what happened. But I couldn't help it. I didn't want to hurt the damn little dwarf in any way. It was simply that I couldn't possibly let her show that snapshot to Rose. No.... She started the whole thing. You could say *she* was the aggressor; she was out to make trouble for me, and plenty. All I wanted was to get that picture back from her and get out.

I may not have hurt her, anyhow. Maybe she had a fit, or something. Probably she's running all around the house now, mad as hell, trying to find "Mister Decker." If I did—do her any harm....

He remembered her with her tongue sticking out, and her eyes bulging....

I didn't want any trouble, he told himself. I'd have paid her for that picture, and got out. But she wouldn't have it that way.

He turned east on Forty-Second Street, deciding to walk uptown to the

St. Pol. *I* didn't want any trouble with that dwarf. I didn't want any trouble with Nellie, either. I didn't believe that tale about a baby. And, anyhow, I don't have to believe it was mine. She was a tramp, a damn little bitch. She wanted to make me marry her. Blackmail me. She said she'd bring one of those paternity suits up in court. You won't get out of *this*, my fine feathered friend, she had said. This time you're going to pay, all right, you heel.

I did get out of it, though, he thought. God knows I'm sorry it turned out the way it did. Naturally, I didn't know anything about the strength of those capsules. I'm not a doctor. I had to get away, that's all. I'm sorry about Nellie. I'm sorry about her sister. I'm sorry ...

I'm sorry—for a lot of things. I'm going to be different. Entirely different, from here on. I mean, I'm going to face things. If I don't get that job in Venezuela, I'll find something here, and I'll go to night school. I'll learn Spanish and—well, accounting, maybe.

I know I've said that before, a lot of times. But this time I mean it; I've had my lesson. I mean, if Rose had seen me in that house—if anybody knew ... I mean, I couldn't say self-defense—and it couldn't be suicide. I mean—I wouldn't get another chance....

He turned up Fifth Avenue, and he thought of some movie he had seen, sometime. There had been a man, walking along a street, and strange music had accompanied him, keeping time to his measured steps. Somehow it sort of frightened you, he thought. I don't remember the picture, but the man had just killed somebody. Or he was just going to kill somebody. Anyhow, he didn't care. He was walking along, smoking a cigarette, and that music was playing....

All right! There's no music here. Unless maybe I'm singing to myself. Everybody does that.... This is the turning point, for me. From here on in, I'm going to be different. I'm sorry for—things in the past, but it is the worst thing you can do, to brood over the past. I'm going to see Doña Luisa....

I love her. I've never really loved anybody else, in all my life. If I'm different now, if I've changed, she's done it. I could do anything for her. I'd die for her.

He called her room from a booth in the lobby. "Doña Luisa, could I come to see you?"

"Certainly! At six, for a cocktail....?"

"If I could come now," he said. "I want very much to speak to you."

"Well ..." she said, with obvious hesitation. "Very well, Monty. In fifteen minutes."

As he hung up the telephone he thought suddenly: What do I want to speak to her about? What will I say when I get there? She'll think there's something important I want to tell her, and there's nothing.... And my hands ...

He looked at them, and the long, deep scratches were crusted with blood. *Got* to think of something.... Maybe I'd better have a drink. It was not his habit, in an emergency, to think of drinking as a help, or a solace, and even now he hesitated. But there was, in his mind, the passionate conviction that this was the turning point in his life, the beginning of a vitally important change, and he did not feel adequate.

He went into the bar and ordered a double rye; he drank it neat, in a few gulps, and then he went to his room. He combed his hair, he washed his face with cold water, he washed, he scrubbed those hands. Bandages? he thought. Sticking plaster? No, that would be worse. More conspicuous. But I've got to explain—say something to her.... All right. I'll say my mother's cat had a fit, and I tried to hold it till the vet got there...

It was more than fifteen minutes now. I've got to think up some reason for seeing her now.... Something that upset me.... Well, what? Hurry up! What? My mother tried to kill herself. That's good; very good. Only not her cat having a fit. That makes it just comic. No.... My mother tried to jump out of the window, and when I grabbed her, she made scratches. Not very good, but I've got to get going....

She opened the door when he rang, and she looked, he thought, more beautiful than ever before, in a long white chiffon negligee, pleated and ruf-fled, a silver belt around her waist.

"Come in!" she said, holding out her hand. "I'm sorry, but this is always my stupid time of the day...."

"I'm sorry I disturbed you. But—"

"That's nothing. Sit down there—in that chair—and you'll have a little breeze from the fan."

She sat down on the sofa herself, and the electric fan, oscillating, stirred her dark hair, fluttered the ruffles about her neck. I'm sorry ... he thought. I'm sorry for everything I've done. Let me kneel down before you and tell you that. And then forgive me—and I'll be different.

"You look very tired, Monty," she said. "Has something gone wrong?"

"Yes ..." he said. "I—had to see you."

"Tell me."

"I can't," he said.

But, after all, he had to tell her.

"My mother ..." he said. "She tried to jump out of the window."

"My poor boy! But why?"

Yes, why? You forgot that one.

"She—I'm afraid she's been taking drugs lately."

"Oh, Monty! That's the saddest thing.... What will you do?"

She was leaning forward a little, looking at him with her eager, warm sympathy.

"I *don't* know yet," he said. "I—"

The telephone began to ring.

"Excuse me," she said, and crossed the room to the foyer, to answer. She spoke in Spanish; she listened; she spoke again.

People always sound excited when they're talking in a foreign language, Monty thought. When she comes back, I'm going to say let's not talk about my mother any more. Her husband is looking after things now, and there's nothing I can do.

"Seguro!" he heard her say, heard the telephone click back into place, and she re-entered the room.

"It was Rose," she said. "She asked if you were here."

Her look, her voice, everything about her was completely changed; no sympathy now, no warmth.

"Rose says you must stay here until they come," she said.

"'They'?"

"She is bringing a policeman."

He sprang to his feet.

"I'm not going to stay! I'm leaving *now*."

"No," she said, still standing in the doorway.

"Let me by, please," he said.

She backed away, swiftly, and stood against the door.

"You must stay here," she said. "If you haven't done anything wrong, you won't mind staying. They will be here in a few minutes."

"I *won't* stay! Let me out!"

"No," she said.

Rose coming—with a policeman. I can't ... I *can* not ...They'll ask me questions—and I can't answer. I'm—I'm too tired. I've got to get away. *And I will.*

"Stand away from that door," he said.

"No," she said.

If Rose is bringing a policeman, he thought, then she's found out—something. I can't—I can't stand this. I'm tired....

He was panting again now; he was again the exhausted, desperate quarry, with the hounds closing in on him.

"Let me *out!*" he said. "Get away from that door—or I'll *make* you go."

"No!"

O God! O God! he was saying to himself. They'll take me to prison. And they'll find that picture in my pocket.... O God! And that alibi isn't any good now, after I said my mother takes drugs.... I've got to get away, out of this hotel, out of New York.

"Let me out!" he cried. And when she did not answer and did not move, he caught her by the shoulder and pushed her aside. But she sprang back, and seized the doorknob. He wrenched her hand loose, and taking her arm, he flung her away, so violently that she fell to the floor.

When he saw her there on the floor, on one knee, he thought this was the end of his life.

But you have to keep running, until the hounds are on you. Her hand was on the knob again, as she knelt there, and he would have to wrench it away again.

The doorbell rang.

Chapter Thirteen

Doña Luisa pulled herself to her feet and opened the door. It was Rose, as Monty had been sure it would be, and there was a policeman in uniform with her, and two other men, a scrawny gray-haired fellow, and standing with them a tall man with a soft hat pulled low over his dark, bold face.

"I'm the Chief of Police from Bagleyville, ma'am," said the gray-haired man. "Name of Lewis. And this here is Detective-Sergeant McGuire of the New York City police." He ignored the cop. "Came here to see a Mr. Duchesne."

"That's me," said Monty.

"Come in, please, and close the door," said Doña Luisa.

They all entered, and they all remained standing, the two women, the four men.

"What's your full name?" asked McGuire.

"Montford Duchesne," he answered, and it sounded theatrical, ridiculous to him.

"Age?"

"Twenty-seven."

"Place of residence?"

"Well, I'm staying here, in the hotel, for the moment."

"How long have you lived here?"

He could not remember how many days.

"Since V-J Day," he said.

"Where did you live before then?"

I don't want to tell him, Monty thought. The Gettys will slander me as much as they possibly can. They could be harmful for me, make a bad impression.

"Where did you live before then?" McGuire asked again.

With his hat off, he looked even more sinister; his thick black hair brushed up behind his ears, like horns, like a devil, Monty thought. He had to be answered.

"In Staten Island," Monty said, and he had to give the Gettys' address.

"How are you employed?"

"Nowhere, just now."

Fine. Fine impression he must be making. Montford Duchesne, my good man, residing at the Hotel St. Pol, and not employed.

"I was working in a shipyard until V-J Day," he said.

"Was you to Bagleyville this morning?" asked Lewis.

"No," said Monty. "I went uptown to visit my mother."

"Miss Brown," said Lewis, "do you identify this here man as the man you saw in Bagleyville this morning?"

"Yes," said Rose.

Monty had not looked at her since she had entered; he could not look at her now.

"That's a mistake," he said. "I've never been to this Bagleyville."

"Where do you claim you saw this man, Miss Brown?" McGuire asked.

"He was in—that house when we first drove past it, on our way to the motel."

"It's not so easy for someone riding in a car to identify anyone inside a house," said McGuire.

"This was easy," said Rose. "It was—it looked so queer. The curtains at the front windows were pulled all the way back, and they were sitting there, Mr. Duchesne and that poor little dressmaker—sitting facing each other, so close their knees must have nearly touched."

"Did your chauffeur see them?"

"No. He was watching the road."

It's just her word against mine, Monty thought.

"Miss Brown's mistake," he said. "I've never been in Bagleyville."

"We-eell …" said Lewis. "I don't know about *that*." He brought a wallet out of his pocket, and took something from it. "Reccernize this?" he asked, holding up something for Monty to see.

It was that snapshot of himself and Nellie.

"Where did you get that?" he asked.

"Right there, alongside the body," said Lewis, with affable satisfaction.

I must have dropped it out of my breast pocket, when I bent over and tried to pull her into the closet, Monty thought. That was the one thing, that was the reason—

"We-eell," said Lewis, "I took and showed this picture to the four taxi drivers we got, out in Bagleyville, and one of 'em reccernized you, right off. Said yes, he drove you this morning out to Mrs. Turner's house. Showed the photo to Mrs. Turner. She was in a real bad state, account of what happened in her house. I never did take to Miss Dobber much, she said, but when you think what happened to her ... Choked to death ... Well, she reccernized you, right off. Yes, says she, that's the young fellow came to my house this morning, to ask had I heard anything from Mrs. Duke. 'I had to be off to the dentist,' says she, 'but Miss Dobber can maybe help you.' She says she left you in the house."

"Good God!" said Monty, scornfully, "this woman—what's her name?—this Mrs. Turner says she saw some man in her house as she was going out. Just a glimpse, I suppose. Then you show her this snapshot that's none too good—it could be anybody, and she says it's the same man."

"Why did Miss Dobber have a snapshot of you, anyhow?" asked McGuire. "Did you know her?"

"No! Never heard of her."

"*And*—" said Lewis, sprightly and pleased, as if he were making a good score in some game, "Mrs. Turner and me, we both reccernized the girl in the photo. She was the one that died, out to Mrs. Turner's motel. The one that was going to have a baby. Called herself Mrs. Dook, but we found a letter in her pocketbook. Name was Nellie Dobber. Suicide, when the man that brought her there walked out on her."

That's the angle, Monty thought. If they do make up their minds that I was "Mr. Duke," I'll say we had a fight, and I went away. I didn't know about this baby.

"Maybe I knew the girl," he said. "I don't remember the names of all the girls I've known. But I was not in Bagleyville this morning. I went up to see my mother, and she'll tell you so, if you want to call her up."

"Mister ..." said Doña Luisa. "Excuse me, please, that I don't remember your names very well. This young man has told me that his mother is a drug addict. If that is the case—" She paused, and now her English had a foreign inflection and accent. "How shall we then believe what she tells?"

She's gone back on me, he thought.

"It's not true," he said. "I told her that, I made up a tale, because she was so jealous—"

"Mr. McGuire," said Rose. "Please take him away. Please—let us rest a little."

He turned to look at her, and she looked back at him.

"He's the most dangerous person—there could be," she said, and tears were running down her face. "There's—nothing—so dangerous—as a coward." She had to stop for a moment. "He'd trample on anyone, he'd betray anyone, he'd *kill* anyone, to get free."

Fight her! Monty cried to himself. Fight, and you could win. He could look at her now, steadily, but behind his eyes was a picture of himself, a figure running down long, long corridors, opening a door here and there, and running out again, slamming it after him.

And something was loping after him, some shadowy beast. His own running steps rang loud in the corridors, but the beast, the hound, padded on in silence. No way out, no end to this flight; all the doors were locked now.

"Please take him away!" Rose said.

"Your evidence isn't so good," McGuire began.

"I did it," Monty said. "I killed them. Both of them. Because—"

He could not see the people in the room now; nothing but those corridors, those locked doors, himself running, and gasping, and the beast loping after him, and all the doors locked. There was a ramp that led up to freedom and safety, but on it, all still as dolls, lay in a row Nellie and Gwen and his mother and the dwarf and Rose. And Doña Luisa. He would have to run over them, to get out.

"I had to," he said.

Someone eased him down into a chair. Someone held a very small glass to his lips, and he sipped a burning liquid. And in a moment he could see again, and hear again. The three men were waiting for him, and he knew what lay ahead of him.

I quit! he said to himself. But how could he quit? They'll put me in jail, he thought. They'll ask me questions; maybe they'll beat me up. There'll be a trial. It'll be months and months before they kill me. I can't take it. I can't take it. I can't wait like that—to be killed.

He got up, and stood, holding to the back of the chair.

"Ready?" asked McGuire. "We'll go along to the D. A.'s office."

He looked at McGuire, and at Lewis, and at the cop. No use asking them to shoot him, here and now. They wouldn't do it. They want me to get the works, he thought.

Now he was able to look at Doña Luisa. She was lying back in a chair, in her pleated white robe; she looked back at him, her dark eyes so sad. Like a saint, he thought, grieving over—the sinner. Rose sat on the arm of her chair; her face was white; she looked ill, and wretched. No help anywhere; all the doors were locked.

But he was going to get out.

"Could I have another drink of—whatever it was?" he asked.

"No. You come along now," said McGuire.

"Oh, let him!" said Doña Luisa.

She rose, and went into the serving pantry; she came with a tiny glass for him.

"It's cognac," she said. "Try to have courage, Monty. Whatever we do, if we are truly sorry, if we repent, we can be forgiven."

I'm not sorry, he thought. I don't repent. I don't want to be forgiven. I— just want to quit.

He swallowed the fiery liquid, and strength was flowing back into him.

He knew what he was going to do, and he would have to do it fast.

"Come on, now," said McGuire. "I can't wait here any longer."

"I just want to get my wallet," Monty said. "I put it down here...."

He pretended to be feeling about among the flower vases on the window sill. The casement was wide open. He pushed a couple of vases aside; then, like a cat, he leaped up on the sill, and dived out of the window. He heard himself scream; he thought that he was spinning round and round, so fast that he could not breathe. He thought that he would go on and on like this, always, that he would never reach the bottom of this abyss.

When he did reach the bottom, he knew nothing about it. He had quit, spinning in the air.

THE END

Elisabeth Sanxay Holding Bibliography (1889-1955)

NOVELS

Invincible Minnie (1920)
Rosaleen Among the Artists (1921)
Angelica (1921)
The Unlit Lamp (1922)
The Shoals of Honour (1926)
The Silk Purse (1928)
Miasma (1929)
Dark Power (1930)
The Death Wish (1934)
The Unfinished Crime (1935)
The Strange Crime in Bermuda (1937)
The Obstinate Murderer [aka No Harm Intended] (1938)
Who's Afraid [aka Trial by Murder] (1940)
The Girl Who Had to Die (1940)
Speak of the Devil [aka Hostess to Murder] (1941)
Killjoy [aka Murder is a Kill-Joy] (1941)
Lady Killer (1942)
The Old Battle-Ax (1943)
Net of Cobwebs (1945)
The Innocent Mrs. Duff (1946)
The Blank Wall (1947)
Miss Kelly (1947)
Too Many Bottles [aka The Party Was the Pay-Off] (1950)
The Virgin Huntress (1951)
Widow's Mite (1952)

STORIES

Patrick on the Mountain (*The Smart Set*, July 1920)
The Problem that Perplexed Nicholson (*The Smart Set*, Aug 1920)
Marie's View of It (*The Century Magazine*, Dec 1920)
Mollie: The Ideal Nurse (*The Century Magazine*, Jan 1921)
Angelica (*Munsey's*, May-Oct 1921)
The Married Man (*Munsey's*, Dec 1921)
The Foreign Woman (*Munsey's*, July 1922)
Hanging's Too Good for Him (*Munsey's*, Sept 1922)
Like a Leopard (*Munsey's*, Nov 1922)
Lost Luck (*The Bookman*, Dec 1922)
The Girl He Picked Up at Coney (*Metropolitan Magazine*, Feb/Mar 1923)
The Aforementioned Infant (*Munsey's*, Mar 1923)
It Seemed Reasonable (*Munsey's*, Apr 1923)
Old Dog Tray (*Munsey's*, May 1923)
The Matador (*Munsey's*, June 1923)
A Hesitating Cinderella (*Munsey's*, July 1923)
The Postponed Wedding (*Munsey's*, Aug 1923)

With Unbowed Head (*The Century Magazine*, Aug 1923)

This is Life (*The Nation*, Aug 15 1923)

The Marquis of Carabas (*Munsey's*, Sept 1923)

Out of the Woods (*Munsey's*, Oct 1923)

Benedicta (*Munsey's*, Dec 1923)

Nickie and Pem (*Munsey's*, Feb 1924)

His Remarkable Future (*Munsey's*, Apr 1924)

His Own People (*Munsey's*, July 1924)

Who Is This Impossible Person? (*Munsey's*, Aug 1924)

Ye Gods and Little Fishes (*The American Magazine*, Aug 1924)

Mr. Martin Swallows the Anchor (*Munsey's*, Sept 1924)

Too French (*Munsey's*, Jan 1925)

The Good Little Pal (*Munsey's*, Apr 1925)

Flowers for Miss Riordan (*Munsey's*, May 1925)

Sometimes Things Do Happen (*Munsey's*, June 1925)

Miss What's-Her-Name (*Munsey's*, July 1925)

The Long Night (*Ladies Home Journal*, Sept 1925)

The Wonderful Little Woman (*Munsey's*, Sept 1925)

As Patrick Henry Said (*Munsey's*, Oct 1925)

The Worst Joke in the World (*Munsey's*, Nov 1925)

As Is (*Munsey's*, Dec 1925)

That's Not Love (*Munsey's*, Jan 1926)

Rosalie Gets Out of the Cage (*The American Magazine*, Feb 1926)

The Thing Beyond Reason (*Munsey's*, Feb 1926)

Dogs Always Know (*Munsey's*, Mar 1926)

Highfalutin' (*Munsey's*, Apr 1926)

Bonnie Wee Thing (*Munsey's*, May 1926)

Vanity (*Munsey's*, Jun 1926)

The Compromising Letter (*Munsey's*, July 1926)

Miss Cigale (*Munsey's*, Aug 1926)

Blotted Out (*Munsey's*, Sept 1926)

Human Nature Unmasked (*Munsey's*, Oct 1926)

Home Fires (*Munsey's*, Dec 1926)

The Grateful Lunella (*The American Magazine*, May 1927)

The Old Ways (*Munsey's*, July 1927)

By the Light of Day (*Munsey's*, Aug 1927)

For Granted (*Munsey's*, Nov 1927)

Incompatibility (*Munsey's*, Dec 1927)

One Misty Night, (*The American Magazine*, Feb 1928)

Derelict (*Munsey's*, Mar 1928)

Half an Hour Late (*Woman's Home Companion*, Mar 1928)

This Road Is Closed (*The American Magazine*, Apr 1928)

Inches and Ells (*Munsey's*, June 1928)

It Is a Two-Edged Sword (*McCall's*, June 1928)

Too Late (*Liberty*, July 21 1928)

Outside the Door (*The Elks Magazine*, Oct 1928)

Hard as Nails (*Liberty*, Oct 20 1928)

Important Things (*Liberty*, Nov 17 1928)

A Dinner Date (*The American Magazine*, Jan 1929)

Vera's Superior Smile (*Pictorial Review*, Jan 1929)

Saving Up (*Liberty*, Jan 5 1929)

Flow and Ebb (*Liberty*, Jan 26 1929)

Without Benefit of Police (*Complete Stories*, Feb 1929)

The Sin of Angels (*The American Magazine*, Apr 1929)

Dare-Devil (*The American Magazine*, June 1929)

Little Deeds of Kindness (*Liberty*, July 6 1929)

Broken Faith (*The American Magazine*, Oct 1929; *Cassell's Magazine of Fiction*, July 1930)

Carline (*Liberty*, Oct 12, 1929)

Rose-Leaves (*Liberty*, Jan 18 1930)

The Chain of Death (*Liberty*, May 24, May 31, Jun 7, Jun 14, Jun 21 1930)

The Girl in Armor (*Street & Smith's Detective Story Magazine*, Aug 8 1931)

It's All Right for Men (*Liberty*, Oct 10 1931)

Brides of Crime (*Street & Smith's Detective Story Magazine*, Nov 7, 1931)

The Preposterous Mrs. Manders (*Woman's Home Companion*, Mar 1932)

Hound's Bay (*Street & Smith's Detective Story Magazine*, Mar 26 1932)

If It Hadn't Been for Laurel (*Liberty*, Jan 28 1933)

A Man Can Take It (*Collier's Weekly*, May 12 1934)

The Green Bathtub (*Collier's Weekly*, June 16 1934)

The Last Night (*The Passing Show*, July 14 1934)

All She Could Get (*Collier's Weekly*, Sept 15 1934)

"I Could Brighten Your Life!" (*The American Magazine*, Jan 1935)

The Bride Comes Home (*Cosmopolitan*, Feb 1935)

The Root of Evil (*Collier's Weekly*, Apr 27 1935)

Nobody Would Listen (*Mystery*, Aug 1935)

Somebody's Cynthia (*Collier's Weekly*, Aug 3 1935; *The Passing Show*, Nov 2 1935)

You Never Can Tell (*Collier's Weekly*, Dec 14 1935; *Grit*, June 1936)

Unscathed (*Ladies Home Journal*, Jan 1936)

Lost (*Redbook*, Feb 1936)

Cross Purposes (*Collier's Weekly*, May 30, 1936)

Can Do! (*Pictorial Review*, July 1936)

Scandal (*Woman's Home Companion*, July 1936)

Night Life (*Redbook*, Sept 1936)

Third Act (*Pictorial Review*, Apr 1937)

Drifting (*McCall's*, May 1937)

Wedding Day (*Cosmopolitan*, Sept 1937)

The Nicest Little Lunch (*Cosmopolitan*, Nov 1937)

Echo of a Careless Voice (*McCall's*, Jan 1938)

Illusion (*Good Housekeeping*, Aug 1938)

They Take It So Lightly! (*Cosmopolitan*, Oct 1938)

Two Passes for the Show (*Liberty*, Nov 5 1938)

So Sort of Proud (*Good Housekeeping*, Mar 1939)

Money Can't Buy It (*Liberty*, Aug 5 1939)

Open That Door (*Liberty*, Aug 26 1939)

Blonde on a Boat (*The American Magazine*, Dec 1939)

Late Date (*Cosmopolitan*, May 1940)

Proposal (*McCall's*, May 1940)

On Yonder Lea (*Good Housekeeping*, Aug 1940)

Tropical Secretary (*The American Magazine*, Feb 1941)

Tomorrow's Not Soon Enough (*McCall's*, Mar 1941)

What It Takes (*Grit*, Mar 9 1941)

Loved I Not Honor More (*Liberty*, Apr 12 1941)

The Fearful Night (*The American Magazine*, June 1941; expanded to *The Obstinate Murderer*)

Another Baby (*Woman's Home Companion*, Nov 1941)

Not Goodbye But Au Revoir (*McCall's*, Oct 1942)

The Kiskadee Bird (*Cosmopolitan*, 1944)

The Old Battle-Ax (1943; abridged, *Liberty*, Mar 18 1944)

Bait for a Killer (*Collier's Weekly*, Sep 30 1944, as "The Blue Envelope"; *The Saint Mystery Magazine*, Mar 1959; *The Saint Detective Magazine* [Australia], Nov 1959; *The Saint Mystery Magazine* [UK], Oct 1960)

The Unbelievable Baroness (*The American Magazine*, 1945)

The Net of Cobwebs (*Collier's Weekly*, Jan 6, 13 & 20, 1945)

Funny Kind of Love (as by Elizabeth Saxanay Holding, *Boston Sunday Globe Magazine*, Nov 11 1945)

"Be Careful, Mrs. Williams" (*Cosmopolitan*, July 1947)

People Do Fall Downstairs (*Ellery Queen's Mystery Magazine*, Aug 1947; *Ellery Queen's Mystery Magazine* [Australia], Aug 1949)

Friday, the Nineteenth (*The Magazine of Fantasy and Science Fiction*, Summer 1950)

Farewell, Big Sister (*Ellery Queen's Mystery Magazine*, July 1952; hardboiled satire)

The Death Wish (*Cosmopolitan*, Feb 1953)

Shadow of Wings (*The Magazine of Fantasy and Science Fiction*, July 1954)

Glitter of Diamonds (*Ellery Queen's Mystery Magazine*, Mar 1955; *Ellery Queen's Mystery Magazine* [Australia], May 1955)

The Strange Children (*The Magazine of Fantasy and Science Fiction*, Aug 1955)

Very, Very Dark Mink (*The Saint Detective Magazine*, Dec 1956; *The Saint Detective Magazine* [UK], Oct 1957)

The Darling Doctor (*Alfred Hitchcock's Mystery Magazine*, Mar 1957)

Suspense Classics from the Godmother of Noir...

Elisabeth Sanxay Holding

Lady Killer / Miasma
978-0-9667848-7-9 $19.95

Murder is suspected aboard a cruise ship to the Caribbean, and a young doctor falls into a miasma of doubt when he agrees to become medical assistant in a house of mystery. "*Miasma* and *Lady Killer* provides an excellent introduction to her world."—Ed Gorman

The Death Wish / Net of Cobwebs
978-0-9667848-9-3 $19.95

Poor Mr. Delancey is pulled into a murderous affair when he comes to the aid of a friend, and a merchant seaman suffering from battle trauma becomes the first suspect when Aunt Evie is found murdered. "A whodunit of the first order."—*Boston Herald*

Strange Crime in Bermuda / Too Many Bottles
978-0-9749438-5-5 $19.95

An intriguing tale of a sudden disappearance on a Caribbean island, and a mysterious death by pills, which could have been accidental—or murder. "The dialog is pitch perfect and Holding writes inner conflict and confusion better than anyone." —Rick Ollerman, *Amazon.com*

The Old Battle Ax / Dark Power
978-1-933586-16-8 $19.95

Mrs. Herriott spins a web of deception when her sister is found dead on the sidewalk, and a woman's vision of a family reunion is quickly shattered by feelings of dread when she answers her uncle's invitation to visit. "A skillfully told tale with deep implications."—*Atlanta Journal*

The Unfinished Crime / The Girl Who Had to Die
978-1-933586-41-0 $19.95

Priggish Andrew Branscombe tries to control everyone around him with such a web of deceit that he is the one finally caught up in its tangled skein. Jocelyn is convinced she is going to be murdered, so naturally everyone suspects young Killian when she is pushed off the cruise ship.

Speak of the Devil / The Obstinate Murderer
978-1-933586-71-7 $17.95

Murder stalks the halls at a Caribbean resort hotel, and an aging alcoholic is called in to solve a murder that hasn't happened yet. "Strongly recommended."—*Baltimore Sun*. "Amazing deviltry."—*Saturday Review*. "As a baffler, it's excellent."—*Waterbury American*.

Two novels in each trade paperback edition from:

Stark House Press
1315 H Street, Eureka, CA 95501
griffinskye3@sbcglobal.net
www.StarkHousePress.com

Available from your local bookstore, or order direct with check or via our website.

www.ingramcontent.com/pod-product-compliance
Lightning Source LLC
Chambersburg PA
CBHW070926190726
48292CB00004B/1123